Anthologies

DARKEST AT DAWN
(*includes* DARK HUNGER *and* DARK SECRET)

SEA STORM
(*includes* MAGIC IN THE WIND *and* OCEANS OF FIRE)

FEVER
(*includes* THE AWAKENING *and* WILD RAIN)

FANTASY
(*with Emma Holly, Sabrina Jeffries, and Elda Minger*)

LOVER BEWARE
(*with Fiona Brand, Katherine Sutcliffe, and Eileen Wilks*)

HOT BLOODED
(*with Maggie Shayne, Emma Holly, and Angela Knight*)

Specials

DARK HUNGER
MAGIC IN THE WIND
THE AWAKENING

CAT'S LAIR

CHRISTINE FEEHAN

JOVE BOOKS, NEW YORK

THE BERKLEY PUBLISHING GROUP
Published by the Penguin Group
Penguin Group (USA) LLC
375 Hudson Street, New York, New York 10014

USA • Canada • UK • Ireland • Australia • New Zealand • India • South Africa • China

penguin.com

A Penguin Random House Company

CAT'S LAIR

A Jove Book / published by arrangement with the author

Jove Books are published by The Berkley Publishing Group.
JOVE® is a registered trademark of Penguin Group (USA) LLC.
The "J" design is a trademark of Penguin Group (USA) LLC.

For information, address: The Berkley Publishing Group,
a division of Penguin Group (USA) LLC,
375 Hudson Street, New York, New York 10014.

ISBN: 978-0-515-15556-3

PUBLISHING HISTORY
Jove mass-market edition / May 2015

PRINTED IN THE UNITED STATES OF AMERICA

10 9 8 7 6 5 4 3 2 1

Cover art by Dan O'Leary.
Cover design by George Long.
Cover handlettering by Ron Zinn.

For my Amanda Martin, with love

For My Readers

Be sure to go to christinefeehan.com/members/ to sign up for my PRIVATE book announcement list and download the FREE ebook of *Dark Desserts*. Please feel free to email me at Christine@christinefeehan.com. I would love to hear from you.

Acknowledgments

I need to thank Domini Walker for doing her best to keep up with me! I need to give a shout-out to all my power-hour partners who keep me on track and writing like a fiend! And always thanks to Brian Feehan for being there with me whenever I call, day or night, to hash out a stubborn scene! I love that you don't mind talking books with me ever.

1

CATARINA Benoit woke to screams. Terrible, frightening screams that echoed through her bedroom. Her heart pounded and sweat beaded on her body. Her long hair hung around her face in damp strands. She clapped a hand over her mouth to still the cries, her throat raw even as her eyes darted around the room. Searching. Always searching.

She searched the high places first—anywhere he could be crouched. Watching. Waiting to strike. She searched the windows. The glass was covered with bars, but she knew that wouldn't stop him if he found her. *Nothing* ever stopped him. He could get inside any house, any building. Any-where. Rafe Cordeau, the thing of nightmares.

She was safe. She had to be. She lived completely off the grid. Underground. She only came out at night. Her one exception to her night rule was her hour of running just before sunset. She worked in a quiet part of town, in a store no one would ever consider she would work in. Rafe would never figure it out, not in a million years. He couldn't find her this time. She'd planned too carefully. She'd even stolen enough money to get herself a start. Right out of his safe. The one no one could crack. She'd done that. He wasn't going to get his hands on her again. Never again.

She fell back against the pillows, drawing her knees into her chest, making herself into a small, protected ball, rocking gently to try to calm herself, to push the terror of the nightmare away. She could taste bile in her mouth.

Drawing in great, deep breaths to try to control her wild heart, she felt something else, something inside unfurl and stretch. It terrified her too. There was something in her, biding its time, waiting for a chance to get out, and she feared it was a monster. She feared *he'd* put it there, he'd somehow made her like him.

She knew she wouldn't go back to sleep. Every window was covered with heavy drapes to block out the sun, but still, she would never be able to go back to sleep. She forced her legs to straighten. That hurt. Every muscle was sore from the terrible coiling in her body. She knew from experience it would be like that all day, her body feeling as if someone had beat her up with a baseball bat.

She sat up and scooted to the side of the bed, first, as she always did, feeling for the gun hidden beneath her pillow. The solid weight of it always made her feel better. She worked out, trained hard, even when she knew she still wouldn't have a chance against him if he found her. Even so, she lived her life. Held herself still. Kept to herself. Reduced his odds.

She took a shower in the small cubicle. It was a rigged hose with a spray nozzle over the top of a tiny booth with a drain. It didn't matter. She was safe. She lived in a warehouse, not her car. Mostly the warehouse was empty, but her martial arts instructor owned the property and he'd allowed her to rent the space when he realized she was living out of her car. He had barred the windows for her. She had put in the double locks herself.

She had done everything necessary to make herself safe, but then she'd made a vow. She would be happy every single second she was living free and alive. She wouldn't hide in the warehouse, shut away from the world, she would *live*. She'd be smart and careful about it, but this time, she wouldn't be a mouse hiding. It hadn't done her much good the last time, and she wasted that little bit of freedom she'd had. The price definitely hadn't been worth it then. She was going to make certain it was this time.

Catarina pressed her fingers hard against her temples, unwilling to revisit the moment when he'd last found her and his terrible punishment. Her entire body shuddered. She'd paid dearly, but that had only made her all the more determined to escape permanently. She'd been terrified and he thought that terror would work to his advantage. She let him think that, and then she'd escaped again.

Her life had really started with her martial arts instructor. Malcom Hardy was in his late sixties and from the moment she'd entered his class, he'd seemed to know something was wrong. He didn't exactly ask questions, but somehow he found out she was living out of her car and he casually mentioned his empty warehouse. That had been the start of their strange friendship.

Catarina had never had a friendship with anyone before, and at first she was distrustful of his motives. It had taken Malcom months to gain her trust enough that she stayed and had a few words privately with him after each class. She hadn't told him her past, only that she was looking for a job and needed a safe home. She'd used the word *safe* in the hopes that he would understand without an explanation—and he had.

When she'd escaped, she hadn't taken tons of money from the safe because she didn't want Rafe to have more reason to come after her if by chance he'd given up on her. That meant she didn't have a lot of money. It also meant, if he had given up on her, he'd send his kill squad after her.

Either way she wasn't safe and she needed to be very careful with her money.

Malcom slowly won her over with his many simple kindnesses. He casually dropped by to put the bars on the windows when she'd mentioned she was a little nervous. He'd also been the one to find her the job after she told him what her dream job would be.

Catarina loved her job. The coffee-house-slash-bookstore was old, the kind where poets and writers came and read their work every Friday. It was a throwback world that suited her. Books were everywhere, and people gathered to talk and read and show off their work. She liked that the place was a tribute to a bygone era and the regulars who occupied it were loyal and definitely different.

She made certain never to stand out. She dressed in loose-fitting jeans. A loose-fitting shirt. Her hair had always grown thick and fast and got worse the more she cut it. She'd given up on short hair so she pulled it back in a ponytail or braid and often wore hats. Since everyone who came to the coffee-house wore berets or felt hats, she wasn't out of place. Most wore sunglasses, even at night, as well, so she did that too, hiding her unusually colored cobalt eyes.

The coffee-house stayed open nearly twenty-four hours, and she had the shift that ran from seven in the evening until three in the morning, when she closed the shop. They got a large influx of people looking to wind down from drinking, dancing and clubbing at the bars that closed at two. She wasn't fond of that particular crowd, but she'd grown used to it.

She spent an hour on working the heavy bag Malcom had hung for her and another hour doing sit-ups and crunches and push-ups. She dressed in baggy sweats and went running. That killed another hour and put her to sunset. Another shower and she headed for the coffee-house.

She tried hard not to allow her heart to do a little stutter, wondering if the new instructor Malcom had hired would drop by again. She liked looking at him. He was a bonus at the dojo as well as the coffee-house. She'd never found herself looking at a man before—she'd never dared to. But he was special. Everything about him was special.

He'd been at the dojo a month, and she'd watched him with the same distrust she had for anyone new who came into her world. He was absolutely the most beautiful man she'd ever seen in her life. He was brutal when he fought, and yet, at the same time, graceful and fluid. Sheer poetry. He was light on his feet, very fast, so smooth. He was always, always utterly calm. She couldn't imagine him ruffled over anything. He embodied the world of martial arts—he lived that way—not just in the dojo but out of it.

Still, she kept her distance, even when he'd noticed her in the dojo and smiled at her a time or two. She didn't smile back. She didn't encourage any kind of a relationship, nor did she want one. Not because she didn't ever talk to people, but because he made her feel something she'd never felt before. But she liked looking at him. Maybe a little too much.

She didn't have flights of erotic fantasy or dreams. Her body had never awakened, on fire, burning with need and hunger. Her breasts hadn't felt swollen and achy, desperate for a man's touch. Not until she laid eyes on Malcom's new instructor. Something moved in her. Something took over, and unexpectedly, at night, when she wasn't having nightmares, she had erotic dreams that burned through her body until she couldn't breathe. Abruptly they'd leave her, and once they were gone her body would settle and she'd be perfectly fine again. He was definitely someone she needed to stay away from, but looking at him was acceptable.

He'd sauntered into the coffee-house two weeks after starting with Malcom. She'd noticed him immediately. How could she not? When he moved, the roped muscles of his body, even beneath his tight black shirt, did a delicious kind of rippling that drew every feminine eye in the place. Ridley Cromer. The name was as strange and unique as the man.

Catarina stood outside the coffee-house just staring into the windows, feeling happy. She always made certain she acknowledged being happy. That was important. She woke up in the morning and always, *always* told herself she would be happy that day.

"Hey, beautiful."

She froze, the smile fading. The other thing strange about Ridley Cromer was the fact that she never heard him when he came near her. He didn't make a sound. She heard everyone. She always knew when someone was close to her. The reason why she excelled in martial arts was because she always anticipated her opponent's move. It was as if she had a kind of radar telling her where everyone was at all times within her space. Everyone but Ridley Cromer.

She turned her head, holding her breath, her smile fading. Her eyes met Ridley's and the impact was so strong the air rushed from her lungs as if she'd been punched. He had beautiful eyes. Intense. The way he looked at her was intense. Everything about him was intense. And Zen. Very Zen.

She forced herself to nod out of politeness. She knew if she tried to speak she would squeak like a mouse and nothing else would emerge. Ridley Cromer was fine to look at. Daydream about. Even have night fantasies over, but there was no talking. No interaction. Not ever. If all the rest of the world of women were smart, they'd adopt her steadfast rules with him.

"You working tonight or just looking for company?"

His voice was low and sexy. Her pulse beat hard in her throat. She swallowed hard. She'd never had a crush on anyone in her life, but he was standing right in front of her. Towering over her. His eyes smiled and his white teeth flashed. He should be locked up to preserve all women's virtues.

She shook her head and reached for the door handle. He reached at the same time, his hand settling around hers as she grasped the knob. A shiver of absolute awareness slid down her spine. Curled in her belly. There was a sudden tingle in her breasts and she felt heat gathering in her very core. Not like her night fantasies, where her body burned up, but still . . .

He didn't let go of her hand, and she couldn't remove hers from the doorknob. His touch was light. Gentle. She should have pulled her hand away but she was frozen to the spot. He stepped closer, so close she could feel the heat of his body seeping into hers. He was hot. He radiated heat. His breath was warm on the nape of her neck, and for the first time she wished she'd left her hair down to protect herself.

"It's Cat, right? Malcom calls you Cat. You're his favorite student. I've never known him to have a favorite. I'm Ridley Cromer."

She closed her eyes briefly. Thunder roared in her ears. Her brain short-circuited. His voice was pitched so low that it seemed to slide beneath her skin and find its way directly into her bloodstream like some strange new drug. No one touched her. No one dared. He had broken that taboo. She didn't know how to feel about it.

"You're quick. Very fast," he went on, as if she wasn't the rudest person in the world for not answering him. "I couldn't help but watch you sparring the other day. You were wiping up the floor with men ranked much higher than you. Men with a lot more experience. It was a thing of beauty."

A thing of beauty. She would hold that close to her and think about it when she was alone. A compliment. Coming from someone who clearly could best anyone in the dojo, probably including Malcom, it was very high praise. Still, she couldn't stand there being an absolute idiot.

She finally found her wits and gave the door a desperate twist, flashing what she hoped was a careless smile of thanks over her shoulder at him. She yanked open the door, but found when she stepped back she stepped right into him. *Right* into him.

His body was as hard as a rock. It was rather like smashing herself against an oak tree. His arms came around her automatically to steady her. The heat radiating from him nearly burned right through her clothes.

To her absolute horror, she banged the door closed again as she threw herself forward and away from him. She nearly ran into the heavy glass, but his hands were suddenly at her waist, gently moving her away from the door.

One moment she was heading for danger; the next he had literally lifted her and put her a foot away from the door.

"Kitten, you'd better let me get that."

Color rushed up her neck into her face. To her everlasting mortification, she could hear male amusement in his voice. She was an idiot—a tongue-tied idiot—and he'd think she was crazy. Still—she gulped air—that was for the best. He'd just dismiss her, hopefully never look at her again. Not with those eyes. Those beautiful, antique gold eyes. Who had eyes that color?

He pulled the door open and held it, waiting for her to go through. Thankfully she found her legs and moved past him, once again throwing a small, hopefully thankful smile at him over her shoulder. She walked stiffly to the counter and shoved her things beneath it on the other side.

She was absolutely certain someone needed to file away books in the back where no one could see her. Someone else could make the coffee tonight and she'd just go hide.

"Cat, great, you're here." David Belmont, the owner of Poetry Slam, threw her an apron. "Get to it, hon. Everyone's been complaining because apparently my coffee doesn't taste like yours. I've watched you a million times and I do exactly the same thing, but it never comes out like yours."

"You don't like making coffee, David," Catarina replied,

and put on her apron. Which she found hilarious because he owned the coffee-house.

The moment she was behind the coffee machine, David moved into position to take orders and money. Clearly there he was in his element, chatting up the customers, remembering their names, talking them into some of the bakery goods sold with the coffee. He even remembered the poetry or short stories they wrote. He was awesome with the customers, and she was awesome with the coffee. They made a great team.

She didn't look up when anyone ordered. It was part of her strategy to keep in the background. The mouse in the coffee-house. Unfortunately, because she was *great* at making any type of coffee drink, the customers were aware of her. She was the reigning barista, and the customers had begun to fill the coffee-house nightly.

She had worked hard to learn what she needed to in secret. She read, watched countless videos and committed coffee books to memory. Before that, she'd had to learn to read. She was a little smug about it. Rafe would never, ever think to find her in a bookstore/coffee-house. *Never.* She was poor little illiterate Catarina.

She kept her eyes on the espresso machine when she heard Ridley give his order in a soft, low tone that set a million butterflies winging in her stomach. She already knew exactly what he wanted, just as she did with most of the regulars. He hadn't been coming in all that long, but she was aware of every breath he took—just as the other women were. She certainly remembered what he liked for coffee.

She knew exactly where he sat without looking up. He always pulled out a book, usually on mediation or essays from a Zen master, while he drank his coffee. He savored coffee. She'd watched him, sneaking looks of course, and he always had the same expression on his face. She knew she put it there. She might not be a conversationalist, but she made spectacular coffee.

She forced herself to make fifteen more coffees before she looked up. Her gaze collided with his. All that beautiful, perfect, molten gold. She almost fell right into his eyes. She blushed. She knew she did. There was no stopping the color rising into her cheeks. He gave her a faint, sexy smile. She looked down without smiling back, concentrating on her work.

One look and her stomach did a crazy roll. What was wrong with her? She didn't have physical reactions to men. It was just not okay. She couldn't ever be stupid enough to wish for a relationship. She'd get someone killed that way. In any case, she'd be too afraid. She didn't even know what a relationship was.

But he was darned good to look at, she acknowledged with a secret smile. *Darned* good. The familiar rhythm of the coffee-house settled her nerves. The aroma of coffee and fresh baked goods swept her up into the easy atmosphere. Once the poetry slam started, darkness descended. There was usually little joy in the poems, but she enjoyed them all the same.

Bernard Casey, a regular who was usually first up at the microphone, accepted his caramel macchiato from David, took one sip, and pushed his head over the counter the way he did each evening.

"Hey, coffee woman. Heaven again."

She shot him a smile. It was safe to smile at Bernard. He loved coffee, his poems and little else. "Hey coffee man, glad you think so." He only looked at her once a day, and that was when he gave her the nightly compliment.

It was their standard greeting. Bernard waved and settled at his usual table right in front of the microphone, making certain he would be the first and last poet of the night.

RIDLEY observed Catarina over the top of the book he no longer had any interest in. She was beautiful and she was scared. Very scared. She thought she'd managed to down-play her looks, but a man would have to be blind not to see through her baggy clothes and attempts to tame her wild hair.

Her sunglasses didn't hide the perfection of her skin, and when she took them off and looked at a man with her exotic cobalt blue eyes, the color a deep intense violet at times, ringed with those long dark lashes—well—the punch was low and it was just plain sinful.

And then there was her mouth. Full lips like a cupid's bow. Turned up at the corners just slightly. Her lower lip could make a man go to his knees and fill his nights with erotic fantasies. When her lips parted and she gave a small, distracted smile, the one that meant she wasn't seeing you, any man worth his salt couldn't help but take on that challenge. When she smiled, like she'd just done to Bernard, the strange poet who poured out his feelings for her through his poems, Ridley knew a man would kill for her.

She was nothing at all like he expected her to be. He watched her at the dojo with Malcom during her lessons and training sessions. She was focused. Intelligent, which, when fighting, was important. She was quick, her reflexes good, and she moved with a fluid grace that took his breath away. He wasn't the only man in the dojo who stopped what he was doing to watch.

He expected her to be a man-killer. She should have been. She had the face and the body. She had the voice. She had a soft drawl, barely there, the kind of drawl that reminded him of drifting down the bayou on a lazy summer night with the sky above him dark and a thousand stars shining overhead and a woman, naked in his arms.

She should have had all the confidence in the world. She had confidence when she sparred with any man Malcom put her against, and so far she'd wiped up the floor with them no matter their rank. She was that fast. She had confidence behind the espresso machines and she had every reason to. She had confidence when she walked home at three o'clock in the morning and she shouldn't.

But she didn't look at men. She didn't talk to them. There was no flirting. He'd never seen her flirt with anyone. Not a man or a woman. She was definitely a puzzle, and one he wanted to solve.

He'd deliberately stepped up close to her, crowded her space, to see what she'd do. She hadn't defended herself. She hadn't told him to get the hell away from her. She froze. Breathless. Terrified. She'd confused the hell out of him, and that didn't happen very often. She'd intrigued him, and that happened even less often. She'd also done something insane to his body.

He was a man always in control. Always. Control defined him. He was a man and lived his life as a man. He was tough and liked things his way, and he always got what he wanted. He was single-minded that way. Women, especially man-killers, didn't do a thing for him. But Catarina . . . The moment her soft body had come up against his, the moment he'd touched bare skin, everything hot and wild and hungry in him responded. He wanted her. And he wanted her for himself. Exclusively. That had *never* happened before.

He looked down at his arms, at the tattoos he'd acquired so painstakingly over the years. He looked rough and mean. He knew that. It served him well to look that way. He deliberately wore his hair longer than most. He served notice to other men just who he was and what he was capable of. Men got the hell out of his way when he was after something. Especially a woman.

Women were easy for him. He didn't have to work hard at all and that was okay, but it never lasted more than a night or two—not for him anyway. But this woman . . . She'd burn up in his arms, and it wouldn't be enough. He got that already just by looking at her. So did every other man who came near her. The difference was, most of them would step back and wait for a signal that was never going to come.

That was definitely not the way to handle a woman like Catarina. A man had to take over and be decisive about it.

Catarina felt the weight of Ridley's gaze on her. She knew he was watching her without even looking up. Her body responded just as if he was standing in front of her. For one moment she felt restless, achy, in need even. That something wild crouched inside of her stretched. Her skin itched. She couldn't breathe and her skull felt too tight. For one terrible moment, her skin went hot and that terrible burn began between her legs. She could barely breathe with the need and hunger.

Horrified, she dragged off the apron and tossed it to David. "I need a break, just a short one."

Even here in her sanctuary, the one place she could go and be around others, her past tried hard to drag her down. She was aware of Ridley's attention settling on her instantly, alertly, but she didn't so much as glance at him. Her past was too close. Even from a thousand miles away, *he* was controlling her. She couldn't look at another man without something inside of her turning ugly.

The book aisles were narrow, the stacks rising from floor to ceiling. She wound her way through them to the back door and pushed it open. The night air hit her face, cool and refreshing, enfolding her in its blanket of darkness. She drew in several deep breaths and stepped outside. The cool air felt good on her skin. She dragged the hat from her hair and sank down onto the steps leading to the back door.

Strangely, she'd always had great night vision, and this last month she'd noticed it had gotten even better. She liked that she could see in the dark. She loved the night. There was an entirely different world going on at night and she was part of it. That made her part of something. And Rafe couldn't take that away from her.

"Kitten?"

She had to stifle a scream as she twisted, nearly throwing herself off the stairs. Ridley stood behind her, in the doorway, his tall body solid, both terrifying and safe. He stepped next to her and closed the door, sinking down onto the step beside her.

"Are you all right? You went very pale in there."

His voice could mesmerize. At least it was mesmerizing her. She nodded, because his eyes refused to leave her face, drifting over her intently.

He frowned suddenly "Are you afraid of me? All this time I just thought you were shy, but you're afraid of me." He made the last a statement.

She looked away from him. Thankfully whatever was inside of her, threatening to burst free, had subsided along with the terrible need to feel Ridley's hands and mouth on her body.

His fingers settled gently on her chin and he turned her face toward him. "I wouldn't hurt you. You don't know me, but I would never harm a woman. I'm not like that. I'm new in town and you're at the dojo and make fantastic coffee, that's all. I wanted a little company. Just to talk to, Cat. That's all. End of story."

It was impossible to look into his eyes and not believe him. Up close she could smell him, and he smelled nice. Very nice. Very masculine. His lashes were long and thick, framing his incredible golden eyes. His tattoos were just as intricate and intriguing as he was. They crawled up his arms, drawing attention to his amazing and very defined muscles.

He was still looking at her and hadn't blinked once. His fingers remained firm but gentle on her chin. She'd forgotten that she'd been so mesmerized by his eyes. Catarina forced air into her lungs and smiled. Before she could speak he shook his head.

"I saw the genuine thing, Cat. You smiled at Bernard. You gave him the real smile, the high voltage one that can knock a man off his feet at two hundred yards. I don't want a pretend smile. Give me the real thing or don't smile at me at all. I'm telling you again, I don't hurt women."

His voice was pure velvet. She shivered, his tone smoothing over her skin. "I'm sorry. I'm not afraid of you." A blatant lie. "I just don't talk much." That was lame. More than lame. She was a total idiot, but maybe that would save her.

Ridley's fingers slid from her chin. He didn't move, his thigh tight against hers on the narrow steps. "Unfortunately for you, Kitten, I am very adept at knowing a lie when I hear one. I've done my best to reassure you, but talk is cheap. I guess I'll just have to show you I'm a nice guy."

She was certain he was not. Oh, not like Rafe Cordeau. Not like that. But he was dangerous. She knew dangerous men, and this one sitting beside her was no domestic kitty cat. He was a tiger, all raw power and razor-sharp focus. But he wasn't *bad* dangerous. He was just plain scary dangerous. And a heartbreaker.

She sighed, hating that she actually felt the loss of his fingers on her skin—hating that every single cell in her body was aware of him. He was a good ten years older in years and experience. There were scars. There were the tats. There was the cool confidence and the lines in his face that only seemed to add to his masculine beauty.

She knew what he saw when he looked at her. She'd always looked young and she was barely twenty-one. He would consider her someone he had to look after, just as Malcom did. That was safe. She needed safe, especially around this man.

"Maybe I am a little afraid of you," she forced herself to admit. "I've seen you in the dojo and you're rather terrifying." That much was true, and if he really were as adept at reading lies then he'd have to hear the sincerity in her voice.

"That's a place of practice. This is a coffee-house. Unless you're going to stand up in front of that mic and read off some really bad poetry, I don't think you have a thing to worry about," he assured.

There was a drawling amusement in his voice, one that made her want to laugh with him, but it was as sexy as all get-out, and she couldn't make a noise. Not a single sound for a few seconds. She cleared her throat. "I'm not good at talking to people."

"You talk just fine to Malcom. In fact, you laugh when you're with him. It's the only time I've seen you actually laugh."

Her heart jumped. She tensed and knew he felt it. Still, as hard as she tried she couldn't relax. Had he been watching her? Why? What did that mean? She bit down on her lower lip, a little afraid that she was so paranoid even such a simple statement could make her want to run.

"Malcom isn't people."

"I know he's your friend," Ridley conceded. "He's very closed-mouth about you and protective."

She turned her eyes on him. Fixed. Focused. Alert. "Were you asking him questions about me?"

"Of course I was. You're beautiful. Mysterious. A turn-on in the dojo. When you move, honestly, Kitten, I've never seen anything like it. You're fast and fluid and hot as hell. You put James Marley down with one punch. One. You hit him exactly on his weak spot and dropped him like a ton of bricks. Your eyes are amazing, and so is your hair. You have the most beautiful face I've ever seen. Are you telling me Malcom doesn't get asked about you regularly? Women like you don't walk the streets alone at night. That's just asking for trouble."

Her breath slammed out of her lungs. "You followed me?" That couldn't be. She would have known.

"Every night that you lock up and walk back to the warehouse. Did you really think I'd let a woman walk alone that time of night? *Any* woman? But especially a woman like you? No fuckin' way."

Something in his eyes made her shiver. Hot. Angry. A flash, no more, and then quickly suppressed. He really didn't like her walking alone at night.

He had been at the coffee-house every night the past two

weeks until three A.M. But she hadn't seen him or heard him or even felt him following her. And that was bad. She couldn't afford to miss a tail. She had a sixth sense about that kind of thing, and yet he had followed her every single night.

"I can take care of myself."

"Cat, even Malcom will tell you that you aren't being realistic. You're good, there's no question about it, but you're small. A man gets his hands on you and you're done. You're smart enough to know that. You can defend from a distance, but if he knows what he's doing he's going to get past that guard and tie you up. Why don't you drive your car? That would be much safer."

She wasn't about to tell him gas cost the earth. He didn't need to know her personal finances, but she wasn't wasting precious gas when she could walk to and from work. It just wasn't that far.

"It isn't any of your business," she said, and knew she sounded uptight and stiff. Well, she was uptight and stiff. *And* it *wasn't* any of his business.

The same flash was there in his eyes. Hot. Angry. Pure steel. Her stomach did another flip. He was both scary and sexy at the same time, a combination she wanted no part of.

"I'm making it my business, Kitten, whether you like it or not. After hours, half the men in here are drunk. Why do you think they're in here?"

"I make a mean cup of coffee and word has gotten around. It sobers them up a little. Coming to Poetry Slam gives them some time to wind down."

He made a sound in the back of his throat that alarmed her. A rumble. A growl. The sound found its way to her heart, kick-starting her into flight mode.

"You can't possibly be that naïve, woman. Just in the two weeks I've been coming, the traffic between midnight and three has doubled. Mostly men. They come here because they're hoping to get lucky. They spend the entire time staring at you and trying to think of ways to get you in their beds. A few of them may have figured out that you walk home and they may make plans you aren't going to like and can't do anything about on your own."

She jumped up fast, but he was faster, his long fingers settling around her wrist, shackling her to him. He stood too, towering over her. His fierce golden eyes stared down into her blue ones, just as intense as she remembered, more so even. His gaze cut right through her until she feared every secret she had was laid bare in front of him.

"Don't run from me. I'm telling you the truth. Clearly you're living in a dream world when it comes to men and their intentions."

She tilted her head to one side, forgetting to keep her attitude in check. "Would you like to tell me what *your* intentions are?" she challenged.

His eyes changed and she knew immediately she'd made a terrible mistake. His eyes went liquid gold, focused and unblinking, locked onto her, and this time there was interest. Real interest. Before she'd been the one locked on to him, playing in her head with silly fantasies, but his motivation for following her had been actually watching out for her—she could see that now, at least she thought she could. Until that moment. That second.

She'd put too much sass into her tone. There was no backtracking from that, not with the stark speculation in his eyes. She forced air through her burning lungs and tugged at her hand to try to get him to release her.

His thumb slid over her wrist, right over her pounding pulse, a mere brush, but the stroke sent hot blood rushing through her veins. She wanted to look away, but there was no getting away from the piercing stare of his eyes.

"Now I'm seeing you, Kitten. And you've got a little bite to you."

"Enough to handle myself if someone decides to attack me on my way home."

"I disagree."

"That doesn't matter," she said, and tugged at her hand again.

His hold didn't loosen. He wasn't hurting her; in fact, the pad of his thumb sent waves of heat curling through her body as it continued to brush little strokes over her pulse.

"It matters to me."

"It isn't your business." Now he was back to scaring her. He couldn't follow her around. Especially not to her home.

She was usually adept at spotting and shaking a tail. She practiced. He couldn't see her practicing. He'd wonder what she was doing and why. She desperately tried to remember if she'd done such a thing in the last two weeks. Usually, after working a full shift, she was exhausted and didn't take the extra time.

"I've decided to make it my business."

His voice was so low she could barely catch the sound, but the tone vibrated right through her body, disturbing her balance. She almost felt as if she was caught in a dream, waking up for the first time, suddenly aware of what real chemistry between a man and a woman was. She was certain she'd been the only one to feel it, and even then, it was just an awareness, not in the least harmful—like her silly daydreams of him.

This was altogether different. Her awareness of him, her reaction, was so strong, almost feral, female reacting to a male on the hunt, wanting him, yet wanting to run. Maybe needing the chase to prove something to both of them. She saw the answering challenge in his eyes. It was impossible not to see.

She shook her head and took two steps back, trying to put distance between them despite his fingers around her wrist. In spite of the fact that she couldn't look away from him. *What was wrong with her?* Her lack of control was frightening. She couldn't blow this. She didn't dare.

"I have no interest whatsoever in a relationship with anyone. I don't do one-night stands and I don't date. I don't want attention from you or any other man. I'm asking you politely to let go of my wrist."

She could barely get the words out. There was something, a part of her she'd never known existed, a part of her that didn't want to walk away from this man. He was beautiful. Sexy. Intelligent. And Dangerous. Everything a woman might find attractive in a man. Everything *she* found attractive when she hadn't even known she could be attracted.

He didn't release her right away. His amazing eyes searched hers for a long moment. His face softened, and the male challenge was gone from his hard features as if it had never been there. Instead, he looked gentle. Still holding her wrist with one hand, he retrieved her hat with the other and gave it to her.

"You really are afraid of me, aren't you? I'm not going to hurt you, Cat. No matter what you think, I won't do that to you." His voice was pure velvet, stroking over her skin, low and vibrant and all male, almost a purr. His eyes hypnotized her all over again. They hadn't blinked. Not once. She was watching to see. He was absolutely, entirely focused on her and her alone.

Her belly did a slow roll and her breasts ached. Each separate spot where the pads of his fingers touched her bare skin felt as if he burned a brand right through her skin to her bones.

She hated that she was so susceptible to his voice. To his eyes. She retreated back to the character that always served her so well. She let her eyelashes fall, and nodded as if she understood. She couldn't handle a man like Ridley. She knew that. She didn't dare chance becoming his friend. She wouldn't know what to do with him.

He let her go. The moment she was free of his grip, she pulled her arm to her, pushing her wrist up against her body as if she could hold in the heat from his touch. She sent him one look from under her lashes and hurried past him back inside.

2

CATARINA looked at her watch for the hundredth time and then looked at David. He rolled his eyes. He held up his hands, fingers spread wide and grinned at her.

"Last call, everyone," David shouted. "If you want a coffee for the road, come get it now. We're closed in ten."

She flashed him a small, tired smile. It had been a great night for Poetry Slam. Business was huge. Huge. The take was the most they'd ever done. The tip jar was overflowing, which meant extra gas money. It had been a great night, but she was exhausted. She hadn't even been able to keep track of how many different variations of coffee she'd made that night. She could do ten more minutes, but beyond that . . .

Three men swaggered up to the counter to give David their closing orders. She avoided looking at them. One of the three, a man his friends called Jase, had twice tried to engage her in conversation. She'd given him a vague smile without meeting his eyes and stayed busy inventorying her various coffee beans both times.

"Hey, Cat," Jase called out to her, overloud.

She winced and forced herself not to glance toward the corner where Ridley continued to read his book. She was all too aware he hadn't missed both times Jase had tried to get her to converse.

"I can hear you, Jase," she answered, without looking up.

"What's it take?"

She made a mistake in pausing as she made his friend Marty his favorite latte. "I'm sorry?" she said, frowning a little, trying to puzzle out when he meant.

Ridley moved. He put down his book and stared hard at Jase.

"To fuck you. Tell me what it takes. We're trying to fig-ure that out and you're giving us nothing."

The coffee-house went utterly silent. David froze. Cata-rina blinked and Ridley was behind Jase, one hand on his shoulder. He spun the man around and punched him in the face. He hadn't pulled back his arm for strength. It was a short punch, but Jase's head snapped back on his shoulders and his legs turned to rubber. The only thing holding him up was Ridley's hand on his shoulder.

"Ridley," Catarina protested softly.

"Don't speak," Ridley snapped. "Just get this place shut down." His eyes moved to each of Jase's friends. "Either of you two got something you want to say before you leave? Because you're leaving right now."

Both took one look at the hard, implacable lines in his face, the smoldering golden eyes, and they shook their heads. Ridley, still holding Jase up, gestured toward the door. Without a word they turned and went out, Ridley trailing them, dragging a rubber-legged Jase with him. He thrust the man at the other two and wasn't gentle about it.

He shut the door decisively and turned and walked back

to his table. Applause broke out. The spectators liked their coffee.

Catarina glared at David, who was clapping along with the others. "You're not helping. Don't encourage him. He thinks I need protecting."

"You do," David said. "Jase is trouble."

"I can take care of myself," she muttered, sending Ridley a look that should have fried him on the spot. Not only did he not appear to fry, he looked a little amused.

She didn't draw attention to herself. Not ever. Thanks to Ridley the entire room was aware of her as more than the barista, a body behind the coffee machine. She sighed and started the cleaning process. The coffee-house shut down at three and emptied. This time Ridley didn't leave. He sat in the corner. She glanced up at him and scowled a couple of times, jerking her head toward him when David looked at her.

"He's got to go, just like any other customer," she hissed.

"I can hear you just fine," Ridley said. "I'm walking home with you, so get used to it, Kitten. Just get your work done so we can get out of here."

"Don't you have anything better to do?" she demanded.

"No." He didn't even look up.

She shook her head, exasperated. Of course Jase would have to act like an ass in front of him and he'd use that to prove his point. She could have handled Jase, no problem.

She accepted her half of the tip money, shoving it into the pocket of her jeans. That much cash made her very happy. It was worth putting up with jerks like Jase until three in the morning to have extra money. She used every little bit she had to get extra lessons from Malcom. She'd been practicing a lot with her gun. That required time at the local range as well as ammunition. It didn't come cheap.

Ridley fell into step beside her. She shot him a look from under her lashes. "You really don't have to do this."

"If you feel as if you owe me something, say thanks."

"I feel as if I'd like to hit you over the head because clearly you aren't listening," she countered. It just burst out of her when she'd promised no sass. No attitude.

Just like earlier, his eyes immediately focused on her. He didn't slow down. Didn't miss a step, but suddenly his golden eyes were fixed on her with the same amused speculation. Total interest. And this time there was something else smoldering in his eyes. Something hot and sexy that sent a wave of fire rushing through her body, burning through her nerve endings and centering squarely between her legs like the hottest fireball imaginable.

Her breath hitched in her lungs. She kept her eyes on the sidewalk, shocked. Embarrassed. Terrified. He brought out something wild in her. Something uninhibited. Something she wanted no part of.

"I'm listening, woman. I'll always listen to anything you have to say. You're just talking a lot of crap right now so I'm dismissing what you have to say as the crap it is. Jase and his friends could just as easily be waiting for you. You don't want them following you home, knowing where you live."

"I'd know. I always know. I've been followed before and I handled it."

He stopped abruptly, his fingers settling around her wrist, dragging her to a halt. "What the hell did you just say?" he demanded.

She blinked up at him. Major mistake revealing that piece of information. She should have kept that to herself. She licked her suddenly dry lips. Her heart pounded. She didn't know how to defuse his anger. In his quiet, cool way he was angry, and that was more terrifying than if he'd yelled. It wasn't his business, but she wasn't going to tell him that.

"Something you need to know about me, Kitten. I don't have a lot of patience. When I ask you something, I need you to answer. It isn't that damned difficult. Just tell me what happened and how you handled it."

His gold eyes burned like a flame, boring through her body. She licked her lips again. His hand tightened.

"And stop that. That's going to get your ass in trouble. Just talk, Cat, say what I need to hear."

She leveled a glare at him. "You are not in the least bit Zen, Ridley. Not even a little bit, and you have crushed one of my fantasies. I have to tell you, that's just plain sad because I could work with that for a very long time."

He blinked. He never blinked. Never broke his stare. That was one of the first observations she'd made about him, and he definitely blinked. Amusement crept right through all the sparkling anger.

"You thought I was Zen?" He began walking again, taking her with him, walking so close she could feel the heat of his body. He hadn't relinquished her wrist, rather his hand slid down her arm to take possession of her fingers.

"The Zen *master*," she said, "Which, by the way, was really cool, and now you've blown that all to hell."

"So you were having fantasies about me?" The amusement definitely deepened.

She sent him a look of sheer reprimand from under her long lashes. "Newsflash for you, Ridley, *every* woman has fantasies about you. That's your gift. But the fact that you just blew one of the biggest parts of *my* daydreams about you took your hotness down a notch or two. Zen was very 'it' for me. You rocked that cool vibe."

"You have fantasies and daydreams about me?"

"Don't pretend you don't know you're freakin' hot. The way you look at women, there's not a doubt in my mind they're all over you, and you've got that hound dog disdain."

His eyebrow shot up. "Woman. You cannot tell me I'm the thing of fantasies in one breath and say I'm a hound dog in the next."

She gave him a serious look. "They aren't mutually exclusive. You are, right? A player? A hound dog? The kind of man who kicks a woman out of his bed right after sex and then loses her phone number?"

His eyes laughed at her. "I don't take women to my bed, I'm usually in their beds, and I get up and leave. They know the score or I wouldn't be in their beds in the first place."

She nodded. "Yep. A player and a hound dog. And just so you know, telling you about my now completely blown fantasy does not mean I'm giving you the go-ahead to make a move on me. Fantasy and reality are two very different things."

"I see."

Catarina secretly hugged herself. She had forgotten it was fun talking to another person. She didn't allow herself that luxury, not ever anymore. Well, sometimes with Malcom, but not like this. Not just saying anything that came into her head. Watching Ridley's face lose the stone-carved effect and replacing it with laughter was fun. Just fun. She'd forgotten what that was like. Or truthfully, she hadn't known about having fun in the first place.

They rounded the corner of the second block and started down the third before she remembered he was holding her hand. Before she realized she hadn't taken a careful look around her to make certain no one was following. The smile inside slipped away. Vigilance was far more important than fun. She actually liked Ridley, even though she was certain he was too beautiful for any woman to ever keep. She didn't want to be responsible for anything happening to him.

Catarina tried to slip her hand out of his, a subtle retreat, nothing overt that he would notice. He noticed. His hand tightened around hers and he looked down at her immediately. He had eyes that saw everything. He didn't fail to see her gaze scanning the rooftops and the fire escapes as they passed the buildings.

"What is it?"

His voice was low. Velvet. So soft and perfect she nearly closed her eyes against the mesmerizing sound. She was fairly certain he could growl, she'd heard him do it once. Now, she thought he could probably purr as well. For some reason, the moment it came into her mind, her body reacted, going feminine on her. She decided it was him. Ridley just had a way with women and he was casting a spell.

"Nothing." She was back to mumbling, her sense of fun fading along with her confidence.

She felt vulnerable and exposed walking beside him. Alone she could stay in the shadows, close to the building if there were no openings, slipping back toward the street if she couldn't see directly into the alleyways and doorways. Ridley walked straight down the center of the sidewalk, head up, shoulders straight, and he looked like a man no one ever messed with. She was certain most men would take one look at him and scurry away.

Rafe Cordeau was not that kind of man. He would walk right up to Ridley, staring him straight in the eye, and without a single word slit his throat. Or his belly. Her fault. She glanced at their linked hands. Rafe would kill him. There would be no discussion and no way to stop him.

Her heart began to pound and she tasted fear in her mouth. "I don't know you well enough to hold your hand and it makes me uncomfortable."

It wasn't a lie, although she'd enjoyed the moment with him, the moment of fun she'd always remember. Still, she was uncomfortable holding hands because she liked it—maybe a little too much. But she wasn't a woman who could ever walk openly down a street with a man and feel comfortable. And she wasn't naïve enough not to realize Ridley Cromer was way out of her league, even if she didn't have hell following her around.

Ridley's piercing gaze searched her face and then their surroundings. His eyes moved in a search pattern around them, the alleys, the streets, the alcoves and doorways. Only then did he look up toward the rooftops and fire escapes as she'd done.

"You're afraid, Kitten, but not of me. Whatever it is you're afraid of, know that when you're with me, you're perfectly safe."

Supreme confidence. Ridley was a man who had been in dangerous situations, she could tell that. In some circumstances he was probably a very scary man, but no one was in Rafe's class. No one. She couldn't explain him to anyone, they'd think she was insane. They'd lock her up and make it easy for Rafe to come get her.

What had she been thinking? She'd let walking with a very attractive man override her good sense. Fun wasn't worth getting someone killed.

She sent Ridley a quick look from under her lashes. It was there again. The expression that told her she'd made a terrible mistake revealing this side of her. She'd suppressed it for so long, it just came out, as unexpected to her as it was to him.

"I'm used to being alone, that's all. I'm careful. I don't want you to think I was flirting with you, I wasn't." And she hadn't been. She didn't even know how to flirt. She didn't look at men. She'd made an art out of finding everywhere to look but at any man in the room with her. She'd trained herself from the time she was eleven years old.

"You don't have to try to flirt, Kitten." Ridley's voice was soft, gentle even.

For some reason the way he spoke made her insides melt a little. Her body reacted to just the sound of his voice. She bit her bottom lip hard to try to counteract the effect.

"You smile at a man, or look at him with your gorgeous eyes, and he's a goner. That's just the reality of it."

She refused to wrap herself up in his compliment. She'd never had compliments before. Not ever. Not personal. About her coffee maybe, but not like this. She couldn't remember anyone being so fun. She'd had her first kindness from Malcom. Now she had her first best time with a man. She couldn't keep him, but she could have the memories, and when she was alone, *then* she'd wrap herself up in his compliments and savor them.

The warehouses loomed on the next block. They turned the corner and crossed the street, angling toward the center one. It looked old from the outside. Old and tired. A single light illuminated a heavy door. There were three cargo doors, all padlocked. Ridley scowled at them.

"You didn't tell me about the time you were followed. I'm still waiting to hear that story."

She snuck a peek at his face from under her lashes. He was like a dog with a bone. She hadn't distracted him at all. She sighed. Loudly. "Seriously, Ridley, it isn't important."

"That's bullshit, Cat, and you know it. You're scared of something. It's not all that hard to tell. You walk everywhere, which means you don't want to drive your car . . ."

"It *doesn't* mean that," she hissed. She stabbed at the number pad a little viciously, punching in the code to unlock the door. "Gas costs money."

She was horrified that she blurted out the truth. It was just that he had such an edge to his voice, as if he knew all about her. She wasn't doing her best job of running him off and she knew it was because she was lonely and he made her feel alive. Okay, happy even. There, she'd admitted it to herself. But it had to stop. She paused before she pushed open the door, her hand on the doorknob.

"Thanks for walking me home. I can take it from here." She used her best dismissive voice. She'd had a *lot* of practice using that particular tone, and it was one of her best weapons. It didn't even faze him. He kept moving, crowding her, pushing her inside.

"Ridley. Seriously. You did the white knight thing. We're good."

"We're not good. What kind of man would let you walk

into a warehouse without checking it out first to make certain you're safe?" His hands settled on her waist and he picked her up, stepped inside and put her to the side of the door. "You stay right there."

It was pitch-black inside, the way it always was. She had heavy drapes on all the windows to block out every bit of light so she could sleep during the day. That didn't seem to faze him, although he swore under his breath as he took a careful look around.

"Light switch?"

For some reason, she thought he had a super power and could see in the dark. Maybe it had been the slow, careful perusal of the empty space, but she just stood there, not breathing, waiting for something, her heart pounding and her mouth dry.

"Kitten."

He just said one word. But it was his voice. *How* he said it. The gentle, amused tone. She felt his voice slide in under her skin, slip into her bloodstream and rush straight like an arrow for her most feminine core. She hadn't expected it.

Instantly there was heightened awareness. She smelled him. That faint masculine, almost wild smell, mountains and jungles and maybe a rain forest or two. He was so solid, all flowing muscle, his shoulders wide and his hips narrow. He moved with fluid grace, and heat radiated off of him, enveloping her.

She stepped back from his sheer potency. His hand instantly went to her waist, slid to settle on her hip.

"Catarina, I'm just going to make certain you're safe."

Thank God he thought she was frozen with fear, not flooded with female hormones at the worst possible moment. She cleared her throat, trying to get past the unfamiliar hunger rising like a tidal wave. The itch under her skin was terrible. It came in a wave, rising and falling, and deep inside something she feared above all else gave a lazy stretch, making its presence known.

She stepped back again and hit the wall, her breath coming in a long rush, but suddenly his touch was too hot, melting through her skin to brand her very bones. She felt something rise in him, wild and feral, trying to break free. The moment was fraught with danger. She didn't move or speak, terrified if she did, something would happen that could never be taken back.

His fingers dug into her hip. Hard. Possessive. She felt the difference. The heat seared her. Scorched like a thousand flames. He went from being protective to predatory in one single moment. She felt the difference, felt the change sweep through him. A single sound escaped her throat. She heard it in the silence of the warehouse. Fear. Pure fear.

Instantly his hand dropped from her hip and moved to the nape of her neck. His fingers curled there. Gentle.

"Cat." His voice was pure indulgence. "Nothing is going to happen to you. Tell me where the light switch is."

She was acting crazy. She was letting fear dictate, fear and imagination. She wasn't over her past. She would never be over it, and she'd never be truly free. She took a breath, forcing air to move through her burning lungs.

"Right by the door as you walk in. Just about a foot above the door handle."

He flicked the light on immediately and she found herself staring up into his eyes. They looked like gold to her. Ancient Florentine gold. His eyes glittered down at her. For a moment she saw speculation. The interest he'd shown when she gave him attitude, but there was no aggression in them. Nothing in the least bit predatory. Just a man being kind to a woman who lived alone. A man taking charge.

"Are you all right?"

She nodded, feeling like a complete idiot. She knew danger and there was none radiating from this man at all. She bit her lip. "I'm sorry. I don't have men in my space." How lame was that?

His hand slid her hat from her head and handed it to her.

"You have a big space here, Kitten. Stay here and let me look around."

His eyes didn't leave her face and she couldn't move, only nod slowly. His gaze drifted over her as if inspecting her carefully. Seeing her. Seeing too much. She had secrets to hide. Not little tiny secrets, huge ones. She couldn't afford a man like this around her. He took in too much. Saw past every guard. And for some reason she wasn't very good at keeping things under wraps around him.

Abruptly he turned away and began to walk around the warehouse. Not walk—he prowled. He moved like a great jungle cat, all flowing muscle, fluid and absolutely silent. He was a thing of beauty to watch. He moved with absolute confidence, and she doubted if he missed anything.

His gaze searched the high places as well as the low. She could see he was systematically checking every concealed space and yet at the same time, seeing everything. There wasn't much to see. Mostly, the warehouse was empty. It was a single story, very long and very wide. What had been an office was now her bedroom.

Malcom had begun work on renovating the warehouse some years ago and then stopped when he met his wife. She hadn't been so enamored with the idea of living in the warehouse district. He had thought it would be nice to have his apartment and dojo together so he'd bought the building. He met his wife four months later.

She was very happy it had taken Malcom four months to meet the woman he had fallen madly in love with. That meant he'd worked on the warehouse. She had a makeshift bathroom and a really good bedroom space. Her kitchen area was the most finished of any room. She had a sink, counter, stove and small fridge. Malcom had started with a kitchen and bathroom, paying most attention to the fact that he liked to eat properly because he worked out so much.

"You have a hose for a shower."

Of course he would notice that.

"It's still in the building phase," she admitted. Since he was talking now, she assumed there was no one ready to jump out and murder her. She trailed after him, moving quickly to catch up.

He was in her bedroom, looking carefully around him. His gaze took in everything, the bed, the small safe on the floor beside the bed and her beat-up chair. She refused to be embarrassed. She'd found the chair at a thrift store and it was comfortable. Ignoring him she went to the safe, opened it and shoved her tip money inside.

The bedroom had three walls. The fourth was open to the warehouse floor. Straight ahead was her heavy bag hanging from the ceiling, a mat and a speed bag. She'd spent precious dollars on her equipment but felt it was a necessary expenditure.

"Nice workout area."

She looked at him over her shoulder, trying not to look too proud. He took up her entire bedroom area. Before she thought it was a lot of space for a bedroom, now it seemed small.

"I like to work out."

"It shows when you're in the dojo."

He wandered out of her bedroom area and into the workout space, his hand moving over the heavy bag. A stroke with his open palm. Almost a caress. Her heart fluttered. They had one thing in common—clearly he liked to work out as well.

"Malcom is a good instructor." He made it a statement.

Catarina was uncertain how to respond. "I think so. He certainly has helped me learn fast."

"You're a good student. I've watched. He tells you something once and you've got it. You listen and you don't get upset when he critiques you."

"I pay him a lot of money. I don't want him to tell me how good I am, I want him to tell me everything I'm doing wrong so I can get better."

"Unusual," he commented, and moved around the heavy bag. His gaze took in her neatly shelved equipment, the gloves and the small weights. "You're really serious about learning."

"I wouldn't spend the money on it if I wasn't."

"Why the gun?"

She stiffened. The gun was hidden beneath her pillow. He wasn't looking at her and his voice was casual, but she knew it wasn't a casual question.

"Cat." Now he did look at her, one arm still circling the heavy bag. "Why the gun?"

She swallowed. Tried to shrug. "Woman alone in large warehouse."

"Can you shoot?"

"Yes. I practice just like I do my self-defense." That much was honest.

"What are you afraid of?"

"I'm not afraid," she denied, a blatant lie this time. "I'm careful."

His eyes cut to her. Looked inside her. Saw too much. She looked away first. "I'm safe, Ridley. And I really do appreciate you taking the time to walk me home and check out the warehouse, but everything's okay now."

He didn't move. Didn't take his eyes from her. She pressed her lips together. Even with the warehouse as large as it was, he took up space.

"You have bars on your windows. You have a gun. You spend money you don't have on self-defense lessons, and Malcom told me you're working on weapons training as well. Knives, arnis sticks. Is someone threatening you?" There was a hard edge to his voice.

She spread her hands out in front of her. "I don't know you."

"You know me well enough. I'm working with Malcom. I teach women self-defense. I don't like when they're threatened. Or if they're afraid."

It was impossible not to hear the ring of truth in his

voice. He was definitely the kind of man who would protect his woman by any means he needed.

"I'm just . . . careful," she reiterated.

"All right. We'll leave it at that, but your security system sucks. You need alarms and cameras on this place. The cargo doors, the windows, front door. Motion detectors. That's my field of expertise, and even with what you've done, you're still vulnerable."

She knew that. She could only do one thing at a time and she had to prioritize. She always divided her money carefully. Bills and paying back the money she'd taken from Rafe's safe first and then the rest on security. "I'm getting there."

"You need to get there faster." Again there was an edge to his voice. Impatience.

She glanced up and her gaze collided with his. It was a mistake. The golden glitter was back and she actually felt the edge of his anger. She moistened suddenly dry lips with the tip of her tongue and his gaze dropped to her mouth and softened instantly.

Her body reacted again, the strange electric awareness she felt in her breasts, up her thighs, in her belly and between her legs. It was instantaneous and powerful, so strong she couldn't move. Her breathing changed. She heard smooth go to ragged. Her lungs burned for air.

His eyes went molten. Hungry. He took a step toward her. Catarina threw her hand up, stepping back, shaking her head. He stopped instantly, his fist closing around the chain suspending the heavy workout bag, knuckles going white.

"I'm not used to having anyone around me for very long," she admitted in a low voice, hoping he would just understand and leave. "I don't have great social skills. This is difficult for me."

"Are you afraid of me?"

She wanted to close her eyes against the smooth, velvet tone. She needed to block out the look on his face. Carved.

Hungry. The hot flames in his eyes. His eyes. She felt as if a ravenous beast of prey had turned his attention fully on her, focused and deadly, and now that she had his attention, he wasn't going to ever be diverted.

She swallowed the lie and went for a half-truth. "Maybe. I don't know." She was terrified of him. She had no idea why he was there or how she'd let him this far into her life. It wasn't like her. It went against every rule she had. It went against common sense. She'd worked hard to get to a place where she could live free and enjoy her life, but at the same time make certain everyone around her was safe. This was not safe. Not by any stretch of the imagination. She had no idea how Ridley Cromer ended up in her warehouse, in her personal living space.

He had to leave. *Right now.* His scent would be all over the warehouse. She didn't even like Malcom to visit, or work on anything because she knew he would leave behind his scent. Ridley's was much more aggressive . . . and . . . and *interested.* She tried not to panic.

"I'm going to design a security system for you," he said, and walked away from her, putting distance between them, studying the lofts that had been built to hold freight. "It wouldn't take that many cameras. A few motion detectors. Nothing fancy."

"I'm saving," she told him, trying not to sound as if she was choking.

"I didn't say anything about paying," he snapped.

She winced. His voice was a lash. He really, really was a nut about a woman being safe. She took a breath and let it out.

"I know you didn't. You're being kind and I appreciate that, but I'll keep saving and eventually I'll be able to pay for a good security system." She was proud of the "firm" in her voice.

He turned his head and shot her a look of absolute impatience. "What the hell kind of crap is that, Cat? You're

living here now. You admitted to me you were followed
once already. A woman looking like you, living alone in a
warehouse in this district, is just plain nuts."

"It's my home and I happen to love it. And this area isn't
that bad."

"The coffee-house is situated on the edge of 'not bad.'
This warehouse is in the 'bad.' We passed three bars. We
passed a pawn shop and two tattoo parlors. A biker gang
hangs out on the third block and they're rough as hell."

She'd seen them. She was very alert to potential problems and that was why she was careful to stay in the shadows and not walk down the center of the sidewalk where
everyone could see her. He didn't get that.

"I'm careful."

He sighed. Ran a hand through his dark, thick hair. He
had nice hair and when he messed it up like that it was even
nicer.

"Your next day off is day after tomorrow. I'll be here in
the morning to install your security system. You know how
I like my coffee."

She glared at him. "How would you know when my next
day off is?"

He flashed her a grin. "Kitten. Come on. I pay attention.
David has a big mouth and he was bemoaning the fact that
half the patrons know when your day off is and they don't
bother to show. Apparently they come for your coffee. I
know when your day off is because I go to Poetry Slam for
your coffee as well."

"You do?" Her heart started beating normally again.
That made sense.

"I do. You make kick-ass coffee. I was hoping you might
have a machine here."

"Those machines are thousands of dollars."

"Still, you make great coffee. You don't even have a
small machine."

"Because I'm saving for a security system."

"I see. Well I'm installing that day after tomorrow so you can use your funds for a small machine and give me my fix while I work."

"You're not paying for my security system."

"Why not?"

"Because nothing in this world comes without a price tag."

For a moment his golden eyes went glittery again and then they seemed to melt into masculine amusement. "You're right about that."

She stiffened.

"My price is your coffee, Kitten. Lots of it. And then, if I get finished, we can spar a little. I've got a few moves that might help you."

He turned and walked away from her toward the door without once looking back. She stood there with her mouth open.

"You going to lock this door?" He paused at the door, turning his head to stare at her over his shoulder, a small grin hovering around his mouth, lighting his eyes.

"It locks automatically."

He nodded and sauntered out. It took her a full three minutes before she was breathing correctly again. She had no idea what just happened or how she was supposed to feel about it, so she did what she always did, she lost herself in her regular routine.

3

THE buzz was persistent. Really persistent. Annoyingly so. Catarina groaned and rolled over, her hair falling around her face, spilling across the pillow and covering her eyes and nose. The stupid buzzer blasted through the warehouse, as if someone leaned on it. It wasn't designed to be musical. It was loud and sounded like an alarm. She put the pillow over her head and held it there in hopes of drowning out the noise, but apparently, whoever had owned the warehouse before Malcom had been totally deaf.

"All right," she yelled, throwing the pillow and fighting her way out of the covers. She kicked several times, destroying her perfectly made-up bed, and sat up, sweeping back the mass of dark, wavy hair. It was everywhere. She looked around vaguely for a clip to tame the thick length, but the buzzer persisted, louder than ever.

"Seriously?" she muttered, and leapt to her feet, stalking through the warehouse to the front door. She flung it open, scowling ominously with blurry vision. "Are you crazy? It's like three o'clock in the morning."

Ridley stood there. Tall. Looking amazing. Refreshed and looking amazing. Seriously hot and amazing. "You. Are. Nuts." She tried to close the door in his face.

He stuck his boot in the door. "Step back, Kitten, I'm coming in and I've got my hands full."

He pushed open the door, and she pushed back. He was stronger, so the door swung his way. She clenched her teeth and stepped back, allowing him entry. He was carrying boxes and bags, which meant his hands were tied up.

"Cat, why are you looking at me like that?"

"Like you don't have two of your weapons and I could kick you in the thigh very hard and give you a dead leg? Like that? And then do a sweep and take both your legs out from under you? Am I giving you that kind of look? And then roll your body right out my front door? Because I'm contemplating how much of an effort that would be."

His mouth twitched. She narrowed her eyes at him.

"Of course, because you're the most annoying man on earth, I'd have to find the wire to cut that buzzer and stop it from ever working. You're the type that would just lay on it and wake a girl up when she just went to bed."

"I always say dream big if you're going to do it," he said, not in the least bit worried. "And it's not three in the morning, baby, it's more like nine."

He stared down at her from his lofty height, which only annoyed her more.

"You walked me home again last night. You know when I got to bed. This is my three o'clock in the morning." When he didn't turn and leave, she threw her hands in the air and then had to shove again at the wild mass of hair tumbling down to her waist.

"Has anyone ever told you that you're grumpy when you wake up?"

"As I don't wake up around anyone, no, they haven't."

His eyes went pure gold, moving over her in the slow, intense way she was coming to recognize as his taking in everything. Her breath hitched in her lungs when he looked at her.

Ridley couldn't take his eyes off Catarina. Her sweatpants rode low on her hips. Her tank molded to her breasts, and she wasn't thin. She had curves, and he liked a woman with curves. She hid them under baggy clothes, but they were there, a little too curvy by normal standards, but certainly not by his. She had a very small waist and a narrow rib cage, which only served to emphasize the curve of her hips and butt and her breasts. Her tank was just that little bit too short, baring her midriff, and she had unbelievable skin. She didn't wear makeup ever that he'd seen. Maybe lip gloss once in a while, but right now her lips were bare, along with her feet.

Her hair was wild. Bedroom wild. Sexy wild. And then on top of everything else she had those eyes. Large, framed with long thick black lashes, her eyes were unbelievable, and he wanted them staring straight into his when he was buried deep in her body. He wanted to see how those eyes changed when he gave her an orgasm.

He swore to himself. She wasn't very old, not in years, but in her eyes, she was a million years old. That wasn't a green light, he knew that. She was terrified, absolutely terrified, and he detested that. No woman should ever have to live in fear. She was always in flight mode. He knew she was preparing herself to fight, but right now, all he'd seen was her hiding herself away, her silence, baggy clothes and downcast eyes. That was Catarina in full flight.

He wanted to help her, to find a way to let her live in daylight. Along with her looks and that smile of hers, she made him laugh. He couldn't remember laughing in a hell of a long time. And then she had that attitude. Looks, humor and attitude—hell—he was a goner. That made the situation a lot more dangerous. The last thing he needed was any chemistry between them. Hell. He was fucked. There were moments when the chemistry was off the charts. He couldn't lie to himself about that. He had to be careful with her. Sex wasn't going to help her situation, at least not now.

"My God, Kitten, you're gorgeous. You're fucking beautiful." He couldn't help himself. He had to tell her, because she didn't know. He knew when women thought they were beautiful, and this one had no idea.

Catarina's heart stuttered. Another compliment from Ridley, and it sounded genuine. She should have been just a little upset over the way he sounded, as if he was astonished, but no one had ever said anything like that to her before. Not ever. She blinked at him and all the attitude melted away. She didn't know what to say so she turned her back on him and walked toward her bedroom.

"Wait." His voice was low. Sexy.

She felt heat spreading. Looking over her shoulder at him, she raised an eyebrow, afraid to trust her voice.

"I brought coffee. I wasn't certain if you were up already, but I couldn't carry it and the boxes. Two cups sitting right outside your door." He didn't wait to see if she'd get them, he just stalked through her living space and left her to it.

Catarina took a deep breath. She had no idea how Ridley managed to get past her guard. No one ever did that, but he didn't even seem to notice she had barriers up at all. He didn't see her shields and she certainly wasn't invisible to him.

"Do you have any tools? I should have asked you that."

She yanked open the door and there were two cups from Poetry Slam sitting right outside where he'd said they would be. She brought them in, taking a sip of the one that was marked *latte*. Not as good as she made, but passable. She needed the caffeine if she was going to deal with Ridley Cromer. Last night he hadn't come inside, in fact if anything, he'd seemed a little distracted. He hadn't mentioned the security system again, so she had hoped he would forget all about it. Evidently he hadn't.

"Tools, Kitten."

"Malcom may have left a few lying around. He keeps most of his things in that corner over there." She waved her hand toward what she considered Malcom's mess. She didn't ever touch his things, so she didn't go near them, otherwise she'd never be able to stop herself from straightening everything up.

The bed was her goal—to make it, not sleep in it. She caught his grin when he glanced into her bedroom and saw the covers all over the floor and partially off the bed.

"You really wake up in a mood, don't you? I can't believe no one's ever mentioned it."

She turned to face him. Throwing coffee would not only be childish, but stupid when she needed it. Besides, if she had to, she could always throw his cup at him.

"No one ever sees me in the morning because I live alone."

"You can't have lived alone your entire life, woman. Someone has to know you're a grump." Amusement crept into his tone.

He sorted through the boxes without looking at her—a good thing, because she stiffened and then froze, her heart pounding in her throat. This kind of thing was *exactly* why she didn't let anyone into her life. She tasted fear in her mouth.

She waited too long to answer and his head came up, his eyes on hers. He saw too much. He knew she was frozen, unable to speak. She could see it on his face. Ridley pushed the box he was opening aside and crossed the space to her. He had a gentle look on his face. He took his coffee cup from her hand and reached for her with the other, his palm sliding beneath her hair to curl around the nape of her neck.

"It's all right, Kitten. I'm not trying to pry. Whatever is in your past, whoever scares the hell out of you, can stay there. I didn't mean to bring up ghosts with my teasing."

Who acted like him? She'd never met anyone like him in her life and she'd been around nothing but men. No one looked at her like that, or spoke in that voice. They weren't kind. Or caring. They always had an agenda. If they were nice to her, it was to curry favor with their boss. If they weren't, it was because they were afraid if they were nice, their boss wouldn't like it much.

She attempted a weak smile. He had to think she was a basket case. The thing was, she was only a crazy person around him. The rest of the time, her rules were in place and she led a happy, disciplined life.

"Tell me you're all right. If you're not, we'll talk about this. And you clearly don't make sense when you wake up."

The affection in his voice would have been her undoing, but he'd managed to annoy her again. "I make perfect sense. And I don't wake up grumpy."

He grinned at her. "I've got tools in the truck. I'll get them. You can sit around, drink your coffee and admire the fact that I really do make perfect sense when I wake up. And I'm not grumpy."

She glared at him. "Do you remember what I said about kicking you in the thigh and rolling you right out of here? The idea is looking better and better."

"One little problem, Cat," he said, and leaned into her.

He smelled as good as ever. Like outdoor, rain forest, jungle after the first rain. She inhaled because she had to, she'd run out of air. She drew his scent deep into her lungs. He surrounded her with heat. Up close he looked even more handsome than she'd first thought. He had a five-o'clock shadow, dark scruff she couldn't help but find sexy. His dark hair was in contrast with his strange but beautiful eyes. He had three scars, one by his left eye, one higher up by his temple and a longer one along his jaw. Even those scars didn't detract from his good looks and instead only added to them.

She refused to back away. "What would that be?"

"My hands aren't full," he said, and threaded his fingers through her hair, a soft glide that ran all the way from the top of her head to the ends at her waist before his fingers fell away. "The coffee I can get rid of in seconds and then you'd be in trouble."

Her stomach did a roller coaster loop just as a million birds took wing, fluttering against her insides when his fingers moved through her hair. He had done it almost absently and he didn't call attention to doing it, but it felt sexy and sweet at the same time.

"And, if you did succeed in dragging me out, I wouldn't be able to install your security system." He flashed a grin at her.

He was dangerous to all women, but apparently to her in particular. Just looking at him turned her insides to mush. He melted her without trying, just by giving her a quick smile. Not even a high-wattage, just-for-her smile, just a casual one that showed his white teeth. And then there was his cocky, arrogant grin. She could weave tons of fantasy and perv around him for a good solid week with just one of his grins.

"Fine, I won't try to take you down before you finish the security system."

"I'm getting the tools out of my truck, so I'll be leaving the door open for a minute or two. Wouldn't want to have to lean on that buzzer."

"I'm already tempted to use that thing for target practice," she admitted, but the coffee was doing its job, putting her in a better mood. Still, she needed clothes. Her tank wasn't covering much and as soon as he was outside, she was rushing to change.

She dragged old faded jeans from the drawers in her bedroom, underwear and a soft T-shirt and raced for the bathroom. She managed to close and lock the door before she heard the heavy front door swing shut. She did a quick once-over, teeth, hair, face, and dragged on her clothes. She rarely wore shoes inside. Mostly she just wore her sweats so she could work out whenever she felt like it.

Catarina loved her days off. She could be herself. She didn't have to be on her guard every moment. She didn't need to expend energy keeping her eyes on the floor and hiding behind baggy clothes and dark sunglasses. She read—*a lot*—listened to her music and spent hours punching and kicking the bag. She stretched and ate ice cream. She stretched more and drank coffee. She was free, and she enjoyed freedom.

"Need some help, Cat," Ridley said as she emerged.

He was up on a ladder. A really tall ladder. He had no problems invading Malcom's corner and confiscating anything he needed. Or maybe he'd brought the monstrosity. Either way, he was on nearly the very top rung and his hands were over his head, fiddling with a black mount.

"What do you need me to do?"

"You afraid of heights?" He glanced at her over his shoulder, his eyes taking her in, taking in the change of clothes and bare feet.

Catarina suddenly wished she'd put on shoes. She could have fantasies about Ridley, but she knew better than to allow anything more than that, and bare feet brought some weird intimacy she hadn't expected. Or maybe it was the look in his eyes when he did just what he was doing now, his eyes, like melted gold, moving over her body with a hint of things she didn't quite understand.

"No. I'm not afraid of heights."

"Good." He turned back to his work. "Climb up behind me, baby, and pull that screwdriver out of my back pocket. I think you can lean around me and tighten that screw for me."

Her breath caught in her throat. Her mouth suddenly went dry. "It takes two people to put one of those thingies up?" But already her hand had curled around the ladder. She wanted the security system up. She needed it up. She had no idea how she was going to repay him, but the idea of a few cameras and motion detectors right now, without having to wait a few months, was a huge relief.

"Not as a rule. I was distracted and chose the wrong screwdriver. The other one is in my back pocket. I've got this *thingie* in the perfect place and you can get it secure for me if you're not afraid of heights."

Amusement and a challenge. "You knew what I meant." She began her climb up the ladder. It was so secure it didn't even shake.

"Kitten. No one says *thingie*."

She loved his voice. His voice could make her forget everything. Even if it was for just a few moments. She had to put her hand on his back and then his shoulder to steady herself as she climbed past him. Pulling the screwdriver from his back pocket seemed more intimate than ever and it was just a tool.

"*Thingie* is acceptable if everyone gets what it means," she insisted, and slid under his arm so that she could maneuver into position.

She hadn't thought about how she was going to have to stand, feet on the ladder, her body inside the circle of his arm, stretched up, so that her butt was against his chest. She tried not to be aware of him as she began to twist the screw into the ceiling. It was difficult because his body was hot and the heat moved straight into her like a living flame, heating her blood and putting all kinds of crazy, erotic images in her head.

"I want you to let me into your life," he said, his voice low. So low she almost didn't hear him.

Her heart did a little stutter. "I don't let people into my life." She tried to be honest. He was so close she could smell him—that clean rain forest scent that took her to another place where there wasn't danger lurking in every corner.

"I know that, Kitten," he said. "That's why I'm asking you to let me in."

His body was rock hard. Oak tree hard. He was all roped muscle. She could feel his muscles through his thin shirt as she carefully turned the screwdriver.

"Ridley, it's too dangerous to let anyone in right now." That was the most she could say, the only warning he would get. "Don't ask me questions, because I can't answer them, but not letting anyone into my life is so I know they're safe."

That was way too much information. She knew she'd made a mistake by the way his body froze. He wasn't the kind of man to walk away from a woman in danger. She knew that. Why had she said something so stupid? Was she trying to get him killed?

He mesmerized her. She just blurted things out around him. Let him see who she was. Made her break every rule she had. But really? Asking her to let him into her life? How amazing was that? How many men were that sweet? He made her want to cry and she didn't cry. She never cried. *Never*. That was a rule too, an unbreakable one.

"I know that too, baby," he said. "I'm not asking for anything but you to let me in. That's all. I've done dangerous before and I'll be careful."

She felt his breath on her neck and she closed her eyes briefly against the tidal wave of need rising. She was so alone. She didn't have friends. She'd never had a friend. She tightened the screw and handed him the screwdriver. She had no choice but to put her hand on his shoulder as she began the climb down.

"I don't want you dead." Catarina didn't look at him when she said it.

He began screwing in the other side. "I won't get dead. We'll work out and I can show you some moves. Have coffee now and then. Sneak in a dinner, even if it's takeout. I like your company. Truth is, Kitten, I haven't had much to laugh about in a long time, and you do that for me."

Her bare feet hit the floor and she rested her forehead on the rung, fists clenched around the ladder, breathing deep. Panic was close. He wasn't going away. She heard that in his voice. She knew he was persistent in his casual Zen way. He wasn't walking away from her and leaving her in her mess of a life.

"I don't know what to do with you, Ridley."

His laugh was unexpected. Low with a hint of gentleness in it. She felt his laughter move right through her body.

She looked up at him, frowning. "Why is that funny?"

He glanced down at her. "I knew you were going to give me attitude."

His eyes were laughing, pure gold this time, and her stomach did that peculiar roll so rough that she pressed a hand to it, hard, trying to glare at him. "I was not giving attitude. It was a simple question. What was funny about what I said?"

"You're the only woman on the face of this earth that would say that and mean it," he said.

"Do you have any idea how arrogant you are?"

"Honest isn't the same thing as arrogant, Cat," he pointed out.

"First, I'm going to bang my head on the wall and then drink the rest of my coffee and then make food. I think you're making my blood sugar drop to zero. Either that or you're just making my head crazy. Either way, I need food. You want some?"

"Absolutely. I'm always ready for food. You getting takeout?"

She gave him a look that should have fried him on the spot, but he didn't seem in the least fazed by it. "Commencing head banging," she said, and walked over to the wall.

He burst out laughing. "Woman, you bang your head on that wall and I'm coming down off this ladder and you won't like what happens after that."

It was a threat, one she didn't understand, so she ignored it and went straight to the kitchen. She loved her kitchen. The only thing it lacked was a view, but if she wanted a view while she cooked, she could sneak glances at Ridley while he worked. She liked the sound of his laughter, and more, she liked the fact that she could make him laugh.

She didn't want him there because it was dangerous for him, but still, she wanted him there because she was lonely and needed to laugh with someone. She took a deep breath and let it out. She was careful. Very careful. Rafe hadn't found her yet, and that just might mean she'd finally figured out how to keep him from finding her. She would never be able to live out in the open, but she was happy and if she let herself have a friend or two, maybe it would work out.

She closed her ears to the voice that told her she was being naïve and it wasn't fair to put good people in danger. She was so lonely she hurt with every breath she took. She hadn't realized just how lonely until Malcom had offered her his warehouse. She'd been so suspicious of his motives, but he'd been kind to her when she needed it the most. Kind when she was totally vulnerable. He hadn't ever once said or done anything to indicate he had a motive beyond that—beyond simple kindness.

She hadn't known that existed until Malcom had come along. She didn't know kind people. She didn't know what to do with them. She found herself smiling as she fixed breakfast, every now and then sneaking a peek at Ridley's very nice behind encased in snug-fitting blue jeans.

Ridley worked hard and fast, meticulously though, adjusting each camera exactly the way he wanted it, so that every single corner of the warehouse was exposed with the exception of her bedroom and the bathroom. He didn't talk anymore, leaving her free to concentrate on her cooking. She loved cooking.

That had been one of the few things she'd been allowed to do and she'd poured herself into learning. She'd excelled to the point that eventually Rafe preferred her meals to the ones his chef fixed. He hadn't ever told her that, but he had fired the chef and one of his men came to her every morning and asked for a list of things she wanted from the grocery store.

She had used the money she saved on a security system to buy a very nice espresso machine yesterday, one of the better ones she could work with to make Ridley his favorite drink. Right now, she wanted espresso with the beignets she'd made to go along with their breakfast.

"Come eat," she called, without looking up. She was nervous. Really nervous. This was important to her, the one thing besides making coffee she thought she was good at and she wanted Ridley to think she was good at it too.

She didn't want him to see her nerves. She tried to be casual as if it didn't matter when she served the Creole red beans under two poached eggs topped with hollandaise sauce. She grilled Andouille sausages and spicy hash browns. The espresso was perfect and the beignets were hot out of the frying oil.

She sat in the chair opposite Ridley's, so nervous she had to twist her hands together in her lap as he sat down. She watched him though. She couldn't help it. His eyes moved over the food and came back to her face.

"Kitten." He breathed his nickname for her.

She had started out hating that name, but now, the way he said it, she loved it.

"You can cook."

"Well, yes. But you'd better try it. I hope you like spicy."

He ate several bites of the egg and red beans, his gaze still on her face. "My God, woman, I need to marry you. Who taught you to cook like this? You're too young to have gone to school for it. Your mom is a cook?"

She closed her eyes and looked down at her hands. It was an innocent question. He liked her food and anyone—anyone—would ask the same question.

"My mother never cooked a day in her life," she blurted out. Her hand actually went to her mouth, pushed against her lips hard. What was wrong with her? That was definitely letting him in. She'd never once said a word to anyone about her mother. Her mother was off limits. Ridley had cast some terrible spell over her and she didn't know what she was doing or saying around him half the time.

His gaze turned speculative as if he knew the subject was taboo. "So if not your mother, Cat, who? Where? Because this is superb."

She shrugged and went with the truth. "I spent a lot of time hanging out in the kitchen and the chef was amazing." She didn't care if she was misleading him in a small way, making him think she'd had a chef growing up because her mother didn't cook. "I was fascinated and watched everything he did and how he did it. Eventually he allowed me to help and then sometimes cook the meal. I loved it."

She pushed the heavy fall of hair from around her face, shoving it back over her shoulder. Heat flared in his eyes, turning them to a molten gold so bright she had to look away again. She managed to pick up her espresso without her hands shaking. She was shaking inside, so that was a particularly good feat.

"You constantly amaze me. I've never had a better meal, or better coffee. Looking like you do, I'd think you'd just sit back and let everyone admire you, but no, you work out in the dojo and you're not there to pick up men."

She smiled at him. "Newsflash, Ridley, the women at the dojo are there to learn how to defend themselves, not pick up men."

"Newsflash right back at you, Kitten, most of them are there to pick up men. Have you watched them working out? Malcom has to tell them the same thing over and over. They don't condition. They don't practice, they just try to look good and bat their eyelashes. Most of them have all requested private lessons with me."

She rolled her eyes at him. "Here's another newsflash for you, Ridley. Anyone with eyes can see you're good at self-defense, the katas and the sparring. So anyone who wants to seriously improve is going to try to score private lessons with you."

"You didn't."

That brought her head up. Her eyes met his and that was a terrible mistake. A really, really bad mistake. Heat moved through her. Not moved. Rushed like a fireball right through her veins and settled low in her body, until her feminine core pulsed with need. She let her breath out and took another sip of espresso.

"I don't let people into my life. Especially not a man the rest of the world is going to notice."

"What the hell does that mean?"

She settled back in her chair, frowning at him, lifting her fork to gesture toward him. "Ridley, come on, you're gorgeous. You're the kind of man other men step aside for. Women can't take their eyes off of you. You have scars and tats and you move like sheer poetry. Everyone looks when you walk into a room. You have presence. I can't be walking around with that. So I'm not going to ask for private lessons even if you're the best there is. Besides"—she smirked at him—"I can't afford you."

Ridley took another bite of the poached eggs covered in hollandaise sauce. She was killing him. She gave him compliments a woman should never give to a man without knowing if he was hers and she did it matter-of-factly, no flirting. She didn't think she was complimenting him, just stating a fact. All the while she did it, her unruly hair tumbled in sheets of waves like a waterfall. Her face was animated, her amazing cobalt blue eyes, so dark they were brilliant, seemed to hold the key to paradise. A man would want to look into her eyes, watch them change, haze over while he buried himself hard and deep inside of her.

She was sexy without trying. Innocent without knowing she was. Lethal as hell to any man with eyes in his head. And scared out of her mind. Still, he was sitting across from her at her breakfast table, eating the most amazing breakfast of his life, and he was finding his way in. Slowly. Carefully. Feeling his way.

"You don't need money to get private lessons, Kitten. Your food will always be enough for a fair exchange. Half the time I eat at a diner or out of a box. I'm no cook."

"What are you? What do you do?"

"Security." He shrugged, a casual roll of his shoulders. "Work for a company and we get sent out on different types of jobs."

She frowned at him. He found her frown adorable but refrained from saying so.

"Like the security sitting in an office building looking at computer monitors to make certain no one's stealing anything? That kind of security? Or the kind that puts you in the path of a bullet because you're guarding someone else."

Catarina's blue eyes moved over his face, and his entire body tightened. Lethal as hell she was. His body was full and hard just from one look under her long sweeping lashes.

"I do install systems once in a while," he admitted, "but I've never actually sat in front of a monitor in an office building."

She slid her lips over her fork, a completely innocent gesture, but his groin throbbed in response. "So the take-a-bullet-for-someone-else kind of security."

He shrugged, concentrating on breathing.

She shook her head. "You're nuts, you know. Taking bullets for other people is just plain nuts. Is that other person worth more than you are? No." That was firm. She leaned toward him, gesturing with her fork again. "The answer, Ridley, is no. They aren't. I don't care how rich they are or how famous. They aren't more important than you are. You have no business risking your life like that."

"It pays well."

She flipped her hair over her shoulder. "Now you're just trying to get a rise out of me." She sat back again and sipped at her espresso, watching him carefully over the rim of the mug.

"Well. Yeah. I have to admit when you get all fired up with that attitude of yours, I'm a goner for you. That does it for me the way Zen does it for you."

She burst out laughing. "Eat a beignet, Ridley, and your fantasies will really take off. They're better than my attitude."

He found himself laughing with her. She was even more beautiful when she laughed. The sound was soft and musical, and her eyes lit up. Her perfect bow of a mouth drew his attention, and his fantasies turned totally erotic just sitting there at the breakfast table. He snagged a beignet. The sugary, doughy dessert was still warm, the taste mixing with the espresso in his mouth, and he knew he would never forget that moment, sitting across from her, laughing and eating the best meal of his life.

No one had ever given him the kind of concern she had, worried about what he did for a living, and damn, she did it looking so beautiful his heart ached. She had pulled her legs up onto the chair and was sitting tailor fashion while she ate her breakfast. It was the first time he had ever seen her truly relaxed. She wasn't thinking about being scared. For those few minutes, he'd chased the shadows from her eyes, and he liked being the one who'd done it.

He was older than she was, and he didn't settle down with women, but he'd had a lot of them. He'd never sat across with one of them having breakfast, so relaxed, and that was saying a lot. He didn't share breakfast with women. They used each other and then he left. Period. No sleeping in the same bed, no breakfast in the morning. He was gone.

"Got to get back to work, but this was fantastic, Cat. I appreciate you going to all the trouble." He stood up and pushed back his chair.

She tilted her head up toward his, her blue eyes moving over his face as if memorizing every detail. "Thanks, Ridley, for the security system. It really helps. You can't know how much."

Her eyes were soft. Her perfect mouth smiled at him. Her gorgeous hair spilled around her like a waterfall of dark silk. His hand moved before he could think. He had no idea what possessed him, but he couldn't stop himself, and he was a man all about control and discipline. His fingers buried in all that silk and fisted there, tugging until her head was back. He leaned in and brushed a kiss across her mouth.

His stomach rolled. His cock hardened. With one touch. One. Fucking. Touch. Electricity crackled and his pulse thundered in his ears. Lightning flashed through his veins so his blood ran hot.

He stepped away and turned without another word, not looking at her face, not daring to. He might have just blown it big-time, but now he had her taste in his mouth and it was far sweeter and tastier than the beignet.

Catarina closed her eyes and pressed her fingers to her trembling lips. He'd kissed her. *Kissed* her. She knew, to him, it was just a small gesture of thanks, or "you're welcome," depending. He probably hadn't felt anything at all. It wasn't like it was a real kiss, with mouths open and tongues involved. It was brief. Hardly there. But she didn't care. It was a kiss. And from Ridley. She could perv on that for months.

She risked a glance and he was back installing cameras, so she rose and did the dishes, hugging the moment to herself. Their perfect moment. No one could ever take that away from her. Not even if everything went south and she was found and dragged back or killed, she would have that moment.

She was wrong to be friends with him. To risk him. But maybe, if she was careful, she could keep the risk to a minimum.

4

"WE'RE going to have to hire some help if the crowds get any bigger," David announced.

Catarina glanced up from behind the coffee machine. The crowd vying for coffee was three deep. She could speed up, but the machine couldn't. "I'm sorry, David, I can only work so fast," she told him.

"No, this is good. I'm loving this," David said. "Your boyfriend's back."

Catarina's head came up and she looked around Poetry Slam. It was crowded, but she knew she would always, *always*, know when Ridley was in a room, and he hadn't come in. They spent a lot of time together, mostly in her warehouse. His latest endeavor was tiling the shower and putting in plumbing.

"I don't have a boyfriend," she denied.

David took another order and then nudged her. "Seriously, Cat, his lovesick poems are getting hard to take. All that unrequited love pouring out for the world to see. You've got to put the man out of his misery and go out on a date with him."

She took a breath. He wasn't talking about Ridley. Ridley came every night to walk her home, but he stayed in the corner after he ordered his coffee, reading. He made certain she was safe walking home, but he never acted interested in her publicly. And since that one brief kiss at breakfast, he hadn't made any other moves.

He did spar with her a lot. She knew she was improving. He showed her all kinds of self-defense moves. He was an exacting teacher and he didn't like it if she messed up. He sometimes scowled at her, his golden eyes glittering with anger.

That will get you dead if you don't do the move right. Pay attention to what you're doing, Cat. If your head isn't in the game, we can do this another day.

He said that a lot. She always paid more attention and tried harder. She kept to her routine, working out on her own, running before work, going to the shooting range as often as she had the money for. She slept a lot easier with the security system. Ridley had placed the monitor right by her bed so when she activated the system, she could see each individual area the cameras covered. She could zoom in and she could record.

Ridley always walked her home, and he never allowed her entry until he'd checked the place out first. She'd been a little uncomfortable with him going into her bedroom the first few times, but she'd gotten used to the way he was about protecting women. Clearly, it was just who he was. And she liked who he was.

Twice he gave her a hard time because she'd left her safe open and the cash in plain sight. Both times he'd been concerned someone had been there, but she'd just forgotten that when she closed the door she had to bang it with her fist to get the stupid thing to close all the way. She'd found the safe in a thrift store and it was old and tired. Still, it worked just fine for her.

"Cat, don't go all silent on me," David cautioned. "I'm just trying to keep Bernard from getting his heart ripped out when the masses rise up and rip the microphone out of his hands."

"Bernard?" Catarina handed David another drink, this one a simple mocha latte, one of the easier drinks those in the crowd asked for. "You think I'm going to go on a date with Bernard? Our main poet? *He's* supposed to be my mythical boyfriend?" She hissed it at David. "I don't date. Not ever. Are you crazy? He doesn't even notice me. My coffee yes, me no."

David rang up two more orders and handed out the mocha latte before he rolled his eyes at her. "Who do you think all those love poems are written to? 'Ode to my Rina'? Is that not an indication?"

If she didn't have such acute hearing she would never have been able to hear him over the buzz of the crowd. She glanced up again. Bernard was in line, second row back. He smiled at her and waggled his fingers. She flashed a smile back.

"Seriously, he doesn't look like unrequited love is happening in his life, David. You've been in the romance section of the books again, haven't you?"

He gave a little sniff and tossed three more orders at her. "You do *not* have a romantic bone in your body," he announced, and turned away from her, his nose in the air.

She tried not to laugh. She didn't laugh at work, but really, David's little snits were hysterical, especially when he guessed incorrectly that someone was fixating on her. Bernard liked the spotlight, plain and simple. He loved writing his poetry and he wanted everyone to hear and admire him. As a rule, everyone did. He actually was quite good.

She made a few more drinks, working fast, trying to clear the crowd when she felt the first tingling of her radar.

Goose bumps rose on her arm. The curious itching beneath her skin came like a wave and receded. She took a breath and didn't make the mistake of looking up right away. Someone was watching her. She felt them. Not like the normal crowd, but someone interested in her.

Alarm bells shrieked at her, but she breathed right through them. Over the years she'd acquired discipline and she used it, calmly making another drink and handing it off to David. He winked at her to show her he was over his annoyance with her. David didn't know how to hold a grudge and if he got irritable it was usually because he needed to eat something. If he got too bad, she left her post, marched around the counter to his side and tossed him a muffin. This wasn't one of those times.

Catarina glanced up just like she always did, letting her gaze scan the crowd for one brief moment. She was good at taking every detail in. She'd trained herself in that too. Observing the enemy. She'd actually studied Rafe's ways and she'd learned from him. She committed to memory every detail about each and every one of his soldiers, the ones that were closest to him, the ones he trusted the most and those radiating out of that inner circle.

She took in as many faces in the now much thinner crowd as she could with that casual glance. No one was familiar, but one man's gaze slid away from her when she touched on him. She kept going, not making the mistake of allowing her eyes to settle on him, but he had definitely been watching her and trying to be discreet about it.

He didn't look as if he was from New Orleans. Too smooth. Hands too soft. Most of Rafe's soldiers had been born and raised around Algiers and they'd worked on the river or hunted in the swamps before he'd recruited them. She made several more drinks.

Bernard took his caramel macchiato, and like always, lifted it into the air in a kind of salute. "Hey, Coffee Lady."

"Hey, Poet."

"Tastes like heaven." He flashed his smile.

She flashed one back and noted the man watching her turned toward Bernard and had a cell phone out. She stiffened. Was he taking a picture? If so, no one she was friendly with was safe. She kept working, her mind racing, but she made every effort to stay calm. Panic got her nowhere. She would make mistakes if she gave into panic, but she did send up a silent prayer that Ridley wouldn't walk into the coffee-house and take it in his head to actually talk to her.

"David," she hissed, and beneath the solid counter crooked her finger at him.

David didn't hesitate, he came right to her. Close. Leaned in. "Get the next man's name, first and last if possible. Somehow." She kept her voice to a whisper, made certain it was in his ear. "I'm going to the ladies' room." She pulled her apron free.

David frowned. "You okay?"

She nodded. "Just be cool about it."

He nodded and called out, "Next."

She turned her back to everyone, completely disinterested, and walked toward the back where aisles of books were. She glanced up at the mirror on the back wall, the one where she could watch the patrons at the counter.

David leaned toward the man. "Name. I'm taking as many orders as I can until she gets back. Give me a name I can yell out."

"Frank. Frank Tuttle." The man pulled his wallet out and shoved some bills at David.

David grabbed a cup and wrote it on the side along with the order. He made the next four customers give him their names as well. Catarina watched Tuttle through the mirror. His neck craned several times as he tried to see her. He even walked partway down the aisle she'd taken. She ducked into the ladies' room and washed her hands, dried them carefully and came back out.

She didn't know the name Frank Tuttle, not that Rafe

wouldn't hire someone outside his soldiers to find her. He
had connections everywhere and most people would love to
do him a favor and have him owe a debt. But still, Tuttle
didn't feel like Rafe. He gave off vibes, but not dangerous
vibes. Creepy maybe. Definitely the kind of vibe she
wanted to steer clear of, but not a Rafe vibe. Still.

She made the next five drinks, one right after another,
without looking up. She didn't want to let Frank Tuttle know
she was on to him, but she watched him walk to the chair
directly opposite the counter and sink into it, pushing the
newspapers aside. Once he was settled, he pulled out his
phone and began scrolling through it. Yeah. He was watching her.

Hours passed fast because they were busy. The theater
got out and customers poured in. Ridley was late. Tuttle
didn't leave. She didn't want to walk home alone with Tuttle
around, nor did she want to walk home by herself. She
couldn't stop her gaze from straying to the door every few
minutes, but he didn't come. For two weeks he'd followed
her home every night. Two more weeks he'd walked her
home every night. Now, the one night some creep was
stalking her, he didn't show.

The bar crowd came in. David and she raked in the
money and the tip jar overflowed. Serious cash this time.
She was happy to see that. She had been saving half her tips
to pay back the cash she'd stolen from Rafe's safe. Of
course she couldn't just walk up to him and give it to him,
but she wanted to have it just in case he found her. Tonight's
take would definitely help her cause.

Tuttle got up and left when David shouted the ten minutes to closing and last call for coffee. Four customers came
up to the counter. She made them drinks and watched as
David escorted them to the door. He closed and locked it so
they could clean and count up the night's take.

Catarina kept an eye on the door. Ridley didn't show, but
she was certain Tuttle was out there. "David. That Tuttle

person creeped me out. He stayed hours, but didn't talk to anyone and only drank two coffees. He wasn't reading books or listening to the poetry either. He left when you announced closing time, but that doesn't mean he's gone."

"You want me to walk you home?" David asked immediately.

She shook her head. "No, but I'd like to leave out the back door. Before you leave out the front, can you give me a fifteen-minute head start? I can go through the back alley and come out down the block. It's probably nothing, but I'd rather not take any chances."

"He was watching you. After you asked me to get his name, I kept my eye on him," David admitted. "He tried to be subtle about it, but even when he picked up the newspaper, he wasn't reading it. He was looking at you over the top of it."

"He's probably harmless," Catarina assured him. "But I really don't want to find out. I'm tired tonight and the thought of having to kick his ass is too exhausting."

David laughed. "The idea that you think you can is funny. Old Tuttle is pretty beefy. He's got a hundred pounds on you, Cat, maybe more."

She put her fists up. "I'm scrappy."

He threw his head back and laughed louder. "Great. I'm all for you ducking out the back, although, if you'd rather, I could call a taxi."

She shook her head. "Not necessary. I can make it home. Just give me my start."

"You got it. Text me when you're home safe."

"David, how many times do I have to tell you, I don't have a cell phone and I'm not getting one."

"Oh. Yeah. I keep forgetting you're living in the dark ages."

Ridley had said the same thing and offered to get her a cell. She'd refused of course. Apparently no one really could exist without a phone. She managed quite nicely.

Phones led to bills and bills were a paper trail. She didn't want that.

When she'd first been hired at Poetry Slam, they were barely scraping by. Most days only a few customers came in regularly unless it was poetry night, then it got a little crowded. David couldn't afford to pay her much so he'd paid her under the table. Once word got out that the new barista was very good at her job and customers began pouring in, David had offered her more money and the chance to go legit. She took the extra money but refused to go legit. No paper trails.

Catarina made her way to the back, David following her, the way they did each night to put the money and receipts in a safe until David could go to the bank. Catarina slipped out the back door. David waited in silence until she searched the alley to make certain no one was lurking there. She gave him the thumbs-up and began to jog back toward the warehouse district.

The alley went down two blocks and came out on a cross street. She didn't make a sound as she moved, and she moved fast. She wanted to be almost home before David locked that front door. If Tuttle was waiting for her, she'd be in her house, locked up tight before he could find her. The danger, of course, was that he already knew where she lived and was waiting for her, but she'd cross that bridge if she came to it. The more she ran, the more she was certain Tuttle wasn't with Rafe. He creeped her out, set off her radar, but not in the way Rafe's men would have.

She slowed her pace, needing to save energy. As she neared the end of the alley, she pulled a small can of wasp spray from her purse and transferred it to her left hand. She stopped at the edge of the alley and moved to the street, staying in the shadows. There were a few straggly bushes trying to live without water nearest the long row of buildings. A few were nearly as tall as she was. None had been pruned and she found it easy enough to slip under the branches and stay inside the planted area that ran alongside the sidewalk.

An SUV cruised by slow and she froze. Movement drew the eye. She tried to blend with the bushes around her. Fortunately, she always wore dark clothes to work, just in case she had to disappear. She believed in being prepared and she'd worked toward this moment. She'd always known it was a risk to settle in one place. She didn't believe Frank Tuttle was Rafe's soldier, but he was too interested in her and she didn't dare take a chance, not when she cared about the people who had given her so much.

The SUV had darkened windows and she couldn't make out the driver, not even with her superior night vision. The vehicle didn't have government plates, but her throat went dry. Tuttle had to be a cop. Her radar had gone off. He was definitely watching her. She was almost positive he wasn't one of Rafe's soldiers. But a cop was just as bad.

She pressed a hand to her stomach, hard, and drew in deep breaths. Nowhere was permanent in her life. No one. That was how it had to be. She knew that. She just liked it there. She liked Malcom. She liked David. She loved her job, the warehouse and most of all her friendship with Ridley.

She hurried home, watching carefully, scanning not only the rooftops and fire escapes, the balconies, and every other high place, but the streets, alleys and surrounding buildings. She took her time, not wanting another mistake.

Approaching the warehouse was always the most difficult. It was open ground. She checked for any parked vans, SUVs, cars or trucks nearby. She knew the rhythm of the place, the traffic, and there was very little. All the parked vehicles were ones she was familiar with. She darted across the street, making it to the shadows between buildings where she stopped again and inhaled to try to find any unfamiliar scents. There were none. She stepped up to her door and quickly hit the keypad to unlock it and step inside.

The dark enclosed her. At nearly four in the morning,

outside the light was beginning to try to streak through the dark. Inside, her cocoon of darkness held. She rushed to her bedroom and threw herself on the bed, heart beating fast, fists clenched tight. Her eyes burned, but there were no tears. She would never cry again. Never, ever.

Life was all about acceptance. She'd known, when she'd managed her escape from Rafe, that if he caught her, the possibility was huge that he'd kill her. She also knew if he didn't he'd never let her go. All avenues of escape would be shut down. Truthfully, she doubted she'd find the courage to go against him again.

Catarina pressed her fingers to her eyes. So she had to leave. She had to go and leave it all behind. She'd traded bad for a semi-life and that had to be enough. Straightening her shoulders, she sat up and pulled her travel bag from under the bed. She had two of them. One was empty, the other was her emergency bag. It had money and enough clothes to give her a start somewhere. She set the emergency bag by the door of her room and began filling the empty one. She had to choose carefully. Her clothes were all from thrift stores. She didn't go to malls or anywhere one might buy a new pair of jeans, but she always loved the items she bought. Still, traveling light was always the key. She hated leaving behind her boots. She only had one pair and she'd paid more money for them than she had most of her clothes combined. But she had to travel light.

When she had the travel bag nearly packed, she opened the safe and counted out the money. She had saved nearly a thousand dollars toward the debt she owed Rafe. With that and her own money, plus her emergency funds, she had enough to take her a few states away.

Catarina changed to her sleeping sweats and tank. She couldn't go out in daylight, that would be a disaster. Somehow she had to go to sleep. As she stretched out on the bed, the door alarm sounded—a long, horrific noise that made her jump out of her skin.

She looked at the monitor and saw Ridley draped against the wall. He looked lazy, arms crossed over his chest, head tilted toward the camera. He looked gorgeous. Perfect. Her heart gave a familiar little flutter and she hit the buzzer to allow him entry. At least she could see him one last time.

"Where are you?" He hit the light switch.

"Bedroom. It's my sleep time, remember?" she called back to him.

Catarina sat up, drew up her knees and put her chin on top of them. She liked watching him walk. He was extremely quiet and seemed to flow across the floor. She'd spent enough time with him in the dojo and now here in her home that she knew he could back up the confidence he displayed.

He flowed into her space, his golden eyes sweeping through her bedroom, taking in everything to settle on her face. "What the hell's going on? What happened?"

"Did David call you?"

Because Ridley didn't show up at five in the morning, and with closing the coffee-house, making her way home and packing, it was already that time. He either walked her home or came over early on her days off.

He shrugged. "I prefer you to tell me what happened."

"Someone came into Poetry Slam today." There was weariness in her voice, regret, sorrow even, in her tone. With anyone else she wouldn't allow it, but Ridley was different. So different. She could have loved him with every cell in her body.

"Someone?" he prompted, and came right to the bed.

Her heart jumped. He was so *large*. Big-boned, raw power, roped muscles. She loved to look at him, especially his face. Right now, there was open concern. For her. She'd never had that either.

"You've given me so many firsts, Ridley," she admitted, because he deserved it. "Thank you. I really appreciate your friendship. You made me feel that I mattered."

"Kitten." He sank down onto the bed and ran his fingers through her hair. "You do matter. Tell me what happened."

She smiled at him. "You can't fix this one, Ridley. He was a cop. I'm sure of it. He had to be."

"You're running from the cops? I thought it might be someone else. Someone bad. A stalker, maybe." He glanced toward the bag at the door and her partially packed one and then over to the open safe. "And you're running again."

She rubbed her chin on the top of her knees. "It really doesn't matter who it is, I can't take any chances. I have to go. I'm glad you stopped by so I can say good-bye."

"You would have left without talking to me first?" Now there was an edge to his voice. His strangely colored eyes went from whiskey to gold and that gold was melting into a glittery, fierce glare that took her breath.

"Ridley, I don't have a phone. I don't have a number to reach you. I don't know where you live. There's no way for me to contact you. I let you in, didn't I?" She meant more than let him in her building. She'd let him into her life. She'd trusted him when she'd never trusted another human being. She'd let him inside of her.

He studied her face. The pads of his fingers came up to brush over her skin, as if wiping away tears. "You have to tell me who you're running from, baby. I can help you."

She shook her head. "There are some people in the world you can't fight. He's one of them. You'd end up dead. Everyone ends up dead. I'm not risking you. I'm not risking Malcom or David. I knew eventually I'd have to leave. It hurts, but still, I had this, I had you, and them, for a little while and I'll never forget."

"You're breaking my heart. If this man is so bad, go to the police, don't run from them. Let's end this thing."

She bit her lip. There was no explaining Rafe Cordeau to anyone, especially not to a man like Ridley who believed he could fix anything.

"Ridley, you have to go. I need to sleep, but before you do, would you kiss me? I haven't had a lot of firsts and I'd rather you kiss me than someone else." It took a lot for her to ask him. He'd been careful not to touch her inappropriately, but she'd never had a man kiss her and she wanted Ridley to. It had to be him.

"Kitten."

He just said it in that voice, the one that went right through her skin and wrapped around her heart and squeezed. His eyes went soft and he reached for her, pulling her onto his lap. Her stomach immediately performed a series of flips. He was strong, so strong he lifted her weight casually, as if she weighed no more than a feather. His heat surrounded her. His arms. For the first time in her life, she felt safe. That was another first he'd given her.

His hands cupped her chin and tilted her head up. Her eyes met his. "Are you telling me you've never kissed another man?"

The way his eyes moved over her face, that male possession, that heated intensity, sent little flames of desire darting up and down her thighs.

"Never."

She felt him go still. Inhale sharply. His eyes changed again, but she couldn't read his expression because his mouth was on hers. Gentle. Coaxing. The butterflies fluttered. Her heart melted.

"Open for me, Kitten, let me in." His voice was infinitely tender and his tongue teased the seam of her mouth.

He was already in so deep she didn't know if she could ever get him out, but thankfully he didn't know it. She had tasted the forbidden and she knew she should leave it at that, but his lips were firm and warm and his body hot and strong and she wanted to know. She had to know. She parted her lips.

Hot. Wet. Commanding. He just swept in and took her over. The world dropped away and she clutched his shoulders, holding on so that she had something solid, an anchor to bring her back. He could kiss. And he did. Over and over. Robbing her of breath, stealing her heart, claiming her body, first with gentleness, then with aggression, then with tender and then with rough.

She melted into him. Became part of him. Let him in further. He lifted his head, his amazing eyes glittering down at her, and there was no mistaking the stamp of possession on his face.

"You can't leave, Catarina. We'll figure this out. I know you're tired and you're scared, but we'll find a way. There's always a way. I want you here, not on the run where I'd worry every minute of every day whether or not you were alive or safe." He pressed his forehead to hers. "I'm asking you to wait a day or two, let me try to figure something out so I don't lose you."

She wasn't going to argue with him, try to make him see reason when she couldn't explain Rafe Cordeau to him. She couldn't mention his name. A man like Ridley would go head-to-head with Rafe, and Ridley would lose. She wasn't losing him. Not like that.

She snuggled into Ridley's warmth so she wouldn't have to lie to him. He was adept at reading lies, and she wanted him to think she'd wait.

"You're a pretty good kisser, Ridley," she said, touching her fingers to her lips. "Just in case none of your many women failed to mention that to you."

She felt him relax. He thought he'd won. The tension went out of all that corded muscle. "Baby, if I'm your first kiss, how would you know?"

Amusement tinged the velvet smooth of his voice. Affection. She let it wash over and into her, pulling the memory into a secret part of herself she would hold on to forever.

"I know," she said firmly.

He shifted her to the bed. She curled onto her side and was a little surprised when he stretched out beside her. He seemed to take up the entire bed. It was only a twin and he scooted her over to the edge, laid back and then tucked her into his side. His hands slid up behind his head, as if he couldn't trust himself not to touch her.

"Your bed's too small."

"I fit in it," she was compelled to point out.

"Yeah, Kitten, I know. But it's not big enough. When we get to the point where I'm staying here and you're staying at my place, we'll need a bigger bed."

She closed her eyes, wishing there was that possibility, knowing she'd never have another time of sharing a bed with him. She wanted to savor every second.

"Okay." That was the best she could do. Even then her voice shook.

Ridley shifted position again, turning on his side, sliding one hand around her waist to pull her into him, and then he settled his hand, fingers splayed wide, on the strip of bare skin not covered by her tank. She felt his palm and every one of his fingers like a burning brand. Her breath hitched in her lungs. Her throat felt raw. She closed her eyes to keep any burning at bay.

She wanted nothing to spoil this moment for her, not even the knowledge that she would never see him again. She let herself have her fantasy. She belonged to Ridley Cromer and he was madly in love with her.

"Don't go to sleep on me yet, baby," Ridley said softly. His hand began to move in slow circles on her belly. "I want to make certain you understand where this is going."

She turned her head and looked at him. His eyes were strange. Different. He had the same focused stare that made her feel as if she were the only person on the planet. The only one on his radar. Still, his eyes were different. The irises were wholly gold. They even glowed a little as if his night vision was every bit as good as hers.

"I don't understand."

"This man you're running from. The cops. They have nothing to do with you and me. Whatever happens, Kitten, it's still you and me. We'll find our way through it all together. I have no problem going with you to the police. I can find you a good lawyer. I don't care what it takes, Cat, I'm not losing you over this."

She swallowed hard and turned her face away from him. His hand moved to her chin and he turned her face back.

"I mean it, Catarina. I know you think whoever this man is that won't get out of your life is bad. Invincible. But you only know my sweet side. You deserve sweet so I give it to you, but that's not who I am. Look at me, baby. Really look at me. I have scars for a reason."

Her gaze slid over his face. She'd memorized it of course. Every line. The little laugh lines around his eyes. The scars that only served to make him all the more handsome to her. He had a man's face, not a boy's. Even when his eyes went soft, his face was hard, carved of stone. He had a strong jaw and always a bit of scruff, as if no matter how often he shaved, his hair insisted on growing.

"I'm not sweet and gentle with anyone else, and I never will be. I can get this man out of your life, but you've got to let me in so I can do my job."

"I let you in," she said softly. She leaned into him and brushed a kiss across his mouth. "I've never let anyone touch me. Get inside. Only you." That was all she had to give him, because she wouldn't give him death.

Talking to him about Rafe would do that, and Ridley Cromer needed to be alive and well somewhere in the world in order for her to keep going. Now she had a reason for being alone and lonely. Now she had a reason to stay in the shadows. And that reason was stretched out beside her, tough as nails, as sweet as the beignets she loved from her home state.

"So talk to me."

"I need more time. I can't just make a decision without considering all the ramifications. And I'm tired. I don't make decisions when I'm tired." She had to let him go before she did do something like talk to him about Rafe. That was how far gone she was. That was how much she wanted him. But even halfway in love, or maybe because of it, she wasn't going to risk his life.

He sighed, but the resignation was in his voice and on his face. "I'll give you a few hours to sleep and then I'm coming back, Cat, and whether you like it or not, we're going to talk."

"Kiss me again."

He shifted his body to half cover hers, his hands framing her face, and he brought his mouth down hard on hers. This was a different kiss entirely. This one said no way was she leaving him. He'd never let her go. This one said she belonged to him and no one else and there were so many more firsts he could give her.

Catarina kissed him back as best she could, following his lead, all the while committing every detail to memory. He stayed beside her while she drifted off, feeling warm and safe. She barely woke when he extricated himself from her and brushed his mouth across hers.

"I'll see you tonight, Cat."

She murmured a soft response and turned over to let sleep and her dreams of him take her away.

She woke sometime later with her heart pounding. She knew instantly she wasn't alone. Someone was in her warehouse and it wasn't Ridley. He had brushed another kiss across her forehead and left her already drifting off. She'd been wrapped in a cocoon of safety, of something close to love, and now she felt threatened on every level.

Her hand went under her pillow to get the gun just as she turned toward the monitor to check the cameras. The monitor was dark. There was no gun. Cursing softly, she slipped off the bed and felt around on the floor for her weapon. She'd more than once knocked it off the bed when she was moving around in her sleep. Before she could find it, lights burst through the warehouse, nearly every bulb turned on.

She leapt to her feet as men poured into her room. Guns pointed. Vests on. Grim faces. She was caught by the lead man and thrown facedown on her bed. She fought, trying to turn over, but he jammed a knee into her back and dragged first one and then the other hand behind her. She felt the bite of the handcuffs. He put them on tight. Still, the adrenaline coursed through her body and that monster inside of her woke.

Catarina lay facedown as the men went through her warehouse, tearing it apart, throwing her things, tossing clothes from her drawers.

"Catarina Benoit? We have a search warrant for this warehouse and your car. We're taking you downtown for questioning."

She recognized the voice. Frank Tuttle. Of course. She'd made him as a cop. They couldn't have anything on her.

"What am I being charged with?" Her voice was muffled against the mattress. Her hair was everywhere. She couldn't see him through the masses of strands falling into her eyes so she forced herself to lie still. Her skin itched horribly and panic was close. She couldn't stop the movement of her hands, trying to find a way out of the cuffs.

Tuttle caught her arm and yanked her to her feet. "Were you going somewhere?"

"To visit my mother," she snapped. "Not that it's any of your business."

"Your mother's dead," he snapped back, and shoved her toward the door.

Catarina deliberately stumbled and went down. She didn't have hands to break her fall and she landed hard. The side of her face hit so hard that for a moment she saw stars and her cheek felt like she broke something. But her handcuffed hand found the small pen lying on the floor beside her overturned bag. She closed her fist around it.

"Damn it," Tuttle said. He crouched beside her. "Are you all right?"

She didn't deign to answer. Silence was a powerful weapon, she'd learned that lesson early, and she closed her mouth, refusing to look at him even when he helped her up. His hands were much gentler, but the horrible monster inside her detested his touch and clawed and raked at her belly, demanding she retaliate.

Catarina kept her eyes on the floor as Tuttle helped her to stand. Retaining possession of her arm, he walked her right out of her safety zone into broad daylight. She could see the police cars around her warehouse. There was no way this wasn't going to make the papers in one way or the other. Her heart started pounding hard and her mouth went dry. She wasn't in the least afraid of the police. But the police had drawn attention to her. And attention was bad. Very, very bad.

5

CATARINA rubbed at her wrists under the table, keeping her eyes down. Her wrists hurt horribly, as did her face from when she had fallen. The cuffs were off, but she kept the pen hidden for two reasons. It was a weapon if she needed one and she could use it to get out of the cuffs if they put them on her again.

She'd been patient, not tipping her hand that she could get loose. She was bruised because she couldn't keep her hands still with her wrists locked so tightly in the metal. Tuttle had deliberately left her sitting alone in the interrogation room for some time. She knew he thought she would become more agitated and frightened. Unfortunately for Tuttle, he didn't scare her. She knew monsters, and he wasn't one.

The door opened and he slipped into the room. She didn't look up. What was the point? She had nothing to tell him, so as long as this was going to last, and she figured it would be a very long time, she would endure.

They hadn't allowed her to grab a sweater and she was cold, and feeling a little exposed, which she figured was also part of the plan.

"Ms. Benoit? I'm Detective Frank Tuttle. We're investigating a man named Rafe Cordeau. I believe you know him."

Tuttle was dressed in slacks and a jacket and he looked far too slick to be anything but DEA. Not that it surprised her. He carried a folder and set it on the table, making a show of it. The thing was, no matter what he said, he had nothing on her and he would have to make something up, or he would have to let her go.

She remained silent. There wasn't a question in his statement.

"Ms. Benoit?" Frank's voice had gone sharp.

"I'm sorry." She sent him a brief look from under her lashes. "I didn't know that your statement required any response on my part."

"Are you acquainted with Rafe Cordeau?"

"You obviously think that I am. Enough that you turned the place where I live upside down. I have no idea what you were looking for because no one had the courtesy to tell me."

"That isn't an answer."

She shrugged. "As I don't know what you're looking for in the way of answers, I can't help you."

"Do you in fact know Rafe Cordeau?" he thundered.

"Is this where I'm supposed to wince and burst into tears?" Sarcasm dripped from her voice. Rafe could make her wince without even raising his voice, but even he couldn't make her burst into tears. Certainly no cop could.

She pushed the heavy fall of hair over her shoulder and for the first time looked Tuttle in the eye. She even leaned toward him. "Everyone who grew up in Algiers knows Rafe Cordeau or at least *of* him. If they say they don't, they are lying. Yes. To answer your question, I know Rafe Cordeau."

"And you lived with him for a number of years."

She stared him directly in the eye and she was very

focused. Intense. She waited. She was good at waiting. Good at the silence game. She'd been taught by a master and she'd followed up those lessons with experiences. She could tell Tuttle was buying into her age. She was young. Barely twenty-one. She'd had her birthday just last month. She didn't look hard, she looked vulnerable. He had no idea the experiences she'd been through had aged her fast.

He sighed. "Ms. Benoit, I'm trying to ascertain how you know Cordeau."

"I'm sorry. You're not very good at this, are you? Again, there was no question for me to answer, and I can't guess at what you want from me."

Tuttle winced. She kept her gaze from the camera, where she was certain other cops were watching on a screen in a control room. Tuttle was going to take some ribbing over that remark.

"I was given to him when I was eleven years old."

"*Given* to him?"

She nodded. "I'm his ward. I was raised in his house."

"And you're engaged to be married to him."

For the first time her heart went crazy, hammering in her chest so hard she feared it would actually break through—or he could hear it. She forced herself to keep her eyes steady on his.

"Why would you think that?"

"There was a write-up in the New Orleans newspaper in the society section that states you are engaged to Rafe Cordeau. Are you saying that information isn't correct?"

No one would dare write an article about Cordeau without his consent. No one. Not even a reporter who wanted a name for themselves. Rafe had planted that article and he was making a statement directly to her.

She shook her head but didn't speak, her mind racing.

"Are you his fiancée?" Tucker asked, his voice a whip.

She shrugged. "If that's what someone wrote in a newspaper, I suppose it must be true."

Irritation crossed his face. He scowled at her. "You aren't helping yourself by being a smart-ass."

She raised an eyebrow. Her wrists throbbed. Her pulse raced, and she had a hell of a headache from falling on the floor. She didn't want to sit for hours in the interrogation room. Every minute that passed was a minute she should be on the road.

"I'm not trying to be a smart-ass, Mr. Tuttle . . ."

"Detective," he corrected.

She took a breath and heaved a sigh. "Detective Tuttle," she said. "I just want you to get to whatever this is about so I can go."

"This is about your relationship with Rafe Cordeau," he snapped.

"I've told you what my relationship is. You seem to have the information already anyway. If that's all you wanted to know, I'd like to go."

His fist banged on the table. She could have told him silence was far more effective. Silence. Staring. And ice-cold eyes. Banging on the table got you nothing. She held still and watched him.

"When was your last contact with Cordeau?"

"I left when I turned twenty."

"So a year ago."

That didn't deserve an answer. He could do math. She just stared at him. Waiting for him to get to it.

"It wasn't the first time you left."

Tuttle knew more than she thought anyone else was aware of. Someone was feeding the DEA information about Cordeau—a very dangerous game to play. She had to go carefully because that meant they had someone in his organization.

"No, it wasn't."

He waited a few moments but when she wasn't forthcoming, he leaned toward her. "You ran away when you were fourteen years old. A woman by the name of April Harp helped you. She was murdered along with her entire family, and you were safe back in Cordeau's house."

It was an accusation. She knew her face had gone white. Her stomach lurched and beneath the table she twisted her fingers together. There were some memories that would never go away and some deeds there was no redemption for.

"Yes, that's true," she whispered.

"Why did you run away?"

"I wanted to see my mother."

"She was already dead."

"I didn't know that," Catarina said. "He didn't tell me."

"He had her killed. Two days after she delivered you to him, she died of an overdose that the coroner said she didn't give to herself."

"That isn't news, Detective Tuttle. I was given that information *after* I was taken back to Cordeau, although how you can attribute my mother's death to Rafe, I don't know. Again, you seem to have information I don't."

"Taken back? You didn't go voluntarily?" He pounced on that.

Now they were treading on dangerous ground. She said nothing, just watched him. He would want to bring kidnapping charges against Cordeau.

"Did Cordeau kill April Harp?" he demanded. "Did he order his men to kill her and her family?"

She remained silent.

"Did you help Cordeau kill her?"

Her stomach lurched again. "If you're asking am I responsible for her death, I believe I am, yes. I didn't kill her, but I left. I knew there would be consequences but I stupidly thought they would be for me, not someone else."

"Were you there when she was killed?"

There was no statute of limitations on murder. She saw where this was going and shook her head. "There is no way, under any circumstances, that I could, or would testify against Rafe Cordeau. None. If that's what your desired end result is, then we're finished here."

Tuttle sat back in his chair. "You know what he is. You know he's killed people. Many people. He runs drugs. Prostitutes. Guns. Still, you aren't willing to help us put him away."

"You've had how many people willing to help you put him away? They're all dead, Detective Tuttle. You can't protect them from him. You certainly won't be able to protect me from him. He owns men like you. He has connections everywhere. You aren't going to bring him down and certainly not with my testimony."

"You *saw* him kill April Harp. You were there."

"I was held there," she spat back. "Fourteen years old. All I wanted to do was see my mother. That was all. I saw a knife go into my friend's belly and she was slit all the way to her breastbone. Then my hands were pushed into the gaping wound so that I would always remember her blood was on my hands. I heard the shots that killed her family, but I didn't see anything else. I couldn't see anything else. I was on my knees screaming and I couldn't even cover my face because my hands were covered in her blood."

She would never forget the horror of that moment. Rafe holding her in front of him. His man, Marcel, holding April. Catarina had been unable to look away, not even when Rafe plunged the knife into April and sliced her open. Blood sprayed all over her, but that wasn't enough for Rafe. He wanted her to learn a lesson.

Rafe calmly forced her hands inside the horrible wound and whispered in her ear. *You did this, my little Catarina. You. Their blood is on your hands. Don't ever be so foolish as to leave me again.* The memory was so sharp, so vivid, she was afraid she would vomit right there.

Rafe spoke softly. He never needed to raise his voice. He simply looked at his men and gestured toward the mess that had once been a live woman, now something he considered trash for them to take out.

April had cleaned their home, and Catarina had followed her everywhere. She'd been one of the few people who had been kind. She'd even helped Catarina learn to read and write, and Catarina had gotten her killed.

"Who killed her, Ms. Benoit?" Tuttle asked. "You didn't say who held you there and pushed the knife into April."

She raised stricken eyes to him. "I don't know. I didn't see his face."

He sighed. "Now you're lying to me."

"My back was to him. He wore gloves. Black gloves. I never saw his face." That was true. She hadn't needed to see his face. She recognized his scent. His hard body. His voice that never changed. He terrified her.

"I'm going to get you some water."

She was surprised by the compassion in Tuttle's voice. He left the room briefly, just enough time for her to press her trembling hand against her mouth. She breathed in over and over, trying to keep from throwing up. She had nightmares and there was no way to ever get that scene out of her head, but talking about it was far worse.

The details. The smell. The horror of it. All along her mother had been dead. Rafe casually told her the truth. That was the thing about him. He didn't hide what he was from her. He didn't lie to her. He always told the truth. She'd been stupid enough to ask him if he'd killed her mother.

She was a whore, Catarina, he had explained patiently. *She didn't need to be, but she turned herself into one because she couldn't live without drugs. Addiction is a terrible weakness. She sold you to me for drugs. Her stepchild she should have loved and protected. I couldn't let her touch you. I couldn't ever allow that woman to harm you through her addiction. She came back wanting more drugs. She threatened to take you back and sell you to men. She claimed that I had conned her and that had she kept you, you would have been an endless source of revenue for her.*

Catarina knew he told the truth, because he always did. The stark truth. He never tried to soft soap it. There were no such things as white lies. Her mother, or rather step-mother, really had done all those things. She was the only mother Catarina had ever known. Catarina, for whatever reason, was under Rafe's protection. She'd been threatened and he'd removed the threat. Just like that.

That hadn't been the only time he'd "protected" her. She'd been sixteen and had become a little rebellious. Not with Rafe. Never with him. But she always had shadows on her. Men who went everywhere she did. She'd gone to a movie and had slipped into the woman's bathroom and she'd stayed there deliberately for a very long time, forcing one of the two men to come in to retrieve her.

She detested Marcel. He'd been the one to help kill April. Marcel had dragged her out and refused to allow her to see the rest of the show. She'd kicked up a fuss. In public, a serious break of the rules. He'd slapped her the moment they were away from prying eyes.

She never told Rafe, but he knew before she got home. He was there and his anger filled the room. *Filled* it. She stood in front of him, bowing her head, terrified of his wrath, kicking herself for being so stupid. She hated having men following her everywhere. She didn't have friends to attend movies with, and she'd overheard the two men talk-ing about how pathetic she was. She'd been crushed.

Rafe caught her chin with two fingers and tipped her face up for his examination. He pressed his palm to the cheek Marcel had slapped. Then he'd raised his eyes to Marcel and jerked his head at two of his personal body-guards. The last she'd seen of Marcel, he was struggling as he was dragged from the house.

Don't hurt him, Rafe. I was upset with them, something they said about me, and I acted stupid.

No one has the right to put their hands on you but me. Never, Catarina, not for any reason. I won't stand for it. If you need to be punished, that's for me to decide, no one else. Any man touches you, you tell me.

That had been the first time he'd ever touched her gently. His hand had skimmed her face and then moved to her hair. His eyes, usually so cold, held something for one brief moment she couldn't understand. But she knew she would never, *ever*, tell Rafe that someone hit her, slapped her, or put his hands on her. She knew it was a death sentence.

Tuttle returned with the water and Catarina drank it down and then pulled her feet up on the chair beneath the table, sitting tailor fashion. She rocked gently, trying to soothe herself long enough to get through this.

"I'm sorry those things happened to you, Ms. Benoit." Tuttle even sounded sorry. His eyes were gentle. "Are you certain you didn't see the face of the man who killed April Harp?"

She swallowed down painful memories and shook her head. "I was forced to face her at all times."

Rafe hadn't tried to comfort her afterward. He'd taken her directly to her room and locked her in, bloody hands and all. She'd spent hours in her shower, sliding down the wall and crying while she scrubbed the palms of her hands raw. In the end she couldn't tell if it was April's blood or her own on her hands.

"You ran away again when you were seventeen."

"Yes."

"Why?"

"I was afraid of what Rafe wanted from me. He looked at me differently. He watched me all the time. I didn't know why and I was afraid. So I decided to try to get away again, but without anyone's help." That wasn't the *entire* reason, but she wasn't going to tell him the rest. She didn't have proof. She never had proof, but she *knew*.

Rafe came into her room at night, his eyes on her. Watch-

ing her. Wholly focused on her. Waiting for something. She
had no idea what it was, but she could tell he was becoming
impatient.

She hadn't left because of that. She'd left because of the
women. The nights he came to her room, prowling around,
his eyes glowing at her, she'd held her breath expectantly.
He hadn't laid a hand on her. But then, after he left, a car
would pull up and a woman would get out. She didn't know
for certain, but she never saw the same woman twice, and
she never saw them leave. Not even when she waited up all
night.

"I didn't get very far. Rafe has eyes everywhere. He found
me within hours." It was more than that, but she wasn't going
to reveal any secrets that would get her locked up. She knew
Tuttle could try to lock her up for not reporting April's murder, but she'd been a virtual prisoner and it wouldn't stick.
They both knew it. "He was angry with me."

"What did he do? And why didn't you go straight to the
police?"

"I was his ward," she reminded him. "He had every right
to haul me back. He didn't kidnap me. And he owned half the
police department." She knew that. She'd seen the fat enve-
lopes that were handed out.

"What did he do?" Tuttle persisted, not denying that
Rafe had owned cops. It was common knowledge.

She moistened her suddenly dry lips. For the first time
she couldn't look at him. There was nowhere to look so she
stared down at her wrists. Already bruises were forming.
She had very fair skin and she'd always marked easily.

"Let's just say, I didn't defy him again until I was very,
very certain I could get away and he wouldn't be able to track
me."

"You lived with him all those years, Ms. Benoit. You
had to have seen him committing a crime. We need you to
be frank with us."

"No one sees Rafe committing crimes, Detective, least

of all me. I can't help you. I really can't. If you don't have
any further questions, I'd like to leave now."

"I have just a few more for you," Tuttle said, giving her
an exasperated look. "You do understand that this man is a
crime lord. You have no reason to feel loyalty toward him.
He murdered your mother. He either murdered April Harp
and her family, or he ordered that hit. Rafe Cordeau belongs
behind bars."

"If all that's true, Detective, why can't you ever find any
evidence? Or witnesses?"

"Witnesses disappear."

"Exactly. That's my point. I was never a part of Rafe's
business. I was a child growing up in his house."

"There's no record of you going to school."

That shamed her and she suspected he'd said it to humil-
iate her. She detested that Rafe hadn't sent her to school or
brought in tutors. She was tempted to lie, but instead she
lifted her chin. "No, I didn't go to school. And strangely, no
one came to ask why."

"He didn't have you homeschooled?"

She shook her head. "No, I was never homeschooled. I
didn't graduate. I didn't go to college. In fact, Detective," she
added a little defiantly, "I could barely read for a very long
time. What does that have to do with Rafe and his crimes?"

"I would say that would be considered an injustice
against you," Tuttle pointed out.

Catarina shrugged. Every second that went by was a
second more Rafe had to find her. Sooner or later a police
officer on the take would notify him.

"Ask your questions. I don't have much time."

He frowned. "What does that mean?"

"It means that sooner or later, word is going to get out
that you have me in an interrogation room. Rafe can move
fast when he needs to. I think it best if I'm long gone before
he gets here."

"We're offering you protective custody in exchange for your testimony against Rafe Cordeau."

She stared at him for a moment and then burst out laughing, noting she just might be on the edge of hysteria. "Have you not heard one word I've said to you? I will not testify against him. I don't have any information to help you. And people in your protective custody are *not* safe from him. He would be able to find me. Once he's here and he gets my scent, my trail, he will find me. He'd kill every single one of you and your families to get to me. He would kill every officer you have guarding me. And then he would kill me."

Tuttle sank back in his chair, smirking. "So he's Superman with incredible powers. Can he fly through the air as well?"

"I want to leave. You aren't charging me with anything, so I want to leave."

"He already knows where you are."

Tuttle dropped the words so softly she nearly missed them. For a moment her lungs seized. Her throat closed. She stared at him. Stricken. Horrified. And then she knew.

"You *told* him. You have someone in his organization trying to climb the ladder and you gave that information to your man so he would gain Rafe's marker. You sold me out and then expected me to put myself in your hands." She whispered it. She knew she was right.

She'd been certain once she'd heard some of the information they had on her that the DEA had a man undercover. They must have fed him her location in order for him to curry favor with Rafe. *They told him where she was.* The police. The ones who were supposed to serve and protect. They'd put her directly in the line of fire. She swallowed terror and looked up at him.

"How long ago did Rafe get this information?"

Tuttle looked at her, noted her shaking hands and tried not to smile. "We can protect you. We'll get you to a safe house."

She stood up, pushed back her chair. "There is no safe house, you idiot. There's no such thing. How long ago did you inform him of my whereabouts?"

Tuttle glanced at his watch. "A few hours before we brought you in."

She shook her head. "You don't have any idea what you've done. You've killed at least three good men. You need to make certain you put them somewhere far from here. David Belmont at Poetry Slam. Malcom Hardy at the martial arts studio. And Ridley Cromer. He'll kill them all to get to me. To teach me a lesson. You can't hang them out as bait and hope he does it so you can build a case against him. You'll never know it was him. *God*. You people. You don't get it."

"I think that can be arranged if you choose to testify."

"Damn you, do you hear yourself? Are you really willing to risk all three of them? I'm not testifying. I don't have anything I can help you with. I don't have one single thing I can help you hang him with. Not one."

"He's been under investigation for over two years."

"And you've got *nothing* on him. You won't get anything on him. He was investigated before that and again before that. What's wrong with you that you'd tell him where I am? Did it once occur to you that you were putting my life in jeopardy? Did you even care?"

"Sit down, Ms. Benoit."

"I want to leave."

"Sit down. You're becoming agitated."

She placed both hands on the table and glared at him. "I. Want. To. Leave."

"I said sit down. If you force me to, I'll put you back in handcuffs."

"I want a lawyer."

"You aren't charged with a crime." He ran a hand through his thinning hair. "Be reasonable, Ms. Benoit. There's a good chance Cordeau is already on his way to find you. We can't protect you from him unless you agree to protective custody."

"You can't protect me, and I wouldn't help you now if my life depended on it. You're no better than him."

"I'm a cop, Ms. Benoit," Tuttle reminded. "It's my job to catch criminals, especially ones as bad as Rafe Cordeau."

"You had no problem throwing me under the bus so you could give your undercover man a leg up the ladder with Rafe. You knew if Rafe found me he might kill me, but that was of little consequence to you, wasn't it?"

"That's not true. We can protect you."

Catarina stabbed a finger toward him. "You were so smug, you were certain I'd come running to you for help. Was that because I have no education and you figured I was stupid and easily manipulated?"

She could tell by the way his face stilled that she'd hit very close to the truth.

Tuttle shook his head. "Please sit down, Catarina. The bottom line right now is that your life very well could be in jeopardy. Whether or not we made a wrong decision is a moot point. We have to keep you alive. That's what matters now." His voice had gone soothing.

She took a deep breath. "I have nothing more to say to you. I would like to leave. You have nothing to hold me on. Nothing at all."

"You do understand if you leave this room I can't guarantee your safety?"

"I understand that if I stay here, I'm going to die. I want to leave."

The argument went on for two more hours. Back and forth until finally Catarina lapsed into silence and Tuttle threw his hands up into the air, realizing he wasn't going to get her cooperation. He swore under his breath and stood up.

"Wait here." His voice was terse. Angry.

It wasn't like she could go anywhere once he closed the

door to the interrogation room. Catarina began to pace back and forth. They'd tried to trap her. She had no idea how the police had found her, but they weren't out to help her, or protect her. They were looking for a way to force her cooperation.

Rafe had once told her, in his casual way, that the police were every bit as corrupt as everyone else. They used people. Informants and snitches. Junkies and prostitutes. They cared nothing about those they tied to them, those risking their lives. At least, he'd said, he played fair.

Some part of her had always thought he'd lied, even though he'd never lied to her, even though his voice rang with truth. Now she knew it was true. The DEA had tried to force her into testifying against Rafe by putting her life on the line. They hadn't cared that they would be putting the lives of her friends there right along with hers.

She would have no choice now, not if she wanted to save them all. Every cop who had searched the warehouse had left their scent behind—a scent once Rafe found he'd never forget. She had to get out fast and try to get Rafe to follow her immediately if she wanted to make certain Ridley was never touched by Rafe. His scent was all over the warehouse. Rafe might ignore Malcom's presence because he owned the warehouse, but Ridley was a different matter.

She froze. *Ridley had been in her bed.* His scent would be on the sheets and pillowcases. Rafe wouldn't wait to find out whether or not Ridley had touched her. He would search for him first and kill him, even before he went after her.

She had to get to Rafe first. He might want her dead, but she'd left before and he hadn't killed her. That meant he might still want her in his life. She could bargain with him. It was a risk, but to save Ridley she would try it. She could offer herself to him. She'd stay with him until he didn't want her anymore, and she'd never again try to escape him, as long as Ridley was alive and well. She couldn't just specify Ridley. She had to include the other two men so it didn't seem like Ridley was any more important to her than the others.

She took a deep breath and let it out. She would be exchanging her life for theirs. Whatever Rafe wanted from her, he was getting impatient waiting for. She had a feeling he was waiting for whatever it was inside of her, the entity that she felt every now and then, the one with teeth and claws, waiting to emerge. As long as she was away from Rafe, she'd been able to keep it under control, but she knew if she went back to him, it was only a matter of time—and then she'd be like he was.

Tuttle returned and she swung around to face him. He handed her a cell phone and a card. "I want you to use this if you change your mind."

"I won't be using it," she said and kept her hands at her sides.

"Take it anyway. I think you'll need it. Word on the street is, Cordeau is on the move and he's heading this way."

"That's no surprise, Detective. I need a taxi."

"I can get one of my men to give you a ride home," Tuttle said.

"I prefer a taxi. Please just call one for me."

"This is suicide," Tuttle suddenly hissed. "You're committing suicide."

Catarina took the cell phone and card from him just to shut him up. She didn't have a back pocket so she kept them in her fist. "That's one way to look at it. Another would be that you and your fellow cops murdered me."

She swept past him into the hall. Tuttle indicated for her to go to her left and she did. Instantly she was surrounded by noise. Conversation. The ringing of phones. Desks and computers and people poring over reports. Normal was going on when her world was shattered. She walked with her head up, refusing to acknowledge she was in her sweatpants and a tank top and nothing more. She knew by the sudden hush that every officer in the room knew who she was and why she was there.

Catarina swept past them like a queen. She'd been raised in Rafe Cordeau's home. All those years growing up his soldiers had treated her differently than they had other women. She'd learned to be composed at all times and that composure saved her now.

She swept by the desks without looking at any of them. Glancing at the exit sign above a stairwell, she headed for that, ignoring the elevators. She had an aversion to elevators, and she needed to move anyway. Her gaze swept the offices and she stopped dead. Froze. Everything in her stilled.

She found herself staring into golden eyes. He was watching her through the glass. Ridley Cromer. *Her* Ridley. Dressed as he'd been the night before when he'd laid in her bed. When he'd kissed her. A kiss she'd asked him for. When she laid her soul bare before him. When she'd trusted him.

She couldn't move for a moment. She couldn't think. Her stomach heaved and she found herself vomiting all over the floor. She didn't care. Nothing mattered. Along with his faded blue jeans and tight tee, he wore a badge. A big, fat shiny badge.

The sense of betrayal, the hurt, was worse than when her mother had sold her to Rafe. Something inside her shattered, broke apart. She felt it go. She felt the knife twisting in her heart. She'd let him in. She'd trusted him. She'd given everything she could to him. She would have traded her life for his.

She vomited again and wiped her mouth after she spit several times, and then she tossed the cell phone and Tuttle's card right in the middle of the vomit. Let the DEA deal with that. Silence surrounded her, but in her head, she could hear screaming. Raw, terrible screaming that rose up like a wail from the dead. She hadn't known another human being could hurt her so deeply.

She sensed movement and she turned and walked straight for the stairs. She didn't run. She refused to give him that satisfaction.

Behind her, she heard Ridley's voice. "She can't leave. What the hell, Frank? She needs to be in protective custody.

You know he'll kill her. And what happened to her face? Her wrists? Damn it, I'm fucking going to kill you with my bare hands."

She let the door swing closed behind her and then she ran, taking the stairs two at a time, and then three. She was fast, faster than she'd ever been as if that being inside of her aided her now, aided her when she was no longer Catarina. Ridley had torn out her guts. Her heart. He'd left nothing at all but an empty shell.

"Cat. Stop."

She heard his voice and it only spurred her onward. She burst from the building and ran to the line of taxis at the end of the street. She had no money with her, but hopefully the police had left her stash behind. She could barely speak to give the driver the address. God. God. She'd been such a fool.

There was no way his name was Ridley Cromer. She should have known he wouldn't be interested in a woman who had never been kissed in her life. She'd said it herself, he was a player, and he'd played her beautifully. She'd kissed a man for the first time and she didn't even know his real name.

He had to have disconnected her security system. He'd taken her gun. He'd left her defenseless. He had tried to get information about Rafe from her, and when his gentle probing didn't work, he'd told the others she was going to run. She buried her face in her hands and kept breathing in and out. She had to keep breathing to keep the terrible black void inside of her from swallowing her.

For the first time in her life she wished she were back with Rafe. He'd never lied, not once. He'd never tried to use her own emotions against her. He didn't hide who he was or what he was. She didn't know how to think. Or function. She didn't know how to be Catarina anymore.

6

THE moment Catarina paid the driver and returned to the warehouse, she realized the front door was intact. Ridley knew the combination to get in. He'd observed her unlocking the door many times, and he must have given it to the police so that they made no noise on entry.

Pressure built and built in her chest. So much pressure. Her heart hurt. Her soul hurt. Her eyes burned and her throat swelled. She heard screaming. Real screaming. Raw. Vocal cord–shredding screaming. She screamed for her dead mother. For April and her family. For Marcel who had slapped her face. For the terrible price she'd paid for trying to escape when she was seventeen.

Mostly she screamed to try to find a release from the terrible hurt that cut through her like a knife. She found herself on her knees, her throat so raw she was afraid it was bleeding. She crawled through the darkness to her bedroom on her hands and knees with the vague idea she'd gather her clothes and leave.

She knew she was in shock, her body refusing to function, when she couldn't find the strength or desire to push herself from the floor and get to work. She crawled to the corner and wedged herself there, drew up her knees and wrapped both arms around them, rocking back and forth. And she wept.

The tears weren't silent at all—they were full body-wracking sobs—soul-wrenching, agonizing sobs. It hurt to cry. Her abused throat protested, swelling so that she had to cough between the choking cries. She couldn't stop once she'd started. She had twenty-one years worth of tears to cry and she shed them all.

ELI Perez slipped into the warehouse. The moment he pushed open the door he heard her. The screams dying away to be replaced by a woman crying. He couldn't even call it crying. He had never heard such anguished screams or such broken-hearted, soul-destroying sobbing. *He* had caused that. There was no doubt in his mind.

Swearing under his breath, he made his way unerringly through the warehouse to the bedroom. He had the eyes of a cat and could see easily in the dark. He moved quickly to the open side of the room.

His first glance took in the bed. The sheets and blankets had been ripped to pieces, shredded the way he'd shredded Catarina's heart. He swung around, carefully scanning the warehouse. She hadn't had time to rip those sheets and blankets, to tear the mattress to shreds. He'd been one step behind her and had heard her anguished screams and then the sobbing. She hadn't touched those blankets. That could only mean one thing. Rafe Cordeau had already found Catarina, and the problem that was Rafe Cordeau was much worse than any of them ever suspected.

He didn't spot her at first in the corner. She was hidden partially by the old dresser. She was so small pressed

against the wall, in a little protective ball, it broke his heart.
He'd done that to her. He knew he had. He swore again.

"Cat."

Her body jerked as if he'd struck her. He winced and
crossed the distance separating them to crouch down in
front of her.

"Cat. Baby. It isn't safe here. He's been here."

She didn't look up or acknowledge that she heard him.
She stayed exactly where she was. He knew her now, knew
she could maintain silence for long periods of time, and
they didn't have a long time.

"He's a leopard. A shifter. Isn't he?" He wanted to shock
her. Get some response from her—any kind of response.

Catarina lifted her head, and his heart stuttered. Her
eyes were absolutely blank. Dead. Devoid of all warmth or
feeling. "Go away, whoever you are."

"Eli, my name is Eli Perez," he said, giving her the truth.
"You know I can't let you stay here," he added gently.
"Look at your bed. He's been here. He's leopard, and that
means he can follow your scent—but you already know
that, don't you?"

"I knew he'd been here the moment I walked in," she
admitted.

Her voice was strained and she kept clearing her throat.
She'd done some damage screaming out her anguish. He
wanted to pull her into his arms, but she had shrunk away
from him, not moved toward him. He kept himself locked
down, under control. He needed to handle the situation
without emotion if he was going to get her the hell to safety.
Clearly she was waiting for Rafe to find her. She wasn't
going to run after all.

"I'll wait for him here. He'll come back for me. He
always comes for me." She confirmed his suspicions, rubbing her chin on top of her knees. "He's probably out looking for you."

That much, Eli was certain, was the truth. If he'd been

in Rafe's place, he would have been out looking for the man
who slept in his woman's bed.

"You have to come with me now, Cat," he reiterated.

"Go to hell."

She wasn't going to hear reason and honestly, he couldn't
blame her, but he sure as hell wasn't going to leave her
there. Sweet didn't work. Gentle didn't work. He reached
out and snagged her hand, jerking her body toward his.

She exploded into action, driving toward him with her
head. She planted the top of her skull hard in his gut, using
the strength in her legs to knock the wind out of him as she
took him down. Straddling him, she punched and she
punched hard. Three wicked blows to his face. One to his
jaw. She rolled off when he went to snag her wrists, and she
kicked him as she rolled away, a hard heel to his thigh.

He caught her ankle and twisted, rolling her over to her
stomach. He didn't want to hurt her, but she was wild, trying to lunge up. He pinned her down with his weight,
caught one of her wrists and snapped cuffs around it.

"Settle down, Cat. I'm not leaving you here for him to
find. You're coming with me."

"You have nothing on me. You can't arrest me."

"I'm not arresting you, I'm taking you out of here. Stop
struggling or I'm going to have to knock your ass out."

That only served to make her struggle harder. He clipped
the other bracelet to his own wrist, caught her free arm and
dragged it behind her back, locking it high.

"You keep this up and you'll break your own fucking
arm. Be smart," he snapped, using his toughest no-nonsense
voice. He was deliberately rough with her. She expected
gentle from him and he wasn't going to give that to her. It
was imperative he got her moving fast and the only way to
do that was to be himself.

He'd never been kind and gentle in his life until Catarina. It wasn't in his nature. He was rough around the edges,
used to getting his way, and when he said move, people

moved. She wasn't doing any of that, and she still looked at him with blank eyes as if she were totally dead inside.

He yanked her to her feet, dragged her to the other side of the bed, where he scooped up her clothes and stuffed them into her travel bag. "Anything else important to you?" he snapped.

She didn't answer. He left the cash behind and dragged her through the dark warehouse toward the door. She tried kicking him twice so he lifted her, one-armed, and tossed her over his shoulder. She sank her teeth into him. It hurt like hell, but he kept walking straight out to his truck.

He dumped her in the cab, unlocked his bracelet, hooked her seat belt and locked her free hand with the other cuff. He then locked the handcuffs to the small bolt he'd installed in his dash. She was forced to lean forward, her head down so she couldn't be seen. He scanned the rooftops and high places as he hurried around to the driver's seat.

A leopard could track his truck. He knew because he was a shifter and he could track almost anything, including vehicles. He should have guessed. He slammed the flat of his palm against the steering wheel. Rafe Cordeau *had* to be a shifter.

Eli glanced over at Catarina, his gaze narrowing. Focused. He didn't have reactions to women like he'd had to her. His leopard didn't tolerate a woman for more than a night or two, but Catarina had been different. When he'd been with her, his leopard had been content. A time or two it had even risen close to the surface as if wanting to be near her. The fact that his leopard recognized her meant Cat's leopard had to be close to emerging.

What did Rafe Cordeau want with her? He already knew, he'd figured it out, but he wanted confirmation. "He took you when you were eleven years old. Had you had your first period?"

She shot him a single look. That blank stare. He wanted to shake her.

"Damn it, answer me. Do you think I'm asking for my health?" He spat the question at her, allowing his anger to fill the cab. She couldn't know that his anger was at himself, at the damage he'd done to her, and at Rafe, for what he'd done to her. She was an innocent caught between two powerful men who played for keeps. He had a very bad feeling she would continue to be caught between them.

"I'm not going to ask you again. Answer me *now*."

She didn't look scared. She looked . . . broken, and he felt like a damn fucking bully, kicking the little kid that was down right there in the play yard.

"Yes. I had my first period at eleven. But Rafe couldn't have known that. My mother was a junkie and she took me to him and offered me to him."

He shook his head. "Think back. It didn't happen that way. He had to have come to your house when you were younger. He had to have looked you over. Decided on you. He was the one who first made the approach. There's a reason he wants you."

He had taken his eyes off the road long enough to watch her face when he told her the truth. He saw he'd scored. She swallowed and looked away from him. He hated that he couldn't comfort her. He hated that he'd cuffed her to his truck and her wrists were already bruised. She had a bruise on her cheek and her face was swollen from crying. He couldn't pull her into his arms and just hold her. First, he had to get them to safety, and it didn't matter to him whether or not she wanted to be safe. He had to make her safe. Not only because he helped put her in this position, but because it was a compulsion and damn it to hell, she'd gotten under his skin.

He waited, hoping curiosity would win out and she'd ask him questions, but she didn't. She didn't look at him again either. She kept her gaze on the floor. Her head had been down the same way, her hair everywhere when she'd bent to vomit in the police station. That was on him too. That had nearly killed him. He wanted to beat the hell out of Frank with his bare fists. He wanted to beat the hell out of Rafe Cordeau. Mostly he wanted to take back everything that had happened and play it all another way.

He pulled into the automatic car wash. He wanted a thorough wash and that meant going through twice. He had no doubt that Rafe had followed Catarina's scent to the police department. He was grateful, at least, that the warehouse had been raided. Rafe would know she hadn't gone voluntarily. If what he suspected were true, Rafe would never kill Catarina. He might hurt her, but he'd never kill her.

"What do you know about shifters?" he asked.

She stared at the floor, but her shoulders shrugged. Her hair covered her face, and her cuffed hands.

"You know Rafe is a leopard. So am I. And I suspect you are as well."

That got him a head turn. Her blue eyes were so dark they looked violet, but again there was no real life in them. Not even the interest he'd hoped for.

"That's why he waited to claim you, Cat. A female shifter doesn't necessarily feel her leopard right away the way a male does. She can't emerge until both the human and the leopard enter the same cycle together." He kept his eyes on hers. "A heat. You both have to be fertile at the same time. When she emerges, both of you are going to need sex. It's hot and wild and not for an innocent."

She blinked, but again, there was no response in her eyes. She turned her head away again.

"Did he mark you? Did you see his leopard? Did he bite you or rake you with his claws?"

She sat up fast, swinging both fists together at his face, slamming into his jaw, snapping his head back. One hand disengaged her seat belt while the other dropped to the truck door and yanked, trying to open it. He'd been smart enough to engage the locks and that second cost her. He gripped her hair in his fist and yanked her hard back to him, so that she fell sideways, her body sprawling across his, her head facedown in his lap.

She cried out and both hands went to his. He didn't loosen his grip, but he did quit pulling so hard. "Are you serious right now, Cat?" he spat out.

He was fairly certain from her reaction that no one had ever manhandled her before, not like this, and he could see the shock on her face. Fear edging in. Good. He was finally getting to her. He'd take fear over . . . nothing. "I'm bigger and stronger. I know your every move." He was secretly proud of her for getting out of the handcuffs. He saw the broken pen on the floor mat.

She went very still, her blue eyes searching his face. He detested the bruise on her cheek. He really hated the bruises circling her wrists. He loosened his grip on her hair, his fingers sliding deeper, massaging her scalp, trying to ease the pain he'd caused when he'd yanked her across the truck to him.

She didn't move. She hardly breathed. She just stared at him like he was a total stranger, not the man who had given her that all important first kiss. The one he could still taste in his mouth.

"Kitten," he said softly.

That got a rise out of her. Her eyes had held just a hint of fear, pushing that blank, dead look—distant. The moment he'd uttered his chosen endearment for her, the name he called her when he was soft inside and wanted to pull her close and hold her forever, the look went from nearly blank to pure fury.

He felt her cat rise and his cat rose to meet hers, clawing and raking at his belly for freedom. He saw the telltale shine in her eyes, felt her body heat. His reacted, going hard, the male cat in him rising to the challenge of a female refusing to submit.

She gasped and pressed both hands to her stomach,

dropping her head to breathe deep. He knew what she was doing and why. Catarina Benoit was terrified of her leopard. She was petrified. She didn't want that gift and she was doing everything in her power to keep it at bay.

Eli smoothed his hand over her hair and helped her to sit up, all the while breathing his leopard back under control.

"Don't call me that. Not ever again. You aren't sweet and kind. Don't use that voice, that lying voice. This is who you are. Violent. Rough. And a killer. You think I can't see it in your eyes? Leopards are killing machines. That's what they do. They hunt and they kill and that's it."

His leopard was far too close for a conversation like this one. Worse, she came close to the truth of it and that made him angry as well. "You left out fucking, Cat," he snarled. "Leopards have lots and lots of sex."

He set her back in the passenger seat and caught up the cuffs. She had gone very pale and shrank back against the seat, her eyes ringed with dark circles. She still looked broken and vulnerable in spite of her sudden fury. Her anger was gone completely. She looked defeated. Completely defeated. He hadn't been going for that reaction either.

She put both hands in the air. "Please. Not again." She didn't look at him.

He took another deep breath, studying the long sweep of her lashes. "Cat, I can't take any chances with you. I can cuff you to me or the bolt. You choose." It was the best he could do. He had the feeling she planned to jump out of the truck on the highway when he was going at a high speed.

They were almost out of the car wash. "Choose, baby, and hurry."

She extended the arm closest to him, turning her head to look out the window. "Just don't talk to me anymore. I can't take any more."

That was a body blow. He could feel her trembling through the connection of metal. "Let's just get somewhere safe where you can sleep," he said. "No safe house or trying to get you to testify. Just sleep."

She swallowed and nodded her head once. Eli supposed that was a better response than nothing. He'd taken the fight out of her, but she was battered and bruised emotionally. He set his teeth and went through the car wash a second time. The moment they were clean, he hit the highway.

He took them out of the city. "Malcom and David are safe. I told them both to get out of town for a while and take a long vacation. They both said they would."

"Thank you."

He hadn't expected that. She sounded like she meant it. "I didn't know they'd gotten word to Cordeau. I didn't have any idea they intended to."

She didn't respond. She kept her head turned away from him and he was afraid the tears were falling again. She made no sound, but that just made it worse. The way she held herself, he knew she wouldn't accept comfort from him.

"I fucked up, Catarina. Big-time. I totally fucked up with you."

She swallowed again, but she remained silent. He drove fast, heading for one of the three houses he kept for safety issues. No one knew about them, not even his friends. This one was situated on a hundred and twenty-five acres and was fairly remote. His ranch bordered another much larger one. The ranch was in his mother's maiden name.

Catarina was asleep by the time he drove down a maze of roads to the dirt track that went to the house. He was grateful for that. She didn't wake up, not even when he parked and sat there in the cab just inhaling her.

There had been something about her from the first moment he'd laid eyes on her. He was often undercover. He was good at it. He was leopard and he could sniff out lies and trail people with no problem. Catarina was correct when she'd said leopards were violent, rough and killing machines. He could kill fast and efficiently when needed, but he certainly didn't kill indiscriminately. He'd chosen the side of the law for his hunting grounds.

Leopards were also fast and cunning, and he was every bit of that. Somewhere in the back of his head he had suspected Rafe Cordeau was a shifter. He couldn't exactly blurt out that information to the team. They would probably freak if they knew about shifters in general, let alone that one was in their midst. He should have put two and two together the moment he met Catarina.

All the signs were there. In the dojo when she worked out, she was just that little bit too fast. She had power when she punched or kicked, real power. Her hair, wild silk that fell down her back like a waterfall, grew thick, much thicker than normal.

Eli uncuffed his hand and swung out of the truck to walk around to the passenger side. He really should have put it all together when he'd reacted to her. Not just physically, but emotionally as well. That never happened to him. Not once. Not on an assignment and not with any of the women he took to his bed.

The fact that his leopard hadn't protested was the biggest sign of all. It was just all so unexpected, and he found himself wrapped up in her. He thought about her day and night. All the time. He couldn't walk into a room she occupied without his body reacting. That gentle side he didn't know he had, the one that had come out when she looked at him with her sad, beautiful exotic eyes, had taken him over and the cop and the leopard had faded away.

"Come here, baby. Let's get you inside. No one will disturb you here," he murmured softly.

She woke enough to push at his shoulder, when he bent over her, getting one arm under her knees and one around her back.

"I'm just taking you inside, Kitten," he crooned. "That's all. Putting you to bed."

He lifted her into his arms. She didn't weigh much. She had curves, beautiful, lush curves, and he'd been looking at her breasts pushing against the thin material of her tank for the last few hours. He could see her nipples outlined there. Her hair was everywhere, brushing against his face as he cradled her tight against his chest. He couldn't resist burying his face in all that hair and inhaling her deep into his lungs.

Catarina didn't protest, nor did she hold her body away from his. If anything, the heat of her body melted into the inferno that was his. That kind of hot he had going usually meant he'd better have sex soon or the rough edges would begin to fray. She'd done that. She'd taken his discipline and control and he'd made a mess of everything.

The only thing he had left to him was to keep her safe. And he was going to do that whether she liked it or not. He carried her into the house. He hadn't been there in a while, but he had the neighbor woman looking after it for him and he'd called ahead to tell her he was coming. She'd had the heat turned on so the rooms weren't ice cold. She always stocked his fridge for him when he called, and he knew there would be food.

He carried Catarina through the open great room to the master bedroom. The bed was made and he made a mental note to be certain to do something special for his neighbor to thank her.

"Sweetheart, you're going to have to wake up. Do you need to use the bathroom before I put you to bed?"

She nodded against his shoulder and he took her on through to the master bath and set her on her feet, one arm around her waist to hold her steady until she got her balance. She swayed a little and clung for a minute, looking around her while he removed the handcuff from her wrist. Her long lashes swept up and down, blinking, and something shifted in his chest. She was beautiful and sexy just standing there half asleep. Without even trying she was under his skin and wrapped around his heart.

Eli pushed back the sweep of hair from her face and bent to her. "You good, Cat, if I leave you here? There are new toothbrushes in the second drawer. And toothpaste. I'll go get your bags if you promise me you won't fall on your head while I'm gone."

She nodded and lifted her hair from the back of her neck, exposing her back. His breath caught in his lungs and his leopard slammed so hard against him, he felt the animal in his throat. Raking. Snarling. Roaring with rage. Mad with the need to be free. Eli's hands tightened on Catarina just for a moment.

A shifter had marked her. Claimed her. A leopard. He could see the top of a rake mark. The unmistakable scar of two puncture wounds up near her shoulder. He'd marked her in a callous, brutal, ugly way. Branded her his. His own leopard responded, roaring against another male trying to take his female.

Eli knew then without a doubt. He knew by his own reaction. By the reaction of his leopard. Catarina Benoit was meant for him. She belonged to him. Cordeau had made certain her leopard would recognize him—accept him—when she emerged, but she wasn't Cordeau's mate. She was Eli's.

Catarina blinked sleepily up at him. "I really need to be alone for a few minutes."

She had no clue. He dropped his hands, and it was a difficult thing to do with his leopard so close. He didn't speak because he knew his voice would be too much of a growl. She was exhausted and he'd wanted to get her in bed. Now he had one more thing to do, and she wasn't going to like it.

He turned away from her and hurried out of the house to retrieve her bags and put the truck in the garage.

Catarina's emergence was close. She was at her time— the Han Vol Dan of his people—where the human's and cat's cycles came together, allowing the leopard to emerge. That couldn't happen until he knew her leopard would accept his as her mate.

Cordeau would be frantic to get to her. Eli knew he would pull out all the stops to find her. Eli knew that because, again, Catarina had been right about him. He was like Cordeau in some ways and if a man took his woman, he would hunt that man to the ends of the earth. Eli knew if he wanted to keep Catarina Benoit, he would have to kill Rafe Cordeau, and he was definitely keeping Catarina.

She was standing in the middle of the bedroom looking around her a little helplessly when he returned. He walked up to her and took her hands, turning them over to examine the bruised ring on her skin. "Fucking Tuttle put the cuffs on too tight, didn't he?"

She gave a halfhearted attempt to pull her hands away but subsided when he tightened his fingers around hers. She nodded.

"I'm going to beat the crap out of him."

He slid the pad of his thumb over the bruises on her inner wrist lightly. She shivered. She definitely wasn't immune to him. She was every bit as aware of him as he was her, but she didn't like it. He had to find a way to change that. Right now, she was too sleepy, too exhausted to protest anything he did so he took full advantage.

He brought her wrists to his mouth and brushed a kiss over each. Her cobalt blue eyes went wider. Darker. Shades of violet. Again he felt her tug and he allowed her fingers to slip from his. She pressed both wrists to her thighs, but he didn't rub his kisses away. He reached out and tucked strands of hair behind her ear.

"You need to climb in bed, sweetheart. You're so exhausted you're nearly falling over." He kept his voice gentle.

Tenderness crept in and that shocked him. He didn't know he knew how to be tender. She stripped him bare, looking so young, the terrible bruise standing out so starkly on her pale skin.

"Something's wrong with me." She whispered the confession to him, her eyes avoiding his. He scented her. The age-old call. The need rising in her. Her breasts lifted, her nipples peaked beneath the thin tank. Her legs moved restlessly and color swept through her body.

The moment she admitted it, tension filled the room. He almost groaned aloud. His cat roared at him, desperate to get at his mate. His body flooded with hunger, the need so strong it shook him. He'd blown it with her once already; he wasn't about to do it again by stripping the clothes from her body and pounding into her.

He took a breath and forced calm into his leopard. "It's not wrong, Kitten, it's the Han Vol Dan. It's as natural as breathing. She's close to emerging and she's giving you a little taste of what it will be like."

"I don't want it."

He winced. Not wanting your leopard was denying who and what you were. Leopard was pure freedom. Once she experienced that, no one, not even her mate, could take that from her.

"You don't want it because you don't understand it. Your experience with shifters hasn't been good, but you're wrong. We're not all killers. We can kill when we have to, but we can choose not to. We don't hunt for fun. Those that do are considered rogues, living outside our laws. Our kind goes after them and removes them from society. Like the police would do." Only rather more permanently, but he didn't add that.

He took her hand gently and tugged, leading her to the bed. With one hand he pulled back the covers. "Get in, Cat. She'll subside in a minute and that need will go away. Just breathe."

"It's strong. Very strong." She frowned and lifted her gaze to his.

He caught his breath at what he saw there. Hunger glittered in the deep blue of her eyes. Speculation.

"I know because I'm looking at you and suddenly wondering what it would be like to have you touching me," she continued honestly. "And I despise you. I don't trust you. I don't want anything at all to do with you. But I'm still wondering."

She had always been honest, or tried to. That was one of the things he admired in her. She'd been frank about what was going on with her when she hadn't been able to share much else of her life. He swept his hand over her hair. "I know, baby. It can be like that. Just breathe. She'll calm down and you'll be able to sleep."

She slipped into the bed.

"Lay on your tummy, Kitten."

"I don't like you calling me that."

She sounded so hurt his heart ached. "I know. You don't have a defense when I do, but I'm not going to stop. I know you think none of it was real between us, but you're wrong about that too. I don't blame you for not believing me, but that doesn't make my feelings for you any less true, or any less strong."

"You're right, I don't believe you."

"Just lay on your tummy for me." He pushed a little more command into his voice. His hands went to her shoulders, urging her to turn over.

Catarina was too tired to fight him, too stressed and the leopard inside her too close. She was terrified of the monster getting out of her, but now, with the burning between her legs and the heat rushing through her body, she feared she might throw herself at this man she didn't know or like and she would never, *ever*, get over that humiliation.

She lay on her belly, her hands under her face, her eyes closed, shutting him out. He was a lot to shut out. He took up space. A lot of space. And he wasn't any less gorgeous. She thought if you didn't like someone they became ugly to you, but that hadn't happened with Ridley—Eli—whatever.

She was aware of every little detail about him. Especially his scent. It called to something wild in her. Something needy and so hot. She wanted to squirm around on the sheets, and it took discipline not to give in to that need. She liked the wide width of his shoulders and the way he moved, the flow of his muscles and the way his eyes went from amber to gold and then molten gold. She'd even dared for one supremely frightening second to drop her gaze to the front of his jeans. It was impossible to miss the impressive bulge there and that just plain freaked her out.

She felt his weight on the bed as he sank down beside her. Her heart began to pound. She couldn't just lay there with him next to her, not feeling the way she was. Her nipples were on fire, moving against the tank and sheets with every tiny shift of her body. She couldn't stop her hips from their restless movements either.

His hand skimmed down her back. "I'm just going to take a look at what he did to you. This was your punishment for running from him, wasn't it?"

She tried not to react to his hand. It felt good, almost a caress, and she didn't want anything good from him. She didn't want gentle or sweet. She wanted him to be mean so she could never associate him with the fantasy man she'd fallen for.

"You heard. You watched." She made it an accusation. Of course he'd listened to Tuttle interrogating her.

"Cordeau did this because you ran from him, didn't he? He showed you his leopard." He ignored her accusation.

She couldn't stop the shudder that had gone through her body. He wanted to know so she told him the stark truth. What did it matter anyway?

"He stripped right there in front of me, his hard body naked, his eyes glittering. I was terrified that he intended to rape me. There was nothing to stop him."

Eli swore aloud, biting out ugly words between his teeth, but his hand never once stopped that gentle stroking. Maybe she wanted to shock him. Maybe she just wanted him to know why she despised that entity inside of her. Either way, she told him the truth.

"His body contorted horribly and then he was all teeth

and claws and fur, stalking me across the length of my bed-room. I tried to run but the leopard caught me easily, bring-ing me down like prey. I felt the hot breath against my skin and knew I was dead, that he was going to kill me."

She turned her head to look up at Eli. "The strange thing was, I didn't care if he did. I wanted it all to be over. But he didn't kill me. He hurt me so bad." She turned her face into the pillow. "So bad," she whispered.

His hand moved under her tank, over her bare skin, his fingers finding each rake scar as he pushed the tank all the way up and out of his way. He shifted the hair off her back to expose the scars even more. She felt the skim of his mouth against each mark and tears burned again. She wanted to roll over, push him away, but she couldn't move.

Her body was no longer her own. The touch of his hands and his mouth proved she had no real defense against him.

"What he did was wrong, sweetheart." He stretched out beside her, his hands continuing to massage her back and shoulders. "All male leopards are affected when a woman goes into the Han Vol Dan, but you don't take what doesn't belong to you. He knows the rules. He knew better."

She kept her eyes closed. His hands felt wonderful and that terrible burning need was subsiding just as he'd said it would. She felt him shift position again, moving almost over the top of her back, and now his mouth trailed kisses over the rake marks again. She should have stopped him, but she didn't. She couldn't. She felt tension coiling tight inside of her. She felt the leopard inside of her leaping toward him.

There was the slide of fur against her bare skin. She felt hot breath against the nape of her neck. Still she couldn't move, not even when the leopard sank his teeth into her shoulder in the holding bite of his kind. Her leopard surged forward toward the male and she felt the larger male's response.

Her body went up in flames as her female neared the surface in answer to the male's call. She cried out, writhing beneath him, but he moved one strong thigh over her, pinning her down, holding her until her female accepted his male. More hot tears soaked the pillow. She went from never crying to a flood she couldn't stop.

The fur was gone, replaced by Eli's mouth moving over the bite with small kisses and a soothing tongue. He didn't bother to try to hide the urgent hunger in his body from her.

"What did you do?" she whispered.

"What I had to do. It's over. There's no need to hurt you, Catarina. Your female will accept my male. She's going to emerge whether you like it or not and you'll need a man, a male shifter to take care of you."

She rolled then, expecting him to move away from her but he didn't. He wrapped an arm around her waist and tugged her body into his. She held her head back, glaring at him.

"If I have to choose between you and Rafe, I choose Rafe." She ignored the fingers digging into her midriff. She ignored the warning in his glittering eyes. "At least he's honest. I know what I'm getting. You're all deception, and you don't care about me any more than he does. Neither choice is ideal but better the devil you know than the one you don't."

His golden eyes moved over her face. Brooding. Moody. Scary. She found herself holding her breath.

"Lucky for me you don't get a choice," he said. "When your leopard emerges there's only going to be me to help you." There was satisfaction in his voice. "Now go to sleep. You're trying to get under my skin and, Kitten, just a little FYI, you're already there. Don't push your luck."

Something in his tone, in the set of his jaw and his molten eyes stopped her from taking another dig at him, although it was tempting. Instead, she turned away from him and closed her eyes, scooting all the way to the edge of the bed, willing him to leave. He didn't. He just pulled her close into his body, spooning her. One leg slid over the top of hers, and his head leaned down to press into her hair.

She stiffened, hating the way her blood ran so hot. Hating that she was so aware of him. Hating the fact that she couldn't fight him, too tired, too battle-scarred already.

"Just go to sleep, Kitten," he said softly.

In that voice. The one she loved. If she cried again, she was going to hit him. She felt the brush of his mouth in her hair and somehow the tension drained out of her and she let herself drift off.

7

CATARINA woke with her body unbearably hot. Her breasts felt swollen and achy. There was a terrible burning between her legs. It was absolutely impossible to stay still. Her body writhed along the cool sheets. It was impossible to stop, even with the knowledge that she was pressed up against Eli Perez. His body had somehow become wrapped around hers, his knee intimately between her legs and his hand shaping her breast.

She tried to breathe away the fire, but the tension in her only coiled tighter. Eli was hot, his skin burning through hers. She realized that sometime in the night he had shed his boots and clothes. He wore only a thin pair of draw-string sweats and he was pressed tight against her buttocks. He felt . . . delicious.

Her heart beat hard and her breathing became ragged. She craved him. His touch. The feel of his fingers on her skin. His mouth on her. She needed to taste him. Taste his kiss. His skin. To feel his heavy erection in her palm, in her mouth, deep inside of her. The craving grew until thunder roared in her ears.

She tried to still her mind. To pray. To fight the chaotic, unbelievable burn that scorched her. That demanded. Craved. Flames seem to burn her skin and the material of the sheet actually hurt her skin. She had to stay still, but it was impossible. She needed, and he was right there. She couldn't fight that terrible, desperate burn one second longer.

She turned, and crawled up his body. *Crawled.* She needed his body tight against hers so she could feel the throb of his cock against her mound. He reacted with a groan and his erection grew harder and thicker. *Perfect.* Just the feel of him there fed the fire burning between her legs and she kissed his chest, sliding her mouth over to his nipples and then down to his flat belly. She traced each rib with her tongue.

Her clothes hurt her skin and she reached with one hand to tear her tank from her body, pull it over her head and throw it away from her.

The itch rose, a terrible wave, but this time it was worse, igniting tiny flames in every nerve ending. Her sweats burned through her pores. "Get my sweats off. Oh, God. Hurry. You have to get them off."

She heard the plea in her voice. She needed the material off of her, but she couldn't stop tasting his skin. He was an addiction now, one she couldn't give up, one she needed to survive.

"Kitten." His voice was raw with need. "This isn't a good idea."

She could barely hear him with her blood roaring in her ears. She moved lower, shoving at his sweats, her fist wrapping around his cock while she dipped her head lower to run her tongue over that velvety smooth head. The moment her lips touched him and she drew the taste of him into her mouth she needed more. Much more.

One hand pushed at the material causing her actual pain,

the other remained tight around his shaft, squeezing gently. His hand covered hers and he drew her hand up and then down, showing her without words what to do.

"Okay, baby, okay. We've got this," he said softly, and his hands hooked into her sweat bottoms and pushed them off her body.

She kicked to get them free of her legs and he tugged them away. The relief was tremendous, but the craving for him worsened. "I need this, right now. I need this. Tell me what to do."

His hands shaped her bottom for a moment, sliding over her firm muscle and then he wrapped her hair in his hand. "Take me in your mouth, sweetheart. Use your tongue." His fist in her hair pushed her head down.

Catarina obeyed him instantly, taking him into the scalding heat of her mouth. Eli nearly lost control right then. She didn't need to know what she was doing, her body instinctively did it for her. Her tongue slid over and under, she suckled, tightening the suction around him and then sliding her mouth up and down all the while working him with her tight fist.

The breath slammed out of him. She was so hot she burned against him. He could feel his leopard roaring and leaping and his own body was so hard, the demand more urgent than he'd ever experienced. There was one fleeting thought to try to stop her, but that was gone in the fierce, raging fire licking at his body.

"Please, please," she begged against his shaft, the soft words vibrating through the sensitive organ so that he threw his head back and with a low growl pulled her off of him.

Before she could protest, he rolled her over and took savage possession of her mouth. *His.* She was his whether she liked it or not. There would be consequences to this, but he could no more stop himself than he could shoot himself. He kissed her hard, over and over, his tongue ruling her mouth.

He dropped his hand to her breast to first cup the soft weight and then to roll her nipple between his finger and thumb, tugging aggressively. Her body arched and the breath hissed out of her. Instantly he covered her breast with his mouth, pulling soft flesh deep inside. She tasted like heaven. Her body felt like sin. Those lush, sweet curves every bit as soft and perfect as he suspected.

He worked first one breast and then the other, using the edge of his teeth, the heat of his mouth and his fingers to drive her up fast. She sobbed against his shoulder, chanting the same little ragged plea.

"Please, please, please."

He moved down her body, kissing, nipping with his teeth, his hands going to her thighs to pull them apart. He could smell her beautiful, exotic scent of spice and honey calling to him and he wedged his shoulders between her thighs, draping her legs over him. He didn't give her a moment to recover. To breathe. He bent his head and plunged his tongue deep. She screamed.

She was a furnace, burning hotter than anything he'd ever known. Her taste was addictive and he couldn't pull the honey out of her fast enough with his tongue. He held her still while he devoured her ravenously, forgetting everything but the need to feed that terrible, wild addiction growing in him. He knew he would never get enough. She would sate him for a short time, and he would have to go back again and again.

He was good at sex. No, he was great at sex and he knew it. He might not be able to tie her to him any other way until her leopard emerged, but he could tie her this way. He drove her higher and then higher, his ruthless mouth demanding. She came hard, her voice hoarse from her sore throat.

He didn't let her go back down but pushed her up again, suckling on her sensitive clit, stroking with his thumb, using his tongue to stab deep and draw out the spice and honey spilling out of her. It was wild. Primitive. Out of control. She came a second time, her hot channel spasming, her belly rippling. He felt it in her thighs.

Ignoring her gasping pleas, he moved over top of her and pushed the head of his cock into that fiery inferno and then stopped.

"Look at me, Cat."

She kept her head turned away from his, her eyes shut tight. He waited. Patient while her body throbbed and burned around his. She licked her lips and he wanted to lick them too. Finally she gave him her wide, blue gaze.

"You look at me. Don't turn your head. When I give you this, I want you to know who I am. You haven't once called me by my name, and you're fucking going to do it when I'm buried inside of you. Do you understand me? If you want this, say you understand and use my fucking name when you do."

He was nearly more leopard than human in that moment. Not his body, but his mind. This was his woman. His mate. She needed to submit to him. To know she belonged. Even if she couldn't wrap her head around the fact, her body needed to know.

Her eyes begged him. He shook his head, gritting his teeth. She squirmed. Writhed. Tried to force him to impale her. He refused to move, although it cost him. Jackhammers tripped in his head. His blood pounded with need. He felt savage. Half angry, half desperate.

"Fucking say my name and tell me you understand what I'm saying to you."

"*God*. Okay. Eli. Just *please* do something."

"You're mine. You know that now, right? *Mine*. No one else ever gets inside your body. Or your mouth. That belongs to me. *You* belong to me."

She pressed her lips together against another sob. He couldn't take the scorching fire beckoning his cock. He surged in hard and deep, driving past the thin barrier of her innocence so she cried out at the shocking bite of pain, arching her hips upward and closing her eyes.

He stilled, watched her face, waited for her eyes to come back to him. Her lashes lifted and he saw himself reflected there. The lines carved deep, the stamp of near brutality, of ruthless savagery. He was leopard all right, but that didn't mean he wouldn't make it good for her. Perfect for her.

He began to move inside of her, pushing through her tight, scorching folds, that fiery inferno that he knew he would always crave. The entire time he watched her face. Watched the tension coiling in her. Watched the beauty of helpless need. He loved the way her breath was so ragged and the way her eyes glazed. Her lips parted, and beneath him her body rose to match the rhythm of his.

He took her with hard, pounding strokes, going as deep as possible, burying himself to the very root, bumping her cervix, wanting to go so deep he would lodge in her belly. He took her up again, loving the way her head tossed on the pillow and her hair spilled around her like living, breathing silk.

He was relentless, refusing to let her go over the edge again, taking her higher and higher until he saw alarm spread and she clutched at his shoulders, her nails biting deep.

"Ask for it, Kitten. Say my name and ask me for it." She had to know it was Eli Perez, not some mythical Ridley Cromer or a bastard like Rafe Cordeau.

Eli was there with her, not either of them. And she was his. She would always be his, because already he could see he'd set up the craving, that terrible addiction he knew came with being a leopard.

For a moment she tried to hold out, but fear skittered down her spine. He could read it in her wild blue gaze. Staring into her eyes, he slipped his thumb into her and pressed against her clit. She gasped. He removed his thumb and tipped her hips to give him the perfect angle so that the friction was on that sweet little button.

"Eli. I need this."

"From me," he prompted.

She nodded her head, then thrashed again. Desperate. Hot. Needy. Scared. "From you. From Eli."

He slammed home, taking her with him on the crazy, wild ride. He felt her body tighten to the point of strangulation but he didn't stop driving into her. She screamed. Her body nearly seized and then the orgasm tore through her hard and fast and mean, a powerful quake that persisted when he was swept along with her. The splash of his seed hot and strong gave her an additional powerful quake.

He buried his face in her neck as the ripples continued and he stayed inside her, riding them out with her. Her breasts felt soft and right against his hard chest. Her body was small, but fit perfectly. He'd been brutal in his possession of her and she was going to be sore. He needed to attend to her, and she was going to be embarrassed and angry when she came down from the high.

He lifted his head and pressed his mouth to the corner of hers. "Are you okay?"

She took a breath and curled her fingers in his hair, looking confused. Her gaze started to slide from his but he caught her chin.

"No, Kitten. We're past that. We're moving forward, and you're not going to be embarrassed at what we did together."

"I don't even like you," she whispered. "I don't even know you and I was all over you. This isn't even your fault. It's mine. I did this. I couldn't stop myself."

He smoothed back her hair, stroking little soothing caresses over her scalp. "It's going to be all right."

"It isn't though. I used you. I didn't even try to control myself. The burning was terrible. My skin hurt, everything hurt. I didn't think about you, only myself and some way to try to stop it."

She sounded close to tears. He brushed kisses on each eyelid and then trailed more to the corner of her mouth. He still felt her tight sheath surrounding him. He should have been empty. Finished. But he was still hard. All that scorching fire and that honey and spice. But she was done. She needed care. Time to come to terms with what happened between them.

"This isn't your fault, Catarina. It just *is*. We're shifters. We didn't ask to be shifters, and this comes with the territory. I know you're afraid of her. Your leopard, but you don't have to be . . ."

"Are you kidding? I would never have attacked you in a million years. She did that. She made me into a slut."

His hands tightened on her and he gave her a little shake. "Don't you ever call yourself that, Cat. She didn't make you anything but what you're supposed to be. My mate. She recognized my leopard and mine recognized yours. It's that simple. She'll give you a freedom you've never had, one that no one can take from you. When you run in that form, there's nothing like it on earth, except this. What we have together."

He forced himself to roll off of her. The moment he was out of her body, he felt alone again, an ache instantly, a need to be connected physically to her. It was all he had with her and he knew it. Having sex, even great sex with her, didn't mean their problems were solved. He'd betrayed her and that betrayal had gone deep.

"I'm going to run you a bath. If you don't soak in hot water, you'll be sore." She was going to be sore anyway. Leopard sex was savage at best. Brutal most of the time. His leopard clawed and raked for his mate. She wasn't ready, but that didn't stop the fierce cat from driving Eli to cement the relationship. Who was he kidding? He was a rough man and he liked sex hard and wild.

He pulled up his sweats and padded across the room to the master bath. He left the door open, keeping his eye on her while he ran the water as hot as he thought she could stand. She didn't speak, but he felt her eyes on him.

"What is it, baby?" he asked as gently as possible.

She looked upset, and he didn't blame her. She was dealing with too many things at once.

"Why? Why did you use me like that?"

For a moment he thought she was talking about sex, but when he looked at the expression on her face, the raw hurt there, he knew what she meant. Her question was a potential bomb. How could he answer that without her feeling even more betrayed? He *had* betrayed her.

Eli was acutely aware of what she'd said about making the choice between Cordeau and him. She wanted honesty. She even deserved honesty. He sat on the edge of the tub and kept his eyes on her face even while one hand trailed in the water to make certain it wasn't too hot for her.

"Looking the way I do, Cat, rough and mean, gives me a certain edge in the kind of work I do. Being a leopard helps me to have a better than average rate for arresting and prosecuting very bad men. What I'm saying is, I go undercover a lot. I live undercover for months at a time. Most of it is bad. Most of it sucks. You live in the dirt long enough, baby, and it rubs off on you."

"But you believe in what you do." She propped herself up on one elbow, watching him just as closely as he was watching her.

He was surprised at that insight. More, he was surprised at her interest. He felt his way carefully, afraid they were doing a little dance and he didn't yet know the steps. Still, he wasn't going to lie to her. Not again. She asked him a question, and she was going to get an answer whether or not she wanted to hear it—or he wanted to give her one.

"It's what I dedicated my life to. My parents were murdered because they were in the wrong place at the wrong time. They'd gone to visit old friends, took a wrong turn and got caught in the middle of a drug deal gone bad. I was just a kid, but I guess that was what first made me decide I wanted to get into law enforcement."

She had pulled up the sheet but it barely covered her breasts. He could see the pale curve of the swell and there were a few marks there. His marks. Had she not been a virgin he would have said the hell with the bath and pounded into her all over again. His cock jerked at the thought of teaching her the things he liked. At the thought of doing the things to her body that she was going to like.

"So is part of your job seducing women?"

Shit. Fuck. Son of a bitch. How the *hell* was he going to answer that? "I didn't seduce you, Cat. I was very, very careful to keep my hands off you, and it wasn't easy. Right from the beginning I knew you were different. You got under my skin. I wasn't going to go there with you. Not you."

She caught her lower lip between her teeth, instantly drawing his gaze, reminding him he wanted to bite her lower lip himself. She was beautiful, bruises and all. Even with dark shadows beneath her eyes and suspicion and hurt in all that wild blue.

"So the answer is yes, you do or have seduced other women as part of your job."

He nodded slowly. "Unfortunately yes. It isn't a part of the job I enjoy, but sometimes it's the only way inside an organization I'm penetrating, or the only way I can get information."

"What makes you different from a prostitute? She trades sex for money, you trade sex for information."

He winced and reached out to turn off the taps. "I never looked at it like that. It's never comfortable, Catarina, and I'm not particularly proud of it, but I wormed my way into a human trafficking ring by sleeping with a fucking bitch who acquired young girls. I shut that shit down. Am I sorry I slept with the skank? Do I wish I didn't have to do it? Hell yeah. But I closed it down and a hell of a lot of young girls were rescued and more saved from being forced into that kind of life."

He worked at keeping the edge out of his voice, but he

didn't like having to justify himself and his choices. He stalked across the room and yanked the covers back, exposing her naked body. For the first time he was able to really look at her body. The evidence of his possession was on her thighs, along with trickles of blood.

She had a gorgeous body. Her curves were definitely lush and soft. Her skin was satin, her hair silk. Even the tiny curls at the junction of her legs looked soft and silky. She blushed and reached for the sheet. He bunched the material in his fist and kept her from pulling it over her.

"I'm putting you in the bathtub, woman. You have to get used to being naked around me." He caught her up, cradling her close to him. Their combined scent made him hard all over again. He liked the way they smelled together, hot and primal and straight out of a rain forest.

She was forced to reach back and hook his neck with one arm. The action lifted her breast toward his mouth. He dipped his head and licked at the nipple. She did a full body shiver and her breath rushed out of her lungs.

He set her down, feet first, in the tub and she sank low, holding the thick mass of hair out of the water. He had forgotten that her hair would be everywhere. He stepped behind her, gathered the heavy fall in his hand and deftly tied a loose knot on top of her head.

"I think we need to get something straight," she said, not looking at him again.

"Eli," he prompted.

Her blue gaze darted to his. She made a face. "Eli, then. It's important for you to know that even though I totally screwed up, it doesn't change anything. It was sex. That's all. Sex. There is no reason for me to get comfortable being naked around you. I don't plan on being naked often. In fact, I prefer that you're not in the room while I'm taking a bath."

He didn't take his eyes from her face the entire time she made her little speech. He felt slow amusement start somewhere in the vicinity of his gut, climb into his chest so his heart felt lighter and a small smile finally reached his mouth.

"Did I say something funny? Because you're smirking and it isn't very nice."

"Yeah, you said something funny. Kitten, we didn't just have sex. That was off-the-chart sex and you know it. I look at you and get hard. You look at me and burn between your legs. You think I don't know when a woman wants me? We're going to have sex, as you so delicately put it, often and in ways you can't imagine in your wildest dreams. So it is *very* important that you are comfortable being naked around me. And comfortable talking about sex, what you like and what you don't."

"I don't like you smirking and being so sure of yourself," she said. Her blue eyes flashed a deep violet that only made her all the sexier to him.

"At least you know your partner knows what the hell he's doing. You're in good hands."

She sighed and closed her eyes, leaning back against the tub. "I don't trust you, Eli. I really don't. I don't want to be with someone I don't trust. It was a mistake having sex with you. I couldn't help myself. I take full responsibility for throwing myself at you, but that doesn't mean I want to repeat the experience."

He made a low sound in his throat, somewhere between a growl and a laugh.

Her gaze jumped to his. "I don't. Maybe my body does. I won't lie to you about that, but that doesn't mean I can't show restraint and learn control."

"You do that, baby," he said, still amused. She had no idea how much she was turning him on with her nonsense. She didn't know the first thing about a wildfire out of control, and that was what they were together. But she'd learn and he was going to have fun teaching her. "In the meantime, while we're here in this house, you can lose the panties and be very comfortable."

She rolled her eyes. "I can see you're going to be difficult."

"I'm not trying to be, Cat, but seriously? You think this is a onetime shot?"

She nodded slowly.

"So when I put my mouth between your legs you're not going to start pleading with me to be inside of you?" he demanded.

Color swept up her neck to turn her face a pretty pink. Her eyes went bright. Hungry. Her legs moved restlessly beneath the water. "I'm not expecting you to put your mouth between my legs."

"You can't give a man a taste of all that honey, baby, and then try to take it away from him. It doesn't work that way. I want to eat you alive. I've got the taste of you in my mouth and it isn't going to go away. I'm not going to be able to be inside you for a little while, a few hours or a day or two so that means I have to sate my desire on your taste. And you're going to learn what to do with my cock in your mouth."

"I'm not your sex slave, Eli," she snapped. "I told you. I don't like you. I don't trust you. I don't even know who you are."

"Well you're finding out fast, aren't you, Kitten," he said.

Eli leaned his hip against the sink and crossed his arms over his chest. Steam rose from the tub, wrapping her in mystery. A light sheen covered her skin, giving her a glow. Her leopard had subsided for the time being. He knew because his leopard wasn't pushing him so hard. A female leopard rising several times close to the surface and then settling was fairly standard.

That was hard on the female human counterpart, but he intended to take good care of her. In the meantime, he had a lot to make up for.

"Are you hungry?"

"Can you cook?"

"Not really." He admitted with a grin. "I told you the

truth. I tried to give you who I really was, Catarina, not some bullshit made-up man. I'll try to cook for you though."

She smiled a genuine smile for the first time. "Do you actually have groceries?"

"I called my neighbor and she sent a supply over. I asked her to pick up an espresso machine as well and some coffee beans."

"Give me a few more minutes and I'll see what you have. I enjoy cooking, and it will hopefully get your mind off sex long enough for me to reason with you."

"I doubt that, but I'm willing to give it a try," he agreed, mostly because she really did look as if she wanted to make breakfast. And he liked her cooking.

"Why did you do that to me?" she repeated.

He sighed. "I told you, baby. It's my job. No one really knew what you were to Cordeau. No one knew why you were in his home or why you left. There were rumors and speculation. I think most people thought you were part of his organization, at the very least his lover. I knew the first time I saw you that you weren't either."

"Still, you came after me. You lied to me. I thought you were my friend. You worked hard to gain my trust and then you betrayed me."

"I know it felt that way to you," he said, "and I'm sorry. I told you I fucked up with you, and I did. I liked being with you far more than I should have. The minute I realized you were an innocent, I was careful with you. I wanted, maybe even needed, the friendship more than you did."

Her eyelashes fluttered and she tilted her head to one side. Once again, her bottom lip was between her teeth. His heart somersaulted and his cock jerked. That mattered to her, his admission of need. He had to give her something of himself.

"A man in my position, Cat, doesn't have family and has very few friends. Not even in the department. I work knee-deep in slime and I forget sometimes what the hell I'm even working for. I can't remember the last time I laughed, not until I was with you. I can't remember feeling light and easy and even happy, not until you. I couldn't stop myself from getting involved with you. Every single day I told myself it had to stop, that I was getting in too deep and it wasn't fair to you, but honest to God, Kitten, I couldn't stop myself."

His voice rang with honesty because it was the truth. She drew up her knees and rubbed her chin on top of them, regarding him with her blue eyes. She liked what she heard, that much he could see. It wasn't redemption, but it gave her something to think about.

"You wouldn't have kissed me if I hadn't asked you to, would you?" she persisted.

"Would I have? I'd like to think I would have been a better man than that. I didn't know about the decision to tell Cordeau where you were, swear to God, Catarina, but I knew you were thinking of running after you spotted Tuttle. Not just thinking about it. I tried to talk you out of it, but I knew you'd made up your mind."

He scrubbed his hand over his face. "Damn it all, I didn't want to lose you. I could tell you I did it so you would be safe from Cordeau. I knew you wouldn't agree to testify against him. I didn't think you really knew anything of use. To anyone else I used that excuse, that I wanted you safe from him, but the honest fucking truth is, I didn't want to lose you. I knew if you left, I'd never see you again."

She sucked in her breath, her eyes glued to his face.

"That's it. That's the real reason. I'm not the white knight. I'm not even a good DEA agent. I'm the man who for the first time in my life wanted a woman for myself. You can't know what my life is like, Cat. I'm alone all the time. I don't have a clue about a real relationship. I'm a leopard, a shifter, so I'm bad-tempered and mean and sometimes violent. I can be as cold as ice or in a fiery rage. That's the life of a shifter. There are few of us and most choose to stay within our kind, in lairs. I don't have a lair. I don't have friends. I do my job and I'm damn good at it, no regrets. Until you came along."

"Eli," she whispered. "Stop talking. I can't process any more. I have to think about everything you've said. I'm very hurt and confused and feeling raw. I'm embarrassed about throwing myself at you, and the things you talk about scare the crap out of me."

He frowned. "I'm not trying to frighten you, baby. I'm trying to make you see where my head was."

"Not about that. About sex. You and me. *That* scares me."

"I know," he said gently.

"You said you wouldn't hurt me, and you did."

"I know," he repeated, his voice dropping an octave. "You need to come out of there before the water cools down. I really don't want you sore."

He had no idea when her leopard would choose to push close to the surface again, or worse, emerge fully. She couldn't be sore for that event. It would be wild and uninhibited, a primal joining and both human and leopard would claim their respective mates. There would be no turning back once Catarina's leopard made her choice.

He removed a towel from a drawer and held it up. "Stand up."

"I'd really prefer to do this alone," she said.

"I know." He stayed where he was, holding the towel so she could step out of the tub and he could dry her off.

"Stop saying 'I know,' that doesn't really say anything at all," she snapped, exasperated. "You just do whatever you want, don't you?"

"Pretty much, yes." He flashed a small smile. He loved her sass. Catarina broken tore his heart out. Catarina full of attitude made his body harder than a rock. "It's the only way with you. I learned that from watching you in the dojo. You aren't predictable at all. Like attacking me in your bedroom. That was the last thing I expected. And you did pretty well. I was proud of you."

She pulled the plug on the tub, clearly resigned that he

would stand there forever, which wasn't true. If she hadn't stood up, he would have hauled her ass out of there and then dried her off.

"I was proud of you getting out of the handcuffs as well. You're no pushover, Cat, and you can't be a pushover with a man like me, but bottom line, when it comes to your safety or health, you're not going to win."

"You're back to being an arrogant jerk."

He enfolded her in the towel and began to rub the material over her skin in order to remove the water. While he did he inspected her for marks and bruising. He crouched down and nudged her legs apart. She trembled.

"Put your hand on my shoulder, baby. I just want to make certain you're okay. I'm not going to do anything you won't like."

"That's not what I'm afraid of," she said honestly.

He wrapped his hand around her calf and then ran his palm up to the inside of her thigh. He couldn't imagine another woman being in her position and being so open with him. But then, she'd done that all along when it came to her emotions. She might have hid her past with Cordeau, but she didn't hold back when the topic was about her and what she thought or felt.

He stroked the inside of her thigh and allowed himself to inhale her scent. Honey and spice. He would always want that, want her. No. He'd always crave her.

"I'd like to make breakfast now." Her voice was tight. Clearly she was nervous.

"I'll get you one of my shirts to wear. It's warm and will cover you easily. I think if you let the air reach you you'll heal faster."

She considered his offer. In the end she took his flannel shirt when he handed it to her. It was soft and warm and far too big for her, fitting more like a short dress than a shirt. He rolled up the sleeves for her and walked her into the kitchen.

"You don't have a phone anywhere that I can see," she observed.

That told him she'd been looking for one. The only person he could think she might call was Cordeau. That didn't sit well with him, but he kept his mouth shut.

"I live off the grid here. Totally self-sufficient. The water is gravity fed. Solar panels for electricity. I've got a garden in and I pay to have it kept up. Grow most of my own vegetables. I'm not here often, but when I quit work, this is where I plan to retire. My leopard has space to run free, and I like the quiet."

"I like quiet too, as long as I have my coffee."

He flashed her a small smile, still wondering who the hell she wanted to call and considering handcuffing her to his bed just to make certain it wasn't Cordeau. "I like your coffee too."

"I'll make that first," she said. "And then I'll look through your fridge and the cupboards to see what you've got in the way of food."

"Emma is pretty thorough," Eli said, still distracted. He caught the back of a chair, spun it around and straddled it, leaning a little forward to look her in the eye. "You going to tell me why you were looking for a phone? You still think you're going to make Cordeau your choice of mate and not me?"

There was no keeping the snarl from his voice. He had gone from mellow to angry—it was there in his tone—and quite frankly, he didn't give a damn if it scared her or not. She had to see the rage in his eyes. It roiled in his gut. "You want to tell me that shit, Cat? Because I can tell you, no fucking way is Cordeau ever going to put his dirty hands on you."

8

CATARINA turned back around to face Eli. He'd been right about the leopard and his temper. The lines in his face were cut deep. There was a hard set to his jaw. His eyes were cat yellow and fixed on her intently. She shook her head and turned back to the espresso machine, concentrating on making that first cup. She needed it if she was going to face him after ripping her own clothes off and jumping him. He obviously needed it just to mellow him out.

"And you call me grumpy in the morning," she muttered.

"What the hell did you just say?" he demanded.

She rolled her eyes at the coffee machine. "Clearly you're the grumpy one in the morning, not me. I'm being all sweet making you a cup of coffee and you're snarling like some raging wild beast."

"Newsflash, Kitten. I *am* a snarling, raging beast. You want to answer the damn question?"

"Not particularly. At least not until I have two or three

sips of coffee under my belt and you have a full cup. What a grouch."

"Don't give me attitude, baby, not when I'm feeling like this," he warned, a low growl rumbling in his throat.

"Don't *you* give *me* attitude when I'm making a master-piece," she countered. She glanced at him over her shoulder.

His hair was all over the place, and she liked it that way. She didn't know exactly what to think anymore so she didn't want to think too much about anything. He'd broken her heart, devastated her, basically kidnapped her and then opened his heart to her—if she could believe him.

There was the problem as she saw it. Could she actually believe anything he said? He was a good actor. She'd fallen for him hook, line and sinker, and he'd betrayed her. She tried hard to keep an open mind. At first she hadn't wanted to hear anything he said. Then she wanted him to be Ridley again. Eli wasn't Ridley, but there seemed to be a part of him that was.

"Woman, you keep it up and you're going to find your-self in trouble."

"Maybe." She turned around again, and this time had a cup of perfection in her hands. "But this just may buy my way out of it." She took him the coffee. "Drink that, Mr. Grumpy Pants, and see if it doesn't improve your disposition."

His gaze moved over her face with a brooding look she tried not to think was hot and sexy, but of course she really did. She began making her own cup of coffee, needing to do something besides look at him. Looking at him didn't help her confusion.

"All right. I've got some coffee in me. Now are you going to tell me why you were looking for a phone?"

She burst out laughing. She couldn't help herself. He was like a dog with a bone. He wasn't going to drop it, but then she was beginning to realize he didn't drop anything important to him.

"You like your way, don't you?" she asked.

"In all things, Kitten. You'd better get used to it," he cautioned. "Now answer the fucking question before I throw you over my shoulder and haul your ass back to my bed to show you who you're supposed to be with—let me give you a clue—his name is Eli Perez."

Catarina heaved an exaggerated sigh. "Seriously, Eli? Are you going to threaten me with sex every time you don't get your way?"

She heard him put the coffee cup down, and the chair scraped. Her heart jumped and she spun around to face him. He was on his feet, stalking her purposefully. She held up one hand to ward him off, laughing in spite of the sudden fear coursing through her body. Fear and excitement.

"Who the hell said anything about sex? I'm considering something entirely different."

She didn't want to test him and she backed up until she collided with the counter. "You do know that your behavior is causing serious disappointment, Eli. I held out hope for my Zen fantasy, and you've buried that deep."

"Catarina." He bit out her name between clenched teeth.

"I noticed you didn't have a phone. It was an observation, that's all. Rafe would be the last man on earth I would call in this situation."

He stopped, towering over her, in her space. She could feel the heat from his body and she remembered how it felt to melt against him. She didn't close her eyes and hold that memory to her, but she wanted to and that confused her even more.

"A situation like this?" he echoed.

"He'd kill you, Eli. He might even kill me, leopard or no leopard. At the very least, he'd make me pay with the blood of the people I care about."

His golden gaze searched her blue one. One hand cupped the side of her face, his thumb sliding over her skin. "That's it. You observed I had no phone and you just confirmed it out loud?"

She nodded. "And don't forget the part where you totally shot down my Zen fantasy."

His smile was slow in coming but it was genuine and it warmed his eyes. "I'll have to see what I can do about replacing that one with something else."

She felt a shiver go right through her. She had wanted to see if she could make him smile like that. He might be the worst grump in the world in the morning with no coffee and he had definitely shattered every dream she had of a Zen master, but he was gorgeous and all man standing in her space, smelling like a rain forest and sex. He looked darkly sensual, and intensely masculine.

"One more thing, Kitten," Eli added, his fingers skimming her chin with the same gentle caress, robbing her of breath. "I wouldn't bet the bank on Cordeau being able to kill me so easily."

She shivered again, this time because he sounded like he meant it. She even took a step back but bumped against the counter. There was no way to look away from his focused stare. She was caught there, her mouth dry, her heart pounding. His dangerous quality was back, clinging to him like a second skin. He wasn't the same kind of dangerous as Rafe, but she could see the predator in him now. She saw the leopard, and there was no doubt in her mind that he could kill if he needed to. That he would kill if he needed to.

"Don't." He said the word softly.

She couldn't breathe. She stared up at him, shaking her head, having no idea what he meant.

"Don't look at me like that. Don't ever be afraid of me. You took a step back and you look as if you think I might hit you. That could never happen, baby."

Clutching the coffee cup, she lifted her hand to her scalp, the memory of his behavior in the warehouse and the truck washing over her. What had she been thinking? That he really was Ridley Cromer just because they'd had sex? Her body ached all over. She had marks on her skin. That hadn't been making love. They'd had sex. Rough sex. She'd suddenly felt all sweet and melty inside. That didn't change who or what he was.

"Kitten." He groaned softly, and his fingers went to her scalp, massaging gently. "I didn't hit you. Remember that when you're condemning me. You attacked me more than once and I restrained you, but I didn't hit you. In the truck, I had to stop you. A leopard can track through scent. Your scent could not be on that ground. You knew he was leopard and you knew you were risking him finding you."

"I wanted to get away from you," she admitted in a low voice.

She hated the way her body went into meltdown at his touch. That confused her more than anything else. She should have been screaming at him not to touch her, but instead, when he did, even in such a simple way, she wanted to get closer to him. Maybe she wasn't slutty, but certainly the leopard inside of her had to be.

"I'm well aware you wanted to get away from me, Cat," Eli said, in a voice totally devoid of feeling.

Her gaze jumped to his. His hooded, sensual eyes were back to moving over her face broodingly. She pressed her lips together and then lifted her chin, forcing herself to look him straight in the eyes.

"Eli, what if I don't want all this? What if my leopard chooses your leopard, but I don't choose you? What happens then?"

His face softened. "Your leopard has already chosen, Kitten. So has mine. I'm the only man who has ever been inside of you and I'm the only man who ever will. If your choice isn't me right now, I'll have to work a hell of a lot harder to make certain it is." His thumb was back to moving gently over her skin. "Too much has happened too fast for you to be able to even have a chance at knowing what or who you want. That's why we're here. Cordeau won't find you here and neither will the DEA. You have time to figure it out."

She didn't take her gaze from his. "Eli, you *are* the DEA."

"Not here, I'm not."

"How do I know what's real and what isn't with you?" Her heart pounded when she asked, but she watched his face, hoping for a clue.

"You don't at first," he said. "That's something I have to prove to you. But I'm asking for you to give me a chance to prove it to you."

She kept her eyes on his. "You didn't answer my question, Eli. What if my leopard chooses you and I don't? What happens?"

He was silent for a long time. She didn't think he'd answer her. His thumb slid over her lips and then down to her chin. Featherlight. She felt his touch all the way to her most feminine core. Her body trembled, but more to the point, she felt the sudden damp heat between her legs. She bit at her lower lip and then sharply inhaled when his gaze settled there. Just the small act of breathing lifted her breasts beneath his flannel shirt and she became acutely aware she wore nothing beneath it. What had possessed her to be so stupid?

He was close. So close she felt heat radiating off of him. She felt every breath he took. She felt his hunger. It was so close to the surface, and it was there in the glittering gold of his eyes. Intense. Powerful. Very focused on her. She had only to take one small step and she'd be in his arms. She wanted to be in his arms and that was just humiliating.

He had all the experience and she had none. Sex could be another way to control her. What if he interrogated her while they were having sex? She'd probably tell him everything. She'd never be any kind of a spy, that was for certain.

Abruptly Eli stepped back away from her, raking his fingers through his hair. "Woman, you have to stop thinking so much. Your face is an open book. I get that I fucked up and I'm doing my best to make up for that, but it hurts like hell when you look at me that way. I'm going to take my shower and you put together breakfast. That will give us both a little time away from each other."

She nodded. Grateful and disappointed at the same time. Which again, was crazy and totally humiliating. She didn't seem to have any self-control around him.

"As for your question, I don't honestly have an answer to that. I don't, Cat. I hadn't even considered that a woman might not want the same man her leopard wants because as a rule, they're mates. The humans are and so are the leopards."

"So it's possible I could still leave if my leopard accepted yours," she persisted. She needed to know. She *had* to know she had a choice.

"I think it would be improbable that would happen, but I think any of us can walk away if we decide we don't want what we have." He stepped into her space again, his fingers on her chin, tilting her head so she could look into his eyes, eyes that were pure cat. "As to whether or not I would turn into Cordeau without you, I can't honestly say." He dropped his hand abruptly and turned and walked out of the room.

Catarina found herself shaking. She walked to the kitchen chair with her coffee, sat down and drew up her legs. What had he meant by that strange statement? He couldn't possibly turn into Rafe. Eli might be leopard, but he wouldn't be a part of the DEA if he wanted to commit the kinds of crimes Rafe did. Rafe's organization spanned three states. He had a large network, and it was growing every day. She just couldn't see Eli running guns or keeping prostitutes in line or creating a drug empire. Killing maybe, the rest of it no way.

How could she want a man so much when she didn't trust him? She was very honest with herself. Eli wasn't Ridley but she was still very attracted to him. Their chemistry was off the charts. Still, sex wasn't making love. People hooked up all the time for great sex, didn't they? Couldn't she just view it like that? He knew about the little hussy inside of her. She could bide her time until her leopard made her appearance, use Eli for great sex and then if things went bad, just walk away.

She sipped at her coffee, surprised to find it was warm, not hot. She'd always been good at figuring things out. She just had to get past the horrible hole in her heart. She still felt as if she'd been ripped to pieces, shredded inside and left empty. The problem was, she only felt that way when she was alone, when Eli wasn't right next to her, and that, she knew, was a very bad sign.

With a little sigh she got up and checked the fridge and cupboards and then found Eli's pots and pans. She liked the kitchen and the views it had. She could look out the wide windows while she cooked and watch the wind playing through the trees. It was beautiful country. She had chosen to come to Texas because she was certain the state was so large Rafe wouldn't be able to find her there.

This countryside was beautiful, with far more trees than she expected. Eli said his leopard could run free here. She wondered what that would be like. What it would feel like. She suddenly had the desire to run free as a leopard, just to experience it. She was afraid, because she'd seen Rafe's leopard and she knew the animal was even more dangerous than the man.

Even as a teenager, Catarina realized the leopard drove Rafe hard and it took a great deal of discipline and energy to keep that part of him under control. The leopard's traits were definitely infused in the man and now, after seeing Eli and knowing what was inside of him, she knew his leopard drove him as well.

She paused in the act of stirring her sauce to press a hand to her stomach. Her leopard drove her as well. She'd been violent with Eli twice. More, she had practically forced him to have sex with her. She gained just a little sympathy for Rafe. Her sauce bubbled and she quickly began to stir it again. Leopards, like people, had to have their own personalities, and some had to be more difficult than others. More prone to violence. More alpha.

She glanced toward the open archway leading toward the master bedroom. The water had gone off. Eli would be with her again soon. His leopard was pure alpha, the same as Rafe's leopard had to be. She couldn't imagine the two men coming together in any kind of agreement. They would each view the other as a threat and would feel the need to neutralize that threat.

She fixed two plates, arranging them artistically, because for her, it wasn't just about really good food, but good presentation as well.

Remembering the look on Eli's face when he'd said that about losing her made her heart beat faster. He walked in when she was setting the plates on the table. He looked good. He smelled good. And when he smiled at her, he took her breath away.

She sank into the chair across the table from him, pulled up her bare feet and sat tailor fashion. "I hope you like it. I made us a skillet breakfast with hash browns and country ham biscuits. The beignets just came out of the oil and are very hot, and you have fresh coffee."

Eli flashed another smile and something inside her responded with a warm glow. "You have no idea what a treat it is to smell food cooking in this house. I bought the place and nearly burned it down the first time I ever used that stove."

"Someday I'm going to have my dream stove, Eli," she said. "I've always wanted a Viking."

He paused to eat two bites of the egg scramble. "This is heaven. Every time you get in a kitchen you produce a miracle for the taste buds."

She laughed. " 'Miracle for the taste buds'? You didn't just say that, did you?"

He shrugged and kept eating. "Sometimes even corny crap is the only thing a man can say because it's the fucking truth."

"You swear a lot."

"Does it bother you?"

"How could it? I grew up in Rafe's home and all his men used foul language."

"House," he corrected. "You grew up in his house. That was no home, Cat, any more than the number of foster homes I was in were homes."

She hadn't known he'd been in foster homes. His parents had been murdered but he hadn't said what happened to him after that. "I'm sorry, Eli, I didn't realize."

"It was a house."

"It was my house," she said. "I didn't know any other way of life."

"Do you love him?" he asked, his fork halfway to his mouth. His body still. Utterly still. His eyes on her face.

Something moved under her skin, rolling through her like a wave. It left behind prickling as if it had agitated her nerve endings.

"Cat?" he prompted.

"I'm not in love with him, if that's what you mean. It was never like that between us. He didn't kiss me or show affection, at least not like other people. I don't know if Rafe is capable of actually loving anyone. I think he wants to, and if he does, I'm probably the one person he does."

He put a forkful of food in his mouth, still regarding her steadily. "That's not an answer. Do you love him? Do you feel loyalty to him?"

Her first reaction was a resounding "no," but something stopped her. He was asking not as the DEA, but as Eli, sitting across from her at the breakfast table. At least she thought that's who it was.

"No. I feel sorry for him. I do. I don't know what his life was like when he was a child, but it wasn't good. I think his leopard is hard to control and enjoys violence. But he does things that are wrong. Morally wrong. More than that. So wrong there's no redemption."

"You know this for a fact? I ask because appearances are often deceiving, especially when it comes to shifters."

"I don't. But women would be brought to the house, prostitutes, always on his bad days. He would come to my room first and just stare at me. I was always afraid. Something in his eyes, feral. Not right."

She shivered and put down her fork. Her thighs tingled. Burned. She rubbed her palms up and down them.

"Did he say anything to you?"

She shook her head. "Never. Not those nights. He left and then the prostitute would come. He would spend hours with her and then he would go out into the swamp in his leopard form." Her voice dropped to a whisper. "I think he hunted and then killed her."

He leaned toward her. "Why would you think that?"

She took a breath. It didn't matter what she told him, she couldn't prove any of it and neither could the DEA. "I would see missing persons signs tacked to telephone poles and the sides of buildings. I recognized more than one of them. I just didn't think it could be coincidence."

There was no way to explain Rafe and the way he was, or the difference in him when he came back from his trips to the swamp. He was more relaxed for a short period of time, less likely to retaliate with violence for some infraction among his business acquaintances or his men.

She pushed at the heavy fall of hair hanging down her back. She should have put it up. The room was too warm. She lifted the heavy mass off her neck and felt the rise of her breasts. Her nipples rubbed against the flannel and the air left her lungs in a gasp as a wave of heat rushed over her to settle between her legs. Burning. The fire came fast, hot and ferocious, a hungry, blistering blaze that ignited before she could catch her breath. Her breasts seemed to swell to an aching need, her nipples pressing against the flannel, liking the feel of the material pushing against their hardened tips.

Her gaze went to Eli across the table from her, taking in

his wide shoulders, his thick, heavily muscled chest. Everything in her urged her to slide from her chair and crawl under the table, pull at his sweats and feast on her prize. Her mouth actually watered, remembering the taste and feel of him. She wanted to drive him out of control, to be the one to bring him to the very edge and push him over.

She gripped the edge of the table, hard. She didn't even know *how* to feast on him, and yet the erotic images were in her head refusing to go away. Her skin hurt, the weight of the shirt pressing into the raw nerve endings. It was happening again and this time felt even worse. She had to be able to stay in control.

She dropped her head and took several deep breaths, struggling with the need to claw at Eli, to rake at him, ravage him, devour him. Her body shuddered and her legs moved restlessly, unable to stop that terrible burning that demanded to be sated.

She wasn't like this. She wasn't. She didn't know the first thing about sex and she didn't want it like this. Not without love. Not without caring. Just tearing at each other, a wild, hard mating that meant nothing at all. She couldn't do this.

"Baby." His voice was soft. "It will be all right. We'll handle it."

He knew. He saw her state, probably smelled her call. He knew—that was even more humiliating than being so out of control.

She shook her head. "This isn't me. It's not me."

Even her voice was different. Sultry. Low. A distinct velvet whisper designed to play on a man's senses. She wanted to scream. Rake the table with her claws. Bite Eli's lower lip and rip the sweats from his body.

Her skin felt too tight. Her breasts were aching so badly it was painful. Her breath came in ragged gasps. She knew in another minute she would pull the shirt from her body and crawl all over Eli. She couldn't do that again. She leapt up, and raced for the door. She had no idea where she was going, but maybe she could run so fast and so far, the fire building so hot inside would go away.

She'd taken three steps when Eli's fingers settled around her wrist. She spun back to him, a low warning growl escaping, one hand swiping toward his face. He was prepared and he moved just in time, the claws missing by a scant inch.

The moment he touched her, she knew she was lost. His fingers burned a brand in her skin. She still tried, still fought the wild, uninhibited creature that she didn't even recognize, but it was too late, she'd already aroused Eli.

His face was stamped with pure male sensuality. His eyes had gone molten, intense, lust rising to match her own. He caught the front of her flannel shirt and yanked down. Buttons popped and he stripped it off of her. The air hit her skin, fanning the flames even more, pushing the terrible need higher. She couldn't think, not with the roaring in her head.

"I have to go" was all she could get out. But she wasn't going. Her hands were already sliding down his chest to find the hem of his shirt.

He caught her face in his hands, yanking her chin up. "Look at me, Catarina. You can't run from this. She's too close. When you're like this, you need me."

She didn't know whether she was going to scream at him or weep. She couldn't stay still, not with the fierce heat sweeping through her like a firestorm out of control. What did a shifter do when they were out in public? It was horrible. Beyond anything she'd ever imagined, and far, far worse than the first time.

She had nowhere else to turn. Only him. Only Eli. It didn't matter that he had betrayed her, or that he might be lying. That he'd brought her to his home without her consent. There was only Eli, and he had to know what to do because she didn't.

"Eli." She breathed his name, looking up at him, feeling helpless and vulnerable.

Eli looked down into Catarina's face. She was so beautiful and she looked so frightened. He dragged her close,
tight into him, fitting her body into his while his hands held
her face tipped upward toward his. He brought his mouth
down gently. He didn't feel gentle, but she needed this
moment. She needed gentle and tender.

He kissed her with love. He even tasted it on his own
tongue. He didn't have a clue when it happened, maybe the
first time he found himself laughing with her, but he definitely knew when he stretched out beside her and tugged
her body into his in bed. He didn't sleep with women. He
had no problems fucking them, but then they were gone. He
was gone. He didn't bring them home, especially not here.

Everything changed the moment Catarina stepped into
his house—everything—because it felt different. It felt like
home instead of a house. So he held himself back, and it
took a lot of restraint to control the wildness building inside
of him. He kissed her over and over, his tongue stroking
caresses, teasing and dueling with hers until her breathing
was ragged and her hands were frantic.

Then he devoured her with a ravenous appetite that knew
no boundaries. He took her mouth like the savage cat he was,
bit her lower lip, the one he couldn't get his mind off. He
loved her mouth and he made certain she knew it intimately.

He left her mouth to burn kisses down her throat. He
liked that she was naked and he was fully clothed. There was
something very decadent about that. He kept her hands from
pulling his shirt off. Instead he dropped his hands to the
waistband of his sweats and pushed them down over his hips.

Her gaze dropped. Her breath caught. He widened his
stance as he bunched her long hair in his fist. Her leopard
was rising close to the surface again, and as much as he
wanted to give her the time to heal, there was only one way
to stop the terrible burn.

"Kneel down, baby," he said, keeping his voice low, an
authoritative whip.

"I need . . ." She trailed off.

"I know what you need, just kneel down, knees wide. I want to see that you're wet and ready for me. I want to see that you enjoy giving your man pleasure." It was subtle enough, he slipped that in there, knowing in her highly aroused state she wouldn't notice that he'd called himself her man. She'd get used to it though.

She moistened her lips and he nearly groaned. She was sexy without trying, her body flushed, her breasts swaying with every move she made. He wanted to touch her, but he didn't allow himself to. That would lead to other things, and right now, he wanted her to learn about pleasing him.

He kept his gaze on hers, not giving an inch when she hesitated, and finally, she dropped her eyes to his fully aroused cock and then slowly sank to her knees. She was graceful, beautiful, her dark hair a sharp contrast to her light skin. Her breasts drew his attention, full and round and high, her nipples taut, waiting for his mouth.

Her hands slid up his thighs and then she was cupping his sac and he wanted to throw his head back and roar with primal need, but he breathed his way through it, using his hand in her hair to pull her head over him.

"That's what you need, Cat, right there. You learned a little last night. You're going to learn more right now." He exerted pressure on her head.

Her tongue licked up his shaft and then up and over the flared head. His breath left his lungs in a rush. She began licking like a cat. Over his balls, under them, up his shaft and back down, and then he was inside her hot, moist mouth and she sucked, her tongue still dancing. She had good instincts and she used them. He let her explore on her own until he thought he might lose his mind.

Breathing deep, he caught her hair on both sides of her head and held her still. He waited until her eyes met his. The cobalt blue had gone a deep violet and he could see her leopard was close. So close. She was wild and needy. He scented Cat's call, and the taste of honey and spice was already on his tongue.

"That's good, Kitten, very good. Right now, I'm going to push a little deeper. I want you to take a breath and relax, let me in. I'll count to ten and give you another breath." He waited until she complied and then he took over, not allowing movement while he gently thrust deeper with his hips.

For a moment he thought she'd struggle. He watched her face carefully. Her gaze didn't leave his and he saw her make the effort to relax her mouth and throat for him. He inched farther into that tunnel of unbearable tightness. He pulled back and let her have air before he thrust again. The pleasure was exquisite. Perfect. He went three more times, not taking advantage, not sliding deeper.

"We'll go fifteen counts, babe," he bit out. It came out more a growl. He couldn't help it. She was beautiful on her knees, her mouth tight around his cock, her legs open so he could see the welcoming moisture collecting at her entrance.

She nodded and he watched her take another breath. He slipped deeper this time, still gentle, still careful.

"Suck hard, baby, use your tongue."

He loved that she complied, that she didn't question him or fight him. Her hands cupped his balls, slid over his thighs, always kept contact with him as he thrust gently deep into her mouth.

The fire in his belly grew, flames leaping and burning and his cock felt scorched in the blaze, enveloped in the inferno of her mouth. He pulled back before it was too late, and pulled her to her feet, no longer gentle. She'd driven him out of his mind with her mouth and he wanted her his way.

He lifted her easily, planted her butt on the edge of the counter, yanked her knees apart, pushed one hand into her belly so she was forced to tip backward, forced to prop herself up on her elbows. That gave him access to everything he wanted. He dipped his head and ate her. Ravenously. Ferociously. A man starved.

He was ruthless. Relentless. This was his and he was addicted to it. Honey and spice, a scorching tight cauldron, all his. She screamed out an orgasm as he took her up fast, but he hardly heard with the roaring in his head and the thundering of his blood in his ears. He suckled, licked, used his fingers and thumb, the edge of his teeth and kept devouring her right through a second and third orgasm.

"I need you. Please, I need you now."

Her sobbing plea finally penetrated. He licked the honey off her thighs and lifted his head, again waiting.

"Tell me what you need, and use my name."

Her breath hissed out, her eyes flashing at him. He dragged her ass right off the counter, her legs over his shoulder, his mouth clamped between her legs, feeding, uncaring that she writhed and struggled. He forced another orgasm, this one so powerful she screamed through it. He didn't stop.

"Eli! Please. Eli." She sounded close to tears, not sobbing with pleasure, but real tears. She didn't like asking. "I need you inside me. Please."

He rewarded her instantly, pulling her all the way off the counter. "Wrap your legs around me, Kitten. Hook your ankles." He was full. Bursting even. His cock felt as if it might explode. His body was hotter than hades and lightning seemed to fork through his veins.

She did exactly what he instructed and he didn't waste time—he surged up as he forced her hips down. Fire streaked through him. His cock drove through hot, tight folds, forcing her body to accommodate his size. Her tight channel squeezed him and the friction, as he pummeled into her, just drove him wilder.

He needed more, and he took her to the floor, pumping into her even as he went down over her. There was no give, nothing to cushion her body, so he could pound into her deeper and harder.

She used her feet to push upward, tilting her hips to allow for even deeper penetration. Her nails bit into his shoulders, scored down his back and the bite of pain only added to the frenzy of need. He allowed himself to lose control. He didn't want to ever stop. He never wanted to be separated from her, and he damn well wasn't going to let her think she could ever live without him. Without this.

He had no other way to tie her to him, but he had this. *This* he was good at. He might say and do the wrong thing, but he *would* tie her to him this way. He moved in her and the earth moved around him. He bent his head to her breast, suckling hard, using the edge of his teeth and feeling the hot wash of spiced honey bathing his cock as he plunged into her over and over.

She came again and then again, gasping for breath, her eyes shocked and dazed, which only spurred him on. He whipped his arm under her hips, lifting her more, pounding deep as fire streaked up from his legs, burst through his thighs and took his cock in a crowning storm. Her body clamped down, a vicious vise around him, locking there as he emptied himself into her, the friction bordering on pain. The scalding heat triggered a powerful quake in her, sweeping through her entire body, a long, hard orgasm that seemed as if it might never go away.

He took a breath, his hair damp, his body covered in sweat, but for once in his life, he was completely sated, limp and relaxed. He let himself cover her smaller body, resting on her soft curves, feeling her heart pounding every bit as hard as his own. He was heavy, too heavy for her, and he levered himself up, staying buried in her.

They were locked tight, their bodies connected and he wanted to stay there. He pushed at her heavy fall of hair. She didn't look at him. She kept her face turned away and her eyes closed tight. He felt the little hitch in her breath. She was going to cry, and this wasn't about pleasure or need, this was something altogether different. This was about shame.

"Don't." He ordered it. Meant it.

Her hands curled at his shoulders. She exerted pressure. He didn't move. He decided on honesty.

"I'm trying to think of something to say that will help you understand what's going on, baby, but all I can think about is how much I love being inside of you. You're scorching hot and fucking tight, wrapped around me and I feel like I'm in paradise. I don't want that to end. Tell me how it feels to you."

Little aftershocks were still going off and he felt every one of them. Her muscles squeezed down with hot greed, still trying to milk him.

"This isn't me."

"It's you, Cat. This is you. You don't just like sex—you love it. You have more passion in your little finger than most people do in their entire bodies."

"I'm naked on the kitchen floor."

"That's right, baby, and it was heaven. I want to do you in every fucking room I have. Outside. Inside. Hell, on the roof."

"This isn't me," she denied, biting her lower lip.

He leaned down and licked along her lip to soothe the sting. The action set off another series of aftershocks and she gasped.

"This is you, Catarina. It was you wanting to please me when I told you to get on your knees. You didn't have to, but you wanted to."

He saw the truth on her face. She *had* wanted to. He leaned closer and brushed his mouth over hers. "I bet my taste is still in your mouth. You wanted all of it, didn't you? You didn't want to stop."

A single sound slipped from her throat. Her lashes fluttered.

"It wasn't about what you could get from me. You knelt in front of me and you were wet, dripping wet with your mouth around my cock. That was you. All you. There's nothing wrong with being that person. In fact, you should be rejoicing. People go their entire lives without ever having what we just had."

"I don't want this to be me. I want to have love in my life. I want to be loved. I don't want to be the kind of person who uses a man for sex and has him use me."

He framed her face again and brushed a kiss across her lips. "Baby, here's a little newsflash for you. There's no way in hell a man could be with you and not fall in love."

9

CATARINA sat in the very comfortable chair on the front porch of Eli's ranch house. She was still warm from the bath he'd run for her and snug in another one of his very expensive flannel shirts. He took care of her. She had to admit that whether she wanted to or not.

Lying on the kitchen floor, totally naked, she'd felt humiliated that she'd jumped him again, and this time it was far, far worse than the last time because she really was addicted to the taste of him. And to his body. And to her absolute mortification, she liked rough sex. On the floor. In the kitchen.

She pressed her fingers to her eyes to try to ease the headache she couldn't quite get rid of. Her skull felt far too tight, as if it no longer fit inside her skin. The worst was knowing Eli knew the truth about her. She *had* wanted to kneel at his feet. She liked his hands hard in her hair, guiding her mouth. She liked the low, almost soft voice that carried absolute command when he told her what he wanted.

She groaned softly trying to get the sounds of her own moans and pleas out of her head. In her wildest dreams she'd never imagined ending up bare naked on the kitchen floor, wild and out of control.

She knew if she'd been with Rafe naked on the floor, it would have ended very differently. Instead of holding her the way Eli had he would have left her lying there, uncaring that she was upset and confused. Uncaring that her body felt a little bruised and battered, although very sated.

Eli had taken the time to talk to her. He'd been honest, maybe even brutally so, but he did it in a way that made her feel she mattered and he just wanted her to understand and accept who she was. He obviously didn't think something was wrong with her.

He had been gentle, carrying her through to the bathroom, running her a hot bath, telling her to clean up and he'd bring her another shirt. He had done the dishes and made fresh coffee by the time she was out. Then he carried her out to the porch and told her to take a little break, he'd be out soon. Rafe wouldn't have done any of that.

There was no sound, but she knew the instant Eli stepped through the door onto the porch. "I brought a couple of beignets to go with coffee, Kitten," he said, and bent to brush a kiss across her mouth. He put the coffee and small plate of dessert beside her on the little end table and then pulled up a chair behind her.

"What are you doing?" She glanced over her shoulder to see him sprawled in a chair, his legs splayed out and around her chair.

"Your hair is bothering you. I'm going to braid it for you."

Her heart stuttered. She had so much hair it was difficult to keep her arms up when she was working with it so often she just clipped it back or wore it in a ponytail.

"Lean back, baby."

There it was again, his low, commanding tone. He used

it often. Now that she thought about it, Ridley had used it as well.

"You don't have to braid my hair, Eli. There's a lot of it."

"I'm familiar with your hair, Cat. When a man is crazy about his woman's hair, he is aware of just about every strand on her head. I'm crazy about your hair. I love the way it looks when you're first waking up. I love the way it feels on my body when you've got my cock in your mouth. I love the way it falls down your back like a fucking water-fall with so much shine sometimes I think it's going to blind me."

Her teeth tugged at her bottom lip. What could she say to that? Absolutely nothing. That was the kind of thing she wanted to hold to her and take out occasionally in secret and listen to all over again. Eli gave her compliments just like Ridley, only maybe better.

She leaned her head back. The brush went through her hair, a long smooth stroke. It felt wonderful on her scalp. He took his time brushing her hair, seeming to enjoy it. The brush pulling through her hair was almost hypnotic. She closed her eyes for a few minutes and just let herself enjoy it.

Peace stole over her. The view was incredible, and for the first time in her life she felt as if she was home. Catarina didn't try to analyze why, she just allowed herself to enjoy the moment. She drank coffee and ate one of the beignets. They weren't quite as good cool as they were fresh and hot, but it was sugar and that went great with the strong coffee. It was perfect.

"Do you let your leopard run free very often?"

He divided her hair into thirds. "I try to every day, but when I'm on a job, sometimes that's not always possible."

"Are you gone a lot, working?"

He tugged gently. "If you're asking me will I be away from my mate now that I've found her, the answer is no. I don't need to work. I inherited a lot of money. It was in a trust and I couldn't touch the bulk of it until I turned thirty-one. I work because I wanted to. Now I don't. I'll be handing in my resignation."

She tried to turn her head but his hands in her hair prevented her from doing that. "Eli. You can't do that. You love your job, and I still feel very confused." Her lashes swept down. "I don't know if I can ever trust you again. It was hard enough the first time. I'm still asking myself if you're seducing me in order to get me to do what you want."

"Of course I am. I want you to stay with me. I know you're not going to testify against Cordeau. But you're mine, Cat, and I'm not giving you up. It's natural for you to be afraid, and I'll have to work at earning your trust back, but I will."

"You lied to me."

"Only about my name. The man who was with you in the warehouse was all me. Maybe not so bossy or crude like I can be, but he was me. I gave you me."

"Where were you that day? You always came to walk me home, but you didn't that day. It was Tuttle, not you."

"He's a moron. He doesn't do undercover work and he sure as hell can't tail someone without them spotting it. I'd heard they were going to move on you and I wanted to stop them. I spent the day arguing. During the meeting I got wind that maybe someone had tipped Cordeau and I needed to run that down. If it was true, I planned to lay the entire thing out for you myself."

Catarina swallowed hard. "Eli, I don't want you to change your life on the chance that I might want to stay. I don't know if I can get that trust back. I don't even know what's going on here between us. Is this just until my leopard emerges? Is this supposed to be a lifetime deal and I've got no say in it? I can't tell you I'll stay."

"You'll stay. Shifters mate for life, Cat. You'll stay."

She winced, afraid he was right. If her leopard only had two choices, Eli or Rafe, and she didn't even know if Rafe would take her back or kill her, she knew she would rather be with Eli. He might never love her, or she him, but he cared enough to take care of her after they had wild, crazy sex. She blushed again just thinking about it.

"You sore?"

She moistened her lips. Her body ached from the pounding on the floor, and deep inside with every movement, she still felt him there, but it was a kind of delicious soreness. She liked it. She liked knowing how she got sore.

"Baby?" he persisted.

She nodded, liking the way his hands moved in her hair. "Not bad. The bath helped. Although I think I have skid marks on my butt."

"I think your leopard is very close, Cat. When she emerges, I'll have to let my leopard out. We'll both be affected by their very unrestrained passion."

She could tell he had chosen his words cautiously. Her heart jumped and she felt a sudden rush of damp heat at the idea of what unrestrained passion was. She thought they'd been pretty darned unrestrained.

"I'm not certain what you're telling me. Is this going to get worse?"

He laughed softly and tugged on her braid. He leaned over and nipped at the soft spot where her neck and shoulder met.

His hands transferred from her hair to her shoulders and he began a slow massage, easing the tightness from her sore muscles. She felt almost as if she were melting into the chair. His fingers were strong and then moved to her neck, back to her shoulders and down her back. She'd never felt more cared for in her life and she didn't know how to think or act so she did nothing at all. Again, she just allowed herself to enjoy the moment.

He pulled up the more comfortable deck chair beside hers and sank down into it, reaching for his coffee.

She glanced at him. "You didn't answer me. Is it going to get worse? The sex?"

"You're such an innocent. Not worse, Kitten, better. You'll like it." He said that with confidence.

"You only say that because you've discovered I'm a perv," she said. There was a part of her that wanted to laugh and another part that wanted to cry.

He laughed. "Woman, if that's you being a perv, I'm all for it." He reached across the small end table and curled his fingers around the nape of her neck. "You're sitting next to the real thing, and I can tell you, absolutely, truthfully, you are not there. I won't mind trying to shape you in that direction. The moment I sat down I thought about sitting out here watching the sunset with a fresh cup of your coffee and you sitting right here between my legs, your mouth very busy."

Her eyebrow went up. "I think you have an oral fixation." She had to make a joke of it, because, honestly, the moment he sat down, she wished he wasn't wearing any sweatpants and she could practice all she wanted to. And her leopard hussy was nowhere in sight.

He grinned at her. "You think? Don't worry, baby, you'll like it."

She already liked it, she just wasn't certain she should like it so much. Because he was talking about it and she was thinking about it, she just had to ask him. She was very grateful she had an excuse to stare straight ahead. "Um. Eli. Why counting?"

He didn't answer right away and she figured she hadn't given him enough information, but really, what was she supposed to say? That she wanted to be really, really good at pleasing him and he obviously liked her mouth on him?

"I didn't want you to panic when you couldn't breathe, baby. You have to learn to breathe through your nose and even then, when I'm deep, if you don't relax and trust me, you might still think you're going to choke, or strangle. First, I wouldn't let that happen, and second, you're learning. I don't want anything we do to frighten you."

His voice was matter-of-fact. They could have been discussing the weather.

"Once I learned to read, I found a few how-to books about sex," she admitted, because he made it easy to talk to him about anything. "I didn't dare go online and look at anything because he always had me watched on the computer and he checked my history and everything else. I knew he tracked the keystrokes on my computer so I used his. He never knew." She said it rather smugly. She felt smug about that.

He flashed a grin at her. "You outsmarted him."

"Yes."

"You read about sex in a book?"

"I was afraid Rafe might want that from me at some point. He'd begun coming into my bedroom some nights and just watching me. I actually went so far as to eavesdrop on some of the girlfriends of Rafe's closest soldiers when they were talking about things they'd done with their men."

Eli groaned softly. He stroked a caress down her hair. "Kitten. Really."

She blushed for no reason. "You've given me more instruction and experience in twenty-four hours than I read in all three books or heard about in a very graphic and rather drunken conversation."

"I want sex to be good for you. Every time. Whether it's rough or gentle or I'm making you beg, I want it always to be off the charts for you. I'll teach you the things you need to know and if you have questions, just ask. If there's something you don't like, tell me. We'll talk it through. If there's something you want, you tell me and it's yours."

She pressed her lips together. She had made up her mind a long time ago that she would be as honest as possible. She was good at deception—at least she thought she was—but she didn't like it. She wanted to be the kind of person who dealt with something and then it was over. And she wanted honesty. Still, Eli was very blunt when it came to sex. She didn't like that she didn't know very much. She didn't even know if it was good for him.

"What is it, baby?" he asked gently, his hand curling around the nape of her neck, his fingers moving into the muscles there. "One of the things I admire most about you is the way you just ask me questions or answer when I ask you. Don't be embarrassed. You don't ever have to be embarrassed with me."

She took a deep breath. "You say that it isn't just my leopard making me so crazy when it comes to sex. I can't stop. I can't control myself when it happens. I don't understand that. I've never been like that in my life. I've never even wanted another man, but with you, I have to have my hands and my mouth on you. I can't wait for you to touch me. It doesn't make sense because I still don't even know if I like you. I don't trust you. If it's me and not just her, why didn't I know this about myself before?"

"Cat, you can tell that I'm experienced. I know women and I know what they like or need. In case you haven't been paying attention, I like control. I like my world the way I want it. I need sex often and a certain way. I knew the moment I laid eyes on you that you'd be compatible with me. Even my leopard recognized it and that was before your female made an appearance. If you weren't capable of matching me in bed, of being what I need you to be, I never would have touched you."

She frowned, trying to deny to herself that she liked sex with him. That was insanity. She loved sex with him. She liked the way he took command. She liked how rough he could be and how absolutely caring he was afterward. Mostly she loved how he could make her body go up in flames. She hadn't known it could be like that.

Catarina bit down on her lip. There was something to what he was saying. She couldn't hide from the fact that even now, and she didn't feel her leopard close, erotic images played through her mind.

"I don't know what I'm doing, Eli," she admitted. "You do make it good for me, but I don't want sex to be all about me. I need to know that it's good for you too."

She was so confused. She didn't even know why she cared whether the sex was good for him too. She was just using him, right? She didn't have a clue what she was doing or even why, but his answer mattered to her.

There was silence. Her heart pounded.

"Cat. Look at me. Right now. Look at me."

She could barely make herself turn her head to him. Her face was red, but it was the truth. She wanted to make him feel the same things she felt.

He caught her face in his hands, his thumbs sliding over her jaw. "I'm not a man who would ever pretend even if I could. If you don't know anything else about me, you have to know that. You please me, baby. You more than please me."

Her eyes slid away from his. He growled low in his throat. "Kitten. I said look at me—that means your eyes are looking right into mine when we're talking about this."

Catarina sighed, but forced herself to look him in the eye again. "It's just a little embarrassing, Eli. I don't know what I'm doing, you have to tell me everything."

"Sweetheart, I love coaching you. I love that no man has been inside you and you're all mine. I love that I can teach you the things that please me and you're so willing to learn. That matters to me, that you want to please me."

"Don't get too used to it," she advised. "I want to kick you more often than I want to please you."

He threw his head back and laughed. "I intimidate everyone, especially women. Where the hell have I gone wrong with you?"

"You intimidate me," she admitted. "But that only makes me want to kick you all the harder."

He stretched his legs out in front of him and looked out over the slightly rolling land. "I fell in love with this place the first time I saw it," he said. "But it never felt right. It never felt like home. Not until you walked through the door."

Catarina didn't like the way her heart melted at his statement. The sex was bad enough, but it was just sex. She could handle just sex with no emotion attached to it. She didn't want to like him so much and the way he talked to her, the things he said, even the way he looked at her, made her feel special.

"I think I was handcuffed and maybe carried," she pointed out.

"Yeah. Like I said, felt like I was coming home for the first time."

His voice had dropped an octave lower, sliding over her skin like the touch of fingers, and she shook her head. The problem was, Eli was a very sensual man and right now, she was finding she liked sensual. She even craved it. So Eli was somewhat irresistible to her.

"I need a few more supplies from town." Changing the subject was the only safe thing to do. "For cooking. A few more spices, just some things."

"You like to cook, don't you?"

She shrugged. "I told you I did."

"Make a list, I'll get you whatever you need. I like the fact that I get to reap the benefits, especially if you're in the kitchen in one of my shirts."

She glanced sideways at him and realized he was teasing her. She took a breath. Oh, God. She shouldn't for one minute trust this man enough to feel like her insides were melting, but she did, she was nothing but goo inside and that didn't bode well for keeping him at arm's length.

"My shirt and no panties," he added.

Her tongue darted out to moisten her lower lip. Of course he had to remind her she'd been a crazy perv, on the floor, for God's sake. On the floor.

"Baby." His voice gentled and his fingers curled around

the nape of her neck. "Stop being embarrassed. What we did was beautiful. I know you're scared right now, but I'll take care of you, get you through this."

"What happens when Rafe shows up?" She asked because . . . well . . . Rafe would find her. He always found her once he had a starting point.

"Catarina, don't ask me questions if you don't want answers," Eli said, and his voice went hard. Scary hard.

She turned her head to look at him again. She'd always thought of him as sweet. Dangerous maybe, but still sweet. There was nothing sweet about Eli in that moment. Danger radiated off of him. He gave off a vibe every bit as scary as Rafe did. She caught her lower lip between her teeth. Maybe it was the leopard in them, but suddenly, she felt a little bit like prey, caught between two powerful predators. Eli hid it better than Rafe, but he was just as lethal.

"Don't." He said it softly.

"Don't what?"

"Be afraid of me. I'm a shifter and my leopard is difficult to handle at times, but I handle it. I don't kill people unless I have no choice. I'm not Cordeau. I wouldn't slash my woman's back to punish her or bite her so fucking deep she has scars. Don't look at me like that, like you're afraid of me."

"I am afraid sometimes," Catarina said honestly. "Right now is the first time I really saw it in you. The stamp of danger that means you've battled and won a million times and you don't back down—ever."

"Why would that scare you? You're under my protection."

Her body jerked. She knew he saw it because his eyes narrowed and moved over her face. "I was under his protection. He told me that a million times."

"Cat. Come here."

Her gaze flew to his. "I'm right here."

"Come here." He said it softly. The command he could put into his voice was there and her heart beat faster.

Catarina slipped out of her chair before she could stop

herself and went to stand in front of him. He caught her wrist and tugged her down onto his lap. His arm slid around her waist and pulled her tight against his body.

"Relax, baby. Just let me hold you for a minute."

Another minute went by. She tried to hold out. It was insane to sit on his lap and allow this kind of intimacy. This wasn't about sex at all. This was about comfort. Caring. She couldn't do that with him.

"Settle, Kitten," Eli insisted, his fingers easing the tension out of her neck.

When he did that, massaged her neck and shoulders, she turned to putty in his hands. She found herself melting into him in spite of her resolve to hold something of herself back.

"That's my girl," he whispered, and skimmed his mouth along her neck and then behind her ear. "Cordeau must have studied your family and realized that there was a good chance you were a shifter. Females are difficult to find. I should know, I traveled the world, all the rain forests, everywhere I knew that there were pockets of us left."

He stroked her hair, and she fit her head more comfortably into his shoulder. He was a big man with the roped muscles of his kind, and he made her feel very safe. She knew she shouldn't allow it, but she'd never had that luxury of safe before.

"He didn't make any effort to spend time with you, or build a relationship. He went about his business, and when you needed a little love and guidance, he hurt you. He's a rogue. You don't understand that term and maybe you never should. Rogues aren't allowed to live. Other shifters hunt them. We have our own police force for that."

"Are you part of that?" she asked.

He didn't answer her question. "I know I scare you, Kitten, but I'm not like Cordeau. Never like him. Do you understand?"

She wasn't certain she did. "What do you mean when you say your leopard is hard to handle sometimes?"

He sighed. "His moods are fierce and passionate. Obviously they affect me. He's bad-tempered and he doesn't like
bullshit. I have to keep a strong hold on him all the time."

She wiggled to get free and was surprised when he let
her go. Surprised and maybe a little disappointed. She
slipped back in her chair and picked up her coffee cup
again. The coffee was cold, but it gave her something to do.

"I want to see him. Your leopard. And I want to watch
him run." The moment she blurted it out, her heart began
to pound. She hadn't meant to say that, it just slipped out.
She'd been thinking about it, but she wasn't certain she was
ready for it.

The smile faded from his face. He took the coffee cup
from her hand and set it on the table and reached both
hands to frame her face. "Catarina, you're terrified of my
leopard. Why would you ask to see him?"

There was no way to avoid his eyes. All amber. When he
looked at her, she always felt like she was the only woman
in his world and he didn't see anything or anybody but her.
That wasn't the truth because he was always aware of
everything around him, but still, he made her feel that way.

"I am afraid, Eli, I'm not going to lie. But I've only seen
one in a rage and he hurt me. It hurt for weeks. I have nightmares about his leopard. I really thought I was going to die.
And then on top of that, I believe absolutely that he allows
the leopard to hunt and kill humans. People disappear and
he's suspected of getting rid of them, but no one can prove
it. I'm terrified and I've got one in me. I don't want to be a
monster. I don't want to live as a monster or knowing I'm
living with one."

He bent forward until his lips brushed hers. "I understand. I know a lot of shifters, Cat. I'll introduce you to a
few someday. They're good people. They risk their lives to
help people in trouble. Their leopards don't hunt and kill
anything human, nor does mine. I would never allow my
leopard to hunt and kill for sport."

Her heart was doing a strange fluttery thing again, just because he was so gentle with her. His kiss was feather-light, barely there, but she felt it all the way to her toes.

"You'll show me then?"

"Why do you want to see him run free?"

She took in a deep breath, let it out. He was still holding her eyes and she couldn't look away, so he would see how important it was to her. "I've never been truly free. If my leopard can do that, it might just be the greatest thing in the world."

Eli's heart turned over. She was right, whether she knew it or not. She wouldn't be free of him—not ever. He wouldn't let her go. If she tried to leave him or run, he would find a way to make her stay and work overtime to try to find a balance with her. She didn't understand yet about the way leopards mated for life. She was holding herself back from him. He knew she didn't trust him, but he'd work on that. Still, she wasn't going to leave him.

He knew what kind of man he was. He didn't try to hide it from her now. He was the head of his home. The man. That wasn't politically correct, but he couldn't be anything other than who he was. He was alpha all the way. He liked to be the dominant in all things, including in bed. He enjoyed taking care of Catarina. He liked doing little things for her and wanted her to feel special. He wanted her to make his house a home, her home. Later, down the road, when they were married with several children and he knew she wasn't going to have one foot out the door, he'd carve a sign and hang it on the gate. Cat's Lair. He'd already made up his mind to that.

"You can run free in your leopard form," he said. "And you'll be there with her. You'll experience it with her. And you'll love it, Catarina; I do."

He let his hands fall away because he wanted her all over again and she needed to heal. Fast. His leopard was pushing close to the surface all the time now, aware of her leopard so close to emerging.

"Will you then? Let me see him?"

"If I'm in leopard form, I won't be able to stand in front of you and shield you if you get too scared, but if you call my name, I'll shift back immediately."

Her eyes lit up, although her hands trembled, her fingers twisting together nervously. "Then you'll really do it, Eli? Let me see him?"

He nodded. "Baby, listen to me. My leopard is big. He's an alpha. But he would never, under any circumstances hurt you. You hold his mate inside of you. You are part of his mate. He knows that and he knows you're mine. I'm not saying this very well, talking, explaining things, is not my forte—but you belong to us. To both of us, and he would die to protect you."

Her small tongue came out and she moistened her lips. "When?"

"Right now. You've got your courage up, let's just do it now."

He saw her take a breath, but she stood up. His Catarina. Yeah, she was scared, but she didn't let that stop her.

"Um. Eli. I'm not dressed. I don't even have shoes."

"You don't need shoes or clothes. You're just going to sit in the truck and watch."

"What if I want to touch him? Can I do that?"

She was killing him. "Yes, baby, if you want to touch him, you certainly can." He got the truck keys and came back to her, reaching out his hand. She hesitated, but she took it.

"I'm going to take us out into the middle of the property, Kitten. That way no neighbor might accidentally stop by. It doesn't happen often but I don't take chances. You always have to remember, you can't take chances either, once she's emerged. She's your responsibility. You have to control her and protect her."

He opened the door to the passenger side and when she stepped up, his hand slid over her bottom, shaping her butt, a small gesture of male possessiveness. He didn't do it with the long shirt over her bottom, he slipped his hand under the material to caress bare skin. She recognized the gesture for what it was. The warm slide of his hand sent heat rushing through her body, streaking through her veins like a drug. Once she was in the seat, he leaned in to fasten her seat belt.

"You do know I'm perfectly capable of putting on my seat belt," she said, mostly because his head rubbed against her breasts, sending sparks of electricity straight to her feminine channel.

"Of course I know," Eli said. "But then I'd miss a golden opportunity." His fingers deftly undid two of her buttons and his mouth closed over her breast, mostly because he couldn't resist her, but also to see her reaction.

She gasped and her arms went around his head, cradling him. That was all his Cat, not her leopard. She didn't realize that she should have pushed him away. Been angry as all hell. She shouldn't have been cradling his head to her while his mouth suckled her breast and his tongue pulled at her nipple. He used the edge of his teeth and felt her shiver. Perfect. She was born for him. If he had any doubts, which he didn't, this would have proven his point. She belonged to him.

Reluctantly he lifted his head and brushed a kiss across her mouth before closing her door firmly. She looked a little dazed, a look he'd come to know and would forever want to see on her face. She was beautiful, his Cat, and she didn't have a clue.

Her fingers went to the two buttons he'd slid open when he got behind the wheel. "Leave it, baby. I like to look at you."

Again, she should have told him to go to hell and slapped his face, but instead, her hands dropped to her lap, her fingers twisting together. His shirt on her was open nearly to her belly button. He could see the curve of both breasts and the darker nipple of one.

"Fucking beautiful," he whispered as he started the truck. And it wasn't all about her looks, although she was beautiful. She suited him. She didn't keep her body from him even though she wasn't certain of them together. He hadn't thought it was possible to find a woman who would take him as he was.

He reached over and captured her hand, bringing it to his thigh. He held it there, needing the closeness, wanting her to understand it wasn't just about sex with her. He knew he made it seem like that, but truthfully, everything about her appealed to him and it had from the moment he'd laid eyes on her.

A man could go his entire life waiting to find that perfect someone—most gave up and settled. He wasn't settling. She was the one. He'd known it instinctively, even before he knew she was leopard. Now he was absolutely certain. He was also certain, if he was Rafe Cordeau, he wouldn't give her up. He would be hunting her. Cordeau was coming. Sooner or later he would find her, but she wouldn't be defenseless anymore. Eli planned to teach her leopard how to fight just as he was teaching the woman. And Cordeau would have to go through him and his leopard to get to Catarina.

They drove along a narrow road toward the center of the property. He wanted her to see how beautiful the land was. It was important to him that she liked it. It would be her home and her leopard would want to run free here. Once she relaxed, her gaze was on the window and he was fairly certain she liked what she saw.

"This is good, baby," he said softly, bringing the truck to a halt. He kept possession of her hand, bringing it up to the warmth of his mouth. "I don't want you to be afraid. We'll open the door . . ."

She shook her head. "I want to be outside. With the leopard."

That surprised him. Clearly she was afraid. He studied her face. "Kitten, there's no need to prove anything to me."

She lifted her chin. "You asked me to trust you, Eli. I'm

going to stand outside with a leopard, and if it attacks me I'll know you're full of shit."

He couldn't help but smile. "That isn't even logical. A leopard can kill in seconds. You know that. Why would you put yourself in jeopardy like that just to see whether or not I'm telling you the truth?"

She didn't answer him. In fact, her gaze slid away from his. His heart stuttered in his chest and he swore under his breath. She thought she was risking her life, and if he wasn't telling her the truth, it didn't matter to her. She had nowhere to go, and after the sex they'd shared, she knew she wouldn't be sharing that with Cordeau. She'd rather be dead. He hooked his hand around the back of her head and pulled her in close to him.

"I'm telling you the truth, Cat, but your thinking is totally fucked up. You know that, don't you? There's always a way out."

"Not with Rafe there isn't. Let's just do this, Eli, before I vomit all over the seat."

He leaned close and kissed her. She tasted as sweet as ever. She wasn't going to puke but she was scared, he could feel her body tremble. "We'll do this then, baby, and you'll see that it's all going to be all right."

10

Eli let his hands slide away from Catarina and, curiously, he felt the loss. She made him laugh more than anyone he'd ever met. She cooked for him. When he got in her space and put his mouth on her breast, she cradled his head to her. He loved the shy hesitation in her eyes and the way she was so honest about wanting to please him. He *detested* that he'd ever made her doubt him.

Eli yanked open her door. She already had the seat belt off. She hadn't done up the buttons, leaving them just as he asked. His heart stuttered again. Who had a woman like this one? His hands spanned her waist and he lifted her out of the seat to carry her around to the bed of the truck.

"Take my shirt off, Cat," he instructed. "A leopard has to stash clothes around the property just in case. I have to be naked to shift."

Her eyes jumped to his. She licked her lips, and he groaned.

"Baby. I need the shirt gone. You need to sit on the tail-gate and I don't want your ass on that cold, dirty metal."

A hint of a smile stole into her eyes and that made him want to groan all over again. She leaned away from him so she could pull his shirt up and over his head. First one arm was free and then the other. He opened the tailgate and laid the shirt down before depositing her there. She didn't take her eyes off of his face.

"Shifting with a hard-on is much more difficult," he growled at her.

Her hint of a smile widened into the real thing. She swung one bare foot. "I'm sure you're up to the task."

"You could help me out . . ." he suggested, not making it a command, just teasing.

She wiggled her fingers imperiously at him to get on with it. Eli grinned at her and pulled off his boots and socks and then his hands dropped to the drawstring of his sweats. She didn't look away. He stepped in close to her, wedging his hips between her legs, pushing her thighs open with his.

"Actually, Kitten, if you want to see my leopard you can do this for me."

She tilted her head. "Do you think I won't?"

Her hands shook but they went instantly to his drawstring. She loosened it and then opened it, her fingers working deftly in his waistband to push the material off his hips. Eli wanted to throw his head back and roar like the leopard he was. She was his all right, every damn inch of her. He was beginning to realize that all the time he'd been trying to hold her to him, she was winding herself around his heart. He was more than halfway in love with her—he was already gone.

His hand dropped to her thigh. Her skin was warm and soft, just like he knew it would be. He had the taste of her in his mouth and his body already recognized the feel of her. He ran his palm up her thigh and then around to the inside. He felt her incredible heat radiating, beckoning.

"Are you wet for me?" he murmured.

"Don't get distracted. You're showing me your leopard," she whispered, but her hand curled over his cock.

His body shuddered. "You aren't helping." He couldn't resist seeing for himself. His fingers found her hot core and yes, she was wet for him. Scared of his leopard and still wet for him. Perfect for him. *Perfect.*

He kissed her hard, plundering her mouth, taking her tongue and taking command. She gave herself to him, her mouth moving under his, following his lead, tentative, but still opening to him. It took a moment for him to get himself under control, to feel the small trembling in her body. When he lifted his head, her gaze shifted from his immediately and dropped to her hands.

"Don't, baby, don't do that." He caught her chin in his hand and tipped her face up. "Don't be embarrassed because you want me. There isn't anything wrong with it."

She nodded, pressing her lips together, but her eyes didn't quite meet his.

"Catarina. You know what I want." His hand went to the nape of her neck, fingers moving gently on her tension-filled muscles.

Eli waited until her eyes were on his. He nodded approvingly. "Thank you, Cat." He kept his voice gentle with an effort. "Now talk to me. What's going on in your head right now?"

"Maybe I don't want to talk about it, Eli."

"I get that." He wasn't used to prying things out of people. He rarely asked twice and very few men argued with him, let alone women. Most recognized the alpha, never understanding a good portion of that was his leopard. She recognized the leopard and she still struggled against his authority. "I do, Kitten. But this is about you coming to terms with our future. If we don't talk, bring things out into the open, how are we ever going to work things out between us?"

"You just keep pushing me, Eli," she said. "I need a little breathing room. This is difficult to come to terms with, all of it."

"You think I don't know that?" Eli raked a hand through his hair. "I'd give you all the time in the world if we had it, Cat, but we don't. She's so close my leopard is getting crazy. We have to be right, you and me, solid. You have to know you can count on me. You'll be scared and you won't know what to do. I'll be the one seeing you through it and I want to make it as easy as possible. So talk to me."

Her eyes shifted again. He waited. He actually counted every one of his heartbeats. He couldn't allow her to win this one. It was too important. She did deserve all the time in the world, but they didn't have it and that was a fact. He remained absolutely silent and still, focusing his eyes on her, his will.

Catarina sighed and lifted her gaze to his once more. "You don't understand. I realized that I can't go back with Rafe, not after everything between us, which essentially means I'm staying with you. But you hurt me. I let you in so deep, and I didn't even know I was doing it. You hurt me far worse than he ever did. I have to get to a place where I can let that go. I don't want to be the type of person who brings up the past and throws it in someone's face, and that means I have to deal with it and forgive you or I can't be with you. More, I have to trust you again. To do that, I'd be giving you everything, stripping myself bare. And if I do that . . ." She trailed off.

He kept his face blank, but it was a body blow. *You hurt me worse than he ever did.* He wanted to roar with rage. He'd handled everything the wrong way with her. *I don't want to be the type of person who brings up the past and throws it in someone's face, and that means I have to deal with it and forgive you.* She'd delivered that in her soft little confessional voice as if she was the one who had sinned, not him. *Giving you everything. Stripping myself bare.*

She was definitely going to kill him if she kept saying things like that in a voice that penetrated through all of his armor and pierced him straight through the heart. He pressed one hand to his chest, hoping he wasn't having a heart attack and it was just penance for betraying her. She had been such a damn innocent and he'd ripped that away from her as well.

"If I trust you again, Eli, you could destroy me. That's what I'd be giving to you. The power to destroy me. That's what you're really asking of me."

There it was. She saw what he was asking—no, demanding—of her. She knew what the ultimate price would be. She was going in with both eyes open, no rose-colored glasses like she'd had in the warehouse. She knew what he was and now, what he was capable of. Still, Catarina was holding out the world to him. That was the one piece she didn't get. What she would be giving to *him*.

She could bring him to his knees without even trying. He didn't deserve her. He had a hell of a lot of sins on his soul, and she didn't. She was clean and good and damn it all, he was keeping her anyway, even when he knew he shouldn't. That wasn't his leopard talking, that was the man.

"I know that, baby, I know what you'd be handing me. All I can do is tell you I'd cherish that gift." He poured sincerity into his voice. She was leopard enough to hear it.

"I don't want to be like him." She rushed the second confession, the words tumbling out fast. "If I'm like him, I want your leopard to kill me. I do, Eli. I don't want any part of him inside me."

"Cat." He framed her face with both hands. Now his heart broke for her. "You're nothing like him. Neither is your leopard."

"You can't know that. You said there are rogues. What if my leopard is like that? The first time when I was with you, it hurt. Really hurt and I didn't even slow down. And then I wanted more. That isn't normal, and no matter what you tell me, I know it isn't."

He winced. There it was again. Cat blaming herself for something he did. Her first time should have been slow and gentle, not ruled by two leopards coming so close to the surface. He was the one who was supposed to have control. He was the one with a lifetime of experience dealing with his savage, brutal, very alpha leopard. Catarina still had no way of knowing what to expect, let alone learning how to deal with her leopard.

"Kitten, if you don't listen to anything else I have to say to you this afternoon, hear this. You're sweet and kind and good. You're an innocent in all this. That leopard inside you, she's just as confused and afraid as you are. She's being driven by nature just the way you are right now. You'll control her because you have to. You'll feel her needs and you'll take care of her. She'll do the same for you."

Her teeth tugged on her lower lip and he stopped himself from groaning, stopped his body from reacting. She needed care. Gentle handling. While their leopards were settled, he knew it was the only time he'd have to give her those things.

"This all happened to me because of her—my leopard. All of it. My mother handing me over to Rafe. Rafe killing April and the others. You taking a job in the dojo and befriending me. All of it, because of her."

He shook his head. "No, none of that was her fault. That was all Rafe Cordeau and your mother." He wasn't going to soft-soap any of that for her. Her mother was just as guilty as Rafe was. "She sold you to a man who took a chance on what you were. He couldn't know for certain and that's why you had more freedom at first but he began watching you closer as you got older."

"If my leopard hadn't emerged, he would have hunted me in the swamp."

For some reason, Eli couldn't bring himself to believe that. He wasn't certain Cordeau was as devoid of feelings for her as she believed. Cordeau had shown a few protective instincts, not just possessive ones. The DEA had quite a long file on the man, dating back to when she was just a child. She'd gone up a tree, a tall one and she'd taken a nasty fall.

Cordeau had been conducting a business meeting with two of his local distributors and he'd launched himself from his chair, sprinting to break her fall. They had a series of photographs and two of them showed his face very clearly. It hadn't been the face of a man who didn't care, but Eli wasn't going to tell her that. Not now, maybe never, and that made him an even bigger bastard. Strangely, both of the distributors had disappeared about two months later, neither body ever found.

"You don't know that for certain, Cat."

She shrugged. He caught the front of her shirt in his fists and tugged her closer as he leaned down and brushed a comforting kiss across her mouth.

"I'm going to shift. I can go fast or slow. Up close or far away. You tell me how you want it, Cat, and it's yours."

She blinked. He realized she hadn't expected any concessions from him. Her deep cobalt blue eyes searched his face for a long time as if looking for something. It took a few moments and then she took a deep breath. "Up close and fast. Rafe was across the room from me and shifted very slowly. It looked torturous and so scary. I've never been so frightened of anything in my life."

He frowned and stroked his hand down the side of her face, more to soothe her than because he wanted to feel the softness of her skin—and he really wanted to feel how soft she was. "Why up close and fast?"

Her chin went up. "You said how I wanted it was mine to say."

He studied her face another minute. "Just say my name," he reminded her.

Catarina nodded, and Eli shifted. It was not just fast, he shifted with blurring speed. He was so fast she nearly missed it because she blinked. One moment he was a large, intimidating man and the next he was a *huge* leopard. The head on the male seemed almost as big as she was.

There wasn't time for panicking, she didn't even scream,

her breathing catching in her lungs and holding there, trapped. Gold eyes locked on her, smoldering, pupils dilated. So gold they were pure fire. Focused on her. Unblinking. Absolutely intelligent. Eli's eyes. She would know his eyes anywhere.

The leopard was all roped muscle and thick, dark fur, a massive black panther. He looked . . . powerful. Invincible. Up this close she could see the shadowy rosettes stamped deep in the dark fur. She recognized a very efficient killing machine when she saw it.

She held her breath, hearing the roar of thunder as her blood pulsed in her ears. She felt her heart hammering hard in her chest. Strangely, there wasn't the terrible fear that still woke her from a dead sleep, the other leopard snarling, rushing her, the eyes intent on her as prey. This leopard was just as deadly, but he was also Eli. She could see evidence of him there in the way his eyes watched her so closely.

Eli always watched her with the same intense stare. The way he looked at her, so focused, as if he could see into her soul, always thrilled and terrified. She felt both emotions right then as well.

Eli's leopard took a step toward her, not the freeze-frame stalk of a leopard hunting, but a slow, measured step that brought the large cat directly in front of her. The way it positioned itself, it was almost as if it was a sentry, a guardian, seeking to keep her safe. She didn't understand why this animal, every bit as large and intimidating as Rafe's leopard, could make her feel so different.

For the first time, once the animal had taken up location in front of her, he broke his stare with her, turning his head and lifting it toward the air. She knew what he was doing, all those hairs, deeply embedded in tissue surrounded by nerve endings transmitted data to his brain. Like a guidance system, the information giving the exact location of vegetation and other obstacles so the leopard could move silently in the dark. The radar system also allowed him to find and identify enemies or prey quite easily.

Like Eli could. Or she could. She'd always known it wasn't just about great night vision, that something else allowed her to move so easily in the pitch-black warehouse without ever falling over an obstacle, she just knew where everything was. She knew she could because she'd practiced. She hadn't known how it worked for her, only that it did, but her warning system was a little spotty at times. It seemed to be growing stronger and she thought it was because she practiced so much, but now she thought maybe it was because her leopard was getting closer to the surface all those times.

It was impossible to be so close to such a large cat, a predator, and not feel the immense power and mystery. Yes, he was definitely a killing machine, the top of the food chain, but he was beautiful, magnificent even. Catarina shifted position carefully, pulling her feet up slowly onto the tailgate. She tried to be silent and stealthy, to not draw the cat's attention. She wanted it to stay facing away from her so she could take in its amazing beauty without any fear, but the moment she inched one foot up, it swung its head around and the stare of golden fire locked onto her own.

She froze. Her heart stuttered to a halt and her breath once more became trapped in her lungs. They stared into one another's eyes for a long time. Time enough for her lungs to burn for air. That long. Still, she couldn't look away, mesmerized by the beauty and focus there.

The leopard shifted his weight and from his sitting position, jumped easily into the back of the pickup truck with her. He landed silently, just to one side of her, but all that muscle was heavy and she felt the truck's bed settle for a moment.

She would not be a coward and call Eli's name. It felt too much like surrender and she'd already surrendered her body to the man. She wouldn't surrender her courage. She stayed very still. It seemed that as curious as she was about the large leopard, he was just as curious about her, extending his head toward her. The head seemed much larger up close than it appeared when the animal had been on the ground.

The leopard shifted position and involuntarily, her body jerked. The animal had to have registered her heart pounding out of control. Still, she wouldn't give in, wouldn't call Eli's name. She felt the brush of the animal's body against her shoulder as he moved behind her until she lost complete sight of him. She froze again, her entire body nearly seizing with fear. She closed her eyes, waiting for the terrible moment when she would feel his claws raking her back, his teeth puncturing her skin.

The leopard made a soft chuffing sound. It was quiet. Nonthreatening. She didn't open her eyes. The animal moved against her back, rubbing his fur over the shirt she wore, his chin on top of her head. She was forced to take a breath before she passed out. She could smell him, his wild, exotic, *feral* scent filling her nostrils.

She wished for her leopard. She prayed for her leopard. "I brought you out here so you could be with him. Go to him. Let me slip away," she whispered to the cat inside of her. "Save me."

Eli hadn't guessed what she was up to. She needed her leopard to emerge right there. Right then. If she could bring her out and keep her out, Catarina Benoit could disappear and she wouldn't have to face either of the powerful predators who threatened her.

She hadn't told Eli the entire truth about Rafe. Rafe was an extremely violent man. His temper was fierce, fast and explosive. Not like fiery passionate. He was all ice, even when he exploded. No, he'd never actually struck her or even manhandled her in the way Eli had, but that certainly wasn't true of any other living soul, man or woman, in their household.

Twice he had punched the wall inches from her face during one of her transgressions. He hadn't said a word to her. He hadn't raised his voice. He'd stalked across the room and punched a hole through the wall, all the while staring into her eyes. She had gone for a swim in the pool, which she did every single day, and she'd slipped on the deck as she was diving, just enough to throw her off balance.

The accident was freaky. She'd somehow curled in on herself and knocked her shoulder against the side of the pool, barely missing her head. She had a nasty scrape down the side of shoulder and arm. The moment he was told, which was the instant he returned home, he had stalked toward her, and *pow*. She could still hear the sound of the blow and see the concentrated venom in his eyes. He'd been enraged at her. Over an accident. That was Rafe. That was her other choice. She couldn't imagine having a child with him and if he wanted a female leopard, it had to be because he wanted a child, another shifter to inherit his business.

"Come on out," she whispered to her female. Invited. Pleaded. "Here's your big chance, girl. He's right there and he looks pretty handsome. You two can run off together and live life free. Live it large. Just for me."

Nothing. Here was the hussy's mate, and she didn't so much as show one bit of interest, not even with him making the kind of soft chuffing that should have won a girl leopard's heart.

Catarina sighed and hung her head. Time for another plan. Rafe was out. He just was. She couldn't have the kind of sex with him she'd had with Eli *willingly* and then have him treat her the way he would. She would be nothing more than a means to an heir, and he would never again allow her to escape. It would be a life sentence in hell with a man who had an empire bought and paid for with guns, drugs and prostitutes. With murder. He wasn't a great choice no matter what she'd told Eli.

She huffed out her breath a second time, this time harder than the first. On to the second choice, which, really, really sucked because there were a few good things about Eli. He could kiss. Really kiss. Okay, the man was seriously good at kissing. Hot, off the charts kind of kissing, and the moment he put his mouth to hers, she didn't have a brain anymore. Everything in her head simply fried.

She looked over her shoulder to stare into the cat's golden eyes. The cat's head was inches from her, his eyes focused right on hers. The impact was terrible to take. He was beautiful and deadly. She saw it so clearly. And those eyes were Eli's eyes. She wasn't going to pretend to herself that Eli wasn't every bit as dangerous as Rafe was. He could be just as violent, and he would rule her life. That was a given.

She couldn't think about the pros and cons of staying with Eli, not with the huge leopard hovering over her. She pointed out to the vast tract of land. "Go run." Like she could order a leopard around. She couldn't order the man around. She clearly couldn't take care of herself, even after all the effort she put into learning how. "Do it or just bite me really hard. It shouldn't take you long to kill me, so that or go run."

Eli. Any relationship they had would be all about sex. Not for a baby shifter, but for raw, insane, scorching hot, burn in hell forever sex. She would be totally consumed by him. Totally. His voice alone made her shiver. He knew how to use his hands, his mouth, his tongue and most definitely his cock. He was brilliant with that.

She knew he was rough and a little crude. He had tats she wanted to spend hours poring over and maybe even tracing with her tongue. She'd considered that in the warehouse before he'd ever kissed her. Amazing eyes. His body was hard and powerful and just plain hot—like his sex.

She wanted to hit her head against a wall. Option number two wasn't looking much better than option number one, because when Rafe chose to end the relationship he'd just kill her. When Eli chose to end it, he would destroy her and leave her alive.

The cat rubbed up against her a little harder, chuffed a little softer and nudged her side as it leapt to the ground.

Option three, death by leopard, was looking slim. The

cat wasn't going to pounce on her and kill her. He stretched languidly, and with one more look over his shoulder, he took off running. The cat was a thing of beauty, the muscles rippling effortlessly beneath the fur, the run silent. The cat definitely looked like freedom personified.

She bit at her lower lip, watching the leopard until it disappeared into foliage. She was alone. The space around her filled up with sound. Birds. Insects. Even a frog, indicating water very close by. Her hands dropped to the buttons of the shirt and slid them back into position.

So that meant she had to come up with option four. She just had to be logical and really think it all the way through. She'd gotten away from Rafe. She'd escaped when everyone would have told her it was impossible. How the DEA had spotted her, she had no idea, but still, she was smart.

People didn't get that she was intelligent because of her lack of formal education. It hadn't occurred to anyone that she might be able to learn to read on her own. There were children's shows on television. Even language shows. And she'd watched every one of them over and over. Children's educational shows. They'd saved her life.

Once she could read enough, she'd used the Internet to find places for math and science. For history lessons. But always, always, she read. Newspapers, magazines, every book in Rafe's house. She read dictionaries and the labels of cans. She read the ingredients of everything that came into the house. She didn't want Rafe to know she could read and she made certain she never made a mistake in front of him.

She knew he tracked her computer, reading everything she did on it, learning everywhere she went, so she used his computer, the one in his sacred office, the one he never once considered she might touch. She'd used his own computer to educate herself and she'd done it right under his nose.

The moment she knew Rafe was a shifter, she tried to find out more about them, but there wasn't really information anywhere, so she read up on leopards and studied their behavior.

Clearly shifters were different. Leopards were loners, they didn't live in groups as Eli hinted some shifters did. Leopards had multiple mates and the females raised their offspring alone. She had the feeling shifters didn't do that either, but she didn't know. It was a possibility and that needed to be addressed at some point if she didn't get away from Eli.

She could do this. She could think her way out of this, or at least hit on some kind of a plan. Part of the problem was Eli. He did more than just melt her body every time he looked at her. She still remembered sweet. Worse, he still gave her sweet. He treated her as if she mattered. He didn't need to look after her the way he did, but then he'd done it before, drawing her in, only to stomp on her.

Eli had tons of experience when it came to sex, she at least recognized that. She knew she could be somewhat submissive. It was impossible not to be, raised the way she was, but it didn't make sense that she found his commanding voice so absolutely compelling. Each time he gave her an order, delivered in a low, sexy tone, her body went up in flames. Was that something to do with being a shifter? His cat dominant over hers? She didn't know. She didn't know why she liked caring for him so much. Or why she liked obeying him when they had wild sex. She just didn't know.

She slipped from the tailgate, caught up his clothing and brought it with her back to the cab. Her gaze slid to the ignition. He'd left the keys in the truck. She'd been fairly certain she'd noticed that little detail, and if she noticed it, he had. So, what was he playing at? Testing her? If so, she ought to drive back to the house and let him walk home. She bit her lip, for the first time finding a little humor in the situation. That was, if she could find the house and if she could figure out how to drive.

She climbed into the relative warmth of the cab. The sun shone through the windows, warming the leather interior. She took the keys out of the ignition and stared at them, before folding each item of his clothing carefully and setting them on the backseat in plain sight.

She was exhausted from all the sex and trying to figure out a future. Her leopard was no help, sleeping or something rather than giving her any clues as to what to do. She went through the glove compartment and found a set of handcuffs, but nothing else that might give her something to get an advantage over Eli.

Catarina found herself shivering at the thought. He wasn't the kind of man to cross. Not in the same way as Rafe; he wouldn't kill someone and tell her their blood was on her hands, but he'd make it known he wasn't happy. She wasn't certain she wanted to find out how.

THE leopard stretched its legs, running along the road and winding through the trees, but always in a tight circle that kept the truck in the center. He detoured when the scent of three men he recognized drifted from just over the edge of his property line. His acreage butted up next to Jake Bannaconni's estate. His neighbor was a billionaire with oil on his property, and twice he'd mentioned to Eli that he was certain there was oil on his property as well.

Eli hadn't cared much one way or the other. Not then. He had plenty of money from his trust and a job that kept him gone most of the time. Still, if Bannaconni said there was oil, there probably was.

He'd met the man through a mutual friend, Drake Donovan. Eli had spent weeks with Drake in the Borneo rain forest, and Drake had taught him more about shifters in those few weeks than his father had ever had a chance to teach him. Bannaconni had somehow tracked him down, explaining Drake needed a bone graft from a shifter, that if he didn't get one soon, he would never shift again and they'd lose him. Eli had immediately volunteered for testing and had been compatible, grateful he could repay Drake for his friendship and knowledge.

He'd refused to take the considerable sum of money

Bannaconni had offered him, but he'd let it be known he was interested in acreage out of the way where his leopard could run free, and to call if they stumbled on anything suitable. Bannaconni contacted him the instant the property next to his came up for sale.

Eli had a lot of respect for Jake Bannaconni. He could have purchased the prime real estate and added it to what he already had, especially suspecting oil on it, but he'd let Eli know it was coming up for sale and when Eli was interested quietly arranged the sale and hid it under multiple layers of his own corporations.

It was Jake's wife, Emma, whom he emailed when he was coming to the property. She personally didn't stock his fridge, he knew better than that, but she had the supplies bought and delivered. The Bannaconnis were good neighbors and Jake certainly deserved a heads-up that a rogue would eventually be coming their way.

He shifted as he got closer. As a rule shifters weren't in the least bit modest, but he was always careful to know who was close by before he allowed himself to be seen.

"Jake?" he called out the moment he identified two of Jake's men with him.

Joshua Tregre and Elijah Lospostos were two of Jake's shifter crew. Eli knew them both fairly well. They'd come from Borneo with Drake to work for Jake. Eli knew Drake was now living in New Orleans but was still very tight with Jake and these two men.

"Eli?" Jake called back.

The three men moved closer to the property line.

"I've been out for a run," Eli warned them.

They didn't hesitate. "I've got a spare pack," Joshua said. "Do you want a pair of jeans?"

"Seems silly just for a short visit. I've got my mate in the truck and she could decide to take off any minute," Eli said.

"Not happy about being your mate, I take it," Jake said, stepping through the foliage. He was a big man, like Eli.

Like all of them, they were built with the roped, powerful muscle of their kind.

"No, can't say she is. She's got a rogue after her. Not only is he very dangerous, but he's built himself a large crime network. He owns just enough cops to get information very quickly."

"You got a name?" Bannaconni asked.

"Rafe Cordeau."

Elijah made a soft sound, a kind of warning growl at the back of his throat. "He's a bad one, boss," he said. "Rumor is that he likes to bring his enemies to the swamp and let his leopard hunt. I heard a whisper that he lost his most prized possession. She with you?" His mercury eyes met Eli's. "Because if that woman is the one he's been looking for, he's going to come at you with everything he's got to get her back."

"I'm well aware of that. I've been chasing this bastard for over two years with the DEA and haven't gotten anything on him that would stick. Every time we had him, our witness disappeared right from under our noses. Every safe house we put them in was found and penetrated, nothing has worked. Now I know why. I had no idea he was a shifter."

"He knows to stay clear of Drake's lair and the Boudreaux boys in the bayou and swamps. They're all in law enforcement in some capacity and Cordeau wants no part of them," Elijah said. "Drake married into that family, and he runs a tight lair. I've had a couple of sit-downs with Cordeau. It was tense, to say the least. My uncle was in power back then. The two of them did business together. Since I've returned to the States, he's put out a few feelers."

"I've got to take him down," Eli said. "If I don't, my woman will never rest easy again."

"You can't keep a shifter locked up," Jake said, watching him close.

"I have no intentions of locking him up, Jake," Eli said, knowing his eyes had gone cool and watchful. His cat surged close. He'd been close all along, but the thought of meeting Cordeau and taking him out permanently had his cat raking for freedom.

"Do you want extra patrols over there? More eyes on your woman?" Jake offered.

Immediately his leopard roared a challenge and he had to fight to keep him under control. "Her female hasn't emerged yet and my male is difficult at the best of times. I wouldn't want to vouch for him right now. She's close though."

"Once she emerges," Jake said, "bring her over to meet Emma."

"Jake." Both Eli and Elijah spoke his name at the exact same time in the same warning voice.

"He kills entire families. Anyone befriending Catarina," Eli said. "I thank you for your offer, but I don't want to put Emma in danger, especially now. I've heard you're expecting again."

A muscle ticked in Jake's jaw. "Emma could use a friend. We're set up for anything and my men will have no problems protecting a woman. Bring her over. I'll show you my setup. Your woman can get comfortable with us and if things go wrong, she'll know she has a place to go."

Eli studied Jake's face for a long time. He meant every word. Eli nodded. "I appreciate it. The only shifter she's ever encountered was Cordeau, and he terrified her. Marked her with scars, and he did it on purpose. He killed a woman, a friend of hers, and forced her hands into the blood. She was a kid. This man, he likes to hurt people, Jake. He gets off on it."

"I've met a few of those, Eli. We can't have your woman thinking that's what all shifters are. Bring her over. We'll close ranks here. She'll know she's protected."

11

CATARINA stood in the police station staring in horror at Eli. He stood with his friends, laughing, telling them how easy it was to manipulate her—how she was so hot for him she'd do anything for him. Laughter surrounded her, horrible male amusement at how weak and stupid she was to fall for him *again*.

She tried to run, but her feet were frozen. She couldn't move, locked there listening. Eli turned his head and saw her standing there, listening to every word. He sent her a cocky grin and turned back to his friends.

She fought to move, to throw off the frozen horror so she could run. She even opened her mouth to scream, but no sound emerged. When she looked again, instead of Eli, a giant black panther stood where he'd been. She whirled to run and came face-to-face with a large leopard, his lips drawn back in a snarl, already advancing on her.

She stood helplessly in the middle of the hallway,

helpless prey caught between the two leopards—and there was nowhere to go.

Kitten. Wake up, now. It's just a bad dream. Wake up.

She clung to the voice, anchoring her. Drawing her back from the edge of madness.

"Baby." Eli's soft voice penetrated, and this time she heard him.

She felt him then, his arms stealing around her, drawing her close to him. The terrible paralysis ended and she was able to fight. She used every trick she knew, everything both Malcom and Eli had taught her to free herself, but Eli knew them all as well. She fought silently, ferociously, dirty, using her teeth and fingernails. She knew she'd scored a couple of times when he swore.

Then she was flat on her back, Eli on top of her, pinning her down, both wrists in one of his hands, her arms stretched above her head.

"It was a nightmare, Kitten, that's all. Just a nightmare. You're safe here with me." His face was dark, lines etched deep. He looked hard and invincible and even a little frightening.

She didn't relax under him, not even when she realized he was right. "Let me up." She whispered the demand, her heart pounding. She was such a fool. She wanted to believe him so she just ignored all the evidence.

"I don't think so, babe. You need to tell me what's going on in that head of yours. I can see that nightmare had nothing to do with Cordeau and everything to do with me." With his free hand, he brushed strands of hair from her face.

She tried not to let his touch get to her. It was that easy for him, one stroke on her skin with the pads of his fingers and she was lost. Her entire body shuddered. She didn't want to feel anything for him. She wanted to curl into a little fetal ball and just cry until the room flooded with tears and she drowned.

"That's fucked up," he pointed out.

"I didn't let Cordeau in," she whispered. "Only you. I let you in."

His hand moved gently over her face. "I know you did, Kitten. I know I hurt you. I can't take that back. I can only tell you it won't happen again."

"How do I know that? How do I know that you're not keeping me here so you can win my trust again and ask me to testify against Rafe?"

He leaned down and brushed a gentle kiss across her lips. "You don't know that, but your leopard does. Your leopard knows a lie when she hears one. When she emerges, listen to her. She'll let you know if I say something she doesn't like."

Eli studied her face. She looked so young, and very exhausted. He'd come back to his truck, half expecting it to be gone, but found her asleep on her seat, the keys clutched in her hand. His clothes had been folded neatly on the backseat. There had been something touching about the fact that she'd taken the time to retrieve his clothing and folded it before putting it into the warmth of the cab.

They'd had a quiet evening together and she'd taken another long, hot bath before bed. He thought she'd settled, but clearly her dream had renewed her doubts.

"Cat, I know you're scared. I did that to you and I have to own it, but you're going to have to get past it so we can work together. I need to teach you how to fight him, just in case I'm not with you when he shows up. My male needs to teach your female how to fight for the same reason. We have to be a team."

He kissed her gently again, pushing back the long silky hair that had come out of the thick braid. He preferred it down, spilling all around them on the pillows. He always wanted white sheets now, just to see the contrast of her dark hair tumbling around them. Her body trembled again, a shiver he felt moving through him. Already they were connected in the way of the shifters. The bond wasn't strong yet, but he was forging it, binding them together with tiny threads she'd never be able to break.

Her brilliant blue eyes searched his. He couldn't see one hint of her cat. She had exotic eyes, like most of their kind. He'd slowly begun learning to identify shifters by their eyes. Hers were gorgeous and very distinct in coloring and shape. Her leopard might have receded, hopefully resting up for the big event, but her eyes would always give her away. He should have known the moment he'd seen her. He'd been drawn to her, even reading her file, but he still hadn't gotten it. Drake would have scowled at him and shaken his head in irritation.

"I'm so afraid." The admission came out softly. "I barely know who I am anymore. I feel lost and alone and I don't have anyone I can trust."

Every word she said was a major body blow. He hated that he'd done that to her. Her voice shook with pain. It was impossible not to feel it. The worst part of it was he could tell she wanted to let go of what had happened and give him the same trust all over again, but she didn't know how.

"I know, sweetheart. I know you are, but I'm not going anywhere. Not ever. If you want a fucking ring right now, we'll go get one and find someone to make it legal. I'd do anything to make you feel you have someone that's going to stay and fight for you." He nibbled on her chin. Her sweet chin that sometimes lifted defiantly and made him hard just watching the tiny little gesture. He loved her rebellious. He loved her sweet. He loved her when she gave him everything.

"You know, Kitten, you do trust me a little bit. When I make love to you, you surrender totally to me. Always. You always give yourself to me."

She shook her head, frowning a little. "That's you, or maybe her. That's not me."

He kissed her neck. Kissed the fluttery pulse right there on her throat. He couldn't help himself, he had to feel it under his lips, the one little spot that confirmed she was alive, was his, lying there under him, looking up at him with her beautiful eyes.

"That's all you, Catarina. Your body knows I'm here to stay. Let me back in, sweetheart. Take another chance on me."

He kissed his way down the valley between her breasts, feeling her shiver again as the shadow on his face rasped against her sensitive skin.

"This isn't okay, Eli." Her hands curled around his shoulders and she pushed, without really exerting much effort.

"What, baby? What's not okay?"

"This. You. This is different." Fear crept into her voice.

He swept his hand down her body, his palm absorbing the warmth of her satin skin. Already there were dewdrops in the tight curls guarding treasure. He slipped his finger deep. She was tight. She was always tight. Sometimes, he thought he might not make it inside her she was so damn tight. But always, always, she was slick and hot and ready for him.

He nuzzled her breast gently, using the rough hairs along his jaw to stimulate her more. He loved the way her body was so responsive. He was the one drowning. He'd been so busy trying to convince her to fall for him, he hadn't realized just how far he'd fallen. He couldn't help himself.

He used both hands to shape her body, to slide over every lush curve and trace every rib along her narrow rib cage. She was his. All his. She might be afraid, and she might be on the verge of running, but when he had her under him, she belonged to him.

He should have taken her gently the first time. Like this. Like she feared he was doing. The rough, hard sex she could blame on their cats, but this, this was all them. The man. The woman. And it terrified her. He didn't take his gaze from hers and her every emotion was there for him to see. Pain. Fear. Need. Even the beginnings of the love he'd seen before, there in the warehouse. That's what scared her. That's what had her hands pushing at his shoulders. She could take his orders. She could take his rough. She couldn't handle sweet or gentle.

"Eli. This isn't right," she whispered again.

"This is exactly right, Cat. This is what you deserve. Slow and easy and loving." He kissed his way back up to her mouth. A sweet, fantasy mouth that left him breathless and gave him one too many erotic images playing in his head all the time.

Her eyes went wide with shock and fear. She shook her head frantically. "I don't want this."

"Baby." Gentle male amusement. He couldn't help it. "You're already wet and hot for me. What kind of man would I be to leave you like that?"

Panic spread in her eyes. She swallowed hard. "I know. It's just that you can't do it like this."

He loved that about her too. Her soft little admission. *"I know."* She didn't think to deny her state to him. She simply admitted it without even blinking. And then her soft trembling. *"You can't do it like this."* It. She couldn't say *fuck* and she wouldn't say *making love*. And that was just it. He didn't want to fuck her. He wanted to make love to her.

He kissed her. He loved her mouth and he loved kissing her. He poured love down her throat. His love. His rough, not so easy to live with, but all-encompassing love. He'd never given himself to a woman before and he never imagined he actually would. He had some stupid, lunatic idea that she would love him and he would cherish her. Care for her, but there would be some part of himself he would hold back. There was no holding back and he didn't even know when it happened. He didn't care. He kissed her with love. His love.

He knew she tasted it because he did. She drank it down her throat, let it settle in around her heart. He doubted she knew what it meant, or what it was going to change between them, but that didn't matter either. He kissed her over and over, long, telling kisses that left him stripped bare, utterly naked and vulnerable to her. Showing her what she meant to him. Without words. He'd never been good talking, but he could use his mouth and his hands and his body to show her what she was to him.

She was everything. Her mouth moved under his. Accepting. Catching fire. Letting him take her in a kind of surrender. He persisted. He didn't just want surrender. He wanted her. Catarina Benoit. The woman hiding inside a frightened girl. His little runaway. She'd been ripped from her childhood and exposed to a monster. And then when she'd taken a chance, opening herself up to him, Eli had betrayed her.

Baby, I'm taking you back. I want your heart and this time, I'll safeguard it for you, I promise.

He poured his promise down her throat and into her body as well, along with his love. He stopped being so gentle with his kisses the moment she responded, the moment she began actively participating in kissing him back. She'd never really kissed him back. Not like this, not moving her body deeper beneath his, her hands sliding around his neck, fingers finding his hair. Her tongue slid along his, danced and dueled, made her own demands.

She lit up for him like a flame. He'd lit the match and she caught fire. Heat swept through his body, turning him rock hard. It wasn't just his cock she affected, it was his entire body. He could feel his need for her in every cell, each individual muscle. His heart pounded and thunder roared in his ears. He could feel the hot blood pumping through his veins, roaring like his leopard did when it was demanding his mate.

This was all the man, not the feral cat. This was all Eli, needing Catarina. Loving her. He took his time, kissing her, making an art of it, feeding on the taste of her, committing the shape and feel of her to memory. Her lips were soft, warm, nearly indescribable for him. He was a tactile man and he loved running his tongue over her lips and tugging on her full lower lip. Little nips. Little bites. God she was gorgeous.

He loved the soft little sounds that came from her throat. She would never be a silent lover. She made noise. Lots of it. Breathy little moans. Soft little pleas. A kind of purr that nearly drove him out of his mind, and when she came, she screamed, or chanted his name. She wasn't embarrassed about sex. She was more embarrassed that she didn't know a lot about it.

He couldn't tell her what a turn-on it was for him to know that no other man had ever been inside her. Maybe that was macho of him, and very unfair, but it didn't matter, he loved that no one else had been in her mouth or her body. That he'd been her first kiss, her first everything. She belonged to him alone. No one else had even a tiny part of her. Not her heart. Not her soul. Just his.

"I've never had anything that I wanted just for mine," he admitted softly against her throat. His hand swept down to her left breast. He loved that she more than filled his large palm. She had curves and he was a man to appreciate curves, especially hers.

His fingers found her nipple and he tugged, catching her breath in his mouth. Catching her breathy little moan. Her nipples were sensitive. He liked that. He liked that she could take rough, but fell apart with gentle. He kissed his way to her right breast, flicking her nipple with his tongue before covering the dark, perfect treat with his mouth and suckling hard.

Her body arched, pressing her breast deeper into his mouth, and when he rolled and tugged on her left nipple, he was so in tune with her, he felt the electricity himself, a straight line from breast to her hot, wet, channel. Her legs moved restlessly and she bucked her hips.

"That's it, baby," he murmured softly, taking his fill of her breasts. He switched from one to the other, using the edge of his teeth and the flat of his tongue to drive her up. "Come to me, Kitten. All the way to me."

She made a soft little mewling sound and the sharp little points of her nails dug into his back. He spent time on her breasts, just the way he had her mouth, sometimes rough and then back to gentle, never letting her find a rhythm. He kept it up until her breath came in soft little gasps. His hand slid between her legs, fingers pushing into her tight sheath.

He lifted his head to watch her. She was sprawled out, her eyes on his face while his fingers stroked deep inside her.

"I'm going to . . ." she broke off, her hips undulating, bucking, needing.

"You're so fucking hot when you come for me," he whispered, meaning it. He loved watching her come. "That's what I want, Cat. Give it to me. Give it all to me." It was always the moment she was the most honest with him because she did give it all to him. To him. Eli. No one else. She came for him.

Her passage, slick and hot, clamped hard on his fingers, so hard he felt the bite right through his cock. She shuddered, cried out his name, her hands sliding down her own body from the sides of her breasts, along her ribs and belly to frame his hand with her own. All the while her eyes clung to his, while her body sucked at his fingers, pulsing around them, the tight muscles working to draw him deeper.

He leaned down and sucked her nipple deep into his hot mouth just as her body was settling. Ever so gently he brought his teeth there, biting down just hard enough that she exploded again, her body becoming a vise while his fingers worked her through her second orgasm.

He loved watching the dazed, helpless expression on her face. He loved the way she said his name, or sometimes, like now, couldn't say it. His name just formed there on her lips and stayed right through her climax. How beautiful and hot was that?

He wouldn't mind using his mouth on her and tasting all the honey spilling from her body, but he couldn't wait. He needed to be inside of her, and she was ready for him. So hot. So slick. So ready.

He pushed her knees up, laying each foot flat on the mattress, spreading her thighs. He'd only gotten into her fast and hard, forcing his way through those impossibly tight folds. This time he wanted her to feel him. To know he was inside of her. Eli was in her, not just his cock.

He let the very crown of his cock nudge into her slick, wet inferno. His body shuddered at the tight squeeze. Her eyes flew to his, her body nearly vibrating with sensation. She tugged her lower lip between her teeth. He nearly groaned. He couldn't stop himself, he leaned down to use his tongue where her teeth had just been. The action pushed his cock just a tiny bit deeper, just enough to feel the ripples of her last orgasm calling to him, beckoning.

"Can I have you, Kitten? Are you going to give yourself to me this time? I want all of you. Let me have you, baby."

She studied his face for what seemed an eternity. He didn't move, just let her body squeeze and burn the hell out of his sensitive crown. His cocked throbbed and jerked, but the rest of him remained utterly still. He saw it first in her eyes. A slow surrender. His heart beat faster. His mouth went dry.

He knew her. He knew once Catarina gave herself to him again it was a done deal until or unless he screwed up, and then he'd never have her again. This was it. Now or never. He watched her little tongue touch her lip where his had been.

"Can I have you, sweetheart?" he asked again. Softly. Letting her see him. What he felt inside for her. "Give yourself to me." Because he was never going to screw up with her again.

She nodded slowly, her gaze clinging to his. Again, her teeth were tugging hard at her bottom lip, a sign of the momentous decision she was making. There was a plea in her eyes that broke his heart. She was handing him herself once again and was terrified of the consequences. She was giving him forgiveness and a chance to start again. It was monumental and her decision humbled him. He didn't deserve it, but he was taking it.

He leaned forward again and took her mouth. Gently. Reverently. In awe of her and the gift she gave him. He slowly raised his head, one hand trailing over her breast, down her belly to the place where they were joined together. "Mine," he whispered softly. "Thank you."

He pushed a little deeper and found himself swearing softly, his teeth coming together as her hot, sweet channel closed around the first inch of him like a vise. "Fucking tight, baby," he whispered, and sank another inch so that his entire crown was totally surrounded by a tight fist of scorching flames. She took his breath away, pushed every ounce of air right out of his lungs.

He forced his body to stay slow, not wanting to be rough with her, but she was killing him. Killing him with some kind of rapture that threatened to take the top of his head off.

She was tense, her muscles taut, and he gently slipped his hands to her thighs. "Open for me, Kitten. Relax and open for me. Let me have you."

She nodded but it took a moment for her to take a breath and consciously open her knees wider for him. He rubbed the inside of her thighs with a gentle circular motion, waiting for her inner muscles to ease just a little for him. It didn't happen. She'd given herself to him, but letting him take her was another matter altogether.

Eli withdrew and she gasped, disappointment flaring in her eyes. "I'm trying, Eli," she whispered. "I really am."

"I know, baby. I just want this to be good for you. Tell me what's going on inside that beautiful head of yours. You always talk to me."

He pushed two fingers into her, stretching gently, finding her clit to stroke with the same gentleness.

"I'm so scared of this. If you're rough . . ." She trailed off when he shook his head.

"I want to make love to you, just like this. I want to feel every inch of you with my body, and I want you to feel me. This is about giving ourselves to each other, not taking the pleasure as high as it can go. This is about me worshipping your body. Because, Kitten, that's exactly what I'm doing."

"I know." Tears glittered in her eyes. "I can feel it, and it scares me, Eli. Giving myself to you scares me so bad."

"I know it does," he said, watching her face as his fingers continued stroking and working her. He watched the helpless pleasure begin to push away the tension in her face. "But you aren't paying attention, baby. I'm giving myself to you. I've never given myself to a woman before. I've never taken the time to love her. To be like this with her. This is me, giving myself to you."

The last of the tension drained from her face and she blinked rapidly to push the tears back. "Then, Eli, you need to be inside of me where you belong," she whispered softly. "Because I feel empty without you."

He closed his eyes for a moment. "Damn it, baby, you're fucking killing me here, saying things like that to me."

He replaced his fingers with the head of his cock, pushing in to feel her silken fist grasp him and try to pull him deeper into her hot depths. The vise took his breath, but still, he couldn't resist licking the honey from his fingers. Her taste was so addictive, already he missed it.

He didn't power through her tight folds, but slipped in one increment at a time, one slow inch, taking a breath each time, feeling her body fight the invasion, but slowly give way, just as the woman had done. She gave way inch by inch. Letting him take her. Letting him have her.

She gasped, her eyes wide with shock at how stretched she felt. At the stinging and burning as his thick, long cock relentlessly but slowly, sank into her. He groaned, a fine

sheen of sweat covering him. Sweat beaded on his forehead. He wasn't altogether certain he could survive long
enough to bury himself all the way inside of her.

He'd never seen anything so beautiful as the sight of
Catarina pinned beneath him, impaled by his cock, stretching her, taking her for his own. Her breasts swayed with the
short little rocking rhythm he'd set to take him into her. His
cock was in heaven or hell, he couldn't decide which. The
pleasure was so intense it was close to pain, her body so
scorching hot surrounding his with so much silk it breathed
over him as it strangled him.

He laid one hand right below her belly button, fingers
splayed wide. "Don't fucking move, baby. I want this to last
more than five seconds and right now, for the first time
since I was thirteen, I don't know if that's possible."

"Eli." Her voice pleaded with him. "I don't think I can
stay still. I really don't." Her breath came in ragged gasps
and her hips tried to buck, to force him all the way inside.
"I want to do what you ask, but . . ."

"But you will, won't you, Kitten? For me. Because I ask
you to. Because you want to please me. You'll stay still for
me." His voice had gone low, velvet and steel.

Her gaze searched his and he saw the exact moment
when she forced air through her lungs in an effort to do as
he asked. Her breasts lifted and fell. Her body stilled around
his so he could only feel her hot, wet channel clamped so
hard around him.

His woman. Listening to him. He loved that. He needed
that from his woman. He needed to know he mattered to
her and that what gave him pleasure mattered to her. His
thumb found her clit and did a slow lazy circle, watching
the helpless pleasure take her over. More honey spilled
around him, fiery hot. He wasn't going to be able to prolong
this much longer.

He wrapped his fingers around the slender calf of her leg
and drew it around his waist. The action allowed him to

sink deeper. He closed his eyes briefly, absorbing the pleasure. He drew her second leg up. "Lock your ankles, baby," he instructed softly. "Hang on to me."

She did, sliding her arms around him, the trust he needed from her there in her eyes. He caught her with one arm around her hips and pushed into her. Her tight folds gave way, and her mouth opened as he took a breath and pushed a second time. Then he was there, balls deep, the very tip of his cock bumping her cervix. He was surrounded by fire, in a tunnel of silk, a fist so tight it threatened to strangle him.

He decided she was paradise. Pure fucking paradise. He swore he could feel each individual muscle wrapped around his cock. Her body vibrated and the feeling radiated up his shaft to nearly blow that ultrasensitive crown right off of him. The tears were back in her eyes. She felt small under him, her deep channel far too tight, but now his body remembered the feeling of moving in her, being part of her.

He bent his head and kissed her belly and then began a slow slide out, withdrawing nearly to the very hilt, loving the way her eyes went wide and her lips protested. He shoved back in hard. Fast. Driving through the tight folds to claim her.

She gasped, her legs tightening around him. He smiled at her. "You like that, don't you, Kitten? You like it when I drive hard."

Her tongue licked at her lips. She nodded. "Please. Yes. Eli, please."

He gave her one more hard, fast stroke, and withdrew very slowly, watching her frown, feeling her hips buck as she tried to get him back.

"Let's see if you like this," he said softly. He set a much slower pace, going deep, but driving in slowly so he could feel the way her muscles grabbed at him. Locked down on him. He kept an easy, almost lazy pace, showing her slow and lazy could be good in a different way. He ground over her little button, keeping the friction there, watching the color spread over her body like a soft rose blush.

"Yeah, baby, you like that too, don't you?" he whispered. He kept his attention exactly where it needed to be, right over her wonderful little sweet spot, so greedy, so in need. He kept a crazy leisurely pace, feeling the power in his body, the gathering, his balls tightening. Fingers of desire, of need, danced up and down his thighs.

He felt a force gathering in her body as she surrounded him. Her thighs tensed, her breath, her arms locking him closer even as her delicate inner muscles locked down on his cock. He pulled back and slammed hard. Once. Twice. Three times.

Catarina screamed as she came, the orgasm tearing through her, taking him with her so they both went flying. He kept driving, once, twice, another time, and then it was impossible as her body flung his somewhere into subspace and he just floated there in heaven for a while.

Eli collapsed over her, holding her tight to him. She felt so small, so fragile, and yet her body could take his. He was a big man and even at his most gentle, he knew he hadn't been quite the way other men would be with her. His heart pounded into hers. He felt her frantic pulse around his shaft and his own heartbeat throb in his cock.

"I'm too heavy for you, baby. Probably crushing you. But I can't move." He didn't want to move. He wanted to stay locked with her just like he was.

She held him just as tightly, her legs and arms still wrapping him up as if he was a treasured gift. He buried his face against her shoulder and neck, turning his mouth so he could sip at the taste of her skin.

"You're the most beautiful woman I've ever seen," he whispered, meaning it, barely able to say the words aloud because deep inside he had fallen apart. He needed a few minutes to pull himself back together. He hadn't expected his feelings for her to be so intense, so overwhelming. To eat him from the inside out.

"No one's ever complimented me before," she whispered back. "I don't want you to just say it."

His heart turned over. He lifted his head to look at her, his eyes searching hers. He was leopard. He heard the ring of truth, but still, was Rafe Cordeau really such an idiot? How could he look at this woman, have her in his home, and not tell her she was beautiful?

"Baby." It was a reprimand. "Leopards don't lie to their mates. You'll know if I do. You really are the most beautiful woman I've ever seen."

She blinked at him. Her long lashes fanning down and then back up. "Probably not, but at least you think I am." A slow smile softened her voice even more than usual. "And that's saying something considering all the experience you seem to have." Her legs slipped back to the mattress, as if she was suddenly too tired to hold herself around him.

He rolled, taking her with him, so that he was still locked inside her, but she was sprawled over the top of him. She was small and light, but warm and soft. He ran both hands down her back to the slope of her butt. He loved her ass. Soft. Firm. The little indentations. His fingers found them and he rubbed there.

"You ever think about getting a tattoo?"

She lifted her head, resting her chin on his chest, one eyebrow raised. "A tattoo? Of what? Where?"

His hands slid up her rounded bottom to find the curve at the small of her back. He stroked caresses there. "Right here. Something sexy and all you. That way when I take you on your hands and knees, I can see it."

Her smile reached her eyes. "Do you think about anything besides sex?"

He grinned at her. "I did until you came along. You messed up my mind, Kitten, so now that's all I think about."

She laughed and turned her head to rest her cheek on his chest. His hands went back to smoothing over her soft skin. Making her his. Memorizing the shape and feel of her. His body enjoyed the occasional aftershock as her body began to relax all the way, her skin melting into the heat of his.

He had never held a woman this way. So intimately. He had never considered he might be a man to want to cuddle a woman, but he wanted her close to him. He wanted to hold her. He wanted to be inside her for as long as physically possible.

"You ever hear of a man named Jake Bannaconni?" he asked.

"Everyone's heard of him, Eli."

"He's our closest neighbor. He and his wife, Emma, own the ranch next door. They have two children and another on the way, and they've invited us to come over and have dinner with them. Do you think you'll be ready for company in a few days?"

She went quiet, the pads of her fingers tracing little patterns over his ribs. She seemed languid, drowsy, her lashes covering her eyes. "It's dangerous, Eli. Of course I'd like to meet our neighbors, but Rafe will find us eventually. You know that or you wouldn't have suggested training me and my leopard. You know he'll come for me."

"Jake and Emma are shifters. His ranch locks down tight and his crew are all shifters. He's dealt with rogues before and he has a sweet setup to protect his family. I'd like to take a look at it, and he wants you to know you've got a place to go in an emergency." He was careful to keep his tone to information only. He didn't want to push her one way or the other. He was already pushing her in too many other areas.

"I'll think about it."

Her voice was so sleepy—sensual sleepy—his body tightened again. That was fine with him. He didn't mind both of them drifting off with his cock still buried inside of her. If he didn't have his cock there, he'd be tempted to put his fingers inside her and then she'd really be shocked.

"I've asked for the groceries on your list and a few clothes. You'll need the clothes for learning to get rid of them fast for shifting. The faster you shed clothes, the faster the ability to shift on the run."

"You left my boots. I paid so much money for them." Her voice was sleepy and he knew she was drifting a little.

"Your boots?"

"I loved those boots."

He made a mental note to replace her boots with something she'd love equally. "I'm sorry about the boots, baby. Are you awake enough to listen?"

She nodded, but her lashes persisted in drifting down.

"We keep extra clothes in vehicles and also around the property. Jake's men do the same on their property. Are you fairly good at reading maps?"

He felt her head nod, but she didn't answer him aloud. He knew he was losing her to sleep. She needed it and she'd need more over the coming days. Once her leopard emerged, they would have twice the work.

He stroked his hand over her hair, his fingers sliding into the thick braid. He'd almost lost her. He'd been that close. He still had to tie up loose ends with his work. He'd already sent in his resignation. They knew he was angry over the way the case had been handled, and the moment his boss had informed him that Rafe Cordeau had been told of Catarina's whereabouts, everyone in the building knew they'd lost him as an agent. He'd nearly come across the desk and punched his boss's face. He knew no one would be surprised at his resignation, but they'd try to persuade him to stay. He'd already had several emails from his boss, Brady O'Connell, trying to backtrack.

He wrapped his arms tighter around his woman and turned on his side as his cock finally relaxed enough to slip free. He rolled her tight against him and locked his arm around her, holding her to him. One thigh slid between hers and he pushed against her buttocks, burrowing between those soft firm globes, so his worn cock had a soft, warm resting place.

"Good night, baby," he said softly. "No more bad dreams."

12

CATARINA busied herself making breakfast. As a rule when she was in the kitchen, she could lose herself there. The kitchen had been her favorite place, her refuge. Rafe often wandered in when she was putting a meal together or baking something for later.

Eli liked to sit in the kitchen and drink his coffee. His presence took up the entire room, despite it being spacious. He also seemed to suck all the air out of it as well. He didn't seem to know it, calmly gazing out the wide panel of windows to the outside where the view was gorgeous.

She snuck another peek at him. He was too good-looking for her peace of mind, in a purely masculine way. There were no boyish features whatsoever on Eli. He was all man, every angle cut strong, the lines in his face carved deep. His jaw was strong, his nose straight, and his shoulders were wide enough to fill a doorway.

He made her feel small and very feminine. Right at this

moment, she was suddenly feeling very shy. That had something to do with the way he looked at her. He was different this morning. Whenever his gaze rested on her, he was focused, just as before, looking as if he could see right through her to her soul, but it was more. It was the way he focused on her.

She moistened her lips and tried not to startle when he moved. The scrape of his chair had her gaze jumping to his. He'd gone from sitting behind the table to crowding her all the way around the counter, his much larger body pinning her against the sink.

"What are you doing, Eli?" She hated that she sounded so breathless. Like a girl instead of a woman. He was always so sure of himself, and she felt very unsure. Her heart got all fluttery—she was still so scared of him ripping it out and destroying her she actually felt fragile.

"Kitten." He said it softly. Just that. His hand came up to frame her face, his thumb sliding gently over her smooth skin. "You haven't looked at me once this morning. Not one single time."

"I have," she denied hastily. "I looked at you lots." She couldn't quite get herself to raise her eyes to his because she'd see that look. She knew it was there and she knew what it meant. She'd given herself to him last night in a way there was no taking back. She'd made a commitment, and now she was terrified.

"You're hiding from me."

His voice was so gentle. The velvet one that smoothed over her skin and sent shivers of heat down her spine. It was pure, utter hell to be so affected by a man's voice. His scent surrounded her, a wild, rain forest, primal scent—when she breathed in, she felt as if she took him inside of her.

"I'm working, trying to make breakfast. And before that I made us coffee."

"You didn't kiss me good morning either."

Now there was humor in his voice. Gentle and amused. She couldn't take the combination, not on one cup of coffee.

"Eli, I'm serious, you're going to ruin our breakfast." Again, without really raising her gaze to his, she tried to step around him.

Eli was a solid wall. There was no moving him even when she put her hand on his chest and shoved. He didn't even rock back.

"At this precise moment, baby, I don't give a damn about breakfast. I want you to look at me."

"Well, I can't." The admission burst out of her. She couldn't contain it. She always seemed to blurt the truth out around him no matter what she vowed to herself.

"You can't?" he echoed, sounding more amused than ever.

"No, I just can't. So go sit down and let me finish making our breakfast."

Catarina sounded snippy. Eli didn't do snippy very well, she was pretty certain of that, especially when one hand moved the pan on the stove from the burner and the other arm wrapped around her waist.

"Kitten, I'm not going the entire morning without a kiss from you. When we wake up, you've got two choices. Your mouth can be on mine, or it can be on my cock. It isn't that difficult. You didn't have your lips wrapped around my cock when I woke up, so I'm waiting for my kiss."

That was just a little shocking. She shouldn't be shocked because that sounded like the arrogant, bossy Eli she was becoming familiar with. Bossy, arrogant, *dominating* Eli was far more familiar than sweet Eli.

"Those are my two choices?"

"Yeah. And some days, I'll expect both."

"How lucky of me. Really, Eli, what other rules do you have? I wouldn't want to break any." In spite of her sudden, weird shyness, he'd made her just annoyed enough that she risked a glance upward.

Big mistake. He might sound amused, but he didn't look amused. His amber eyes had gone golden. Burnished gold.

Almost liquid, which she knew was a bad sign. His hand settled in her long hair, fisted there. He pulled her head back, using his grip on her hair. Rough. Not at all gentle. A bite of pain in her scalp sent heat rushing through her veins like hot lava flowing straight to her deepest feminine core.

Oh, God. Why did she have to find everything about him scorching hot? She gave a soft protest, "Eli." Her stomach did a funny flip. He could make her want him with one touch. One look. He terrified her the longer she spent time with him. What had she done? How had she made such a stupid commitment?

"You don't get to take yourself back. You gave me you last night," he said, his eyes burning fiercely.

She could see the leopard in him, a ferocious, feral animal, lurking close to the surface, needing his mate to submit to him.

"I'm not taking me back," she whispered, awed by the power she felt running through him. His body was hard and hot, his strength barely contained.

"Then what the hell are you doing?" he demanded.

She counted her heartbeats. She heard her pulse pounding in her ears. One hand was a flimsy defense, there on his chest. She could feel his defined muscles coiled with tension beneath her palm.

"I'm . . . ah . . . taking a time-out."

He let his breath out in a slow hiss of annoyance. His hand never loosened in her hair, preventing her from moving her head. "A time-out?"

She moistened her lips, and for the first time, she really looked at him. Looked into his eyes. Immediately she found herself caught and held there, a prisoner in all that gold. She swallowed hard. "I'm not taking anything back, Eli. I'm just overwhelmed. I don't know how to act. I'm still just a little freaked out and I'm sorry if that upsets you."

He stared down at her with the unblinking, focused stare of the leopard for what seemed an eternity. His face softened, although the grip on her hair didn't. "Kitten. You can't hide from me like this. If you're freaked out, you talk to me. If you're overwhelmed, you tell me. I'm not the kind of man to guess what's going on with my woman. You have to come right out and tell me."

She swallowed hard again. "Okay."

"I'm going to kiss you good morning," he said softly. "That's all, just kiss you. That shouldn't scare you. You've kissed me before, so why does it freak you out this morning?"

"We never stop at just kissing, and I need to process. You confuse me, Eli. I can't think when you're kissing me or your hands are on me, and I seem to do the craziest things."

His lips whispered against hers, the lightest of touches, but he might as well have sent a flaming arrow straight between her legs.

"I love how honest you are, Cat," he said softly, his mouth on hers.

The way he did that, talked right into her mouth was just as hot as if he'd kissed her. Well . . . maybe she was wrong about that because then he was kissing her and the ground shifted out from under her feet. The room spun. Her body melted into his. She didn't even feel his hand loosen in her hair. Her arms slid up his chest and curled around his neck to bring his head closer. He kissed her and then he devoured her as if she was all he wanted for breakfast.

Eli broke the kiss and looked down into her dazed eyes. His heart stuttered in his chest. She was beautiful to him. Not just the outside packaging, but the way she gave herself to him when he touched her. The way she answered him so honestly, even if she was revealing things to him she'd prefer to keep hidden.

Her lips were parted just the slightest bit, looked swollen from his kisses, moist and soft and inviting him back. He didn't try to resist the invitation, even though he'd promised her he would only kiss her. He knew she wore nothing beneath the shirt, because he'd asked her not to wear anything else. His woman always did what he asked, because for some reason, if it mattered to him, it mattered to her. Even when it was difficult for her.

Like this morning. Overwhelmed by her commitment to him, but not taking it back. He lifted his head again and ran his hand gently over her face. "You okay now, baby? We need to talk more?"

A hint of amusement crept into the dark blue violet of her eyes. "Is that what you call that? Talking?"

"It's how I do my best talking. That said good morning to my woman. That said you're safe with me. Did you feel it?"

"I don't know. I'm still trying to put out the fire you started. You always scramble my brain."

But she was smiling. Looking at him. Before she'd been afraid to even chance a look. Eli stepped back away from her before it was too late. He prowled across the room, paced back and forth to release the energy built up in his body. He was a man who needed sex. Lots of sex, but now, with her so close to him, he needed it all the time. His leopard was a handful on the best of days, but with Eli's body painfully hard for what seemed like every minute of the day, his leopard was roaring for Catarina's submission.

"I'm making another coffee," he announced. "Do you want one?"

"Sure. That would be nice," she ventured.

She just stood there, her back to the counter, her long hair gleaming like a waterfall after midnight, her eyes still a little dazed and if she didn't move, he was going to sit her up on the counter, put his mouth between her legs and have her for breakfast.

"Baby." He sighed the endearment.

"Mmm?"

His cock jerked. Threatened to burst through his jeans. "Fix our breakfast."

"Oh. Yeah. I knew I was doing something."

That made him smile and the fierce edge to his temper was gone just like that. He went to the coffee machine and began the process. "I want to make certain you understand the rule we've got going in this house." He kept his back to her. He could hear her chopping vegetables and she was fast at it. There wasn't a second's hesitation. She'd be good with a throwing knife.

"Rule?" she murmured, already distracted.

He didn't want her distracted. "Cat, look at me." He turned his head to look over his shoulder, waited for the full impact of her beautiful blue eyes on his. "When you wake up, where does your mouth go?"

"Seriously, Eli? That can't be a rule."

"It's a rule."

"I might have morning breath. Or I might have to go to the bathroom. Or I just might want to wake up before you and sit on the porch with a cup of coffee. That can't be a rule," she protested.

She stood there, gesturing with the knife, a little frown on her face. Her eyes were bluer than the deepest sea, and her hair was everywhere, falling in sheets to her waist. Her beauty took his breath.

"It's a rule," he repeated. "You wake up, your mouth belongs either of those two places. After that, you can do any damn thing you want."

"Lucky me." She went back to her chopping.

He found himself smiling. She didn't argue with him and he was fairly certain he'd made his point.

"Speaking of kissing, Kitten," he said, paying great attention to the coffee machine. He didn't understand why her coffee was so much better. He followed her instructions to the letter, but it just didn't come out quite the same. "That same rule applies at night when we go to bed."

"Oh, for heaven's sake. What about your mouth?"

He laughed softly and toed a chair around so he could straddle it as he watched her work. "It's only fair if the same rule applies to me. I wake up, my mouth is on yours or between your legs. Whichever works best at the time."

She nearly choked. The blush stole up from inside the shirt to her neck. "I see," she managed to get out.

He liked watching her cook. She enjoyed it. There was no doubt in his mind, she would be happy in his house, making it a home for them. He liked sitting in their kitchen with the smell of coffee and breakfast surrounding him. He liked having her scent in his lungs and the taste of her in his mouth. He especially liked knowing her naked body, warm and soft, was wrapped in his shirt while she worked. He felt comfortable teasing her, and watching a blush steal up her neck and into her face.

"Did you think I was going to neglect you?" he persisted.

She narrowed her eyes. "Quit trying to distract me. I'm working here."

"I just wanted to make certain you know I'm not altogether a selfish bastard. Well, now that I say that, maybe it isn't true. Maybe I am. I like my mouth between your legs, taking all that sweet honey from you. It's mine, right? Belongs to me. A man ought to be able to harvest honey anytime he gets a notion if it belongs to him."

"I've got a knife in my hand," she reminded him. "And you're trying to embarrass me."

"Kitten," he said softly. "I'm doing a damn good job of it."

She laughed, and instantly the kitchen flooded with warmth. She didn't laugh that often, not like this, not for real and the sound felt a little like music.

"You are," she admitted. "I'm almost finished. The beignets are almost done and the omelets are perfect. I didn't have a lot to work with. We really need groceries, Eli, and I can do so much better."

She arranged his omelet and hash browns mixed with ham onto his plate and set it in front of him with his silverware. The way she arranged everything with such care made his heart melt around the edges. She liked taking care of him. He hadn't had anyone want to take care of him since his parents had died when he was a boy. She liked it. He could tell by the way she put a napkin out for him, checked his coffee and put the basket of fresh, hot beignets in front of him before she settled with her own food across from him.

"Never going to give you up, Catarina," he said firmly. "Not ever. I'm going to take such good care of you, you'll never want to leave me."

She sent him a small smile and pushed her hair out of her face, tossing the long strands over her shoulder in a purely feminine gesture. She was sexy without even trying. Still, she had an expression that told him she wasn't certain he meant what he was saying.

Eli leaned across the table toward her. "We're shifters, Cat. Shifters mate for life and beyond. It's said we find one another over and over, that sometimes we can even remember things about one another. Leopards smell lies and that makes it impossible for mates to lie or deceive one another."

She frowned. "Why didn't I know you were a cop?"

"Because your cat wasn't close enough to recognize mine. I didn't know you were leopard and you didn't know I was. But we're mates. You'll know. So will your leopard. I'm not telling you lies when I say I think you're the most beautiful woman I've ever seen. Or the sexiest. Or that I want you every fucking time I lay eyes on you. Or when I tell you I'm never going to give you up."

Her eyes searched his for a long time. "Then I guess I made the right decision. I think you're so beautiful you take my breath away."

He tried not to let the sound of her voice and the way she said the words, the ring of absolute truth get to him—but it did. His heart turned over. His belly knotted and his cock was as hard as a damned rock. Love and lust mixed into some terrible combustible chemical, just waiting for a match. "Baby. Men aren't beautiful."

"You are. The way you move. Your eyes. Your mouth. Especially your voice." She sent him another small smile. "It doesn't hurt that you have a scorching-hot body and you know how to use it."

His eyes met hers. It was all he could do not to come over the table and drag her into his arms. He had the feeling that he was just getting in deeper and deeper with her. She wasn't ready yet. She needed a little space and she'd made that clear. He wanted to give it to her. He took a deep breath, lifted his fork and saluted her. "Kitten, you have to be the best cook I've ever been around. I watched you make this, saw every ingredient you put into it, but I've never had eggs like this. Not ever. You must be magic."

She looked pleased. "Wait until I actually have some spices and things to work with. I love this kitchen, Eli. It's beautiful."

"I'm glad. Anything you want different, let me know and I'll see what I can do about it. I told you, I'm no cook, but I can grill a mean steak." He forced himself to sound offhand. He didn't want to spook her, but he'd get her anything at all she asked him for. He'd pull down the damn moon for her if she asked him.

"That's good, because I don't always feel like cooking," she admitted, sneaking a little glance at him over her coffee.

Eli frowned. "You don't have to cook for me, Catarina. I didn't bring you here so you could wait on me. Any time you don't feel like cooking, just say so. I'll take a turn or we'll eat out."

"We can't eat out, Eli. Even *you* can't eat out." She raised her head, her blue eyes meeting his, anxious.

Eli liked that she looked alarmed. For him. Not for her. She was worried about him. "I'm not afraid of Cordeau, baby," he said softly.

She shook her head. "Eli, he'll know I'm with you by now, and the minute you surface somewhere, he'll find you," Catarina cautioned, carefully choosing her words,

trying not to sound like she was challenging him. Or boss-
ing him.

His heart turned over. He put his hand over hers, his
thumb sliding along the bare skin of her inner wrist. "We're
going to be ready for him. I don't intend for us to hide forever. Just long enough for your leopard to make her appearance, and for us to be ready."

Catarina tilted her head to one side and her long, gleaming hair fell around her shoulder and tumbled down her
back making his cock jump. He loved that simple little gesture and she did it a lot when her hair was down. He liked
her hair down.

"Just how does one get ready for a man like Rafe
Cordeau?"

"In a fight, Kitten, sometimes it comes down to conditioning. I know that sounds simple, but whoever is in shape
is sometimes the one left standing. So we're going to start
training camp today. We'll run, work on the bags, kicking,
punching, crunches, push-ups and the medicine ball. I want
you shooting a gun every day and I've got a couple of practice knives we can use. You get hit with one, it raises a hell
of a welt and you know you would have gotten cut."

"Sounds fun," she said, and took another sip of coffee.

His eyes narrowed on her face. "This isn't a game we're
playing with Cordeau."

"I'm not complaining. I was already training," she
pointed out. "It's just that, well, I can't see me besting Rafe
at hand-to-hand combat."

Eli frowned. She'd grown up with Rafe being the sole
authority around her. Everyone was afraid of the man.
Everyone. Especially Catarina. To her, Cordeau was the
ultimate, invincible monster. Eli hunted monsters, both
human and shifter. He'd been doing it a long while, and the
other shifters he knew had been doing it even longer.

"He isn't invincible, Cat. He's dangerous, but he isn't
invincible. I've met quite a few men—and rogues—just

like him. I'm still alive and they're not. I put the humans in cages if I can and the shifter into the ground because we can't afford a rogue loose on the world."

She dropped one hand under the table where he could see her anxiously rubbing her thigh with her palm. "I know you're all macho, Eli. I can even tell you know how to fight. But he's not right. He isn't. I never really wanted to look too closely because he's all I had, but there's something not right about him."

He knew what she meant. Rafe Cordeau was a sociopath, and it made it all the worse that he was a shifter. His leopard craved the hunt for humans and Cordeau gave that to him. He enjoyed the power of life and death over those around him. He couldn't imagine what it had been like for a young girl to grow up in Cordeau's house. Or the courage it had taken for her to leave.

"I'm truly sorry the bastards gave him your location, Cat. I didn't agree with the decision, but still, I was a part of it."

She shrugged. "I was too comfortable there. In the end I would have stayed too long, and I would have made a mistake. That's the worst part, figuring out when you have to make the move, after all the time and effort you put into a new life."

"Not here," he said. "Not now. This is going to be your home. Right here. My Cat's Lair. It's all yours, Catarina, so do whatever you want to it."

"You mean that, don't you?"

"I want a home. I figure you know what you're doing in that department a whole hell of a lot more than I do. And baby, working in the coffee-house, I don't care how loose you wore your clothes, every man for miles was already lining up trying to figure out how to get in your pants. With your face and body and all that hair, hell woman, men were leaving the bar early to come to the coffee-house just to see you. Most of them were jacking off in the restroom at the sound of your voice, and the image of you in their heads."

She gasped. "That is *so* not true. I was flying under the radar. And men don't see me like that."

"I'm a man, Kitten. What the hell do you think I was doing every night after leaving you?"

She blushed again. "Seriously, Eli, the way you talk to me is so crude sometimes."

He kept his eyes on her face. "That bother you, baby? The way I talk?"

She opened her mouth to say something quickly, a fast answer, but then she stopped herself and shook her head. "Not really."

"Growing up the way you did, I figured maybe the way I talk wouldn't bother you so much. I go undercover for months at a time, Cat. The places I go, the people I rub shoulders with, they aren't the kind that talk polite. I talk this way because if I don't think this way, I'm a dead man."

"I understand. It doesn't bother me. I just never thought in terms of a man looking at me and needing to go into a restroom for . . . um . . . relief."

"It's the truth. You wouldn't have lasted another two weeks without drama. I was going to have to kick some ass, and it wouldn't have been pretty."

"You would have kicked ass for me?"

"Baby, I would kill for you. Man touches you, he isn't going to live long. Not then and not now."

"Don't say that, Eli. *He* said that. I don't want you to say that ever again."

"I know, Cat, I know he said it, but I mean it in a different way. I mean any man who tries to harm you."

She let her breath out slowly, clearly not wanting to continue the subject. "Why has my leopard gone so quiet all of a sudden? Could I have missed her emerging window? I didn't want her to appear. Maybe I repressed her with all my doubts."

"I don't know if that's actually possible, Cat," he admitted. He hadn't thought of that. "I figured she was resting up for the big event."

He finished what was left on his plate because no way was he going to leave one bite of food that Catarina had cooked for him. He leaned back in his chair and reached for a beignet to go with his coffee.

"I hope so. Now that I've seen your leopard and it didn't eat me or anything, I kind of like the idea of her."

"She'll be tough to handle at first, but you're strong and you've got courage. You'll do fine with her."

She looked up at him from under her long lashes. "Do you know how many times you've said nice things to me, Eli?"

"Someone should have been saying nice things to you your entire life, Kitten. You shouldn't have had a junkie for a mother, or Rafe for a guardian. You should have grown up in a house filled with love. I can't do a thing about your past, but I can make damn certain you feel loved in your future. And when we have kids, we'll be saying nice things to them a hundred times a day."

Her gaze clung to his. Again he saw hope there—and fear mixed up with it, like she was still afraid to believe, but willing to try. "I'll get the dishes. You get dressed to work out. Have you climbed before?"

"Climbed in what way?"

"Up a mountain. A boulder. A climbing wall. Anything at all."

"They don't have mountains where I come from, and Rafe would never have allowed me inside of a place where there was a climbing wall. I had men following me around all the time."

"How did you get away from him this last time?"

"He had sensors on the windows and doors. He forgot the floor. I was careful, so there was no evidence I was pulling up the floorboards so I had a space big enough to drop down into. He didn't put cameras in the bathrooms or the bedrooms, other than mine. I just had to take my time. I figured out how to beat the combination of his safe so I'd have running money. I learned to read by watching children's shows.

He'd hear them on and it would only reinforce his belief that I wasn't too bright."

"Cordeau didn't want you to be educated?" He was beginning to detest the man. He felt the leopard rise close to the surface in direct response to his rising temper. He knew his eyes glittered because he could see heat waves banding across his vision. Cordeau wanted a teenage girl so trapped and so alone she had no friends and nowhere to turn. He also ensured she would feel bad about herself, inferior to him.

She licked her lips, drawing his instant attention. "No, I asked once if I could have a tutor and he got mad at me. Not just mad, but scary mad. You're the only other person that can do that."

She was plucking at the silverware on the table and he reached out to lay his hand over hers, stilling those restless fingers. "What do you mean, 'scary mad'?"

"When you're angry, Eli, you can walk into the room and I feel it, the sudden onslaught of frightening, intense, very powerful heat. The energy is so strong, I sometimes think you could knock someone over with it."

He knew what she was talking about and he couldn't deny it. He could shut down a room full of macho men with his anger. It wasn't that difficult to feel the presence of his cat, a moody, brooding, vicious, bad-tempered animal that could tear a man apart in seconds.

"I know, baby," he admitted softly. "I can get like that. I can be mean. I got a temper. For you, I'll try to keep it in check, but if I get ugly, you have the right to say so. Just don't walk out on me. If I say something that hurts, let me know. Don't hold it inside. You have to learn to live with me and I'm not saying that's going to be easy. I told you, I like things my way, and I'm not taking any chances with your safety. I'm guessing we're going to butt heads a few times."

"When you say I'm your woman, Eli, what does that mean, exactly? For me. What do you expect and what can I expect?"

His thumb slid over the inside of her wrist, checking her pulse. Her heart beat just a little too fast. She was scared, but she was determined.

"When I say you're mine, it means you're my mate in shifter terms. My wife in human terms. We build a life together. That's what we're going to do. I'll have your back and you'll have mine."

"So a partnership."

He saw instantly where this conversation was going. He had to be honest with her about who he was. He wasn't going to change, not with his leopard so dominant. Not with so many years of being the man he'd become. He liked the way he was. It was important for her to know the truth of him, even if it was a little risky so early in their relationship.

"Yes and no, baby. I told you, I like my way. My rules, my way. That's just how it is. I'll make certain you're happy. Just like the way I talk sometimes. You don't always like it, but you're okay with it. I think you're in danger, you will do exactly what I tell you when I tell you. It's that simple."

"I see. So really a dictatorship."

He shrugged. "I don't give a damn how you want to label it, Kitten. The bottom line is we'll work it out. You don't like something, you tell me. We'll work it out."

"Will we, Eli? Will you listen to me?"

He heard the slight tremor in her voice. She was being very brave, trying to get a sense of her future with him. He didn't want to lie to her and paint a pretty picture. He wasn't going to be easy to live with, but he'd been with her enough to know she fit with him. She didn't know it yet, but he knew it. He felt it.

He brought her hand to his mouth and slowly pried open her fingers. Pressing his mouth to the center of her palm he looked into her brilliant blue eyes. She was really trying for him and he appreciated it. His heart turned over, like it often did when she looked so fragile.

She had grown up in a terrible household and she knew

the criminal world, but in many ways she'd been sheltered. Cordeau hadn't wanted her to know too much about anything in the world so that when her leopard emerged, she would be totally reliant on him for anything, including information she would need.

Had Cordeau planned to shape her into the kind of mate he needed for his killer leopard? Would he have tried to force her to hunt humans with him? If she had done so even once, thinking all shifters did, the shame and guilt would have tied her to Cordeau for eternity.

"I'll listen to you, Catarina, I promise. I'm going to make certain you're happy here. I've noticed you don't need much to make you happy. Laughter, music, great coffee and a kitchen. And boots. I have to get you killer, sexy boots." He was rewarded for remembering by her quick smile and he vowed to get right on finding boots for her.

She took a breath, studying his face, her eyes searching his. He knew she was looking for hope. "Do you really think we have a chance to live a life here, Eli?"

"For a while. We've got time. He can't trace us here. The ranch can't be traced to me. Even the DEA doesn't know about it. Cordeau's got eyes and ears, but we're gone. My neighbor will close ranks with us, and once your leopard emerges we'll be able to figure out our next move."

"You said we'd visit the neighbor after my leopard emerges. Why not before?"

He leveled a gaze at her. "Baby. Really? And when she suddenly comes close to the surface and you need me riding you hard, we going to do it on the neighbor's kitchen floor?"

She blushed again and gently removed her hand from his to push at her long hair. "I see. I hadn't thought of that. I guess I thought I'd gain control."

"There is no controlling a mating heat, Cat, no matter how much we both might want to. When she decides to show herself, you'll be on fire. I'll be on fire and both the cats will be. We just have to hang on to each other wherever we are and ride it out."

She tugged her lower lip between her teeth. "How much longer?"

"I don't know. No one ever knows. The male shifter is aware of his leopard almost from birth, but the female knows absolutely nothing until the human cycle lines up with the leopard's cycle."

"Um . . . Eli," she said softly. "You aren't using birth control."

"It doesn't work on shifters. You either get pregnant or you don't."

"Condoms?" She raised her eyebrow.

"You've seen me, babe, how I'm built, and we don't just have sex. We have rough sex. I've never known condoms to work on a shifter either."

"What about when you have sex with a woman who isn't a shifter?"

"Birth control works on humans." He pushed off the table. "Get dressed, Kitten, let's start our conditioning."

She stared up at him for a few more minutes as though she might protest the truth of what he said. But it was truth, and he had no more to give her. He wanted time alone with her, but if a baby came along, he was fine with that. He hoped she would be too.

"You could have warned me," she pointed out.

"Would it have made any difference when your leopard was close?"

She shook her head. Honest. "No, I guess not."

He watched her walk away, wishing he could read her mind.

13

SUNSET. The sky turned orange and red as they jogged together, turning back toward the house. The wind shifted subtly and Eli instantly scented the males. They were close. Too close. He wanted Catarina to know where the property lines were and to familiarize herself with the way to the neighboring ranch, but he hadn't expected to meet anyone along the way.

He was too pent up sexually. His leopard prowled too close. He cursed under his breath, knowing he had no choice but to introduce Catarina to Jake's crew.

"What's wrong?" she asked softly.

Her voice only added to the increasing frustration. Working out with a permanent hard-on was becoming nearly impossible. He hurt like hell. Every muscle in his body hurt thanks to the hunger crawling through him, raking at him. And now this.

"Come on. They heard us and asked for a meet. You stay close to me, do you hear me?" He growled the words at her, his features set in hard lines.

"Are you angry with me?"

He was totally pissed. Not at her, at the situation. At himself for allowing it to go this far. Hell, he was no teenager. He'd gone weeks without sex before he'd met her. He didn't have to like it, but he did it. He couldn't go four fucking days without his temper getting out of hand? What kind of crap was that?

Eli clenched his teeth and made his way slowly to the fence, dropping his arm around Catarina and pulling her into his side. His hand slid down from her waist to the curve of her bottom. He kept his palm there, knowing he was making a show of being proprietary, and uncaring that she might not like it. He didn't want any other shifter around her, not when the emergence was so close.

"Eli?" she asked again, turning her face up to his, trying to read him.

Day four of their conditioning training was going very well. He couldn't fault Cat for anything. She did every single thing he demanded of her—and he pushed her. He pushed her hard. They ran together long distances and did wind sprints. He worked self-defense moves with her and sparred with her. He didn't ever take it easy on her. If anything he was harsh. She never complained.

"Just stay close," he warned.

She'd climbed her first boulder and her hands were sore, the skin was torn off a couple of her fingers. She didn't say a word. They spent several hours a day on the gun range, firing a variety of weapons, and she was a very good shot. Still, he refused to let up. He pushed her so hard, that every night she looked exhausted. She fell asleep in the large tub and he took her out, dried her off and carried her to bed.

Right now she looked upset. Hurt. Great. He was going to

walk her right up to three men—three single shifters—with
her looking vulnerable. His mean temper was getting meaner
and becoming a problem.

She kissed him in the morning. She didn't wrap her lips
around his cock. She kissed him. Now, watching the three
men staring at her, he was damned sorry he didn't wear her
out another way. He should have spent more time making
certain she knew who she belonged to. He should have spent
a *lot* more time ensuring *he* was tired out from claiming her
every way he could. His leopard was riding him so hard he
could barely talk without growling. Now, he could only stand
and be gracious when he wanted to snarl and roar.

He walked up to the fence and halted on his side of it,
clamping his arm around Catarina, his fingers pressing into
her bottom. She trembled. He forced his hand to smooth out
and gently rub, trying to convey he wasn't angry with her,
just the situation. She wouldn't have understood even had
he tried to explain it to her.

"Cat, this is Joshua Tregre, Elijah Lospostos and Trey
Sinclair. They work security for Jake Bannaconni." He
knew Trey from the rain forest. The man had recently come
to work in the States for Bannaconni.

Eli heard the growl in his voice, that warning that came
from every male shifter when his woman was close to the
Han Vol Dan. Fortunately for all of them, Catarina's leopard was being very stubborn, hiding away from her, otherwise she would have set off every male in the vicinity.

He felt Catarina's body jerk. She actually tensed, moved
closer to him, her eyes suddenly downcast.

"Catarina and I have met before, haven't we?" Elijah
said, his voice gentle.

Eli narrowed his eyes, his gaze settling on Elijah. When
they'd talked a few days earlier, Eli had mentioned Rafe
Cordeau, and Elijah had admitted his family had done business with him. Elijah's family was mired deep in the inter-
national drug trade. He wasn't surprised that Elijah and

Cordeau had crossed paths, but he was shocked and not too happy that Elijah and Catarina had already met.

"Funny, you didn't mention that the other day when I brought up Catarina." Eli kept his voice neutral. Elijah was a good friend of Drake's and he'd worked with Drake's crew for a long time.

"I was at more than one meeting my family had with Cordeau," Elijah said. "But only once at his home. That's where I met Catarina."

Cat didn't say anything, but again he felt a small shudder run through her body. "He isn't one of them," Eli was compelled to say. "His family is part of a cartel, but Elijah is not in that business. He isn't a friend of Cordeau's. You're safe here."

She didn't speak. She didn't look at any of them. Clearly she thought she'd perfected the art of disappearing into her surroundings by simply remaining silent and not looking at any of them. He knew better. She was a beautiful woman. She had lush curves and gleaming silk for hair. It was pulled back and clipped at the nape of her neck, but there it was messy, and sexy and impossible to ignore.

His cat snarled. Raked at his belly. "What's the word on the street?"

He knew that's what he'd been called to the fence for. Elijah had heard something and was passing on information.

"Cordeau's pulled out all stops, called in all favors. He's hunting, Eli. He's pushing all the way to the lowest ranking member of his network from those on the streets to favors from other crime bosses. He's even hitting up the cops on everyone's payroll. I heard someone in your branch as well; he's threatening everyone he knows to get information. There's a hefty reward. I heard it was up around a million. People would kill their own mothers for that kind of money."

Eli nodded. He'd expected nothing less from Cordeau. He would have done the same thing if he had the money and resources and he'd lost Cat to another man.

Another shudder went through Catarina's body. He

glanced down at her. Her face was utterly still. Frozen. She never once raised her eyes toward the three men. She looked almost as if she was in shock.

"Kitten?" He used a soft, gentle voice. Inquiring. She didn't blink. Didn't look at him. "Are you all right?"

She was terrified, and it had something to do with seeing Elijah Lospostos. Clearly she believed he was a friend of Cordeau's.

"Baby, I'm telling you, Elijah is clean."

"Not clean," Elijah denied. His voice held the ring of truth. "I'm a Lospostos. My family goes way back in the crime industry. I've worked hard to get out, but that doesn't mean I didn't have to do a few things that were illegal along the way. Cordeau was in bed with my uncle. My uncle killed my father. I'm no friend of Cordeau's. You have nothing to fear from me, Catarina."

Eli liked the way she was tight against him, almost under his shoulder, burrowing close, seeking his protection, but he didn't like her being afraid. There was no way to salvage the situation, not there with Elijah so close.

"You were, what, fifteen? Sixteen? You fixed the meal that night. It blew my uncle away that you cooked for us all yourself. He asked to meet you. That was unusual, wasn't it?" Elijah persisted. "It was unusual and it scared you."

For a long moment, Eli didn't think Catarina would answer.

"He wanted to scare me. Your uncle. He wanted Rafe to know he knew who I was." She spoke in a low tone.

Eli frowned. Catarina had grown up in Rafe Cordeau's home. It stood to reason he'd kept her away from his business. No one really thought, even if they could get her to do it, that she could testify about anything other than April Harp's murder. Rumor had it Catarina had been there. Something in the way she revealed that she knew Elijah's uncle's motivation in asking to meet her made Eli rethink his position on Catarina inside that household.

She'd taught herself to read. She'd learned how to make coffee. Not just make coffee, but became a leading barista, someone who was great at what she did. She was quiet, and she downplayed her looks. She listened. Really listened when others were talking. She looked so young. She'd learned to play to that too. Only when her body betrayed her with its lush curves was it necessary for her to run.

He swore under his breath. He'd been such a fool. They all had. Sweet little Catarina Benoit was not just sweet, fragile and uneducated, she was extremely intelligent. Off the charts intelligent. She probably knew more about Cordeau's business than Cordeau. She'd been there, a fixture in his household, one he intended to keep, a beautiful trophy he intended to mold into his likeness.

Catarina had been Cordeau's chosen mate. She'd been a sponge in Cordeau's house, soaking up everything she heard, learning as much as she could. She'd learned sex education by listening to two of Cordeau's crew's girlfriends talking. If there'd been a wall close Eli would have been tempted to smash his head on it. He'd been so obtuse, buying into the image she projected.

He tightened his arm around her, not knowing whether he wanted to shake her, or kiss her. She was damned brilliant. But if he was right and Catarina did know everything there was to know about Cordeau's business, that meant she knew everyone he was in bed with. His partners wouldn't like that. They wouldn't want anyone running around loose out of their control.

Eli understood the million-dollar price tag. This wasn't all about getting Catarina back, it was also about protecting her. She wasn't where Cordeau could keep her from his partners and he was letting them know she was still under his shield.

Elijah nodded his head. "Yes, my uncle needed some kind of leverage against Cordeau. Cordeau didn't have any weaknesses."

"With the exception of Catarina," Eli said. "She was the one thing that made him vulnerable in a world of other sharks."

Beside him she stirred, tension coiling even tighter. He kept his eyes on her but she didn't look up at him, she was looking at Elijah.

"He made it clear that day I wasn't anything to him."

Eli's belly knotted. Was there hurt in her voice? Of course there was. She'd been a child and back then, she had no one else but Cordeau. If he'd shown in front of company she was nothing to him, she would always feel like nothing.

"He did," Elijah said.

"How?" Eli asked.

She flinched. Hard. For the first time she tried to pull away from him. His fingers dug into her waist, holding her still, holding her to him. Her hand slid over his, fingers trying to remove the vise-like grip he had on her.

"He insisted she read to us, and when she stumbled through a passage, everyone laughed. He laughed the loudest and said something about Catarina being an empty but decorative head."

Eli felt the sudden heat in her body as she flushed a deep rose. She was humiliated all over again. He hadn't expected that either, but it stood to reason. Childhood experiences shaped everyone. Catarina's childhood had not only been traumatic, but she'd grown up thinking she wasn't worth anything to anyone.

She was beginning to actively struggle against him, fighting, not him, but her past. Elijah had brought it too close and the dark ugly memories were flooding her mind.

Eli leaned down, his mouth a whisper from her ear. "Settle," he advised softly. "This is all crap. It's over. You aren't with him, and you aren't what he said you were."

He transferred one hand to the back of her head, shaping her skull with his palm, pushing her face into his rib cage and holding her there. Was it possible they all had Cordeau wrong and Catarina meant far more to him that he let on?

That entire time, when he was convincing everyone around him, Catarina included, that she meant nothing, that he was even embarrassed by her, was Cordeau really protecting her from his associates?

Eli didn't want to think so. He didn't want to see Cordeau as having any redeeming qualities, but the truth was that no one was one-dimensional. All that time, Cordeau could have been pretending indifference to protect her. He tried not to think about the incident when she'd fallen out of the tree and Cordeau had nearly lost his mind. Had that been the act of an indifferent man?

"It wasn't even a difficult piece, that poem," Catarina said, her voice devoid of all emotion. "A child could have read it."

Eli's heart bled for her. "Let's go home, baby. It's been a long day. We've still got a ways to run this evening before we're done."

She turned away immediately, not looking again at Elijah or the other two men. As soon as they were away from the fence, she stepped away from him and began to jog back in the direction of the ranch house.

Eli stared after her for a moment and then turned to wave at the three men. Elijah lifted his hand in salute. All three men wore somber expressions. Eli couldn't blame them. It was impossible not to feel the pain radiating off of Catarina. She'd been cut deep more than once. How many cuts like that could a person take before their soul was ripped away?

He fell into step behind her, jogging easily, covering the ground with his longer legs to catch up to her. She'd never had a chance. Not a single chance. She was beautiful and intelligent and so sweet he wanted to eat her up like candy, but never once had she had any real choices. If he were any kind of man at all, he'd let her go and hope she came back to him, but the Han Vol Dan was too close and his leopard would never allow its mate out of his sight. Did that make him every bit as bad as Cordeau? What the hell did that make him?

It took a good half hour to get home, and that was with them making good time. Catarina set herself a grueling pace. Twice he'd tried to slow her down, but she didn't even acknowledge his warnings. He let it go when ordinarily he would have forced her to stop. Yeah. He was that kind of a man. He controlled things. He got his way. He looked after his own. Was he just like Cordeau? Did she see him that way?

He cursed with every step he took. Darkness streaked the orange sky in long layers, stacking one on top of the other, first sandwiching the orange and then squeezing slowly until all that color was gone. He thought he had a kitten on his hands, and he'd actually acquired a little tiger. Because Cordeau had essentially taught her she was nothing, she didn't recognize that she was a tiger, not a kitten.

The house was dark when they arrived, but neither switched on any lights. Catarina held herself away from him, averting her face as he reached past her to open the kitchen door. He stepped back to allow her inside.

"I'm going to take a bath," she announced.

He wasn't surprised. She spent a lot of time in the bathtub and he knew it was a form of escape. Not certain what to say, he simply nodded his head. He watched her go, his heart sinking. What kind of man was he? He clenched his teeth. He already knew. He'd made the decision almost the moment he laid eyes on Catarina. Some part of him recognized her and what she meant to him. She'd given herself to him, committed to their life together. Maybe it wasn't perfect, that decision, but there was no real choice for her. No other choice.

He jerked open the fridge and pulled out two bottles of water. He needed her. His body needed hers. He ached, and not from the run or their climb or the bag work. He ached because every muscle in his body felt cramped and tight. Catarina Benoit belonged to him and he wasn't giving her up. Not even for all the right reasons, because, damn it all, he wasn't a good man and truthfully, he fucking didn't care.

He walked into the bedroom and glanced toward the master bath. The door was closed. The sound of water running was muffled. The scent of honeysuckle drifted from under the door to envelope him. Instantly the taste of her was on his tongue, in his mouth and his cock swelled alarmingly.

He'd waited for her to come to him. Was it really that damned hard? He'd been pressed up against her body every night. She couldn't fail to read the signs, but not once had she made a move. Even her morning kisses were tentative and chaste. She wasn't getting away with that crap anymore. He'd waited for her to make her move and tried to drive himself to exhaustion while he waited. She had his body—and him—in knots. He was done with being the nice guy.

He felt the edges of his temper expand. He was already in a foul mood. He stalked to the door and found it locked. His temper flared instantly, hot and violent. He didn't knock. He didn't ask her questions, he just kicked the door hard. The doorjamb broke instantly and the door flew open. He stepped inside.

She stood naked beside the tub, her hands over her head as she put her hair up. Startled, she spun around, her breasts swaying invitingly, her eyes wide with shock. "Eli?" Her teeth tugged at her lower lip.

"Don't fucking lock that door again, you hear me?" He took a step toward her, his eyes blazing with fire. "Not now, not ever. I don't give a damn how angry or upset you are, you don't lock me out of any room you're in."

She didn't flinch. She stood her ground. "I take it that's another rule."

"Damn straight it is, and you'd better remember it."

"Perhaps you might tell me all the rules so I don't keep making mistakes."

He studied her face. Her brilliant cobalt eyes. "Are you being a smart-ass right now? Do you think that's really wise?" It was difficult to judge her mood. More than anything she looked defiant. He didn't do defiant very well and his leopard liked it even less. He forced the cat under control when it rose snarling and raking at him with demanding claws.

She shrugged and stepped into the tub. He was close enough to see the small shiver that ran through her body. She wasn't nearly as sure of herself—or of him. He stepped close to her. Very close. Close enough for her to see the bulge straining against his trousers, but then she'd been seeing it every day for four long days and nights and she hadn't done a damn thing about it.

"You've got twenty minutes and then I want you out of here. I'll be on the kitchen porch. I want you to join me."

"I'm tired. I thought I'd just go to bed."

His gaze slashed her face. "I'm restraining myself here, Cat. Keep it up and you're going to find yourself in trouble and believe me, baby, when I say you won't like the trouble you're getting into. Join me in twenty minutes and don't be late." He shoved the bottle of water at her. "And drink this. How many times do I have to fucking tell you to hydrate after working out?"

She took the bottle of water, her eyes searching his face. He kept his features hard. Implacable. No give. He wasn't feeling like giving. He was feeling like taking. He'd had enough of waiting for her to come to him. She wasn't going to do it, and unless he wanted to wait for her reluctant leopard to emerge, he was never going to have her soft body surrounding his with heat and fire. He turned and abruptly stormed out.

Catarina slowly twisted the cap off the water bottle, all the while keeping her gaze on the empty doorway. Her heart hammered too fast. Too hard. Too loud. Had he heard? She wouldn't be surprised if he had and if he had, he hadn't cared enough to do anything about it. The story of her life. She had planned a good long crying fest, a pity party right there in the bathtub.

Elijah just had to tell that horrible, humiliating story to

Eli. She pressed the cool water bottle to her hot face. As a temptress, she was an utter failure. She had no idea how to entice Eli into touching her. She didn't want to make the first move because she felt awkward.

Where was that hussy of a leopard when she needed her? Eli had all but retreated from her. He was angry, but she wasn't certain why. She'd done everything he'd asked of her, no matter how difficult, no matter how tiring. She could only guess that he wanted her so tired he wouldn't have to touch her. Now, after hearing what Elijah had said, he really wouldn't want to touch her, but he needed sex all the time, so she was rather handy to have around.

Eli was nearly always hard around her. She couldn't miss the state of his body, yet he hadn't even tried to have sex with her, not even when they lay naked in bed together and his cock was pressed so tight against her. Was she really that awful? Or was it because the challenge was gone? She'd given herself to him and since then, he'd rejected her.

She drew her knees up tight against her chest. Eli had been bad-tempered, moody and even mean with her since that first morning after. She'd never been able to get Cordeau's attention and as a child, she'd tried. She'd been desperate for someone, anyone at all to take an interest in her. He never had. She'd been cared for just the way he cared for the objects in his home. Now she had the same problem with Eli. She didn't know how to get his attention.

Eli had used that voice, the one that made her shiver. The one that made her go hot. The one that always sent fire dancing between her legs. Did he know what that voice did to her? Did he realize just talking to her like that made her weak with need? She sighed and pressed her fingertips to her eyes.

She knew that these past four days she did what she always did when she didn't know what to do. She retreated. Withdrew. Eli had let her. He'd acted almost disinterested in her.

He was more worried about how fast she ran and how far. She hadn't made one complaint, not one, no matter how sore she was or how bad it hurt when they were sparring. She had done every single thing he asked and she cooked the best meals she could think of. Still, that hadn't been enough for him.

Eli had been in a foul mood every single day. She didn't know what she'd done or what she was supposed to do. She just knew it wasn't good enough. Nothing she did was good enough. She contemplated defying him, but it wasn't worth the effort. She really was tired of it all. She just wanted to go to bed and pull the blankets over her head and just hide.

Catarina dried off slowly and pulled on one of Eli's flannel shirts. At least she felt clean and alive again after their workout. She wandered into the kitchen. The dishes were still in the sink so she rinsed them and began to put them in the dishwasher.

"Kitten. Come here. Now."

Catarina heard the rough in his voice. His sensual, sexy growl that always made her wet. Her body reacted with hunger. With anticipation. Excitement. At the same time, she was tired of being ordered around by a man who didn't care enough to talk to her. To explain anything. She didn't deserve his foul mood.

She wandered over to the screen, pushed it open with one hand and stood in the doorway looking at him. He sat in the shadows, in his favorite chair, his hair damp from his shower and his eyes all cat. And maybe that was the trouble. He was more leopard than man. "What is it you want from me, Eli?" she asked softly. "More sex? That seems to be all you want from me, but only when you want it. I don't right now."

His eyes narrowed. Fury burned. She didn't care. She stood her ground. She wasn't backing down.

"Do you think I don't know when my woman wants me?"

"You're talking about my body, Eli, which strictly speaking isn't all me. My body wants you. I'm not denying that. But I don't. Me. The woman. You hurt me. You didn't notice, or you didn't care. You demand all the time that I talk to you—that I tell you everything going through my mind, but you don't bother to give me that same courtesy. I asked you if you were angry with me and you refused to answer. I have no idea what I've done to set you off and quite frankly, right at this minute, I don't even care."

That was such a lie. She did care. It hurt to have him upset. She'd trusted him all over again. Given herself to him. Declared she'd stay with him and start their relationship over. She knew she was going to cry and that upset her more. Those leopard eyes staring at her without blinking, coming out of the dark like they did, were terrifying. But she refused to back down.

"You'd better start caring, Cat," he snapped back.

"Why? So we can have sex and you can walk off a happy man again? That's all that matters to you, isn't it, Eli. If you'd just left it there it would have been fine. We could have sex and you could be in control and I'd just go along with it, because really, in your eyes, that's all I'm good for."

"Do you really believe that the only thing I value you for is for sex?" he demanded, his voice harsh.

"Why would you value me even for sex?" she shot back. "I don't know the first thing about it. You tell me to put my mouth on you in the mornings when I wake up and you did so knowing I couldn't possibly do more than give you a brief kiss. That's a set-up, kind of like when Rafe forced me to read that poem so he could make fun of me. For you, I'm more like a body you can use, and if I don't do exactly as you say, you go up in flames."

His face changed. The anger glittered in his eyes, and the lines in his face hardened more. He was up, crossing the distance between them so fast she almost didn't see him move. He was intimidating up close. He smelled wild. Feral. His hands belied his scent and those golden eyes. He reached for her and drew her reluctant body against his—and he was gentle when he touched her, which shocked her.

"Catarina, I don't understand how you could think you mean so little to me. Or that I'd be capable of making fun of you when you do something so beautiful and giving as waking me up in a loving way in the mornings."

She turned red. She felt the color sweeping up her neck into her face. At night, erotic images played through her mind. His body heat scorched her. She could taste him in her mouth. Feel him on her skin. Sometimes she even felt him inside of her. She wanted to be able to match him in every way, but she didn't know what she was doing. He knew that.

"Why are you angry with me, Eli? And don't say you're not." It was painful to ask him. She'd done everything she could to please him and it wasn't enough. *She* never seemed to be enough, no matter how hard she tried.

His hand moved through her hair, as if soothing her, yet his eyes were still all predator watching prey. "I've given you every opportunity to think about it, but you chose not to take any of them." The edge in his voice increased and his eyes went from amber to a fierce golden liquid, taking her breath.

"I don't know what that means, Eli," she admitted.

"It means, baby, I'm done with the fucking bullshit. I've wanted those lips of yours wrapped around me every fucking morning but you haven't exactly been cooperative."

"You wanted your cock in my mouth?" she echoed, thinking of every morning when she'd been too shy to do what she wanted, which apparently was what he'd been waiting for. "You were waiting for me to . . . um . . . initiate it?"

His expression softened. "Yes, Kitten. That's what I was waiting for. I'm always the one initiating sex. Just one damn time I'd like to know you wanted me for a change."

The raw loneliness in his voice took her breath away. How could he not know she wanted him? "I attacked you first. More than once," she said. He always seemed so confident, arrogant even. For just that moment he seemed almost insecure.

He shook his head. "Not the same thing, baby, and you know it. That was the leopard's heat talking mostly. But then, a few days ago, you gave yourself to me and then you took you away. You dangle paradise in front of a starving man, give him a taste and then take it away, he gets angry and he isn't going to accept that loss."

She didn't understand and it made her more frustrated than ever. He held her close to his side, his arm around her waist. His body language, face and eyes said anger, but the gentle way he held her said something altogether different.

"My parents died and my life turned to total shit, baby. Not like yours. Not even close, but I had this leopard and he was riding me hard, struggling for control. I was always in fights. Didn't matter where I was, honest to God, or how much I wanted to stay there, I couldn't stop the fights. And the need to fuck. All the time. It never let up. If I didn't give in and find myself someone to ride hard then I was beating the crap out of someone. I was a teenager without direction and a leopard that needed sex and violence all the time. That got me kicked out of a dozen homes in a few very short years. It also got me pitted against the male adults in the homes where I stayed. That meant fists and beatings and forcing me to hold my leopard back. Once . . ."

He closed his eyes briefly. When he opened them again, she could see that leopard, feral and wild with hunger and needs of its own. She held her breath and her fist twisted in his loose shirt.

"Not just once," he confessed, the words sounding as if each was bitter and disgusting. "Many times, I had to fight my own nature. My leopard wanted free rein. I was young and it felt like protection, but he would have killed them. I knew he would have. I couldn't allow it and it just made it all the more difficult to take those beatings when I knew I could let him loose and it would be over."

She inhaled sharply, her natural compassion rushing to overtake her.

"I've never told a damn soul this fucking shit, baby," he confided. His hand slid under her chin and he tipped her face up to his. "Just you. Because I trust you. Because you make my life worth something. You make all those years worth fighting and being strong, learning control. I know I'm controlling. I know I can get mean. I'm trying, Kitten. Really. My life has to be control. I can't take too much chaos, because as I've grown stronger, so has he."

She pressed closer to him. She didn't know what to say. "I have no idea how I make your life worthwhile, Eli."

"Are you fucking kidding me, Catarina?" He all but snarled it. "Look around you. Look at our home. You made this place a home. You take care of me. No one has done that for me. It isn't that you cook for me, it's that you love cooking for me and I can taste it in every bite I take. When you give yourself to me, it's full surrender. Everything. All of you. In the mornings when I wake up, you're cuddled into me all soft and warm and you always smile. Always. The sun rises right there. I know my day is going to be good because you smiled at me. I could give you a million more reasons, and I know I'm being damned selfish that I wanted—no I *need* you to make a move on me. I have to know that you aren't staying with me because I fucking forced you to."

God. He was giving her everything. Stripping himself of pride. Of his ego. Of the confident, arrogant, *controlling* man that he was. She fell a little bit more in love with him. How could she not?

"I don't know what I'm doing," she admitted, embarrassed. Not just embarrassed—humiliated. Nearly as humiliated as when Rafe had insisted she read a poem to his visitors. "And it's mortifying. You're so experienced, Eli, and I hate doing anything wrong in front of you because I don't want you to think I'm stupid."

"Baby," he said gently, cupping the back of her head in his palm. His eyes softened. His face gentled. He slid his thumb over her lips. "Is that what you've been afraid of?

That you wouldn't do it right? And never again, *ever*, believe that I would think you were stupid. I'm very aware how intelligent you are. You not only outsmarted Cordeau, but you fooled me a time or two as well." His head dipped down to hers, his lips feathering gently over hers. "You really didn't make a move because you were afraid you wouldn't do something right? Baby, there is no right way."

She nodded, miserable. "I hate not knowing what I'm supposed to do. And there might not be a right way, but there's a way you like it. That's the way I want to do it."

"What did I tell you about that, Cat? When you need something, talk to me. You want information, especially about something as important as this, you talk to me. Kitten, I like anything I can get from you. Anything. Any way. I need to know you're with me because you want to be with me, not because you have to." He shoved a hand through his hair, messing it up.

She liked his hair messed up. Already her body was heating up. Needing. Hungry for him. She let it happen because this time she was going to ask. If he needed to know she wanted him as much as he wanted her, she could show him that.

"I thought tying you to me with sex would be a good idea, Catarina," he confessed. "But in the end, all it's done is make you think that's all I want from you. I have to admit, I'm very sexual, it matters. I'm not saying it doesn't. But all the rest of it, all that you give me, the way you give it to me, your surrender to me, putting up with my shit, that makes the physical take a backseat. You get me? Do you understand what I'm saying to you, baby? Because it's important you know that."

She nodded. Took a breath. Made a decision. "I'm going to get your coffee for you. I want you to take your clothes off and sit in your favorite chair and wait for me. I'll be out in a minute and I'll expect a little direction."

His golden eyes searched hers for a long time. A slow

heat crept in. Hunger. Desire. Lust. She watched it build. *She* had put that look there. He liked control, but she was taking charge and he liked that too.

"Don't be long, baby. I'm already dying here a little."

He leaned down and took her mouth in a long, slow kiss that only added to the fire burning so hot in her veins. When he lifted his head, she saw it. Stark, raw love. He took her breath away, but then he always did. She turned back to the kitchen, needing a little space to collect herself. She'd tamed the leopard. It was powerful and exhilarating. She'd made her stand, and he'd listened to her. He'd shared himself with her. He'd given her his childhood and his struggles.

As she made his favorite coffee, she realized he had the same struggle all along that Rafe had. His leopard was a dominant male, fierce and wild. Rafe had lost control, but Eli had taken control. That was why he was so overboard about control in the world he'd created for himself.

She stripped off her shirt and went to him naked. She stepped onto the porch and immediately saw him in the shadows. He sat in his chair, following her instructions, naked, his cock already hard and thick. One hand fisted the length and slowly, casually moved up and down in a mesmerizing slide. Her mouth watered. She loved seeing him do that. That simple action turned her on all the more.

She set the coffee down on the small table beside him. Her courage was beginning to fail a little. She still didn't know what she was doing.

"I'm not certain I'll be able to drink that coffee with your mouth wrapped around me, baby," he confided, his voice low. Husky. Sexy. "I think that might be too much of a distraction to enjoy the coffee. But, baby, if that's what you want, then that's what I'll do. Or I'll try."

She found herself smiling. She knew he was deliberately putting her at ease. "I thought, at first, you could let me . . ." She trailed off, hesitating. He waited, and she sighed. "Explore."

He smiled at her. "I get that. I'll just sit back and drink my coffee. We're not in any hurry, although this might just kill me. There's no right way or wrong way right now. I want you to do some exploring. Whatever feels good to you. Get to know the shape and feel of me, you'll know what I like and what I don't. I won't like the feel of your teeth, but I'll love your tongue."

She took a breath, her eyes searching his face for a long while. He was patient. Her gaze dropped to his cock still wrapped in his hand. He was big. Long and thick. The crown was broad and looked silky. She loved to look at him. He was all muscle, all power and danger. His cock matched the rest of him.

"Keep telling me what to do, Eli. When I hear your voice, it's reassuring to me. I need to know you're there. I like it when you give me guidance." That was her confession. Her surrender. She hoped he understood what she meant.

Of course he knew. He immediately complied, using that low, commanding tone she loved. The one that vibrated between her legs and made her burn hotter.

"Kneel, Kitten, with your knees wide. That lets me see you like what you're doing. That's important to me, knowing you're enjoying yourself."

She moved into position between his legs. His skin was hot and smelled a little wild, feral, definitely primitive. She liked the way he smelled. There were two pearly drops on the silken head of his cock and she leaned into him to lick them off as she opened her knees wide.

His taste was addicting. She didn't know if he was that way naturally or if it was the things he chose to eat, only that she loved the taste of him and always craved more. For her, this moment was huge. She wanted to know she could please him just the way he pleased her. She needed to feel on the same level with him, that he wanted her just the way she wanted him, that no one else would do. And she needed to know that she could bring him to the very edge of his control, or even, possibly, tipping him past it. She liked that he cared enough to give her power. And she knew this was very powerful.

Eli dropped his hand to the top of Catarina's head and brushed a caress over her hair with one hand while he reached casually for the coffee cup with the other. There was something very decadent about sitting on his porch in the late evening, a cup of coffee in his hand and his woman kneeling between his legs, her hands caressing his balls, her tongue gliding over the crown of his cock.

She looked so anxious that he cursed himself that he hadn't seen the problem. He should have known she wouldn't have the confidence to initiate sex, particularly sucking his cock in the early morning hours. He wanted to groan aloud at the thought of her looking at him and wondering what to do.

She stroked her tongue over his shaft, and then flicked it underneath the broad head. His body shuddered and fire raced up his shaft to radiate into his belly. His balls burned. Maybe this wasn't such a good idea. He wasn't going to be able to last very long, not when he'd gone so long without her.

"Take your time, baby," he murmured softly. She needed to know what she was doing was perfect, whether or not it was killing him.

She ran her lips up and down him, over his balls and back up to the crown, learning the shape and feel of him with her mouth and hands.

"That's it. Pay attention to the cues I give you. Changes in my breathing. If I put my head back or tighten my thighs." He took a sip of coffee and watched her tongue lick at him like an ice cream cone. That was enough to make him moan.

"Deeper, baby, take me deeper," he encouraged.

Catarina did what he said, and he put down his coffee cup. She liked it a *lot* better when he put the cup down and she knew she had him, that what she was doing was getting to him. She found if she suckled strongly and did a little moaning of her own, the sensation really got to him. She found the most sensitive spots, and she worked them, enjoying every shudder of his body.

"That's perfect, baby," he praised. "You're already a master at this, and you want to know why? Because it matters to you. You really do want to please me. You're beautiful, Cat, so fucking beautiful."

She loved the rasp in his voice. The way he was always so decisive and commanding. She loved that he gave her praise when she did something right. She loved her mouth on him. His taste. The way his body shuddered with pleasure. And she especially loved that she was the one giving him that pleasure.

"That's so good, Kitten, but I think you're ready for me to take over. I'm going to go a little harder and a little deeper than last time we did this. When I go deep, it might be more like twenty seconds instead of ten and you might begin to panic. I want your eyes on me the entire time. That way I can see if you're panicked but can take it, or panicked and we have to stop for a couple of minutes. Do you understand?"

She nodded, too caught up in what she was doing to really pay attention.

He narrowed his gaze. "Baby, I don't want you afraid. If you start to panic, I need to know. I have to be able to read you. Tell me you get that."

She fought down a smile. He was more anxious on her behalf than she was. "Yes, Eli, I understand, I'll keep my eyes on yours."

"I want you sucking me and using your tongue while I go deep. Relax for me, just like before."

She was so wet between her legs, her thighs felt creamy. Her body tingled from head to toe. Her mouth watered. She couldn't take her eyes from his, from the dark intensity of his hunger. He looked darkly sensual, his features carved with lust, his eyes hooded and hungry.

"This time, I'm not going to stop. You understand?"

She swallowed. He was scaring her just a little bit, but

she was excited at the same time. "I understand, you're not going to stop."

His hands went to her hair, fisting on either side of her head. "Tilt your head and keep your eyes on me. Don't look away. And put both your hands on my thighs and keep them there." He stood up, towering over her, the head of his cock at her lips.

She brushed a kiss over the silky head and then licked again at the white drops that told her she was doing her job. She pressed her palms to his thighs, feeling a little vulnerable without the ability to control how deep he drove into her. Still, that in itself added to the thrill and sensuality of the act.

He pushed his cock into her mouth, holding her head still, his eyes pure cat. Focused. Unblinking. He filled her mouth, driving deeper than he'd ever been, and he was right, it was a little scary, but she didn't look away from his eyes and that held her steady. The fire between her legs grew. Hot. Needy. Urgent. She loved this too.

She used her tongue when she could. She sucked hard when he was deep. Twice she nearly struggled, afraid she couldn't breathe and she'd choke to death. Both times he soothed her. She nearly forgot and brought up her hands to stop him, but recovered both times without him having to remind her and that made her even happier.

"Baby, you're doing great." His voice was hoarse. His head was back. She could see his muscles standing out. A fine sheen dusted his chest. "A couple more seconds. Breathe through your nose. This is paradise. You're giving me fucking paradise."

She wanted to give him paradise and she could see it on his face. His eyes were completely molten, his face carved with pure sensuality. He was holding back for her and she didn't want him to. The fists in her hair pulled at her scalp with a bite of pain and she felt the answering rush of hot liquid between her legs. Determined, she suckled him as hard and as tightly as she could.

When he drove deep, she forced air through her nose and tried to relax her throat. The sounds he made, long feral growls, drove her out of her mind with lust. Her breasts hurt they were so achy. Tremors raced through her body and she was certain, absolutely certain if she dropped one hand and pushed her finger between her legs she would explode, but she didn't, because she wanted to give him this, just as he'd given her so much pleasure.

He went deeper again. He was hotter than before. Thicker. She felt his cock pulse. Throb. She used her tongue along the underside of the broad crown, and sucked hard, hollowing her cheeks, wanting everything he could give her. He threw back his head and roared to the night. His body shuddered. She felt the muscle of his thighs tighten, dance with pleasure as he erupted.

His fists held her head perfectly still while he poured down her throat, the hot, thick length of him filling her. The sensual sounds he made set off a series of mini-quakes in her body so that her sheath contracted hard and her womb spasmed.

Very slowly his hands loosened in her hair. His eyes blazed down into hers. He looked hungry enough to devour her, and that was almost as thrilling as knowing she'd put that look on his face.

"So good, Kitten. Perfect."

His voice was a rough velvet that sent tremors through her stomach. She felt his legs tremble when another shudder went through his body. He didn't release her, not even when he sat down.

He leaned back in the chair, relaxing, even closing his eyes as she bent to him, lapping gently with her tongue. She liked the way the tension slipped from his face so she took her time, taking care of him while she had the chance.

His hand went to the top of her head. "You're the most amazing woman in the world, Kitten. I never once imagined I'd ever have a woman like you."

14

CATARINA Benoit would forever be his obsession. His love. Eli hadn't known it was possible to feel the way she made him feel. He was totally at peace. He couldn't remember a time, from the moment he'd entered puberty, that he'd ever felt at peace. Every muscle in his body was warm and relaxed. He could barely open his eyes, just enough to see her. To watch her.

She was the most beautiful, exotic woman on earth. He hadn't expected her to care for him, not in the ways she showed him care. The minute attention to detail. She was meticulous when it came to the effort she put in lavishing attention on him.

He managed to slide his hand from his thigh to slip his fingers back into her long, dark hair. He'd spent a good deal of his life traveling the world looking for the right woman and he'd been close to giving up. There was only one. He'd known that from the moment he began having sex with women. He'd known because his leopard was doubly dangerous around the women and he didn't always trust that he could control the animal.

The moment he'd laid eyes on Catarina, everything had been different, even the sex. Especially the sex. He'd had great sex before, but he'd never imagined the places her body could take him. Mostly, he never imagined the depth of emotion she could create inside him.

He was a difficult man. He knew himself very well. Shifters had to be in control at all times, especially the males. He lived for control, and he knew he was domineering. There had always been a part of him that feared a woman wouldn't be able to take his rough insistence on dominance. More, he was rough and he liked his sex that way. He certainly hadn't expected a woman who could take his kind of sex and give back the way she did.

He studied her face. Her beautiful, flawless face. Her long lashes and gorgeous eyes. Her perfect sinful mouth. It didn't seem possible that she could be his. He needed to take better care of her. Instead of letting his foul temper smolder for days, he should have recognized that she would be shy with him.

That hadn't really occurred to him either because she was completely uninhibited when they had sex. He knew he loved her. The terrible feeling inside him couldn't be anything but love. It ate him up and made him look at himself, really look at who and what he was. With her, he had to be better. He wanted to be better. She deserved better.

"I can't tell you how much you mean to me, Catarina," he said. He had to clear his throat when her gaze jumped to his and he nearly fell into her eyes. His voice growled, his emotions so strong, so intense he nearly shook with them.

She sat back on her heels, her eyes soft. Something else was there too and his belly knotted fast. She was definitely afraid of her feelings for him, but she had them. At least the beginnings of feelings, and he wanted to nurture that, make certain it grew.

He reached down and drew her gently to him, cuddling her in his lap. Her body was very warm, despite the cool evening. She fit. There on his lap. Wrapped in his arms. She fit. He caught up the bottle of water he had sitting by his coffee and handed it to her, nuzzling the top of her head.

"I've fallen in love with you." He stared over her head into the night as he made the confession. His heart twisted into knots. His blood surged through his body, a rush of adrenaline at the stark, raw admission he never thought he'd ever make to anyone. He felt as if he was baring his soul, and maybe he was. "I don't know how it happened, Kitten. I was so busy worrying about your leopard for my leopard, I suddenly found myself completely obsessed with you."

He could feel the change in her instantly. She went very still. She didn't pull away. Catarina stayed snuggled into him, a part of him, curled up like a little cat on his lap, but she didn't move a muscle, not even to bring the water to her mouth.

He tipped her head up to force her gaze to meet his. "It's true. I love you more than anything on this earth. It isn't about the leopards anymore. I don't give a damn about Rafe Cordeau or the DEA. For me, there never can be anyone else but you."

Her blue eyes searched his face for a long time. She looked close to tears.

"Baby, I'm not asking anything of you," he said softly. "I know you're not there yet. You still have no reason to trust me, but you committed to me a few nights ago. You gave yourself to me, put yourself back on the line, and not once in the last four days have you brought up the fact that I lied to you when we met. Not one time. You were true to your word and you're trying to put it behind us. Do you know how big a gift that is to me? What you gave me? Do you have any idea what giving that to me means to me?" She was the most unusual woman on earth. He couldn't imagine another woman forgiving him and putting herself in harm's way again, not like that. And not throwing it in his face at every opportunity.

He reached around her to take the cap off the bottle and hand it to her. "Drink. You have to be thirsty after all that. I intend to take the best care of you. The kind of care you give me, Cat. You make me feel loved whether you know it or not."

"I've never had anyone love me." She made the admission in a small, shaky voice and immediately took a drink. Her hand trembled as she held the bottle to her mouth so he steadied her hand for her with his own.

His heart turned over. Melted. "That isn't true."

"No. It is. It is true. My birth mother died having me. My father remarried when I was about two. He died a year later. I don't remember much about him and nothing about my birth mother. He left me with Tracy and for as long as I can remember, she did drugs and drank. She was the only mother I ever had, the only person I had growing up, but I was definitely in her way. And then she gave me to Rafe."

He brought his hand up to the nape of her neck, fingers working at her muscles there. "Tracy Benoit isn't your birth mother?" Why didn't anyone have that information? It wasn't in her file.

What he really wanted to know was her reaction to his admission—his confession. She looked a little shell-shocked. His Catarina could take him being rough and bossy and arrogant far easier than when he was loving and kind to her. Now he knew why. She'd never had loving and kind. She didn't know what to do with that.

Catarina shook her head. She was stunned. Shocked. Unable to process what Eli had just said to her. She heard the ring of truth in his voice. Her leopard might be quiet, but already her senses were stretching Cat's. Eli loved her. She wanted to wrap her arms around herself and hug that declaration to her. Instinctively she knew he wasn't a man to use the word *love* if he didn't mean it. Even meaning it, saying it would be difficult.

"I've never told a woman I loved her, because it wasn't

true," Eli said. "Not even when I was undercover. I refused to ever take it that far. I knew if I ever got the chance to say it, I'd want it to be only for the one woman I really loved. Somehow it felt if I said it when it wasn't true, it would cheapen it for the woman I loved. So there it is, baby. It's you. Only you."

Her heart actually hurt, a physical pain. She couldn't say it back because she didn't honestly know what she felt. She was still afraid of him—of them. No, that wasn't the truth. She was afraid of herself. She didn't understand relationships and she was leery of committing her heart and soul too far. She'd just opened herself up to him when he'd betrayed her and that had hurt so bad. If she allowed herself to really feel everything for him, the way she wanted her relationship to be, that intense, that strong, and she lost him, she would be totally destroyed. She was too fragile.

"Thank you for telling me, Eli," she whispered. "I want us to work. I don't want our relationship to be just about our leopards or the sex." She didn't even know if that was the truth. Part of her wanted to keep it simple. The leopards. Sex. That wouldn't hurt so much if she lost it. But the biggest part of her wanted the fairy tale. She wanted what Eli was holding out to her. She just didn't know if she was brave enough to grab on with both hands.

"Let's get you inside before it gets any colder."

"I don't feel cold." She liked being snuggled so tight in his arms. It felt intimate.

"I know, but I still have a few things I'd like to do this evening and it's late. We have to work out tomorrow. I know I'm pushing you, Kitten, but if we're going to be ready for Cordeau, then it's necessary to condition and keep learning how to defend yourself. You still think of him as an invincible monster. I don't want you to freeze when the time comes. If self-defense is ingrained in you, if it's an automatic reflex, you'll have a chance to get away from him if he ever gets his hands on you."

A little shudder went through her body at the thought of

Rafe finding her. Finding them. Rafe would want to kill Eli. She was beginning to believe killing Eli would prove to be much more difficult than she first thought. Living with him made it impossible not to see the danger that surrounded him. He was every bit as lethal as Rafe, only in a different way.

She had equated his gentleness with her as a weakness. She was learning Eli didn't have a weakness—unless it was her. He'd made himself vulnerable by telling her he loved her. She hadn't expected that and her eyes burned. There was a lump in her throat threatening to choke her at the sound of his soft voice whispering to her. Telling her things she knew he'd never told anyone else.

"I guess I do think of Rafe that way. He's so big in my mind. So scary. His word is law." She pulled away just enough to tip her head up and look at him. "Kind of the way you expect your word to be law."

He grinned at her, getting that she was teasing him. "I like that you're not afraid to spar a little with me, baby," he said. "Everyone else is terrified to give me a hard time or argue with me. You're getting there."

"I wouldn't want you to think you're going to get your way in all things," she said. That wasn't entirely true. She wanted to make him happy. She didn't know why it was important to her, but she wanted to be the one that kept the soft look on his face.

His grin widened. "I'll get my way, Kitten. You can count on that. But I'll make certain you're enjoying yourself when I do."

She blushed. The heat inside her body seemed to grow until she thought her skin might be glowing. Or maybe she was glowing because he'd told her he loved her.

Eli laughed softly and stood up with her in his arms. She felt his muscles ripple but the move was fluid and effortless. He walked back inside without even breathing hard, as if her weight was nothing whatsoever to him. He carried her through the house, not turning on any lights, but then he rarely did at night. He had excellent night vision and she did as well.

Her heart began to pound when they entered the bedroom. There was something very purposeful in the way he walked. He tossed her onto the mattress, onto her back. She landed right in the middle, sprawled out. He stood over her, tall and broad-shouldered, his features a mask of sensuality. He took her breath away. She knew that expression. His eyes had gone to liquid gold, the gold spreading until it nearly covered the surface of his eyes.

"Put your hands above your head, baby," he instructed. "Grip the headboard for me." His voice had gone rough. Husky. Low. Commanding.

Instantly, heat flooded her body. Just his voice. That was all it took. Adding in his eyes and the way his body came alive, she was lost. She slowly complied, not taking her gaze from his face. She loved the way he looked, the implacable single-minded focus in his expression, the heat and lust building in his eyes. She recognized the third emotion—love—mixed with the hunger there. Her hands gripped the thick dowels above her head. She had to stretch her arms out all the way to comply.

"That's my woman. I love how you look right now. Open your legs wide for me. Are you already wet? Do you know what I need right now?"

She moistened her lips with the tip of her tongue. Her heart began to pound. She felt the answering pulse in her hot, wet channel. "I'm already wet," she admitted.

He knelt between her legs and, still holding her gaze, slipped a finger into her. Instantly her greedy body grasped at him and tried to pull him deeper.

"I like that you get wet for me. So slick and hot. All that honey. I dream about the way you taste. Sometimes it wakes me up. I want to let you sleep. You're all curled up beside me like a sleepy kitten, and I hate to disturb you, but I can't go back to sleep thinking about devouring you.

Sometimes I just want to eat you up, baby. Never stop. See how much honey I can harvest before you go up in flames."

Her nipples beaded. A small tremor sent a spasm through her channel. He pushed another finger into her, scissored them apart to stretch her. He did it casually, still watching her face, holding her gaze captive with his. A small burn as he stretched her sent heat spiraling through her sheath, rocking her. He was barely touching her and she thought he might make her explode.

Her hips undulated, pressed into his hand so that she tried to ride his fingers. He withdrew them immediately. "Lie still for me, baby. I'm going to eat you. Do to you just what I've wanted to do every night we've been in bed together."

His eyes burned her, they were so hot as they moved over her body. His face was a study in raw, masculine beauty. She loved his face, especially when he looked at her with such command, such stark sensuality. He was the epitome of sexy to her. His rough tone coupled with his explicit intent sent more honey and spice spilling from her body in anticipation. She tugged her lower lip between her teeth in an effort to keep her hips still for him, wanting his fingers back. Aching for his mouth.

"When I wake up needing my mouth on your breasts, between your legs, Kitten, do you know what I decided I was going to do about it from now on?"

She shook her head. She was trembling all over now. So hot. So needy, and he still hadn't even really touched her.

"I'm going to do whatever the hell I want to do," he said softly and gripped her hips in his hard hands.

The breath slammed out of her. She actually began to feel a little feverish. A little desperate for him. She wanted to plead with him to stop talking and get to it, but she knew that if she did, he'd make her wait longer, building that tension already coiling so tight in her body.

His hooded eyes moved over her then, his carved features stamped with possession. His hands followed his gaze, moving down from her shoulders to her breasts. She waited, holding her breath, needing him to suckle, to lavish attention, to tug and roll her nipples the way he did, but his palms just slipped over her curves and moved down her rib cage to her waist and then lower to her belly.

"I'd like to see that tattoo on you, baby," he said. "On the small of your back, but right here, I'd like a little ring so I could put a chain around your belly and play with it when I make love to you."

He was killing her. It took every ounce of self-control she had not to allow her legs to shift restlessly, or her hips to move. He was killing her with the soft brush of his fingers and his erotic images.

"Would you do that for me?"

"If you asked me to," she admitted. Because she'd do anything for him to make him happy. If that was really something that mattered to him, then it mattered to her. She didn't mind tattoos. In fact, she loved his. She'd never thought about piercings, but a small belly ring might be sexy.

"If I asked you to?" he repeated, his hands sliding lower to frame her mound and then slip lower still to sweep over her inner thighs. He frowned a little.

"I meant if I thought it mattered to you," she hastened to explain. It was difficult to think straight when her body was on fire. "I've never considered either, and I really like tattoos. I hadn't thought about a belly ring, but it might be nice."

"You'd do it for me if it mattered to me?"

His eyes were back on hers and her stomach did a crazy flip. She'd said the right thing, she could see how pleased he was. Her answer mattered to him whether she did it or not. She loved that she'd put that look in his eyes.

"Of course. I like doing things for you," she admitted.

His smile took her breath away. He stretched out on the bed, on his belly and put her legs over his shoulders. Her breath hitched again. He looked so sexy, his gaze focused now, this time on the junction between her legs. He looked hungry, like a predatory animal about to feast. The raw sensuality was carved deep into the lines of his face and there in his eyes.

Her body pulsed and throbbed and without any more encouragement than his focused stare, more hot spice slipped out. His hands stroked her thighs and her temperature rose until she felt as if the very blood in her veins had caught fire.

She closed her eyes when she felt his warm breath first. The smallest of things, yet her inner muscles reacted, pulsing with need. She felt as if time had stopped. She heard her heart beat. The clock ticking. The wind in the trees. He had to do something or she was going to die.

He made a single sound, low in his throat, like the snarl or growl of a leopard about to devour a meal it had caught. Her heart nearly exploded and she tightened her fists around the thick dowels to anchor herself.

His tongue slid through her hot, slick folds like a caress and her entire body jerked. A low cry escaped her throat before she could hold it back. His eyes jumped to her face, a golden, hot gaze that warned her not to move, not to disturb him, that he would go at his own pace.

Catarina forced her twisting body to still. To give him all the control. She realized in that moment he was already in control of her, but not so much of himself. He was truly one with his leopard, and he wanted his feast and was going to take it. The primal frenzy was on him and it only made her burn hotter for him.

Eli began licking her like a cat might lap a bowl of cream. His tongue rasped over and into her, sending her nearly spiraling out of control at the first touch. Electrical currents raced to her breasts like tiny bolts of lightning, making them sensitive and achy. Her stomach muscles coiled so tightly it hurt. She fought for air when her lungs burned, reminding her she had to breathe.

Eli's arm held her pinned down, his wide shoulders ensuring she was wide open to him. He kept licking up the honey spilling out of her body, a relentless unhurried pace, ever the cat enjoying his meal. He didn't change his rhythm, but she never knew where his tongue was going to swipe next. No matter how hard she tried, it was impossible to hold still. He kept the lower half of her body exactly where he wanted it, but her head thrashed wildly on the mattress and her knuckles turned white holding on for life to the headboard. Her muscles spasmed again, sending endless amounts of that hot spicy cream to his greedy mouth.

Her entire body nearly convulsed with pleasure. Strong, rippling waves started deep in her core and spread through her body, down her thighs and up her belly to her breasts. The moment the quake started, instead of backing off, Eli drew more spice out, catching the hot liquid on his tongue, pushing deep for more. His teeth raked her clit and she screamed, exploding a second time, right on the heels of the first.

Her body was so hot now, she couldn't stand it. Even with his mouth on her, his tongue wicked, never stopping, forcing another orgasm, his teeth and fingers and mouth so greedy she couldn't find a way to breathe, it still didn't stop the fire that began to spread through her like a wildfire.

Catarina's low, keening cry pierced through the chaos reigning in Eli's mind. He was lost in her body, in the sweet taste of her, in his need to own what he knew was his. In his greed for the treasure that was all his. Catarina wanted to please him and he needed to take full advantage.

His gaze jumped to her face. There was stark fear, nearly amounting to terror. Desperation. Hunger. Her eyes glowed, and he realized her body was scorching hot. Not just her feminine channel but her skin. All of her. His leopard shifted inside him, leapt toward the surface, snarling, raking with claws, roaring for domination. The animal went nearly insane with need, clawing for freedom, desperate and wild.

Catarina's eyes glowed at him, going from a brilliant cobalt to a deep violet. Her skin was nearly translucent, burning like the exotic cat's eyes. She had never looked so alluring or passionate. Her gaze devoured him, hot and hungry, her need as primal as his own. His blood surged hotly, flowing like lava in his veins. His body had already been on fire, but now, drinking in the pheromones her body was throwing off and seeing a look of such stark hunger on her face, there was no going back. No stopping.

"Eli." Catarina sounded frightened. "I'm burning up. Seriously burning up and I need you inside me, right now." Desperation edged her voice.

She couldn't stop moving, squirming, rubbing her thighs together. One hand drifted down past her belly to the junction between her legs. He could see the tiny beads of honey still dampening her mound and creaming her thighs. She curled her fingers into her, working them with soft little pants. Her other hand went to her left breast, finger and thumb tugging at her nipple. She threw back her head, a moan escaping.

Eli thought he might explode just watching her. He still tasted her in his mouth. He breathed her scent into his lungs, the hot, needy siren's call of honeysuckle and spice. She was wild, writhing on the bed, pleading with him, and he'd never seen anything more beautiful.

He stood up abruptly and caught at her wrist, the hand at her breast. He yanked her up, right off the bed and his mouth came down on hers. Hard. Brutal. Savagely. He heard his own feral growl as he took her mouth, sharing the taste with her, kissing her over and over.

He was savage, a wildfire out of control. He devoured her mouth. Fed on her. Gave her no chance to breathe or think. He poured himself into her, every bit of himself, giving her everything he was or would ever be. His hands were rough sliding over her skin, claiming her, fingers biting deep.

The little desperate noises she made, a keening coming from her throat nearly drove him mad. He could feel her nipples, hard and erect, pressed tight against his chest. With her every ragged breath, her breasts rose, dragging the stiff pinpoints of sensitivity against his muscles.

He pushed her against the wall, his hands coming up to

capture the soft weight of her breasts, bringing them up as he bent his head to draw her left breast deep into his mouth. He used his fingers ruthlessly, tugging and rolling her right nipple, so that electric shocks spread from his fingers straight to her clit.

She caught at his head, arching her back like a cat, holding him to her while her cries filled the air. She moaned and writhed, cradling his head to her while he fed on her breasts. He used the edge of his teeth to scrape her nipples and nip the soft sweet curves. He used his tongue ruthlessly, flat and broad and then long, slow licks easing every ache before suckling strong enough to elicit gasps and cries.

She was ultrasensitive to the touch of his hands and mouth, her skin burning against his. She radiated heat and he caught fire. One leg wound around his hip and she pressed her sex against his thigh and ground down, frantic for relief. Her hips bucked against him, a sob choked her throat as she writhed in his arms. It was the hottest, sexiest thing he'd ever witnessed. She was like a living flame, unable to contain, unable to put out the burning heat.

Catarina was on fire. Every cell was inflamed and deep inside, she burned so hot she thought she might die. Her body didn't feel as if it belonged to her at all. Every inch of her was so sensitive she hurt. She was desperate for Eli's body against hers, yet even that seemed to make her ache more. Her skin was just too tight. Her joints ached. Her hair was too heavy for her head and her skull felt as if it might explode.

The absolute worst was the terrible heat burning through her like a firestorm. She couldn't breathe with wanting Eli. Her mind was in chaos, the need so terrible she thought she might go insane. She couldn't stop the undulations of her body, or the need to press over his thigh and grind down hard. Her hands were everywhere, touching him, fingers spread wide to take in as much of him as possible. Her mouth moved over his chest, his belly, along his rib cage. She couldn't get enough of touching him.

The beat of her heart was insane. She felt the throb between her legs, pounding urgently, a feral, primal drumbeat of relentless hunger. She couldn't stop herself, licking at his skin, reaching for him with desperation.

"Do something, Eli," she pleaded, so insane for him even her voice wasn't her own. "I need you touching me. Your mouth. Your fingers. I need you filling me. Take it away. You have to make it stop."

"I've got you, Kitten," Eli assured her, jerking her chin up so he could take her mouth again.

He was addicted to the taste of her, the way all that honey poured down his throat and invaded every organ of his body. The mixture of honeysuckle and pheromones spread through his system like wildfire until she was branded on his tongue, down his lungs and in his very bones.

She sobbed his name, over and over, a desperate keening mewl, and he couldn't stand it another minute. He whirled her around and bent her over the bed, pressing her head down with one hand hard in the middle of her back until her head touched the mattress, the action pushing the firm globes of her buttocks into the air.

When her hand went between her legs, he caught it firmly and stretched both arms out, so that her hands were forced to grip the opposite sides of the bed. He didn't wait. He couldn't. Not with her frantic cries and the way she pushed back against him, rubbing her buttocks along his aching shaft.

He caught her around the hips with one strong arm and slammed into her. She screamed and instantly clamped down on him, gripping with tight, spasming muscles. Her orgasm was long and wild and he pistoned into her over and over right through it.

"Harder. Eli, harder," she sobbed, gasping for breath.

His thrusts were brutal and hard. He took her roughly, savagely, while the fire tore through them both until neither could breathe through the pleasure. The tension wound

tighter and tighter, the frenzied thrall driving them almost
past sanity, as each fed on the other's lust.

His hands were brutal, digging into her hips as he pow-
ered into her over and over, sending lightning crashing
through her body. Twice more she came apart, but he didn't
stop or even slow his ferocious pace. Each savage thrust
rocked her body, driving her head into the mattress as he
forced her hips higher so he could go deeper.

He was relentless, ruthless, taking her higher and higher,
her cries and pleas urging him for more. Always more. Her
mind didn't think she could take it. She thought she might
go insane with the frenzy of lust growing between them,
but her body refused to be sated no matter how many times
he sent her crashing over the edge. He was so thick and
hard, a battering ram that forced its way through her tight
channel so that the friction increased to the point she feared
they'd both burn from the fiery contact.

He slammed into her over and over, jerking her body to
meet the hard thrust of his hips. His face was a mask of sensual fury, of utter resolve. He wouldn't stop. He couldn't stop.
A sob escaped and fear skittered down her spine, but she kept
pleading for more, she needed more. She didn't want him to
stop even if it killed her, because if he didn't make the terrible
burning between her legs stop, she would die anyway.

The fire built into a raging inferno, spreading through
her body like a firestorm, picking up speed until it felt like
hurricane winds had swept the flames through every part of
her. The tension coiled tighter and tighter. She felt him
swell, filling her beyond her capacity to take him, stretching her, burning and stinging until even that was swept
away in a vortex of intense passion.

His cock swelled more. Pulsed. Imprinted itself on her
inner muscles, branded her there with—him. With Eli. She
went rigid as her body clamped down viciously, strangling
his cock, forcing the fire into the friction as his body continued to invade hers with hard, driving strokes. His muscles

bunched. He drove deep again, once, twice and then jet after jet of hot liquid hit the tender walls of her sheath and filled her with his burning seed, marking her internally once again as his.

Her body still wouldn't let him go, milking him greedily for every pearly drop, squeezing as she clamped down around him hard. He couldn't leave her. He just couldn't. He had to stay inside her and burn with her because it wasn't stopping. Ripple after ripple, quake after quake and still her body demanded more.

Catarina slumped over the mattress, her hands clenching the sheets hard. She tasted blood on her lip where she'd sunk her teeth deep. If it wasn't for Eli's iron arm holding her hips up, she would have just collapsed. All she wanted to do was cry. The fire between her legs wasn't gone. Even after all that. Worse, her skin was hot, and far too tight. Her hair was too heavy, pulling at her scalp. Everything hurt. Every joint. Her jaw. Her fingers, even her toes.

Eli didn't pull out of her, nor did his cock soften. He remained in her, stretching her, and as he bent forward over her, the heavy length of him rubbed along her clit and her body exploded again. He licked at the tiny beads of sweat on her back, his tongue stroking caresses along her spine. Her heart pounded and she pushed back into him, tight, a small sob escaping.

"It's all right, baby, I've got you," he whispered against her shoulder. "I'm right here with you. Don't be afraid of this. Let it take you. Let it happen."

She felt her then, her leopard, rising toward the heat and fire. Rising toward the wildness she sensed in Eli. A wave rose just beneath her skin, a terrible itch, pushing from underneath, determined this time, grounded in the fire that burned between her thighs.

"She wants out. I don't know how to bring her out," Catarina whispered into the mattress, on the very edge of despair. If the leopard didn't get out of her, she was going to burst into flames and turn to ash. She couldn't stand the heat or the terrible burning that refused to stop between her legs. She didn't even know anymore if she was the one burning or her leopard was, only that she had to find a way to help the other get free.

"I know what will call her, Kitten. Trust me now. Let me do this for you."

It always came back to Eli—everything. She needed him. She wanted him and God help her, she loved him. She knew he would see her through this. "Please, Eli, please help me with her."

At once she felt the slide of fur up by her shoulder. A hot burst of air hit her and then teeth sank deep. She forced herself to breathe, accepting the bite, knowing his leopard called to hers. It was Eli's hands on her, his body locked with hers, but somehow he had managed to shift his head and allow his leopard to call to the female. She couldn't believe he had that kind of control.

Catarina breathed away the pain as she felt the female leap toward the male leopard. At once, Eli slipped out of her, and stepped back, still holding her up.

"We've got to get outside. Can you walk?" His voice was rough. Growling, already animal.

Her stomach cramped and she slipped to the floor on all fours. Pain was back in every joint, and her skin itched so bad she wanted to scream. Eli didn't ask again, he swept her up, cradling her against his chest and ran through the house with her.

"Breathe deep and don't try to hold her back. You won't disappear, baby, even though the first time is scary and painful. You'll be with her and you'll feel a sense of freedom that's unbelievable."

"I want this." She tried to tell him but her voice was different. "For you, to be with you." She wanted him to know. She was afraid, and yes, it hurt, but she knew Eli's leopard needed her female the way Eli needed her—and she needed him.

By the time Eli had leapt from the porch with her in his arms, her body had begun to contort. Sweat beaded on her skin and she scented the feral creature. The female leopard was as afraid as she was and that made her all the more determined to make certain she could shift properly.

"Tell me what to do."

"Breathe and relax. Let it happen. Don't fight it, baby. I'll be right here with you. The whole time, I'll be at your side."

She believed him. She knew beyond a shadow of a doubt that Eli would stay with her and guard her in any form she was in. She just knew. She breathed deeply, trying to push through the pain to relax her body enough to accept the shift. She even crooned softly to the female leopard, coaxing her out.

Her body contorted again, joints popping. Cracking. Pain burst through her but she ignored it. She forced more air through teeth that were too large for her mouth, through the lengthening jaw and hands that disappeared under fur and claws. Pain radiated through every part of her body as fur rippled over her. Her lungs burned and she looked down at the ground and then at her limbs.

Where there had been a woman, now there was a leopard, a small female with luxurious rosette-covered tawny fur. Elated, she turned her head to look at Eli. In his place was the large black leopard and his eyes were on her as if he might devour her at any moment. The small female turned and with a warning switch of her tail, took off running.

15

Eli woke feeling as if he was hungover. His head pounded and his body ached. He moved and instantly was aware of the slight weight on his belly. He was on his back, Catarina's body curled against him, her head resting just over his belly button. She had one arm flung over him. Her wild hair was everywhere, forming a silken blanket over his cock and thighs.

His body instantly stirred at the intimacy of her position. He breathed slowly and deeply, drawing the scent of her into his lungs. His hand immediately threaded through her hair before he'd even thought of putting it there. He found himself smiling. He loved everything about this woman, especially the way she went wild when he had her body under his.

Catarina Benoit was full of surprises. He knew she was afraid of shifting. Everyone was afraid the first time. It was painful and wrenching to every bone in one's body. She had looked to him with her wide, blue eyes, trusting him to get her through. *Trusting* him. That was worth everything right there to him. She listened and did just as he said.

He was leopard and his male had risen fast. He could scent her fear, but she didn't hesitate and she shifted fairly quickly because of her determination.

Eli ran his fingers through Catarina's thick silky hair. She moved slightly and a soft groan escaped. He pushed back the sheet covering her body and took a good look at her. There were bruises and marks all over her body. Mostly from him, from his hands and mouth during the frenzied thrall of the Han Vol Dan.

He closed his eyes for a moment to block out the sight of her soft skin covered in dark smudges. She definitely was small for a leopard, although she carried the curves and hair, but her body type made her seem far too fragile for the rough sex and rough mating of shifters.

The leopards had been together all night. His male had claimed the female fairly fast, allowing her to run for a short while before taking possession. He was fast and vicious, serious about staking his claim. He was every bit as rough as Eli and just as controlling—even more so.

The two leopards had played hard and rough through the night and most of the next day. The male had been on the female every fifteen minutes or so, using his heavier frame to hold her in place and his teeth in her shoulder to pin her down. The love fest had gone on for hours, as often happened with leopards, all night, all morning and most of the afternoon. When Eli had finally managed to convince the male to bring the female back to the ranch house, it was already nearly sunset.

Eli smoothed his hand over her dark hair. Catarina was exhausted, both emotionally and physically. He'd carried her into the house and she'd fallen asleep in his arms. He'd run a hot bath and actually got into the tub to hold her in the water, hoping that would help to reduce soreness. She'd roused a couple of times to shift position and each time she moved, she moaned softly.

He held her while she brushed her teeth and then he'd slipped her under the sheet and climbed into bed beside her, holding her close to him. Sometime in the night, she had flung one arm around him and laid her head on his belly. He liked waking up with her there. He liked having their legs tangled intimately together and her mouth a breath away from his cock. He liked her warmth and her laughter.

"I'm a goner, baby," he said softly, aloud.

She moved, stretching just enough to groan again and stop when her body protested. Her arm tightened around him. He felt the brush of her fingers along his ribs and the warmth of her breath on his skin. He even felt the flutter of her long lashes on his belly.

"It isn't morning, yet, is it?" she murmured.

"It's pushing nighttime, Kitten. The leopards were out playing all last night and most of today. We slept a few hours. Are you hungry?"

The pads of her fingers made lazy circles along his hip. The touch wasn't meant to be sexual, but it was intimate. She traced along his bone and then into the defined muscle there.

"Not really, but if you are, I can make you something."

Eli smiled, happiness bursting through him. His chest ached in the vicinity of his heart, and for one moment he found a lump in his throat so big he couldn't talk. He swallowed it down and dropped his hand to the nape of her neck, massaging gently.

"You're not going to fix me anything to eat, baby. You're going to lay right here and rest. I was offering to fix something for you."

She turned her head just enough to press a kiss into his belly. His cock jerked in reaction. His belly knotted and his breath hissed out between his teeth. Deep inside his heart stuttered.

"That was a nice thing to offer, Eli. Thank you." Catarina rested her cheek back against his belly. Her hand slipped lower, her fingers smoothing along the column of his thigh. "I'm so tired I can't really think. I like lying right here. You're warm, and when I'm with you like this, I'm not afraid."

This time she turned her head to look up at him. She looked drowsy. Comfortable. Beautiful. Her lashes were longer than he'd first thought, the same dark gloss as her hair, framing her incredible eyes. He couldn't believe she was draped over him, her fingers idly stroking his thigh while she drifted, still a little dazed from the experience of shifting. He couldn't believe she was his.

"Were you afraid?" he asked gently. He liked that she wasn't afraid when she was with him. That said a lot. With Cordeau putting up reward money for information on her, she had plenty to be afraid of. She'd probably been afraid most of her life.

"Yes. But I knew you'd get me through it. And I wanted her to come out. I wanted to make certain she wasn't a killer."

Her hand moved back up to his body and once more she turned her head to press a kiss into his belly. He felt the sweep of her silky hair over his belly, along his thighs, and God help him, tangling over his cock. Heat moved through his veins straight to his groin. He had to admit, he liked waking up this way.

"She's not a killer," he said.

"No, she's not. She was just as afraid as I was. Your male is a lot like you."

There was the tiniest bit of censure in her voice and he found himself smiling. She was definitely annoyed on her leopard's behalf.

"I noticed," he agreed. His hand tightened in her hair. "He knows he has to keep his woman in line because she's a little headstrong."

Her laughter was muffled by his stomach. He felt her soft lips trailing little kisses along his belly. Lazy kisses. Gentle. Barely there.

"Are you implying I'm headstrong?"

She turned her head again to look up at him. Her blue gaze moved over his face, and his entire body tightened. His fingers tangled in her hair again, this time a little tighter, a little more possessively.

"So beautiful, Cat, and all that beauty, all that sexy, is mine. A man finds a woman like you and he walks on water to keep her. You understand that, right? You understand I'm going to love you with everything in me. But I'm keeping you. You can't show me this, this kind of wake up. You can't give me this and then expect me to live without it."

"I understand you don't hear me when I'm talking to you," she murmured, and her mouth was back on his belly, her tongue stroking a caress before her lips trailed a blaze of fire from his belly to his cock.

Her mouth slid over him. Hot. Tight. Moist. Like a velvet fist. Her hair draped over his lap and his thighs, spilling across the sheet like a dark waterfall. His head exploded. Fire raced through him. His heart exploded. A storm of emotion. He heard her. Loud and clear. He heard her. His eyes burned and that lump was back in his throat.

Very gently he tugged on her hair to lift her mouth away from him. It was one of the hardest things he'd ever done, leaving the haven of her mouth. He drew her up over his body and rolled gently to tuck her under him. He felt her wince and another small sound escaped, a little groan that strengthened his resolve.

His hands framed her face and stared down into her incredible cobalt eyes. Right now they were deep blue with shades of violet and she looked at him with such a soft, loving expression he nearly lost his resolve with the need to join their bodies together. There was no better place than inside her.

"Baby, I hear you loud and clear. More than anything I want your mouth on me, letting me know how you feel. You can't know how much that means to me, but even more than that, I want to take care of you. You're exhausted. You need rest. I'll settle for kisses this evening. And then I'm going to feed you and massage you. The leopards are going to want out again soon and you'll need stamina. When they get erotic, so do we. Our emotions are tied together."

Before she could say anything he took her mouth with every bit of gentle and tender he had in him. It wasn't much, but all of it was hers. He poured love into her mouth, hoping she could hear him. He was talking to her just as she'd been talking to him. He lifted his head and saw that tears swam in her eyes. Yeah. She heard him.

"Do you need me to help you get into the bathroom?" he asked softly.

She shook her head. One finger came up to trace his jaw. Then his lips. Her touch was light, barely there, but he felt it like a brand in his bones. He opened his mouth and drew her finger deep. Her eyes went wide, then sexy.

"Baby"—he laved her finger with his tongue and then released her—"I asked you a question. I thought we'd established I like answers."

She smiled again. Her smile could move mountains. "That's not fair, you distracted me, probably on purpose so you could use that bossy tone."

"You like my bossy tone."

"True. But it makes me all hot and bothered, and you made it clear we're not going there right now, so you can't use that tone."

His smile widened until he felt it in his gut. She did that. Brought sunshine into his life, even there in the night. He brushed a kiss over her mouth just because he couldn't resist.

"My bossy tone makes you all hot and bothered?"

"You know it does."

Yeah. He knew. "You're wet for me right now, aren't you? Hot and slick and dripping honey."

She arched an eyebrow. "Probably."

That was a clear challenge. She wasn't going to tell him. She was teasing him. *Teasing* him. He liked it too. His palm shaped her breast, his thumb sliding over her nipple. He felt the answering shiver in her body and her eyes went violet. His hand kept going, down her rib cage to her waist. His finger dipped into her belly button and then circled it before sliding down to the soft nest of curls. The shiver grew into a tremor. She tugged her bottom lip between her teeth.

He liked this too. Playing gentle. It felt a lot like love. He sank two fingers into her. She was hot. She was slick. And there was plenty of spice calling to him. His woman was as perfect as she could get. She squirmed beneath him, her breath catching. He grinned at her.

"You are. Nice and hot too. It's a damn good thing I'm a strong man." Deliberately he brought his fingers to his mouth and licked her right off, making a show of it. "You taste so fucking good, Kitten, I could spend a lifetime eating you up."

That got him a full body shiver. He rolled off her before it was too late. Teasing was one thing, but he wasn't testing his discipline, not when it came to her. "Take care of the bathroom, Cat, and come on out to the kitchen. I'll make us a sandwich."

"Coffee," she murmured, not moving when he got up.

He stood over her just looking down at her. So much love. The intensity was overwhelming. She hadn't moved. She lay on her back, looking at him, her hair spilling around her like a halo, her body bruised and battered but looking sexier than ever. He had to admit, there was a primitive, savage part of him that liked seeing his mark on her.

She lifted a hand, brushed his cock with languid fingers. "I like this part of you very much, Eli. You really are a beautiful man."

Her touch sent a shiver through his body. "Glad you think so, baby," he said. "Since it belongs to you." He should have moved, but something held him there. He'd never had this—quiet intimacy. Both knew she was in no condition for sex—especially his kind of sex—and this felt loving. Right. He loved that she was his.

"I do think so. All of you. Every inch. And I'm glad every inch of you belongs to me."

Her voice was soft. A thread of sound really, but it made its way inside of him. Her eyes met his. Her fingers still moved against him, stroking his shaft with gentle, loving caresses. "Just me, Eli. Right? That's what you mean. I know I don't know what I'm doing yet, but I'm a fast learner."

She took his breath away. She gave herself to him. Admitted, in her way, that she loved him, but she still wasn't sure of him. She still wasn't sure of herself. Damn Cordeau for making her think she was nothing.

"Just you, Catarina. How could I possibly want another woman after having you? It would be impossible. Now get moving and stop trying to tempt me. I'm taking care of you, remember?"

She leaned into him and licked up his shaft like a cat licking cream. Her tongue teased and danced under the sensitive crown. Fire shot through his body. There was nothing gentle about his body's reaction as her mouth slid over him like a tight glove. She suckled, her tongue dancing. A low moan escaped, vibrating right through his cock. Then she was gone, her blue eyes dancing with mischief.

"Just making certain you heard me right," she said.

"That earned you a spanking."

She laughed. "I'm so scared." She didn't sound in the least bit scared.

She rolled up and he stepped back before her hands could reach her intended target. There was only so much teasing he could take, and he knew she was sore and swollen. He wanted to kiss the little smirk right off her face, but that would definitely lead to other things.

"Hurry up," he growled, knowing he'd lost this battle. Even if he did put her over his knee, he had a feeling she'd turn the tables on him and it would turn erotic.

He snagged a pair of soft sweatpants on his way out of

the room. Her laughter only made his body harder and he knew she'd used her soft, sexy tone on purpose.

He was laughing when he got to the kitchen. His life had always been grim. He was okay with that. He did his job and he was good at it, and there was satisfaction in taking down criminals. But still, it was a grim life. Even after he'd traveled the world looking for other shifters. After he'd found Drake Donovan and had been introduced to the men who hunted rogues and took down criminals throughout the world. Shifters he could admire. Shifters who taught him the ropes. Even then, his world was grim. Until Cat. Cat changed everything and he didn't know she'd done it until it was already done.

He looked around his kitchen. It was the same, yet different. There were flowers in a vase on the table. Pots and pans hung on the rack, but they were arranged by size and were sparkling clean. The differences were small, and subtle, but they were there. She'd already put her touch on things, especially the kitchen.

She'd set up a coffee station with the ingredients from her grocery list. Joshua had brought the groceries and clothes he'd requested and she'd been ecstatic. He hadn't shown her the clothes yet—or the boots he'd ordered—but she'd pounced on the groceries, *oohing* and *ahhing* over every object—especially the coffee items. She could make their favorites drinks and when she did, they were every bit as awesome as he remembered from the coffee-house.

He pulled out the deli meat, turkey for her and roast beef for him. Cheese slices, avocado and condiments. He knew the moment she entered, but he didn't look up. He smelled her—that honeysuckle scent that drove him mad. She didn't make a sound as she padded barefoot across the floor straight to the coffee machine.

"Want one?"

"Kitten."

She laughed. "It's amazing how much you can convey with one word."

He went to her, silent as well. She didn't know he was behind her until he was already on her, turning her into his arms, taking a fistful of hair to pull her head back. He took her mouth. Rough. Hard. Possessive. Staking his claim in no uncertain terms. When he lifted his head to look into her cobalt eyes, he saw she got it. She knew his way of talking. He smiled down at her and brushed her lips gently with his. At the same time his hand slid under the hem of the shirt she wore to find her naked bottom. He caressed the firm globes with his palms before stalking back across the room to the center island, putting it between them.

"Our communication seems to be improving."

Catarina burst out laughing. She touched her trembling mouth and wondered if her shaky legs would hold her up. Happiness burst through her veins like champagne bubbles. He had a sense of humor under all that alpha leopard macho nonsense that she found hotter than anything. Which was unfortunate because he already got his way in all things. She just liked taking care of him.

"Is it now?" she prompted as she ground up the coffee he liked.

"You're wearing my shirt and no panties. And you know when I'm telling you that you fucking belong to me. So, yeah, communication is getting better."

"I'm not so afraid all the time," she admitted. She kept her back to him while she made his favorite cup of coffee. He liked caramel. She'd been surprised that he was a caramel man, but when he had something sweet, it was coffee and caramel and he liked two shots with that. She was careful to make it perfect for him.

"Kitten."

His voice turned her heart over. It was amazing to her what that tone could do. She immediately became aware of her breasts because they ached and her nipples scraped against the soft flannel of the shirt she wore. Little fingers of desire teased her thighs, and if he asked, she'd have to admit she was getting damp for him. With just his voice. How far gone did that make her?

"Well, it's true. You gave that to me, Eli. I've been so afraid for so long that I almost don't know how not to be. But you took that away . . . mostly." She had to add the last because she was being strictly honest with him. She still couldn't quite make herself look at him.

"I don't want you ever to be afraid, Cat. Not anymore. We'll make you safe. The more you know about self-defense, the better you are with a gun and other weapons, the more you feel you're in condition, the safer you'll feel by yourself. My male will teach your female how to protect herself, but always, always, know I'm going to defend you and protect you with my last breath."

She glanced over her shoulder at him. He looked— invincible. Maybe it was that strength in him. She saw him naked, all the flowing power, the roped muscles and easy, fluid way he moved. He was fast, and when he shifted, he could do so on the run. His presence made her feel safe, but more than that, she liked that it was important to him that she learn to defend herself. He wanted her strong. He wanted her to feel as if she could survive an attack. That meant something to her.

Catarina cleared her throat. "There really isn't any information on shifters so after I learned about Rafe, I studied leopards. They mate and then the female raises her young alone."

Eli didn't make a sound. He waited in silence. He knew it was an effort on her part, he could tell by the way her body stiffened, but she forced herself to turn around and face him, to walk toward him with his coffee, but she studiously looked at the floor while she did so.

"Baby, are you asking me a question? Because if you are, I need your eyes on mine." His voice was low, but it held a clear command.

Her lashes fluttered and then her gaze jumped to his. He

took the coffee. It smelled almost as good as she did. He couldn't resist smoothing his hand over her bare bottom again. Just having her standing there so close made him hard. He knew it wasn't all about how she looked, or even the fact that she was a wildcat in his bed. There was far more to it than that.

It was this. Her bare ass, no panties under his shirt because he'd asked it of her. It was her inexperience, her shyness, yet her willingness to learn from him, to let him guide her and teach her the things she wanted to learn. Her trust in giving him her body—that trust—in spite of his earlier betrayal of her. How could he not be so in love with her that it hurt? How could he possibly be with her and not know she was his world and always would be?

"I suppose I am. How do shifters handle that sort of thing?"

"Shifters mate for life. Over and over. They find one another and they choose each other. I would never leave you, or take another woman. When you carry my child in your belly, baby, it will only make me love you more. I'm not going anywhere."

Her eyes began to move away from his and toward the floor. She tugged her bottom lip between her teeth.

"Keep your eyes on mine. You hide when you avoid someone's eyes. You've practiced it enough, for years, obviously, but there isn't a reason to hide anymore. I want to know what you're thinking, so you look at me not the floor."

"I'm thinking you're extremely bossy," she snapped, her eyes coming back to his.

Deep blue. Flirting with anger. That made him hard too. He'd seen her a lot of ways, but anger wasn't really one of them. Hurt, yes, anger not so much.

He grinned at her and then took a sip of coffee. "My woman makes a great cup of coffee, and she has a temper."

"Why would that make you happy?"

"Best kind of sex there is, baby. Make-up sex." His grin widened when her eyes turned a deep blue and flashed at him. There was just a hint of a smile in the midst of her mad.

"You do know you can be annoying, don't you?" she demanded.

"I think you're a little grumpy because you haven't had your coffee and you just woke up." He stepped close to her, crowding her, inhaling her scent. She could strip him bare, right to his soul, with her eyes. She just didn't know it and he thought it best that she never did. "What is it about having babies that scares you, Kitten? Talk to me. Let me help with that."

Her eyelashes fluttered, but her eyes didn't leave his and there was an instant melting around the region of his heart. He admired her courage.

"I've never even held a baby, Eli, let alone taken care of one. I've never been around a child. I don't know the first thing about raising children."

She didn't know it, but the way her gaze clung to him, the expression on her face, she looked to him like he was her lifeline. He wanted to be that lifeline. He wanted her to always look to him when she was scared or confused. He stepped even closer to her, one arm sliding around her waist to lock her to him, the other putting down his coffee so he could shape her face with his palm.

"Don't be afraid of a child, baby. We'll sort that out together. We're both smart. We aren't going to fuck up our children. You'll be sweet like you are with them, pouring out all that love you've got, and I'll growl and snarl and protect them. We're going to love each other and them so much, they'll be swimming in love."

Her eyes searched his face. She swallowed twice before she answered. "Eli, has it escaped your notice that I can't even say that word?"

"When it comes to you, Kitten, nothing escapes me. Not ever." His thumb moved gently along her jaw. "You were made for love, Catarina. To love your man. To love your children. And for them to love you."

She blinked, clearly surprised. A faint blush stole up her cheeks. "You say the most amazing things to me, Eli."

She never knew what to do with him when he was giving her compliments. He figured she would have a lifetime to get used to it because he intended to give them to her on a regular basis.

"Only because they're true. We both know I'm brutally honest." He bent his head and brushed a kiss across her lips. "Make your coffee, baby, and let's eat."

"Okay." She smiled up at him.

He couldn't resist another kiss, this time sliding his tongue along the seam of her lips in a silent command for her to open to him. He slid both hands under the hem of the flannel shirt to cup the bare firm globes of her ass. She had a perfect butt. He loved watching her walk. He loved smoothing his palms over that wonderful curve. He loved looking at her bottom when she lay on her belly in their bed, or was on her hands and knees. Just like that, his cock reacted, straining against the material of his sweats. Hungry. Greedy.

She didn't pull away from him. If anything she pressed tighter into him. That was another thing he loved. She gave him access to her body when he needed or wanted to touch her. She didn't make a thing about it, she just did it. Caring for him. Loving him without words. He heard her talking, even if it was in silence. He heard her loud and clear.

"After dinner, Catarina, I'm going to see what I can do about those very sore muscles of yours. First the hot tub, then a hot shower and then I massage you."

She turned her face up to his, her blue eyes searching his face. A slow smile took his breath.

"Massage?" She licked her lips. "That sounds like fun. Do I get to give you a massage too?"

She was killing him. He cleared his throat. "Would that make you happy?"

"Yes. I like touching you."

The way she made the admission, so honest, made his heart stutter. Sometimes just looking at her hurt, she was so beautiful. But this, the way she moved into him when he touched her, the way she allowed his hands on her so willingly, and her ready confession, meaning it, that she liked touching him, nearly brought him to his knees.

He didn't answer her immediately, he was too busy fighting for air. Fighting to keep his hands off of her and his cock out of her while she healed.

She tugged at her lower lip again with her teeth. "Your muscles have to be sore too, Eli. You were conditioning just like me, and your leopard was crazy last night. But if you don't want me to . . ."

He stopped her with another kiss. "I want you to. Coffee. Eat. Hot tub. Let's get it done so I can feel your hands on me, Kitten."

He smacked her on her bare bottom and then slid his palm over the heated skin. Her eyes went wide. He grinned at her. "I owed you that, remember."

"I didn't think it would feel like that if you actually did it," she said.

"Baby, I love seeing that wild look in your eyes. I love what wild does to your body and then what your body does to mine. I'm going to think up all kinds of creative ways to keep that look there." He let her go, stepping back because it was either that or lift her into his arms and slam her body down hard on his pulsing cock.

Catarina went back to the coffee machine and he put the sandwiches on the table. He'd started to put them on plates but at the last minute put them on napkins. Straddling his chair, he snagged one of the roast beef sandwiches and dug in, all the while watching Cat at the coffee machine. It was a thing of beauty seeing her work, the concentration on her face.

"Stop staring at me." She didn't turn around.

Eli found himself smiling. Her leopard senses were becoming acute. Either that or she was really aware of him. Either way, it was a good thing. "I like looking at you. Especially when you're making coffee."

She laughed. He loved her laugh. He watched her while he ate his second sandwich and she delicately picked at hers. She definitely enjoyed the coffee and she looked far mellower. He was glad she didn't want a second cup to take with them out to the hot tub. She hadn't even said a word about the napkins versus plates, although she had raised her eyebrows and her little smile was very amused. He didn't want her smile to disappear when he told her he didn't want her drinking more than one cup of coffee.

"You like my bossy," he announced.

She nearly spit out her coffee. "Where did that come from?" She narrowed her eyes at him. "You were thinking about ordering me around again, weren't you?"

"I spend a lot of time thinking about ordering you around," he admitted, unrepentant. "It's a good thing you like it."

"I think shifting into your leopard yesterday has made you a little crazy. Just drink the rest of your coffee, you'll be all right."

He threw his head back and laughed. She also made him happy in ways he hadn't imagined.

She barely ate her sandwich and he let her get away with it because he could see she was still exhausted and he wanted her in the hot tub. He rinsed the coffee cups before she could and tossed the napkins before grabbing her hand and taking her out to the lower deck where the tub was.

"I don't have a swimsuit," Cat pointed out as she stood uncertainly, watching him take the cover off.

He glanced at her. "Kitten." Amused. "I'd just take it off of you anyway. Have you not figured out yet that one of the greatest joys of my life is to look at you naked?"

She smiled at him. "I guess I missed that."

He stalked over to her, caught the hem of the shirt and pulled it over her head without unbuttoning it. There was very little moon, but he could see her lush body. His mark was still everywhere, the finger smudges and small bite marks. He brushed his hand down her left breast, watching her face. She was sensitive. The shiver ran through her and her eyes heated.

"Get in, before I decide I need you right now."

Her gaze dropped to his fully erect cock as he shed his sweats. "Any time you need me, Eli, I want you. You have to know that. I'm never going to be too tired or too sore."

She trailed her fingers over him and his cock jerked in response. His belly tightened. That was his woman. "Look up at me, baby," he commanded softly.

Her gaze jumped to his. He saw the heat. The fire. The sexy. He nearly groaned aloud, not believing the miracle that was Catarina.

"I really mean it. Not just for you, but for me too." The last was admitted in a low voice, but her gaze didn't waver from his.

"I know you mean it, Kitten. I love that you mean it. Stop tempting me and get the hell in the hot tub."

She laughed softly and climbed in. He watched her, shaking his head, still having a hard time wrapping his head around the fact that she was his. He watched her face carefully as she sank a little gingerly into the hot water. She winced just enough that he knew he'd been right to ensure she had a break. She still looked exhausted, and he made up his mind he would postpone his own massage in an effort to get her to relax and go back to sleep. If she had her hands on him, he doubted if he had the discipline to keep from taking her. And he knew she'd offer because she was just that generous.

The night was cool enough that steam rose from the water's surface. He adjusted the jets on her body, and sank down onto one of the lower seats so the jets could hit the back of his neck and shoulders. Catarina was right when she said he had to be sore too. He felt as if he'd wrestled his leopard and lost.

Catarina put her head back and closed her eyes. It gave

him the opportunity to study her profile. She was beautiful any way he looked at her. Her long sweeping lashes and the curve of her cheek, the high cheekbones and softly rounded chin, all her gleaming, glossy hair she'd tied up in an intricate knot.

"You're staring at me again." She kept her eyes closed.

"I told you, I like looking at you, especially when you're bare-ass naked two feet from me."

"All this time I thought it was when I was making coffee."

"Kitten." He waited until her lashes fluttered and rose just enough that he could see her blue eyes. "I like looking at you all the time."

She laughed softly and closed her eyes again.

16

"YOUR woman has a beautiful laugh," Jake Bannaconni stated.

The sound of Catarina's laughter felt a little like music. Eli tilted his chair back, sprawling his legs out in front of him, the bottle of beer in his fist. He could listen to her laughter all day long and never tire of it. She sounded carefree. Happy. He knew he had a hand in her happiness and that made it all the more sweet.

"You are gone, Eli. A total goner. That woman has you wrapped around her little finger, and you're never going to get the upper hand."

He grinned at Jake Bannaconni. His neighbor looked relaxed sprawled out next to him on the long, wide verandah outside the kitchen.

"Catarina doesn't know she has the upper hand and I intend to take full advantage and savor every moment as long as I can before she realizes I'd do anything for her."

Jake laughed and saluted him with the beer bottle.

"She was terrified to come over here, but Emma's put her at ease. I can't thank her enough for that. Catarina needs to know she can have friends. She thinks she's going to get everyone around her killed," Eli said softly.

"That's not going to happen," Jake said, and there was a hard edge in his voice. "This won't be the first time we've faced this kind of thing, a rogue coming after one of our women. Emma will sort it all out with her." He had absolute faith in his wife's ability to ease Catarina's mind.

"I'm counting on that," Eli admitted. "Have you looked into Rafe Cordeau?"

Jake nodded. "He's related to a family from the New Orleans area. Woman was killing using her leopard. He's a cousin a couple of times removed. Leopards can be vicious, as you well know, and if you don't keep them in line, they can take control of you. Cordeau is a very vicious killer. I'm surprised Catarina managed to escape him. From what I understand, he's called in every favor ever owed to him trying to find her."

"She's smart, Jake. And I mean real smart. She kept a low profile in his house, learned to turn herself into a little mouse. He didn't want her educated and she managed to get an education right under his nose. She cracked his safe. Used his computer when he had hers rigged so he knew what she was doing on it. And she got away from him. She'd still be under his radar if he hadn't been tipped off where she was." Eli didn't bother to keep the admiration out of his voice.

"She'd have to be very intelligent to survive his household and come out intact. Do you know much about her lineage? I made inquiries after you told me Tracy Benoit wasn't her birth mother. Drake knew of her mother's line. She was from the Borneo rain forest, and he knows her family. Her father we're still tracing, but he thinks he comes from a branch of shifters around Panama."

Another wave of laughter came from the kitchen,

catching both men's attention. Catarina had argued with
him about coming. She'd gone silent once she realized he
was insisting, and his belly had been tied up in knots. He
knew she expected the wife of a billionaire to be haughty
and look down at her for her lack of education. She'd even
murmured that at the beginning of the conversation, before
she'd distracted him with fears of Cordeau finding out.

Her lack of self-confidence seemed to come back to
that—no formal education. Her laughter eased something
in him he hadn't known was so tense. He couldn't help but
listen in on their conversation. He knew, sometime in the
future, if it were still important to her, he would make certain she could go to school and get a more advanced education. Not that he thought she needed it, she'd certainly
continued with acquiring knowledge, but he wanted her to
have whatever was important to her.

"I *love* this stove," Catarina said to Emma. "Love, love, love
it. I saw it in a magazine once and then looked it up and read
all about it. I have to admit I covet this stove, although I don't
need one quite this big. It's always been my dream stove."

"I do need the larger one," Emma said. "Quite often the
boys come up to the house to eat so I make certain there's
plenty of food. And I'm with you, this is the best stove *ever.*"

Eli glanced at Jake. He was listening too, and he had a faint
smile on his face. When he caught Eli looking his smile widened to a grin. That grin said he was reading Eli's mind and
he knew Catarina would be getting a new stove very soon.

"Emma always feeds my crew. That's just her way."

"You don't have a chef? Or a housekeeper?" That surprised Eli. The house was very large, and it was rumored
Emma had a difficult time carrying her last baby.

"I hire people all the time. Emma fires them. Well, she's
too sweet to fire anyone, but she refuses to allow anyone
else to cook the children's meals or mine. We have people
come in a couple of times a week to do the bulk of the

cleaning, but that's about all I can get away with. The woman isn't the least bit afraid of me."

Jake said the last as if he'd failed miserably. Eli hid his grin. Jake, like Eli, needed control, especially around those he loved, yet he didn't sound too upset that Emma wanted to run her household.

Eli was surprised that Emma insisted on doing the cooking for her family. He liked that. He liked that it mattered to her, and he could see Jake liked it as well. Jake looked like a happy man, and when he rested his gaze on his wife, the dark, intense look of love and possession was starkly there on his usually expressionless face.

"We're lucky men," Eli observed. "Catarina likes to cook for me as well. Here's to our women and the way they care for us." He tapped the long neck of Jake's beer bottle with his own.

Jake smiled at him. "I like that your woman cooks. They've been talking nonstop about recipes and brands of pots and pans and now stoves for the last hour. Emma sounds happy."

"I've been taking notes," Eli admitted, with a small grin. "I don't forget much, and when it comes to something Cat wants, I especially pay attention. She wants that stove. She's mentioned it a few times now."

Jake burst out laughing. "I knew you'd be ordering her that stove."

"She wants it, she gets it."

"You've got it bad, Eli."

"You have no idea," he admitted, surprised that it didn't matter that Jake knew that Catarina had somehow become his world.

The smile faded from Jake's face and he looked toward the kitchen. "Emma is my life. Without her, I've got nothing. I would kill to protect her, and I have. I understand the concept of giving her whatever she wants because in return she gives me everything. It isn't easy for women to live with men like us, Eli. Your woman is fragile right now. I can see that. She's just learning what shifters are and what drives them. I run roughshod over Emma at times and she handles it because she knows how."

"I hear what you're saying," Eli said. "My leopard rides me pretty hard, especially when it comes to Catarina. I can't lose her, and she's definitely in danger. I'm trying to teach her as much about self-defense as I can and my male is working with her female. She's gotten beat up in the last couple of weeks, but she never complains."

"I made a lot of mistakes with Emma," Jake admitted. "I was just lucky she hung in there with me."

Eli's eyes met Jake's. "I don't like the fact that Catarina never had a choice, because I'll never know if I am her choice, but I'd never let her go. I don't care what it takes, but I'd find a way to keep her. Sometimes I wonder how much that makes me like Cordeau in her eyes." He admitted the truth quietly.

Jake studied his face for a long time and then took a long pull on the beer. "I'd never give up Emma. If I had to, I'd lock her in my house and work my ass off day and night to figure out where I screwed up and how to fix it, but I wouldn't let her go. She knows that. She accepts that in me. She accepts a lot of things in me. Because she does, I work hard to make certain she's happy and that she stays that way. When something's important to her, I give in, even if it goes against everything protective in me."

Eli frowned. "Such as?"

"She loves the ranch, but we're isolated. I think it will help with Catarina being close, given the things they have in common. But once in a while she wants to go for a ride by herself, or go into the city to shop. She doesn't spend money and she's always a little shocked when I give her extravagant gifts, but she likes to just be what she calls normal."

"Of course she can't. You have enemies."

Jake nodded. "No, she can't. But I want to give that to her, because it matters to her. Kills me to let her go off in a car by herself. I've got tracking on it and on her. And my boys are all around her. She knows, but as long as they don't make it obvious, she doesn't bitch at me. Shopping, she's surrounded by a crew. Best I can do for her. She doesn't like it, but she knows it's got to be that way. She never objects when it comes to security for the kids, but it's much harder to accept it for herself."

Eli stirred uneasily. "You let her go shopping in the city without you? And drive her car around aimlessly?"

"Do you ever try to imagine what it's like for our women to live with men like us, Eli? We're not easy and we'll never be easy. I don't like her out of my sight. That can smother an ordinary woman. I'm the one in control, although I've done everything I can to make certain she feels she's on equal footing with me, but we both know the bottom line is I'd never let her go. She's my world. I swear to God, I lose that woman and I'm lost too, kids or no kids. And I love my children with everything in me."

Eli raked his hand through his hair. He'd already known what Jake was saying to him. He wasn't an easy man, and he didn't have a lot of friendships. He was rough and arrogant and bossy and he liked control. His emotions were generally held in check, until Catarina came into his life. Suddenly everything was different. His feelings for her were intense, bordering on obsession. Letting go, even a little, was terrifying. He didn't know if he was that strong.

"You get me, Eli?" Jake said softly. "She has to know she's your world if you're going to be you. You have to allow her to see all of you, even the worst parts. She has to accept and love those parts too. Then it's her choice. She stays because she loves you no matter what."

"You have no idea how fucked up I can get, Jake," Eli said. "She's already experienced some of it."

Jake shrugged. "We're shifters. That isn't an excuse to treat our women rough, or get away with crap, because we're in control of our leopards, and that means being in control of us. But we're going to screw up. Catarina's strong or she never

would have survived Cordeau's household. She can take you
on and tame the wild when it comes. Let her. Give her that.
I'm talking from experience. I'm no picnic, and Emma,
well . . ." He trailed off, and looked toward the kitchen where
another burst of laughter warmed both of them.

"Emma loves me the way I am. She knows what I need
and she's willing to give it to me. In return I give her every
damn thing I can think of that might make her happy." He
hesitated. "Including that baby she's carrying. I didn't want
her to risk it. She nearly died that last time and I was done.
We've got two, Kyle, who is about to turn four, and
Andraya, who is eight months younger." He gave no explanation how the children could be so close in age. "We love
them, and as far as I'm concerned we were complete. She
wants a couple more. Took me a long time to let myself
realize it mattered to her. So I gave in, but I don't like it."

"The idea of more children, or Emma at risk?" Eli
watched him closely. He wanted children. A lot of them.
He'd always wanted a family, and he wanted that family
with Catarina. It hadn't really occurred to him that a man
might lose his wife in childbirth. Clearly Jake had faced
that nightmare already with Emma.

"I love the idea of more children, but I wanted to use a
surrogate. Emma wanted to carry them herself. Emma
won, but I don't sleep so good at night right now. Sometimes I just lay there next to her and listen to her breathe."
While Jake spoke, he was looking through the sliding glass
door to his woman.

There was raw, naked love there for the world to see. Eli
wondered if he got that same expression on his face when
he looked at Catarina. He certainly felt it. He felt stripped
bare, his soul exposed, naked and vulnerable and it wasn't
a comfortable state of mind for a man like him. He realized
that was when he felt the most aggressive. The most dominant toward Catarina.

Already he didn't like being too far from her, but he

enjoyed watching as she bent to check something in the oven and the two women immediately went into a discussion about how the moisture from the mushroom roast flavored the potatoes as they were grilling in the natural juices. It was all Greek to him, but he loved the way Catarina's voice was soft and excited and happy.

Andraya, Jake's little girl, came running into the kitchen, clutching a little stuffed leopard. Both women immediately turned toward her, Catarina automatically closing the oven door and blocking it with her body as she crouched down to be face-to-face with the child. Eli found himself smiling. She didn't think she was good with children, but she'd instinctively protected the child and crouched low to greet her. Yeah, his woman was going to be great with their children.

"Drake told me that the shifters in the rain forest talk to their girls about their leopards and how it all works. They don't want them to be afraid, and they don't hide the men shifting from them. We've decided to do the same with our children. Andraya has already seen both of us shift and she shows no fear when either of our leopards enter a room with her. She knows not to ever talk about it with anyone else. So does Kyle."

"I think I have to agree with you on that," Eli said. "Not knowing what was going to happen to her and thinking her leopard would be a killer like Cordeau's made Cat fearful." He took another drink of his beer, still watching Catarina smiling and accepting the little stuffed leopard, her face animated as she conversed with the child. "She was so courageous. Made me proud of her."

Jake laughed. "Eli, seriously. You didn't have to tell me that. I can see it on your face. I know you think you need to thank me for the invite to dinner, but I owe you one. I'm watching Emma and she's really happy. She needs a friend, especially now. I'm worried the doctor will put her on bed rest. She doesn't like anyone else taking care of us. With your ranch right next to ours, the two of them can go back and forth and it will be especially good to have Catarina occupying her time."

"Cat loves books. You have an entire library. I've ordered a number of books to surprise her along with a desk and laptop. Joshua and Trey are setting it up for me while we're here," Eli said, knowing Jake would know exactly what his crew was doing. Still, he liked the idea of saying it aloud—his secret surprise for Catarina. "She'll love it, but when she sees your library, I figure I'll be adding on to my house in a big way."

Jake laughed. "I'll make it clear she can use it anytime she'd like. Emma paints. She's really good. The first time she did anything it was for my birthday present. She had the boys help her put together a studio in the barn and she painted there in secret. I was a bit of a jealous ass when I found out." He grinned at the memory. "That woman of mine has a temper. She doesn't let it fly often but when she does, she's unpredictable."

Eli accepted the cold beer Jake held out to him. "Mine's got one too. Didn't know that, but I have to say, I like it. She's got attitude, and it comes unexpectedly."

"I intimidate powerful men and other shifters," Jake lamented. "But not my wife. She rolls her eyes at me."

Eli smiled. "Catarina's not there yet. She's still finding out she doesn't have to hide who she is, but it's coming." He took a long pull on the beer, his eyes still on his woman, on the child and the way the two laughed together.

Catarina straightened abruptly and indicated that the child should move away from the stove. She picked up the heavier bowls and took them to the table, preventing Emma from lifting them. She did it smoothly, so Emma wouldn't notice. He glanced at Jake. Jake noticed.

"Your woman is observant," Jake mused.

"Yeah. She pays attention to detail."

"Do you think she paid attention to detail in Cordeau's house while she was growing up?"

"That's the crazy thing. As intelligent as I know she is, as resourceful, it wasn't until a couple of weeks ago when we ran into your crew at the fence line and we were talking with Elijah that I realized she probably knows everything about his business and the people he does business with. Before, under Cordeau's roof, she was off limits, and they all thought she was just an uneducated mouse. Now, they're most likely thinking she's a threat to them."

"She is a threat to them if she can name names and pinpoint who's dealing what. There's a trail, Eli. She might just be the key to that trail."

"I'm not using her to get Cordeau. I quit my job over that shit and it isn't happening again." There was a hard edge to his voice. He liked Jake, but he wasn't going to back down. He didn't have that in him. He'd protect Catarina even at the risk of his friendship with Jake and the other shifters.

Jake laughed. "You're too much like me. That's not what I meant. You're still thinking like a DEA agent. You have to think like a shifter."

"I'll kill Cordeau when he comes after Catarina. Won't lose any sleep over it and won't hesitate."

"I get that. Any of my boys or me would do the same. He's rogue. He's got to go. Probably have a couple of lieutenants that are rogue as well. We'll have to find out which ones. I'm a businessman. I go after wealth and businesses and take my enemies down that way. If your woman knows bank accounts and partners, if she knows the kinds of deals going down, Elijah, you and I can take Cordeau's empire apart bit by bit. The men he's in bed with won't see it coming and won't know what hit them until it's too late. They'll turn on one another. They always do when suddenly irrefutable evidence of their guilt is all over the papers and agents are on their doorsteps."

Jake leaned toward Eli, his eyes suddenly intent. Serious. Burning. "We hunt, Eli, just as you've done, but we do it our way. Join us. Let's start with Cordeau and his partners.

You can sound Catarina out, see if she's comfortable help-ing. If she isn't, we'll still take them down. It will take a little longer, but we'll do it. You aren't going to sit on your ass in that ranch house, it will make you crazy."

"You offering me a job?"

Jake grinned and settled back. "As such. It's really Drake's operation. I'm the information man."

Eli knew Jake Bannaconni was far more than an infor-mation man. He was a wheeler and dealer. He was well known in business circles, and grown men cried when he turned his sights on them.

"I'll talk to Cat, but I'm not pressuring her. She has to make up her own mind. I promised her I'd never put her in that position and I intend to keep that promise."

Jake nodded and both men put down their beers when Emma opened the sliding glass door. Jake's gaze was on her face immediately.

She went right to him, leaned down and brushed a soft kiss across his mouth. "Dinner's ready. Cat fixed a couple of sur-prises. We exchanged recipes. I had so much fun." Her tone was honest and clearly she was conveying something to Jake.

Eli had the feeling she wanted him to take extra care with their guest. Jake was right when he said Emma was very astute. She had sensed how uncomfortable Catarina was and set about putting her at ease.

Eli rose and went straight to Catarina. Her gaze jumped to his as he stalked across the room to her, moving in close. Possessively. He hadn't been away from her for so long since he'd brought her to his ranch. His hand cupped her face, thumb sliding over her warm, satin skin.

"Missed you. Got used to having you right next to me."

She smiled at him and leaned into him. Giving him her closeness. Her fingers curled in the hair at the back of his neck and he was suddenly very glad that leopard's hair grew so much that most of the time his was a little too long. He liked feeling her fingers there.

"I'm having fun, Eli. Thank you for convincing me to come. Emma's . . . great."

"I want your mouth."

"We're not alone," she reminded softly, her gaze going from amazing blue to more blue violet.

"I want your mouth, and I don't give a damn who's around," he growled, just as softly.

Her mouth curved and she turned her face up to his. He was gentle, his lips brushing hers tenderly, his tongue teasing for just a moment before he pulled back, pleased with her. She gave him what he needed, in public or not. She let others know he was her man and that meant everything to him, although he was convinced he'd almost gotten the eye roll from her.

When he lifted his head, her eyes sparkled with happiness at him. "Can you believe this kitchen, Eli? The stove is like the best, although it's a commercial one. That convection oven is perfect. And a double oven? Love that." Her hand swept around the room. "Emma let me do some of the cooking and we sort of compared sauces and breads. Her breads are killer, but she'd never made beignets before. She has a killer fryer." The words tumbled out, nearly running into one another.

He found it interesting that she spoke in a low tone, as if sharing a secret with him. There was joy in her voice, and he knew Emma and Catarina had connected and bonded almost immediately. Both were lonely. Both took care of their men. Both were chained to dominant shifters. They understood one another. But she was still being careful, not wanting to be too loud about making a new friend.

"Emma cooks too?" he asked, inviting conversation. He wanted her to talk to him about Emma without being afraid.

He allowed his gaze to sweep the kitchen, noting the stove in particular and the pots and pans he'd overheard her saying she'd always wanted. He didn't really understand or give a damn why one skillet or pot would be better to cook in than another and he really didn't care, except that

Catarina did—and that made it important. He didn't ever want to pass up anything important to her.

"She's a really good cook. And she bakes too. A lot of people love to do one or the other, but like me, she enjoys both. She has some great recipes. We cook different things, because I'm from New Orleans and she's from the west, but the more we talked recipes, the more we realized we liked the same things. We've decided to swap recipes."

He circled the nape of her neck with his palm. "I think that's great, Kitten."

Catarina glanced over her shoulder at Jake and Emma, who were laughing together as they walked inside hand in hand. "I'm hoping if she has to go on bed rest that she won't mind me bringing a few meals over to help out. She's adamant she doesn't want anyone else taking care of Jake and the children." She raised her eyes to his. "I understand. I wouldn't like someone else taking care of you."

His heart stuttered. Her admission was under her breath, almost as if she was afraid it would upset him. He bent his head to hers. "I wouldn't want anyone else taking care of me. I'm fond of the way you do it."

That got a smile.

"You two ready?" Emma asked, as Jake called Kyle and Andraya back into the room. She indicated the two chairs facing the sliding glass door so they'd have the view.

Jake swung both children into booster seats and secured them, dropping kisses on their heads before seating himself beside Andraya. Emma sat next to Kyle.

"Mommy's going to have another baby," Kyle announced solemnly.

Catarina smiled at him. "Really? That's wonderful. What do you want, a brother or sister?"

"A sister," Kyle said firmly. "Sisters are really good, but you gotta take care of them, right, Dad?"

"That's right, son," Jake agreed, putting roast and potatoes on Andraya's plate and then his own.

Andraya scowled. "No, brothers are better," she announced. "Don't like sisters. Brothers are the best."

"That's nice that you think so, Draya," Emma said gently, "but no matter if we have a boy or a girl, all of us are going to love it and take good care of it, right? We talked about it together. The baby will be all of ours to protect and treasure."

Kyle's brows drew together. He turned his eyes on Eli. Eli could see the leopard was already strong in the little boy. The eyes were definitely Jake's.

"Do you like kissin' girls?" he asked.

"Kyle," Emma admonished.

Jake grinned and coughed when Emma looked at him.

"I like kissing Catarina," Eli confessed. "I like kissing her a lot. But I don't kiss any other girls."

"Daddy only kisses mommy," Andraya announced knowledgably. "And us."

"Your daddy is a very wise man," Eli said.

"I think so as well," Emma said, her voice full of laughter.

Catarina seemed to be concentrating on the roast. She glanced up at Emma. "I don't think I could ever get the gravy like this. It's wonderful."

Jake patted his flat belly. "I have to do a lot of . . . um . . . exercise to keep in shape with Emma's cooking."

Emma rolled her eyes, a faint blush stealing up her neck into her cheeks at the obvious implication.

Eli laughed. He couldn't help himself. Catarina looked so happy he reached out to connect with her. He knew he did it often, but that was who he was, and she never seemed to mind, not even in front of others. His fingers settled around the nape of her neck and stayed there for a moment.

He liked to slide his fingers around her neck to her throat right over her pulse and feel her heart beating into his hand. Right now, he was content with just her nape. She'd put her hair up in some complicated braid that looked beautiful, but that was coming down the moment they were in the truck and on the way home.

"Isn't this good?" Catarina asked, her gaze flicking to his the moment his hand settled around her neck.

He went very still. She knew. She knew he *had* to touch her. He could see the knowledge in her eyes. It wasn't just a compulsion. It wasn't because he was creating intimacy or ownership. He needed that connection and she knew. She got it.

Her eyes warmed, turned a deeper shade of violet through all that blue. "Baby? Emma gave me the recipe. Do you like it?"

Baby. She had never once referred to him as anything but Eli. Not once. An endearment? Even if she was echoing one of his for her. He was grateful for the table to hide the response of his body, but he had to put his other hand in his lap to keep from giving away the sudden tremor in his hands.

He loved her. Plain and simple and every single day, every hour, she was giving him more reason to love her. He was fairly certain he could spend the rest of his life concentrating on Catarina alone and never find out all of her.

"I think it's excellent, Kitten. I have no doubt you can reproduce this very good gravy. I've never had a single meal that you've made for me that I didn't want to overeat."

The corners of her mouth turned up and she shook her head. She glanced at Emma. "He does that a lot. He gives me the best compliments, and I never know quite what to do." She swallowed. "He's sweet."

Eli groaned. "No, Kitten, I am *not* sweet. Don't say 'sweet,' especially in front of another man. I'm rough and tough and scary."

Even the two children laughed. The rest of the evening was spent with a lot of laughter and Eli enjoyed it because most of the time he was watching Catarina have fun. She seemed startled by the fact that she could have fun, and every few minutes her blue gaze would settle on his face and her features would go even softer and warmer than normal.

Mostly he paid attention to how tired she got. They'd both been working hard on conditioning and self-defense, mostly hand to hand, but she put in time on the gun range as well. He wasn't easy on her, in spite of the long nights of frenzied sex and their leopards being just as crazy, driving them both without mercy. The moment he saw her stifle a yawn, he was up, taking her hand and making their good-byes.

Catarina lingered, chatting with Emma, promising another visit soon when he caught the second yawn. He tugged her away from their friends, walking her out to the pickup. Before she could protest, he caught Catarina around her waist and lifted her into the cab, reached across her to snap her seat belt, firmly closed the door and walked around to the driver's side. Jake's laughter followed him every step. No doubt the man knew exactly what he was thinking, but Eli didn't care.

He waved as he drove out, past the guards at the gate and onto the road leading back to their home.

"That was fun," Catarina said. "I didn't expect it to be. Thank you for introducing me to Emma. She's wonderful. And she knows so much about shifters."

He glanced at her. "Anything you want to know about shifters, baby, you just have to ask."

"I know. You always answer my questions, Eli, and I love that about you. I can't tell you how important it is to me that you care enough to answer my questions." She glanced out the window into the night. "You've made my life so different."

"I want your life to be everything you've ever dreamt about."

Her head turned toward him. Her eyes were soft. "I never dreamt about anything but getting away from Rafe. I don't think I know what normal is, but I'm happy. Really, really happy, and you've done that."

He reached out and tugged at her braid, a reminder that he liked her hair down. "I want you to feel safe as well, Cat. I don't like that you were still afraid to meet our neighbors because you thought Cordeau might hurt them."

There was no hesitation. None at all. Catarina's hands went up to her hair and she began removing pins until the thick braid fell free, snaking down her shoulder to pool on the seat. She began working on the tie, absently, as if she wasn't paying the least attention. "I was afraid. I think it's an automatic reaction, but it's getting less. I wasn't so paranoid that I refused to go."

"You could have," Eli said. "You know that, right? You don't have to do everything I say."

Her eyes went soft. "Seriously? Eli, I know that. I like doing things for you, but if I didn't want to, I'd let you know. We'd argue because you like your way, but I'd stand my ground. I'm not afraid of you."

He opened his mouth to respond but stopped, going over what she'd just said. Playing back every inflection of her voice. *I'm not afraid of you.* That wasn't an idle statement. She was giving him something else. Something important. Something sacred. It was big, and he needed to get it.

"Never be afraid of me, baby. No matter how much I growl at you, and it will happen. I'm not always nice. We both know that, but I'd never hurt you, not in a million years."

"I know that, Eli. I really do." Her hands loosened the weave of the braid. "I'm not afraid in our home at all. I was at Emma's because I think I've been afraid for so long that I couldn't help myself."

He reached over and took her hand, pulling it to his thigh and holding it there. "Time will fix that, Kitten. I'm glad you had fun with Emma. Jake is worried about her. She nearly died during her last pregnancy, and she still wanted another baby."

He pulled her hand to his mouth and nibbled on the pads of her fingers for a moment before returning her palm to his thigh. "Jake wanted a surrogate, but Emma insisted on carrying. He gave in." He took a breath and looked at her. "I wouldn't have, baby. I want to give you every damn thing you want, but I wouldn't have been able to give you that."

He wanted her to understand. He'd thought a lot about what Jake said, and he understood that he'd have to give concessions to her when things mattered. He knew that and he would. But not when it came to her health. Not when it could be life or death. She was so inside of him that he knew he wouldn't have a life without her. It didn't make sense. It happened fast. He hadn't even known he wasn't living until she smiled at him. Until she laughed with him. Until she looked at him with trust in her eyes.

"Eli, I'm not going to have trouble carrying babies. Emma was in a terrible car accident. She told me about it. She told me she knew she'd have to go on bed rest, but the doctor assured her she shouldn't have the same problems delivering. They're going to take the baby early, do a C-section."

He pulled onto the private road that led to their home. "Still, you have to know there's some things I can't give you. No matter how much I want to, I won't risk your life for any reason."

He felt her eyes on him but he didn't look at her. He couldn't. He was still inside. Waiting. This moment was too important to him. Her acceptance of who and what he was. He wanted to give her the real Eli, good and bad, and let her make her choice—she was seeing it now. He would be implacable, immovable, when it came to safety and health issues. She had to see that in him. He would ride roughshod over her and he'd win—even if it meant losing in the end.

"Okay, Eli. I get that," she said softly. "We'll work it out. You always tell me to talk to you when things are important to me or if I have questions. I'm learning to do that. You have to promise to do the same. Don't dictate to me when it's an important issue to you. Talk to me about it so I understand what it means to you."

Sheer relief had him tightening his fingers around hers. "That's a promise, baby." She was his. She was perfect for him. She "got" him and took him just the way he was. She wouldn't always like it and she had an unexpected temper that he liked, but she was still choosing him.

17

"Eli." Catarina stopped abruptly as they walked up to the front door. Her heart jerked hard and began to pound. She tasted fear in her mouth. "Someone's been here." Even her leopard had gone on alert.

Eli's arm snaked around her waist and he pulled her body into his, leaned his chin over her shoulder and placed his lips against her ear. "Good girl. I was hoping you'd feel it. Inhale and let your leopard senses free. Tell me who was here."

Catarina pushed down the fear. Eli wasn't pushing her behind him as he normally would if there was danger surrounding them. She did as he said, took a deep breath. Immediately her leopard rose to aid her. There were three distinct scents. All male. Leopards. Her female knew that. She had smelled them before.

"Joshua," she said.

He nodded and brushed his lips against her ear. "Good, baby, he was here. Who else?"

She made a face, even though his warm praise made her glow inside. "Elijah."

"He isn't part of the criminal world, Cat."

She heard the quiet patience in his voice. "He's head of a major crime syndicate, Eli. You don't have to believe me."

"I'm not denying he's part of that family and he inherited the mantle, but he's been working to get all their businesses out from under everything illegal. The first to go were the drugs. That was the most difficult for him. Supplying drugs made a lot of money, and his people didn't want to give it up. He had to find ways to make the money for them without the drugs. There was a war and a lot of people died. He had a price on his head for a long time from some of his own people."

She didn't answer him because she didn't know what the truth was. She knew Eli believed leopards could smell lies, but she had seen Elijah there at Rafe's home, making a deal with him. It made her uneasy to know that she'd met Elijah at Rafe's. Rafe Cordeau had never once invited a decent person to his home. Every man or woman who had come, and some had been cops, were dirty. They ran guns, drugs or prostitution rings. They murdered for hire.

No crime was too big or too small. But everyone who came was a criminal in some way or other. One had even been a Catholic priest who had a weakness for prostitutes. Rafe may have started out by blackmailing him, she honestly didn't know, but he often came to give up the major sins of his congregation when it earned him favors.

"The third man is Trey." She turned her head to look at him over her shoulder, lips just a whisper away from his. "What were they doing here? You obviously know."

"I have a surprise for you," he said. "In the house."

She froze. Her heart did a funny little contraction, almost hurting. "A surprise? What kind of surprise?"

"Kitten." Masculine amusement. He said it softly in the tone that always melted her insides and teased her thighs and feminine sheath so beautifully. "If I told you, it wouldn't be a surprise, would it?"

She still didn't move, even though his body put pressure on hers to step forward. "You planned something for me? You actually planned it yourself? I'm going to cry. I can't help it."

"You don't even know what it is yet."

"It doesn't matter what it is. You thought of doing something for me, Eli. No one's ever done that before."

Eli laughed softly. "Get used to it, baby. I plan to surprise you quite often. Let's go inside."

She blinked back tears, and he had to step around her and tug on her hand to get her in motion. The moment he opened the door and stepped inside, he felt as if he'd come home. He'd been to the ranch several times over the last couple of years, but he'd never really felt that particular emotion until this moment.

He expected Catarina to ask him where her surprise was, but she didn't. She tightened her fingers around his, and actually slowed her footsteps to the point of dragging. He could feel a tremor running through her body.

Eli pulled her in tight against him. "This is a good thing, Kitten. Nothing bad is going to happen."

She turned her face up to his and his heart stuttered in his chest. She looked stripped down, vulnerable. Afraid even. "It's a big thing, Eli, something sweet, no matter what it is and I don't know what to do with that."

He ran his thumb down her cheek, tracing her beautiful bone structure, and then dipped his head to brush a reassuring kiss over her mouth. Her lips were trembling. He couldn't stop himself from pulling her tight into the shelter of his body. The moment he did, she melted into him, her arms circling around his waist, her hands bunching in his shirt as she held on tight.

"Catarina, listen to me. I love you. Those aren't just words to me. You matter to me. You matter more than I could ever express in words. I like giving you things. I like letting you know how beautiful and special you are to me. That's never going to stop." His palm cupped the back of her head and held her face to him. "This isn't supposed to distress you."

"I know. I do know that, Eli," she said, her voice muffled by his shirt. She took a breath, straightened her shoulders and stepped back to give him a tentative smile. "Show me. I'm really excited about it, I just got a little emotional for a minute."

She looked like she was being led to her doom, but he didn't point that out. She was too adorable, trying to appear matter-of-fact when she clearly was ready to cry.

He took her through the house, not bothering with lights until he came to the back where his office was. The room was large, built in light oak. When he flipped the switch the walls appeared golden. She'd been to his office before, commenting that it looked a little bare with just his desk and computer in it.

The office had been completely remodeled. There were floor to ceiling bookshelves on two of the walls. In the center of the room two desks faced each another. His held his computer and his usual stack of papers and receipts he could never quite get filed. Hers held an unopened box with a brand-new laptop in it. The books behind her desk were mostly reference, books on the rain forest and various countries. Books he'd chosen because he thought she'd like them. On the floor beside the chair were the all-important boots. Soft, gray leather, lace up with ruffles made of leather on either side of the lace. He'd chosen them because they reminded him of the ones he'd seen her wear. He'd paid a fortune for them, but he hoped they would make up for the ones he'd left behind.

She stood uncertainly in the doorway, her gaze sweeping the room. She looked stunned. Eli cleared his throat of the lump that had formed for no apparent reason.

"The laptop has never been used. I wanted you to take it out of the box yourself, set it up with your own password so you know you have complete privacy and the ability to go anywhere on the Internet and learn about anything you would like. We'll set up accounts at a couple of the bookstores online so you can order any books you'd like."

She didn't take a single step into the room. Her hand clung to the doorjamb as if it was the only thing holding her up. She had tears in her eyes and she shook her head, her teeth tugging at her lower lip.

He dipped his head again, this time to brush the top of hers with another reassuring kiss. She was killing him with her reaction. Never in her life had anyone given her anything. He hadn't considered the enormity of that.

Catarina pressed her hand to her mouth. "Eli, I can't ever do anything like this for you. I don't have anything to give you. There's nothing I could ever think of that would even begin to compare with such a gift." She gestured toward the boots and then up to the laptop. A soft sound of distress emerged.

He used his thumbs to try to erase the tears streaming down her face. "Baby, this is supposed to make you happy, not sad. You give me far more than I could ever repay." His hand moved through her hair.

"Not like this. Never like this."

"I matter to you, Cat. You show me that in everything you do. I matter. I don't think I've ever mattered to anyone since I lost my parents. You do the things I ask of you even when you're tired or exhausted. You never object when I need to kiss or touch you. Do you have any idea what it means to a man like me that you enjoy cooking for me? Or making this house a home? That you come apart in my arms every single time I touch you? You gave yourself to me, gave me back your trust after I let you down and you've never brought it up again. Whenever, wherever, *however* I want you, you give your body to me and make me aware you enjoy it. There aren't very many women who would take that kind of care with their man."

Her hands went to the front of his shirt, fisting there. She shook her head. "It isn't the same thing, Eli. Not like this. This is huge. I don't even have money to try to buy you a gift. You left everything I had in the warehouse. You grabbed my bag but didn't take a cent of the money and the safe was open."

"Because you were saving it to send back to Cordeau. I know you were. You didn't have to tell me, but you had start money and that had to come from him. You would never be okay with stealing, and you weren't using the money even for gas, so it had to be money to pay him back with. He'd been there and he was coming back. When you left that place I didn't want you to owe him a damn thing."

She laid her head against his chest and slipped her arms around his waist. "I don't know what to do with you when you're like this, Eli."

"You like it then?" he prompted gently.

"You know I love it. How could I not? A laptop in an unopened box? My boots. I love the boots. They're perfect. I hear what you're saying, Eli, and I'm telling you I don't know what to do with this kind of sweetness. I trust you, you know. You aren't Rafe. I wouldn't think you'd rig my computer to see what I'm up to."

"I want you to be confident in that, Cat, never to wonder. I know I'm like him in some ways and that has to make you think twice about a relationship with me."

Her gaze jumped to his. She shook her head. "You aren't, you know."

"I made you stay with me, Catarina. Just as if you were a prisoner."

A slow smile brought a curve to her soft mouth. "Is that what you think? That I had no choice in all this? I weighed every option carefully, Eli. If you weren't my choice, I'd be scheming and planning to escape, no matter what you said or did. I wouldn't snuggle close to you at night, or want to cook for you. I gave myself to you because of who and what you are. Because of how I feel about you. Don't you know that yet?"

He brought his mouth down on hers, hungry for her. Ravenous. He was addicted to the taste of her. To her warmth. To the way her body melted into his and her arms slid around his neck to hold him closer. He kissed her over and over, long, hot kisses that took her breath so he had to breathe for both of them. Still, it wasn't enough. He wanted more. More of everything.

With a soft groan he broke contact with her mouth. Her eyes were dazed, her lips swollen and inviting, and she moved against him restlessly. He loved her hair all over the place, looking as if they'd already had wild sex.

Normally he would have taken her right there on the floor, or on the desk, but he wanted a long night with her. He picked her up, cradling her close to him as he took them on through to the master bedroom.

Eli put her down right beside the bed. "Get your clothes off, baby. Hurry."

Her eyebrows shot up and her mouth tilted at the corners. Her hands went to the buttons of her blouse, but she didn't move fast. Instead she cocked her head to one side so that the long sweep of hair slid over her shoulder. "Hurry? You want me to take off my clothes fast?"

He growled at the playful, teasing note in her voice, stalked back across the room and caught the front of her blouse.

"No," she said.

It was too late. He stripped the blouse right off of her, reached around her to the closures of her bra and removed that as well, spilling her breasts into his hands. His head descended immediately, and he pulled a soft mound into the heat of his mouth.

She cried out, her arms immediately cradling his head to her while he suckled. While he used the flat of his tongue and the edge of his teeth. He was growing wild and he didn't care. He needed this. Needed her. Needed the sweet, spicy honey spilling from her body. He was already reeling out of control, but she was his woman, and his woman always was able to handle it when his hunger overcame him.

"I liked that blouse," she murmured, but her hands were in his hair, fingers curling through the longish ends at the nape of his neck.

He lifted his head just enough to look at her in warning. He knew his eyes were glowing, showing the cat in him. The feral cat. A leopard on the brink of wild and dangerous. "I'll buy you another one. Kick off your shoes." He growled out the command and went back to devouring her breasts.

His fingers tugged and rolled at her nipple, rough, hard, so that she squirmed and whimpered. He kept at it, scenting her call, inhaling the need in her that only fed his hunger more. She was obedient, removing the small flats that had been part of the bundle of clothing Emma had sent over, clothing that allowed for fast removal when she needed to shift—or her lover demanded she rid herself of clothes quickly.

She panted against his shoulder, dropping her head there, her hips moving restlessly against his body. He pushed his engorged cock tight against her, and once again lifted his head.

"Get rid of the jeans. I need them off you right now. From now on, I think you'll have to wear long skirts. Or short ones. No panties."

Her hands dropped instantly to the waistband of her jeans and she quickly unsnapped them and lowered the zipper. "I have to wear panties, you crazy man."

He used his teeth again, nipping along the underside of her breast, and then over the smooth curve, his tongue easing the ache. He wanted his mark on her. He loved that. Loved to see his prints on her skin.

"Why? I see no reason at all for panties," he replied, half serious.

She pushed the denim over her hips and he let her go to yank them down. The moment she stepped out of them, he caught her around the waist and tossed her onto the bed.

She hit the mattress, her arms and legs sprawling out. He didn't wait for her to recover, but went down over top of her, straddling her hips, still fully clothed. Catching her wrists, he stretched her arms above her head and pinned them to the mattress. Leaning over, he opened the drawer next to his bed and withdrew his handcuffs.

"Eli." For a moment fear skittered through her eyes. Fear and excitement. "What are you doing?"

He cuffed her and then hooked the cuffs to the headboard. "What does it look like, baby? I want you at my mercy."

"I'm always at your mercy." She pulled a little on her arms. "I'm not certain I like this. I feel . . ." She trailed off when he moved down her body.

"Vulnerable? Helpless?" He used his hands to pull her thighs apart, wedging his body between them, spreading her open. "That's how I want you to feel. Vulnerable. Mine. Your body is mine. I like it that way and I'm going to make certain you like it that way too." While he explained, he drew his T-shirt over his head and tossed it aside.

His eyes on hers, he removed his shoes. "I want to spend time with you tonight. My way."

She pulled again on the cuffs, her breasts heaving, swaying invitingly. He liked looking at her there, spread out on his bed, completely defenseless and exposed to him. Her nipples were taut pebbles, hard and erect, and her breath came in little ragged gasps.

"It's always your way, Eli," she whispered, her head tossing a little. "But I don't know about this."

His hand slid down her belly to her mound. Two fingers slipped inside her hot tunnel. She was wet and slick. He withdrew them, held them up for her to see. "Yeah, Kitten, you like this." He licked his fingers, enjoying her taste, knowing there was so much more for him.

All the time he watched her eyes. She had beautiful eyes, very expressive and she was getting hotter by the minute. She might be a little nervous, but it added to the climbing heat in her.

"What are you going to do?"

"Anything I want, but I'll make certain you enjoy it. I've always wondered how many times I could make you come. We've got all night." He slipped his jeans from his body, his cock hard and erect.

Her gaze dropped to the heavy erection, her breath catching in her throat. He didn't blame her. He was long and thick and he looked far too big for her little body. But he fit perfectly. She was made for him. He craved her tight, scorching-hot tunnel and the way she grasped at him so greedily with her silken muscles.

"Eli." Just his name.

"It was 'baby' earlier. Now suddenly I'm Eli again. I wonder what it's going to take to get you to call out that little endearment." He stretched out, his shoulders spreading her thighs even wider. His hands held her open to him. "Such a beautiful little flower, and all mine. It is mine, isn't it, Catarina? This is all mine."

His tone demanded an answer and he waited, blowing warm air over her slick entrance. There was a moment of silence. He didn't look at her. He looked at the feast he was about to devour instead. But he waited.

"Yes." Her voice was so low he barely caught the sound, even with his acute hearing.

"No man has ever touched this. Tasted it. It's all for me. Every damn inch of you. All for me. Isn't that right, baby? This is all mine."

He lowered his head and took one delicious swipe with his tongue, dragging out the honey he craved. He stopped instantly, letting it dissolve in his mouth while he waited for her reply.

"Yes."

"Yes what?"

She hesitated again, and he took another sample. Her

body shuddered with pleasure and he blew more warm air over her. Waiting. He let her know he was waiting but he didn't look away from his prize.

"Yes, that's all yours. I'm all yours. Every inch of me."

"Belongs to me. Your golden mouth. Such perfect breasts. An ass that can bring men to their knees. And this beautiful, perfect flower. Belongs to me."

He didn't allow for much movement, but she managed a little. Her hips bucked again. Her legs moved restlessly.

"Yes," she whispered. "Eli."

She was drenched. He wanted that. Even needed it. Her scent called to him, and the craving grew beyond anything he'd known yet.

"I'm addicted to this taste, Kitten," he admitted. "I think I could eat you all night and never get enough. This time, you want my cock in you, I expect I'll be holding out for something from you. Something I need from you."

"What?" She gasped the word. "Eli, tell me what."

"You figure it out, Cat. Maybe after you've given me ten or fifteen orgasms, you'll figure it out."

He didn't wait. He couldn't. Not even for the pleasure of torturing her slowly, knowing every moment he had her spread open, every word out of his mouth was only making her hotter. Only causing the tension to wind tighter and tighter in her.

He needed. And he needed now. His mouth clamped over her slick, hot entrance and he plunged his tongue deep. She cried out, tried to move, but his arms pinned her down, refusing to allow her to wiggle away or even toward him. This was his. This was for him. He was taking what belonged to him. What she gave him.

He used his tongue ruthlessly, devouring her ravenously just like he said he would. She tasted better than he remembered. Hotter. Sweeter. Spicier. He ate her like he was dying for her taste, because he was. He'd had the taste of her in his mouth from the moment he'd heard her laughter in the kitchen with Emma.

He heard her ragged breathing, the desperate little mewling cries as he ate her. He loved her cries, music to his ears. He loved her body, and it belonged to him. He loved that the more he took from her, the more golden cream spilled out.

He felt her body coiling. "That's it, baby," he murmured, his face buried in her. "Give it to me. I want it now. Give it to me." He pressed his mouth over her clit and suckled, using his tongue in little butterfly strokes to stimulate her further.

She screamed and went wild around him, hips really bucking, body writhing, head tossing. He could feel the powerful orgasm sweeping through her body, the tight muscles clamping down hard. He was ruthless, refusing to stop, to give her any break.

"More," he demanded. "I want more from you."

His tongue pulled at the molten gold, all the sweetness her body gave him. He plunged two fingers deep and used his tongue and the edge of his teeth to drive her back up hard and fast. He loved the sensations, her cries. His.

He let go just long enough to raise his head slightly and make his demand. "Give me more, baby. I'm not done. I want more." He was greedy for it. For her honey and her orgasms. For her musical mewling cries. For the way she chanted his name, so breathy. So needy.

His tongue was back immediately, pulling more spice from her. He could hear the nearly feral growls coming from deep in his throat, rumbling in his chest. His cock swelled to the bursting point, aching and hard with its own demand. Still he couldn't stop, licking and sucking and once again using his teeth and fingers.

Her body stiffened. Shuddered. He felt the rewarding clamp of her muscles, a vise around his fingers. Her cry was lower, more muted, but pulled from somewhere deep inside of her. This time the orgasm was even stronger, like a powerful tsunami that gathered strength as it rocked through her body. He rode it out, catching the spilling liquid, flicking her sensitive clit with his tongue, stroking her thighs and using his fingers to press deep into that tight channel.

"Eli." She gasped his name. "You have to stop. I can't take any more."

"Yes you can. You will. Your body was made for this. Sex. Sin. Everything. Whatever I want. You'll love it, baby. You'll come to need it, just like I do."

She pulled at the handcuffs, trying to twist her body, trying to dislodge his mouth, but he'd already clamped down again, taking her over, taking what he wanted, driving her right back up hard and fast. Ruthlessly. Brutally. He heard her breath catch on a sob, but her body still spilled that hot, addictive liquid gold right into his mouth.

Catarina was afraid now, the fear skittering like tiny footprints down her spine, terrified she might lose her mind. He didn't know it, but she already needed this. Needed his mouth and his hands and his cock. She couldn't imagine her life without it. But he was going too far, taking her too high. She thought she might go insane, lose her mind at the pleasure spilling through her, overtaking her, pushing her so high she feared she would never come back.

Her body didn't belong to her anymore. It belonged to him. She couldn't think or reason when he was touching her. Her mind was in complete chaos and the tension in her body just coiled tighter and tighter. She needed another release. Desperately. Only it didn't come. She got close, reached for it, and he backed off, flicking his tongue until she wanted to scream with need.

"Eli." She could barely get his name out.

"Hmmm?" He didn't look up. Didn't stop tormenting her. He licked more. His hands framed her entrance so that he could dip his tongue into her again and again while she writhed under him. "You know what I want from you."

She couldn't think. There was no way to think. No way to remember what he wanted. She'd give him anything. Do anything. Let him do anything. Wasn't that enough? She bit back a sob of frustration as once again she got so close, the burning between her legs nearly exploding, and then he lifted his head as if he knew—and he probably did. He licked along the insides of her thighs.

Shards of desire clawed and raked at her. Streaks of fire rushed from her breasts to her core. She needed him. Was burning up with that need. She couldn't stay still. His mouth and fingers were relentless. He pushed her up and up until she thought she would come apart and never be put back together, but just before she could make that drop, he slowed his feast and left her panting and pleading.

"I don't," she admitted, her voice trembling, her mind in such chaos she wanted to scream with frustration or sob with need, "I don't know what you want."

He took another long, slow swipe with his tongue and she nearly shattered. Nearly. She came off the bed, or tried to, but she couldn't move her hands and he had her pinned down and completely open to him.

"I want more than 'Eli' from you. And I want you to say, in words, how you feel about me." His voice was a command. A threat. A promise.

She went still. Her heart thundered in her chest. His mouth went right over her slick entrance, his tongue plunging deep, and she did sob as the pleasure pushed to the point of pain. She needed to come. Needed to shatter.

"Honey, please." That was the best she could do. The best she could come up with when her body wasn't her own and her brain couldn't think. "Please. Please. Please."

"Please what?" he murmured, not lifting his head. He began a lazy, languid licking of her body. Flicking his tongue. Using his teeth and fingers and then retreating when she went mindless and boneless just before she could tip over the edge.

"I need you in me." She was begging and she didn't care.

"I need something from you, baby. I need it more than you need what I can give you, so let's trade." Again he didn't look at her. He was too busy with his clever tongue and his exploring fingers.

She swallowed fear. This man of hers made her crazy, there was no doubt about it, but he was hers. She'd given herself to him for a reason. He was her choice and he had been since the first time she'd even seen him in the dojo, instructing advanced students. She'd known then that she could belong to him.

She had never given her trust to another human being. Not ever. Eli had been the first person she'd given even a part of herself to and now he wanted it all. Demanded it all, which was just like him.

"Baby?" he prompted gently. "Give it to me. I need to hear it."

This time he raised his head, his glittering cat's eyes suddenly focused completely on hers. Her heart pounded harder. She tasted fear. She tasted love. She didn't want to love him. She wanted to belong to him, but she didn't want to love him. Loving him was terrifying. He already had too much of her, and what if she disappeared when she was just finding herself? What if she couldn't stand up to him? He was a dominant male and he'd be more so if he knew.

"Baby?" he coaxed again, his gaze holding hers captive. "Say it. Tell me. Give me what I need."

Tears tracked down her cheeks. "What if I can't?"

"You can. You're just afraid. Say it once. Give that to me." With his gaze still on hers, he pressed little butterfly kisses up and down her thighs, his tongue lapping at the spilled spice coating her there, fluttering along her skin until she thought she might go up in flames.

Catarina swallowed fear. He knew. He already knew. What difference did it make that she say it aloud to him? Why was he making her? She forced herself to really look at him, to get past the haze of hunger and lust driving her.

His face was carved with lines of need. The set of his jaw, so stubborn, the straight nose and hard features that were purely masculine. But it was there, in his golden eyes, eyes that had gone molten and nearly all leopard. She saw the truth there. The need. He wasn't just playing some sexual game, out to force her to obey him. He was telling her the absolute, stark truth. He needed to hear the words from her. They meant something to him.

She exhaled and hadn't known she'd been holding her breath. He had told her he loved her first. He'd put himself out there, but somehow, she hadn't considered that it was really true. How could it be? What was she giving him? She didn't even have a high school diploma. How could he possibly love her? How could he need her the way his eyes said so starkly that he did?

"Damn it, Cat, give it to me." Now it was a demand. A growl. Dominance winning through all his lazy sensual facade.

He'd given her two orgasms but her body was so greedy that she needed more. She was on fire. An inferno. The growling demand nearly sent her over the edge. She loved his voice. Loved it when he narrowed his eyes and focused with ferocious, furious intent. Her body always responded, going hot, blood rushing through her veins. She came alive.

Her hands gripped the headboard tightly. She needed to hold on to something. Anything. Because what she was about to do was enormous to her. That last piece of her. The one she'd kept for herself. The one she protected. He was demanding it. He knew. Somehow he knew, and he wanted all of her. He wanted the last piece of her that she'd been guarding. Holding safe.

She moistened her lips. "I do, Eli. You know I do."

"You do what, Catarina? Say it, damn you. Do you think I'm going to accept less than all of you? Say it out loud. Right now. And know what it means." His voice had gone harsh. Low and harsh. Velvet soft, but filled with iron. Steel. He wasn't going to back down and his mouth and hands kept the fire inside her roaring.

Catarina knew she was going to give him what he wanted. What he demanded. There was nowhere to hide. He didn't let her. She felt stripped down. Bare. Completely vulnerable, and it had nothing at all to with the way he held her body open to him. She could easily give him her body. Even maybe her heart. But he demanded her soul.

His teeth nipped. A sharp, stinging pain. All the while those golden eyes blazed into hers. Intense focus. A leopard's stare when he claimed his prey.

She swallowed again and let go. Let herself fall. "I love you, Eli. You know I do. I love you with everything in me."

She watched his eyes when she said it. He looked merciless. Ruthless. The moment the words were out in the open between them, those eyes went soft. Melted. She saw absolute, raw vulnerability and the flood of love there. She'd never seen him like that, or imagined him like that. Naked for her to see into him. Her stomach clenched. Her channel spasmed, and her heart turned over. She needed to hold him, to put her arms around him and get as close as possible. She wanted to cry seeing the look on his face because in her wildest dreams, she never imagined he really felt that way toward her. That soul-searing deep.

"That's my Kitten," he whispered softly. "So brave."

She couldn't stop the warm glow that spread at the thought of putting that look on his face, of giving him something that obviously meant everything to him.

Eli moved then, fast, coming over top of her, blanketing her completely, pinning her under him. His mouth went straight to her breast, his hand slipping between her legs to position himself at her entrance. She tried hard to push herself against him, to impale herself on his gorgeous, erect shaft, but his weight made it impossible to move. He held her there, watching the helpless pleasure on her face. Loving that.

"Eli, honey, I want to hold you. I want to be able to touch you." She whispered it, half desperate to feel his skin with her hands.

Without hesitation, he reached for the key on the nightstand and deftly stretched one arm up to unlock the cuffs. He tossed them aside along with the key and caught her wrists to look at them quickly.

She didn't care about her wrists. She wanted him inside of her. She wanted to feel his hot skin under her palms so she wrapped him up as quickly as she could, as tightly as she could. Her arms. Her legs. She hooked her ankles around his hips, her breathing ragged, while her nipples rubbed tight against the heavy muscles of his chest.

She ran her hands up his chest to his shoulders, over and then down his back, taking him in, pulling him closer. She couldn't get enough of him.

"Honey, you have to be inside me," she whispered against his chest, her tongue licking at his skin. He tasted wild. Masculine. Like rain forests. Her fist clenched in his hair for a moment, pulling his head back. She felt wild with pleasure, with hunger. "I need you inside me, Eli."

His eyes glowed like those of the leopard he was. Hot. Golden fire. Piercing her soul. He was hers, as wild and primitive as a man could be. A shifter. Dangerous and dark, but he loved her. And he could bring her to ecstasy.

His cock slammed deep into her, driving hard, forcing her delicate, tight muscles to give way for his intrusion. At first, like it always did, her feminine channel resisted, but there was no holding back against such a force.

She knew he thought he held her prisoner, just as Rafe had done, but she knew she could get away from him. He would never hurt her. He would never kill to force her to stay. "You saved me," she whispered. "Eli, honey, you saved me."

His head reared back, those beautiful, golden eyes blazing with heat. Then her ability to think was gone entirely. He thrust hard and deep, over and over, a wild, primitive taking, a claiming. She recognized that much, but her body was making a climb, tension coiling and flames racing.

Eli watched her face carefully as he pistoned into her

body with hard, deep strokes. She gave him everything. Surrendered everything to him. She gave him control of her body, trusting him to give her pleasure, to make certain she was never harmed. She gave him so much that the only way he could give back was this wild, driving force inside of him to possess her. To love her. To give her more pleasure than any other man possibly could.

He took her savagely, almost brutally, feeling her wildness, feeling her spiraling out of control. He loved to see the dazed look in her eyes, the flush on her body. Her nipples like hard little pebbles tempting him.

She was beautiful all the time, but especially so when she came apart in his arms. He felt her surrounding him with her soft body. Her arms. Her legs. Her sweet, hot channel squeezing the life out of him.

He loved her soft, ragged pleas. Her gasping, broken cries. Her music only added to the agonizing pleasure through every cell in his body. She bared his soul to the world, and she had no idea she did it. He needed the desperate hunger flowing through her body just as much as he needed air to breathe. He could give her this. So much pleasure. She had no idea how high he could take her, but he pushed her limits just a little more each time.

His body wasn't his own anymore. It belonged to her. To Catarina. He was hard every damn time he looked at her. His needs and cravings only grew with his addiction to her soft cries, her tight, hot body and the pleasure coursing through her at his touch.

"Eli."

A plea. Music. Such need. Such surrender. She never held anything away from him, not even her emotions, not even when she feared what they were together. She gave and gave. He needed to give just as much. More.

He poured himself into loving her. Bringing her as high as he dared, watching her face for signals, for when the pleasure was too much for her, her body too sensitive and

the need too great. Her eyes widened. Her mouth opened in
a long wailing scream as he sent her crashing over the edge.

He loved her body clamping down like a scorching silken
vise, milking him, gripping so hard his cock was strangling
in all that hot, wet silk. He felt the explosion start, a wild
ecstasy, somewhere in his toes, rocketing through his body,
straight to his skull. His cock swelled, pushing back at those
tight, vise-like muscles, stretching and burning her to the
point where pain and pleasure came together in a single point
to set off another wild, earth-shattering quake in her body.

This time she took him with her, her keening cries and
breathless whispers nearly shattering him just as much as the
hot sheath surrounding him and her sweet declaration of love
and surrender to him had. He threw his head back, wanting
to roar with the shocking pleasure. It had never been like
this, an all-consuming passion that wrung him inside out.

No other man had ever had her. He was the one to be
gifted with such a sensual woman, to teach her, to mold her
into the lover he wanted and needed. She matched him, fire
for fire. He closed his eyes and buried his face in her neck,
holding her tight, feeling her body surround his, the aftershocks that shook them both. Her ragged breathing. Her
hands in his hair, gripping and stroking as her tight delicate
muscles did the same to his shaft.

"God, Kitten, it's a damn good thing you have no idea
how much I love you," he whispered into her soft skin.
Feeling her pulse. Feeling her tight, feminine channel
spasm around his cock at the admission. She could destroy
him. So easily. So very easily.

He had no idea when he'd surrendered himself body and
soul to her, but somewhere along the line it had happened.
He'd never felt more stripped down and vulnerable to a
human being, but she needed to hear it. She needed the
reassurance, and he wasn't about to allow pride or ego to
get in the way of giving her anything she needed.

She didn't say it back, didn't whisper in his ear, but her

arms tightened around him possessively and her soft mouth moved on his chest, kissing him. He rolled, taking them to his side, not wanting to let go of her.

"I like you close, baby," he said softly. "Skin to skin. Part of me." It was a small warning. He wasn't going to allow her to slip away from him and roll into that little ball as she sometimes did. "You get me?"

She surprised him with her soft laughter. "Another Eli rule?"

"Absolutely."

"You're making this up as you go along, aren't you?"

The laughter in her voice kept him semihard, enough that his body stayed connected to hers. "Gives me the upper hand." He stroked his palm down the curve of her spine to the curve of her buttocks, possession in his touch.

"You always have the upper hand." There was no complaint in her voice.

"Glad you think so, Cat," he acknowledged.

"Eli." Her voice went serious. "Thank you for today. For Emma. For the laptop and books. For my gorgeous boots. Mostly thank you for understanding what something like today means to me."

His heart jerked. He brushed her temple with a kiss. "Go to sleep, Catarina. You need your rest." He didn't want to exhaust her, but if she kept talking, he was making love to her again. Slow. Easy. Lazily. Until it turned rough and wild like it mostly did. She needed care. Love. Rest. He took that seriously, even if it meant lying next to her as hard as a rock.

Eli didn't even mind that. He liked holding her close, his body alive, listening to her soft breathing. Knowing she was his.

"Good night, honey," she whispered.

He closed his eyes. Savored the moment. She was nearly there. She was trying—for him. He loved her all the more for that. He answered with a comforting kiss, too choked up to say another damn word.

18

THE storm came out of nowhere. Sheets of lightning lit the sky and thunder crashed with resounding booms, shaking the house. The rain poured down, the skies opening up to spill a wealth of water across the land, pounding into trees and grass to pool in small puddles everywhere.

Dressed in Eli's flannel shirt, her wardrobe of choice late at night, Catarina wandered out to the porch with her coffee, enjoying nature's display. The turbulent weather reminded her of Eli. Wild and untamed. Fierce. The thunder and lightning also corresponded with her restless mood.

She'd felt the buildup for a while now, the gathering tension that had spread across the sky, matching the ominous dark clouds, the jagged forks of lightning and roaring thunder. He was coming. He was close. The nightmares had started again, just like they had right before he found her the last time she escaped. Rafe was coming, and her perfect dream world was about to be shattered.

She was so in love with Eli. She might have a difficult
time articulating her emotions out loud, but she tried her
best to show him. The days passed and she never thought
of leaving. The ranch had become her home, a real home.
She found herself smiling most of the time. She couldn't
mention liking or wanting anything without the object
appearing a couple of days later. Eli liked to give her things.
He liked to surprise her, and he did it often.

Her kitchen had been transformed. A gleaming new stove,
the exact model she'd dreamt of, was installed there. Along
with the stove was a set of cooking pots and pans, hanging
now from the rack above the island. She'd ordered books and
they'd arrived and were on the shelves behind her desk.

Emma called her twice. A friend. They'd chatted and
laughed and made plans for coffee at Emma's house. Life had
been good—until now. Until this terrible tension had begun to
coil in her gut. Until the nightmares had begun again and she
couldn't stop wondering when she would lose it all—because
she would. He would come. Rafe would come for her.

She suspected Eli knew something about Rafe. Three days
ago, Eli had shut down, become quiet, more watchful, his
dark, brooding, moody behavior making her feel more nervous than ever. She'd waited for him to tell her something—
anything at all—but he remained stubbornly silent and that
only added to the terrors surrounding her nightly.

Just a half hour ago, she'd woken from her nightmare, Eli's
arms around her, his voice soothing, his hands caressing, his
lips gentle on her forehead. She clung to him, to his protection, the shelter of his body, as he'd drifted back to sleep, but
she couldn't forget the echoes of the terrible moment when
Rafe's face, a mask of cold fury above her own, had forced
her hands into a dying woman, smearing blood everywhere.

Emma. Eli. Emma's children. If Rafe knew about them,
they would live under a death sentence, there was no doubt
in her mind. Eli drove her day and night, especially this
past week, determined to get her in shape, to be able to fight

in either form—human or leopard—as if he believed she
could defeat Rafe.

He didn't know Rafe. He'd never seen Rafe's leopard.
He'd never seen Rafe's evil glowing eyes, or the madness in
them. The rage. Life had not been kind to him, and she knew
he was so twisted that the only peace he ever found was in
other people's pain. He enjoyed watching others suffer.

She took another sip of her coffee and stepped closer to
the edge of the porch, the very edge of the storm. Sheets of
rain pounded into the ground and she felt the spray as the
wind shifted just enough to push droplets under the roof.

Rafe had only looked at her with madness a couple of
times—those times when she had escaped his control, even
for a few hours. He had hurt her in unbelievable ways. Killing others. Hurting others in front of her. Showing her his
leopard. Raking and biting her back and shoulder. But he'd
never beat her or struck her. He'd been careful with her.
Sometimes when he'd looked at her, she could actually see
affection stirring behind the mask he wore.

She sighed and set down the coffee to circle the porch
column with one arm, resting her forehead there. She couldn't
deny that Rafe had some feelings for her. They were nowhere
normal, they were twisted just as he was, but he had them.
Perhaps if she'd been older she might have been able to help
him, but she was far too young and terrified of his reprisals.

"Kitten." Eli's arms stole around her. "What are you
doing out here? It's three in the morning."

She never ever heard him walk. He was a big man and
she should be able to hear at least a footfall. He pulled her
back into his arms so her back was to his front, his hands
clasped at her waist. His chest was bare, but he had pulled
on some soft cotton drawstring bottoms.

"I didn't mean to wake you," Catarina apologized. "You
don't sleep as it is."

He rubbed his face in her hair. "I sleep when you're in
my arms, baby," he said softly. "Tell me what's wrong."

She turned her head to look over her shoulder. "You tell me." Her eyes met his. "Do you think I don't know you well enough to know that you've been hiding something from me for the last three days? Actually, it started before that. When we went to see Jake and Emma—you've been pensive ever since."

She felt his response more than saw it. His expression remained the same. His focused gaze didn't so much as flicker, but somewhere inside her, she felt him flinch.

"I should have known I couldn't hide anything from you, Cat." He sighed and dropped his hands from her waist to slide his palm down her arm to catch her wrist.

She always felt shackled when his fingers settled there. Shackled and then fluttery when he stroked caresses on her inner wrist so gently. He went for the chairs. She followed because she had no real choice in the matter. When Eli moved, she moved with him.

"Sit down, Kitten. You're right, of course. I've heard some news and I've considered the best way to tell you."

Tiny knots formed in her belly. She felt each one like a spike settling deep. She knew. She knew it was bad. And she knew it was Rafe. Her heart pounded, slow and hard, hammering in her chest as if trying to destroy her. The coppery taste of fear was in her mouth. She sank into the chair, grateful that Eli's fingers were around her wrist, holding her to him. She needed the connection, needed his strength and confidence. There was a reason Eli was arrogant.

"Just tell me, Eli. When Rafe is involved, there's no way to pretty it up."

His hand swept through her hair. His eyes went soft. "No, there isn't. I wanted to spare you, Cat, but I also don't like keeping anything from you. It smacks of deceit, and I promised myself I wouldn't deceive you no matter what the issue was. Even if that meant we clashed over it."

She was grateful to hear that. She'd known he was bothered and brooding. "I prefer to know everything when Rafe is involved. I probably know him better than anyone else. If anyone can predict his movements, it's me."

"Cordeau found Poetry Slam."

He shifted position, his hand slipping from her wrist, the connection lost. She heard herself scream. The sound never came out of her, but it was there inside, a long, low wail of pain.

"Who did he kill? How many?" She looked down at her hands. How much blood did she have there? How could she ever wash it off? Scrubbing her skin didn't work, she'd tried. The skin had come off, but not the blood.

"David Belmont, and Bernard Casey. He also killed the man, Jase Fulton, who made a pass at you that one night. David was supposed to have gone on vacation. I warned him. He said he would, but he didn't. I guess he was afraid of losing more business and he went back after a couple of days. Malcom is safe. I hadn't considered Cordeau might think Bernard or Fulton were any threat to his hold on you."

She shook her head. "You say that so gently as if he stole softly into their rooms, the silent angel of death, and just struck them down in their sleep. He tortured them, didn't he?" She looked up, her gaze meeting his. "Didn't he?"

She saw the answer in his eyes. The wariness. The sadness. He was watchful of her, knowing how she felt. She waited. She knew, but she waited anyway. The silent screams kept coming but no one heard them but her.

"Yes, Cat," he said on a soft sigh. "He tortured them."

Her heart took a battering. Sore. Bruised. Her chest hurt. "How close is he to us? To Jake and Emma and their children?"

"He can't touch them. I warned Jake. He won't find us."

"He'll find us. You know he will, Eli. He's close. I can feel him. We have a connection. His leopard and mine. You don't want to hear that, but you know he made certain of our connection. She's out now. I let her run every day. Your leopard teaches her how to fight. His leopard feels her and he's coming after me that way. It's the only way he had, but he's using it." She knew with absolute certainty.

Eli winced. He didn't like knowing about the connection between the two leopards. He didn't like knowing any man or their beast had a thread to his woman. She was hurting. He had known she would. He wanted to protect her from it, but deceiving her would have hurt her more.

"Give me the rest, Eli. Knowing Rafe killed three people because of me has to be the worst of it, so just tell me the rest. Whatever Jake told you."

Eli studied her face. She looked fragile. Vulnerable. He wanted to gather her into his arms and shelter her from everything, but she held herself too still. She didn't want his touch. She didn't want him close. Her body was stiff and her eyes too bright. Her teeth tugged hard at her lower lip, biting down until he feared she'd draw blood.

"I told him how intelligent you are, Catarina," he admitted. "When we were talking at the fence line with Elijah, you said something that made me realize just how smart you really are. You educated yourself right under Cordeau's nose. You were able to get into his safe, and you managed to escape more than once. You lived with him, Cat. Right there. You made yourself disappear and no one noticed you, but you were there, listening, learning and you know every connection he has. Everyone who does business with him. You know which of his men are leopards and which aren't. I'm betting you know his deals and how to follow the money trail."

He watched her carefully as he spoke. This was the worst for him. She knew what was coming, she was too intelligent not to know. He saw the reaction in her eyes. The wariness and suspicion. He hadn't wanted to discuss this with her for that very reason. He didn't ever want to see that look in her eyes.

She didn't speak. She kept looking at him.

Eli sighed and pushed his fingers through his hair. "Baby, I don't want to have this conversation with you. I know you can't help but think I'm speaking on behalf of the DEA, but I'm not. Rafe Cordeau can never be taken into custody. There can be no prosecution. When he's found, he's got to die and his body be burned. He's leopard. A shifter. A rogue. We have no choice but to hunt him. That's what we've been doing. Jake's men and me, trying to get a line on his whereabouts. We have to find him before the law thinks they have enough on him to arrest him."

She kept looking at him. Watching him. She didn't blink and he could see her leopard there. The stillness. The focus. Eli cursed silently. Cursed Jake. Cursed himself for ever mishandling the situation with her. For betraying her trust.

"Jake takes down businesses. He takes them apart. He hunts and destroys differently than the law. He can bring down Cordeau's business partners and find the money with your help. That's it. That's everything. I don't like it, but it can be done if you want to cooperate. We're not talking a court of law here. We're just saying we can take down that entire network Cordeau built so no one else can step into his shoes when he's gone."

Her lashes swept down, veiling the look in her eyes, but her face was pale. "I can't breathe right now."

His heart stuttered. He reached out to touch her but she drew back, shaking her head. "Kitten. Let me help you."

She shook her head. "I can't breathe. I just can't."

His heart broke for her.

Abruptly, Catarina stood, a fluid, easy movement, all cat. She pulled the shirt over her head and flung it onto the chair even as she leapt off the porch into the rain. She was fast. He was faster. She ran, naked, shifting on the run just as Eli had taught her. A thing of beauty. A creature who had come into her own. She was running on bare feet one moment and on four paws the next.

He shifted with her, keeping pace just behind her, the larger male protective, but staying back to let her work it out in her mind. Eli knew she had submerged herself in the little female. She needed time to process what he'd told her. He wished she would have flung herself into his arms and clung to him, but whatever she needed, including space, he would provide. He didn't have to like it, but he'd do it.

The rain slid off her fur, feeling like thousands of fingers brushing over her thick coat. Catarina sank deep inside her leopard, just allowing sensations to penetrate. Her little female was happy to run free, to give her human time to process. She ran to protect Catarina from the overwhelming grief and fear. Catarina could feel her leopard's determination to surround her and keep her safe from everything and everyone—including the large male prowling behind them.

It's all right, Cat whispered to her leopard. *He's giving me time. He knows I need this. He's just making certain we're safe.*

He was. She knew she was right. Eli wasn't trying to pressure her into spilling everything she knew about Rafe. Why then, was she so reluctant to help others destroy him? He'd just killed three innocent human beings who knew absolutely nothing about her whereabouts. He'd tortured them, and he'd kill others to find her. Bernard and Jase had nothing really to do with her. They'd exchanged a few words. But David . . . She wanted to scream with anguish.

What was wrong with her that she didn't leap on the chance to help Jake and Eli? She had to know why, because something was wrong with her that she couldn't turn completely on Rafe when she knew nothing—no one—could save him.

She ran in the rain, listening to the sounds of the drops hitting the leaves and the ground. There was a rhythm there that soothed her. Even within her leopard, holding herself still as she waited for her heart to slow and her eyes to quit burning, the rain reached her and calmed her.

Rafe had no one else. No one to love him. No one to care whether he was alive or dead. No one loyal to him, not without his money and fear of him. He was alone. She had felt the weight of that since she was a child. She'd tried so hard to get him to care for her. Nothing had worked—at least she hadn't thought that it did, not when she was a child and needed someone to care about her.

Her leopard cleared a large tree trunk down across the path. Smoothly. Easily. Landing lightly without a sound. Eli had taught her how to move through the heavy brush silently, stealthily, pulling in every bit of information her surroundings could give her. He wanted her to have every advantage. He'd prepared her. He hadn't thumped his chest and told her to stay in the safe house, instead, he'd been tough on her. Conditioning with her, running every day, teaching her martial arts. Shooting with her on the range. Using weapons. Climbing boulders.

Her training hadn't stopped there. He worked with her on shifting fast. Shifting on the run. Disposing of her clothes in record time practically as she shifted, so she had every advantage. He'd made her practice over and over, hundreds of times until she was absolutely smooth and fast at it.

Still there was more. His male had taught her female how to maneuver, to get under her opponent, to avoid the stranglehold of his teeth. How to use her claws to her advantage, to turn in midair and to land in a defensive or offensive position.

Eli had cared enough to prepare her. Still, when he reluctantly told her Jake and he could bring Rafe down with her help, she'd felt sick inside. Part of it, she conceded, was that Eli had tried to force her to help them when he worked for the DEA. A tiny, tiny part of her was afraid he'd set her up again. She knew better. Deep down, she did. She knew better. But the nagging little monster that told her men like Eli couldn't possibly love her had reared its ugly head.

Still, all that aside, and that was clearly her own sad little issue, why was it that she felt the need to protect Rafe? He was a killer. He needed to be brought to justice. Every minute he was loose in the world, innocent people could be killed just for his pleasure. His enjoyment. He liked to hunt them. He liked to kill. He would come back from his trips to the swamp almost euphoric.

And he hadn't been the only one. She knew, even if Eli and Jake managed to kill Rafe, there were at least three more men under him who hunted victims let loose in the swamp with him. Women mostly, but occasionally someone who double-crossed Rafe.

My little leopard, can I just stay here, tucked into the safety of your protection, and never come out again?

If she could have, she would have put her hand on the animal and just held on. She needed something to hold on to. Someone to hold on to. To steady her. To tell her it was okay to the do the right thing and stop Rafe. That she wouldn't be abandoning him as she'd felt so abandoned.

Her throat ached. Her eyes burned. The little leopard faltered. Stopped. Stood, head down in the middle of the path, shaking. The rain continued to pour down. At once the male moved close, rubbing his fur along the female's side. Nuzzling her. Chuffing softly in inquiry. He extended his neck, chin on top of her head protectively.

Rafe had killed David Belmont, because of her. She'd liked David a lot. He owned his own coffee-house and was proud of it. He was funny and smart, and he'd taken a chance on her. She liked Bernard as well. He wrote great poetry and lived in a fantasy world, another era, but still, he was a unique and wonderful man and he didn't deserve to die at the hands of a madman. She didn't know Jase, only that once he'd drunkenly made a pass at her and displayed incredibly bad judgment. Eli had taken care of the situation and that should have been the end of it. The man probably didn't even know her last name, and he certainly hadn't deserved to die just because he'd crossed paths with her.

If she didn't help Jake and Eli bring Rafe's business down, someone else would take his place. They wouldn't hunt in the swamp, but they killed in their own ways, by running drugs, and arms. By beating up and cheating the prostitutes who worked for them. Or giving the women to men like Rafe who murdered them.

She had no choice. There was no other choice. Her heart ached and she felt guilty, but even if she was silly enough to think she could help Rafe by going back to him, she knew she couldn't. He was too far gone. Whatever had happened to him in his childhood, whatever had transformed him into a monster had a hold of him and wouldn't let him go. She couldn't save him. Sacrificing her happiness and Eli's wouldn't solve anything at all.

She shifted on the path, needing Eli's arms around her. Needing the solid weight of his body surrounding hers. She didn't try to stand, the heavy male's head still was over hers, but she felt no fear. His fur was slick with rain, but soft and comforting against her bare skin.

Then Eli was there, his body wrapped around hers. His chest was over her back and his breath was warm on the nape of her neck. One arm slid around her waist.

"What is it, Kitten?" he asked softly. "Tell me what you need."

Tell me what you need. His voice was there to steady her. A soft whisper of truth. All she had to do was say it, want it, wish for it, and Eli moved heaven and earth to provide it for her.

"You. I need you, Eli," she answered, staring out into the trees, into the dark. She should have been afraid, on her hands and knees there in the rain, out in the open on a narrow path, with lightning forking in the distance and thunder rolling loudly. She should have been cold, but she wasn't.

His hands answered her. His palms stroked her breasts, cupped them, fingers finding her nipples to roll and tug until fire streaked to her tight sheath. The sensation was incredible with the cool of the rain and sudden heat of her body.

His mouth whispered over her back, down her spine in little kisses. His tongue lapped at the droplets, until he found the dimples just above the curve of her buttocks.

"Right here, baby. We need to get that tattoo. It's killing me. I can look at you, you belonging to me, whenever I take you like this."

She turned her head then, her gaze burning into his. "You really want me to get a tattoo?" She watched him closely.

"Only if you want one." His eyes held hers for a moment before he dropped his head to follow a little stream of rain along the slope of one firm cheek.

His tongue felt like hot velvet. He lapped at her, pushed at the insides of her thighs to force them wider so he could dip his head and taste her. Not just taste her. Eli never just tasted her. He devoured her. He became ravenous with the first dip of his tongue, and the sounds he made were those of a predatory animal, claiming his share of the food supply and declaring to the world he'd fight to the death for it.

His hands moved over her body possessively, strong. So strong. She loved that about him, the enormous strength she felt each time he touched her. She could count on it. She needed that right now. He stroked her, kneaded and massaged, all the while his clever mouth, his tongue and teeth coaxed more and more honey from her.

When she was panting, and her mewling cries filled the air, he suddenly dragged her hips back into him, slamming his cock into her fiercely, forcing his way through her tight delicate folds to bury himself deep. The breath slammed out of her lungs and her soft cry mingled with his harsher one.

"Don't stop. Please, Eli. I need you."

She didn't have to ask him twice. He surged into her over and over so hard the only thing keeping her up was his arm, a tight band around her waist. He pounded into her, the friction exquisite, as the rain bathed them in cool drops, nearly hissing on their hot skin. She felt alive. She felt loved. She knew exactly where she belonged and to whom. Eli was her man, and she loved being his woman. She loved that she asked him to take her in the middle of the path and he hadn't even hesitated.

She knelt in grass, but the water was a good inch around her knees and legs and Eli hadn't cared. His body was a fierce machine, streaking fire through her. Flames raced up her skin. Electricity arced from his skin to hers. The sensations just built, one on the next. He never stopped, a relentless force driving her up higher and higher until she knew in another moment she would fly apart, shatter into a million pieces.

It didn't matter, because Eli would find every single broken piece of her and put her back together again. Her breath hissed out of her lungs. She needed to fly. Wanted it. Reached for it.

"Not yet, baby. This time with me." He wasn't done. He kept going, forcing her to go with him.

"I don't think I can wait," she gasped, her voice a half plea.

But she would. She would wait. She would do as he demanded because he was Eli and she loved him. She loved that he was taking her on a wild, crazy ride she could barely comprehend. It was Eli and it didn't matter that the pleasure threatened to kill her, she would do whatever he wanted, including getting his tattoo for him. Because she loved pleasing him and he moved heaven and earth to give her anything she wanted.

Her breath came in short ragged sobs and the tension coiled tighter and tighter until she thought she might really go insane with the need to explode. She clenched her teeth, using every ounce of discipline and self-control she had to hold back the orgasm that was so close, threatening to roar through her. Her body shook with the effort.

Eli reached around and caught her nipple between his thumb and finger, clamping down so that the pleasure streaked to her clit at the same time his cock bore down while he thrust deep.

"Now, baby," he commanded softly. "This time with me. Together. Fly with me."

His voice was hoarse, insistent, triggering the massive quake in her body. It rolled through her so hard even her stomach spasmed. There wasn't a single cell in her body that didn't feel the strength of the tidal wave as it ripped through her. She opened her mouth to scream her pleasure, but even her throat convulsed.

Her body flew apart, not her own, but he was there,

surrounding her, holding her close to him, his breath warm on her back, his lips against the snug place where he wanted the tattoo. He nuzzled her with his rough, shadowed jaw.

"You better, Kitten? Need more? Because I can do more."

She took a breath. She needed more from him. Not sex. Not making love, and he *had* made love to her, as rough and as aggressive as he was, she felt it.

"Tell me, baby. Don't ever be afraid to ask me for anything you need," he whispered. His teeth nipped the nape of her neck. His tongue followed, easing the slight ache.

"Hold me for a minute, Eli. I want you to hold me while I tell you this. And don't ask me to look at you. I know you prefer that, my eyes on yours, but I can't do that, not when I tell you this. It . . . shames me."

Eli allowed his body to slip from hers. She shuddered as his cock dragged over her sensitive little bud, the knot of nerves that were already screaming in bliss. He stood carefully and reached down for her, lifting his face for a moment to the rain. The storm had lessened in strength, the lightning moving off to the south. Still, their hair was plastered to their faces, hers down her back in a long sweep.

He drew her into the shelter of his body gently, holding her face to his chest. "You never have to be ashamed of anything you feel, Catarina," he assured. "Just talk to me. Let me help you."

She pressed her burning face into muscles cut so deeply in his abdomen. Her arms circled his waist and she held on tightly.

"I don't want to hurt him any more than I already have. He's so alone, and it breaks my heart that I couldn't make him different. That I couldn't make him better. I wasn't strong enough, or smart enough. Nothing I did helped him, and I tried. I know I'm not responsible for the terrible things he's done, but still, I feel if I could have been just a little better at caring for him, I could have helped him. That's the reason. That's why I don't want to help anyone hurt him."

She made the confession in a small, muffled voice. Eli could hear the tears.

"I wanted him to love me. He was all I had. I tried so hard but I could never do anything right and I could never take away his rage that always burned just below the surface. Only hurting others ever did that. When I knew he was going out and something terrible was going to happen, I tried to hold him there. It never worked. He'd grow worse, pacing, snarling, scaring me and everyone else. Eventually he'd go and when he came back, it was the only time he looked at peace. Relaxed. It never lasted."

Eli kept his mouth closed tightly, wanting her to tell him everything. The level of trust she had for him was growing or she never would have told him such a deeply private emotion she was clearly mortified of having.

"I feel guilty and ashamed that I couldn't help him. He needed me, Eli. He really did. I don't care what anyone says. He needed me and I let him down. All those people died because I couldn't help him."

Okay. That was enough. He caught her chin firmly in his hand and tipped her face up to his even as he bent his head. He captured her mouth, effectively silencing her. He kissed her over and over. Long, hot kisses, demanding her response. He didn't let her breathe. Instead he breathed for both of them, exchanging air, exchanging breath. Making love to her with his mouth. Telling her what she meant to him in one of the few ways he was good at expressing his love to her.

When he lifted his head, both of their faces were wet and he put it down to the rain, although he suspected it was something altogether different.

"I love you, Catarina, because of the kind, generous soul and heart you have. Cordeau loves you in his own way, but you and I both know he's beyond saving. A child couldn't possibly have saved him anymore than an adult could now. He allowed his leopard to get the upper hand, probably when he was very young and things were happening around him he couldn't control. Abuse isn't an excuse for any of us. We can feel sad for the person, but there are many abused people who choose not to go down that path. You can't sacrifice yourself, Kitten, it would be useless. He won't change and he wouldn't, maybe couldn't, when you were a child."

"How do you know?"

"Because he knew you are leopard. A shifter. A female. He had a treasure, a rare, precious treasure and if he was going to stop himself from that kind of behavior, he would have done it then. He knew, deep down, he couldn't have both. You aren't corrupt. You don't have a hint of madness in you. You're sweet and loving and generous. You're too compassionate for your own good and that meant your leopard was the same way. He knew that. He saw that and he still didn't stop. He never will, and his behavior, his choices, have nothing to do with you."

Eli brushed her upturned mouth gently. "You don't have to help us bring him down, Cat. That's my job, not yours."

She moved even closer to the heat of his body. "He feels invincible. Terrifying. I don't want you anywhere near him." She shuddered against him.

Eli caught the long sweep of hair in his hand, wrapped the thick mass around his wrist and pulled her head back, forcing her to look up at him. "You persist in thinking of him the way you did when you were a child. You bested him. Do you realize that? You outsmarted him. Do you have any idea how intelligent you have to be to do that? You lived in his house, right under his nose, and you educated yourself using his personal computer and he never suspected."

She opened her mouth to refute his statement and he tugged on her scalp until she quieted.

"Do you have any idea what courage you have? Grown men didn't leave his organization because they feared him. Witnesses refused to testify against him because they feared him. You escaped, more than once. You tried repeatedly.

You risked everything when others refused to. What does that say about you, Catarina?"

She moistened her lips and then tugged her lower lip between her teeth. He had no choice but to sweep his tongue across that temptation.

"Kitten, when he comes for you, and tries to intimidate you, tries to make you feel less than him, look him in the eye and believe in yourself the way I believe in you. See yourself the way I see you. You'll have nothing to fear. You're prepared. And I promise you, I'll be coming to help you. I'll come."

She knew he would come. He saw the knowledge in her eyes.

She nodded slowly. "I told you all this, Eli, because I know I have to help you and Jake. Thank you for saying I didn't have to, but I know I do. I can't allow him to keep killing people. The businesses he has are bad enough, and the men he associates with are equally horrible. The bottom line is, I have to help or I'm just as bad as he is. Tell Jake I'll give him names, dates and as many deals as I can remember. I have bank account numbers as well."

Eli felt a rush of pride for her. He knew how difficult the decision had to have been on her. His fingers gentled in her hair, moving through the silken strands to ease the ache in her scalp.

"Baby, what I asked of you, helping us, that doesn't come from having been an agent. I don't want you to think, even for a moment, that I would trade what we have for anything. Or use it against you. I love you. If you can't do this, I understand."

He watched her eyes change. They went from a beautiful soft blue to a deep cobalt, almost violet. He saw her so clearly. The cat in her. The love in her—for him. His heart jerked hard and his stomach twisted. He brought his mouth down on hers, all the while falling into her eyes. At the last moment, her lashes swept down, thick crescents that veiled her soul, but it was too late. He'd already seen. He already knew.

She'd given him a gift. She kept giving to him. Eli

kissed her gently, and then fiercely. Ferociously. Like the prime male leopard he was. Dominant and aggressive, he took her mouth, pouring himself into her. He was possessive and he knew it. He could be jealous and he had a hell of a temper. But he had this for her. Love so intense, so passionate, every time he looked into her eyes the emotion overwhelmed him. And it continued to grow in him.

Her arms stole around his neck, her mouth moving under his. There in the rain, he took her again, lifting her, urging her legs around his waist, settling her over his cock, her sheath a scorching, tight glove of silk wrapping him up the way her legs did.

He was a little wild. A little out of control. He loved feeling her breasts pressed so tight into him. Her head tipped back and her long hair, now soaked with water, hung down her back like a dark pelt. The rain sizzled on their hot sensitive skin, lending the sensation of a thousand tongues lapping gently at them.

She matched his wild, out of control mood, riding him hard. Fast. Her soft little cries, music in his ears while he surged into paradise over and over, the pace almost frantic. He thought he'd hold out a long while, he'd taken her just a few minutes earlier and he usually had great control, but the little downward spirals, the way her delicate muscles gripped and milked had him losing himself in her far too fast.

He felt the explosion building from his toes and moving through his legs. His teeth settled into her skin, the soft perfect junction between her shoulder and neck. He bit down and her entire body shuddered, clamped down like a vise on his and squeezed. He roared her name as she took him with her, as jet after jet of hot seed splashed deep into her.

He knew instantly. Even as his body shuddered and rocked. Even as hers gripped his and milked. He knew. This time, right there in the rain, they had created something beautiful and precious between them. He lifted his head to look down at her. He knew his eyes had gone leopard. Possessive. Satisfied. How could he help it? She was his and always would be his.

"What?" she murmured sleepily. She kissed his shoulder and then his throat.

Still locked inside her, surrounded by her, held by her, he gave a little growl. "Give me your mouth."

She obeyed instantly, tilting her head so he could kiss her. So he could lose himself there. She was sacred. The mother of his child. His lover.

"Marry me, Catarina." It wasn't a question. He wanted it to be, but it didn't come out that way. It was a demand. An order. He made the command against her soft lips.

He felt her mouth curve against his. He pulled his head back to look into her eyes, even as he eased her feet back to the ground. He hated slipping out of her body, losing the ultimate, intimate connection between them.

"Are you asking me or telling me?" she answered, her hands smoothing down his arms.

He studied her face. "That depends. You saying yes, then I'm asking. You hesitating, then I'm telling you." He was honest. How could he not be? It was the truth. He wanted his ring on her finger and her name to be his. She belonged to him. With him. More, he was hers, body and soul.

She laughed softly. "That's so you, Eli. So romantic."

He looked around him at the steadily falling rain, the thirsty trees lifting leaves toward the drops. "This is romantic."

"I'll marry you, baby. Someone has to take care of you properly."

Her voice was filled with love. She didn't declare her love, but at that moment he didn't need her to. He heard it in her soft response. Elation swept through him. He would have taken her again, right there, but he couldn't very well lay her down in the wet grass, and she looked exhausted.

"Right away. Immediately." Definitely a command. Accompanied by a growl.

She laughed and shifted, her little female leopard leaping

away from him, sprinting toward the dense grove of trees. He ran after her, shifting on the run, feeling his answering laughter. His answering happiness. He didn't know how he managed it, he knew he didn't deserve her, but she was his all the same and he knew he'd do anything to keep her.

I love you, Kitten, he whispered from deep inside his male.

The female teased and flirted with the male leopard over and over and he allowed it, staying close, rubbing along her fur, approaching cautiously when she crouched invitingly and leaping back when she halfheartedly swiped a paw at him. They tumbled together, rolling around in the grass, playing, but always, the male moved his female toward him. Toward the ranch house.

The much heavier male took her there on the porch, pinning her in the way of the male leopard, locking them together, staking his claim.

Eli let his male have his time with his mate, but once he was finished and just rubbing lovingly along her fur, as she lay exhausted and panting, he forced him back and shifted.

The little female didn't move. He dropped his hand into her thick fur. "Shift now, Cat." He poured command into his voice.

She obeyed automatically, but she didn't move from the floor. He reached down and lifted her exhausted body, cradling her against his chest.

"You sleep in this morning and then we're going to take care of it."

She rubbed her face sleepily against his chest. "Take care of what?"

He strode into the house. "Go to sleep. Let me take care of you. We'll get the paperwork done and get married at Jake's."

She burrowed closer. "I think I'm being railroaded."

He laughed softly. "Bet your life on that, baby. I'm not wasting time and giving you the chance to change your mind."

19

CATARINA pushed away from her desk, stood up and stretched. She loved this room. Their shared office. There was so much space. It was nice sitting opposite Eli, looking up every now and then from her laptop to see his golden eyes on her. The way he looked at her always made her shiver in anticipation. He always looked at her as if he might devour her at any moment. In fact, it was true. More than once he'd ordered her to strip and climb on his desk. More than once she'd dared to crawl under his desk and open his jeans to get what she wanted.

She loved the books that slowly were filling the empty shelves. She knew she spent too much on books, but it was the only thing she spent money on. She threw out her arms and spun in a circle, unable to contain her happiness. The dread was still there, deep in the pit of her stomach and the nightmares had increased so she knew Rafe was closer than ever to her, but still she couldn't help but be happy.

She might not spend money on herself, but Eli kept her supplied in clothes—especially lingerie. Silky, lacy camisoles. He especially liked red on her. She had a lot of lace and red. She could never really understand why because it never stayed on her more than a few minutes, but she liked to wear the silk and lace under her clothes, especially her everyday clothes, just to tease him. He always wondered.

Eli made her laugh. He was bossy, even arrogant, there was no doubt about it. He was super controlling, but, she found, it was mainly when it came to sex or her safety or health. In every other area, he was gentle with her and seemed to want her to grow confident and spread her wings.

She had more boots in her closet than she could possibly wear in a week. She never asked for them. She was careful, even, not to look at anything too long in any of the cool stores she'd found on the Internet, but the boots kept coming and she loved every pair. She didn't wear them often, but Eli always assured her, when the danger to her was past, he would take her out often and she could wear her beloved boots.

"Kitten, where the hell are you?" Eli sounded irritated and bossy. Just like him.

She didn't shout her answer back to him because she knew from experience he detested that. When he called her, he wanted her. Right there. In front of him. And when she came into the room he wanted her kissing him.

Catarina moved quickly through the hall down to the kitchen where Eli paced with a scowl on his face. The moment she entered, he whirled around and stalked toward her, looking aggressive, a leopard on the prowl. Her heart stuttered, just as it always did when she first caught a glimpse of him.

Tall, broad-shouldered, his body cut with heavy, defined muscles. His face was that of a man, no boyish features at all. Right now his jaw was set tight and his eyes were very focused, predatory. She went straight to him, meeting him in the middle of the kitchen, going up on her toes to press her mouth gently to his frown.

He always responded the same way. The moment her lips touched his, his mouth took over, his tongue demanding entrance. He slipped his hand under her shirt to cup one breast, his thumb sliding over her nipple as her mouth met his. She wasn't certain why he always touched her so intimately when she kissed him, but she liked it, almost as if it was his personal brand of ownership.

She had a brand of her own. When she stepped back, she allowed her hand to run down his chest, feel the tight, cut muscles of his abdomen and then brush lightly over his heavy, thick cock. He was nearly always semi- or completely erect after kissing her. Sometimes she wondered if he was always in a permanent state of arousal.

"Where the hell did you go when you left my bed this morning without waking me? And why?"

This time, his hand didn't drop away from her breast when she stepped back. His thumb and finger caught her nipple and tugged hard. Rolled deliberately. Fire shot straight to her center. Heat burned. Her gaze jumped to his face.

"I just went out to the porch and sat for a while, Eli," she said, puzzled.

"And nowhere else?"

It was a demand. He didn't let go of her breast, but he cupped the soft weight and his thumb gentled, stroking there deliberately.

She moistened her lips with the tip of her tongue, trying to think what else she'd done. "I practiced shifting," she admitted, still not understanding why he was upset. She practiced every chance she got. He'd told her to. Even in the bedroom sometimes she tried to best her times of removing clothes and shifting on the move.

"What did I tell you last night?"

Hard hands bit into her waist. He lifted her up abruptly and set her on the table, hard. One hand went to her shirt, yanking it open, uncaring of the buttons that flew in all directions. Her breasts spilled out through the open edges. He placed one hand on her chest and pushed, forcing her to lean back until she had to catch herself with her hands.

"I don't know. What? You're scaring me a little bit, Eli. I can't think straight."

"I told you not to go *anywhere* without me. I told you it wasn't safe."

Her heart tripped hard. He felt Rafe close. Fear made her mouth dry. She tasted a metallic flavor that always scared her. They'd had nearly a month since he'd given her the news about David and the others. She'd allowed herself to live in a dream world again, lulled into a false sense of security because so much time had passed.

"Eyes on mine," Eli snapped. "If you're going to be afraid of someone, it had better be me, not that bastard."

He was really angry, she realized. He'd never actually been angry with her before. Impatient maybe, but not angry. What had he said? He had a temper. He might say and do things she needed to be able to get over. What did that mean?

Reluctantly she lifted her gaze to his. His golden eyes blazed down into hers. "You knew damn well you weren't supposed to leave my side."

She shook her head. A slight tremor shook her body. He was really frightening standing over her with his eyes furious. He was fully clothed, and she was sprawled out in front of him entirely vulnerable. She tried to shift position just a little, to close her legs, to give herself any kind of edge she could.

His hand smacked the side of her buttocks, the sound loud. Fire spread through her. She couldn't help the small cry that escaped. His palm was there, rubbing, soothing, even as his other hand slipped between her legs to feel the rush of damp liquid.

"Can I just say 'ouch'?" she asked.

"Say whatever fucking thing you want to say, Cat, but don't you fucking move."

Two of the f-bombs in one sentence. Clearly he was *really* angry.

"I just misunderstood, Eli. I didn't think you meant here at our house. In our home. I didn't even think about that."

"Where the hell else do you go, Catarina? Nowhere without me. So if I say it isn't safe, not to go anywhere at all without me, that means *anywhere*."

She wanted to roll her eyes, but she thought better of it. He wasn't calming down. If she shifted positions she could maybe touch him, get a hand on him, but the way he'd forced her to lie back, she needed both hands to hold herself up.

"I'm sorry, Eli."

"You aren't. You think I can't read you like a fucking book, Cat? You're trying to think of the right thing to say or do, but you still don't get it. You still don't think you have to listen when I lay down a rule for your safety."

Okay, that was true. Her home felt safe. They had a security system. She knew every shadow, the layout of the furniture, where every weapon was placed, scattered around the house, in each room, taped under furniture and in small cracks and down the cushions of the softer armchairs and couch, everywhere throughout their home. She felt safe, because even if she went on the porch, all she had to do was call and she knew Eli would come.

His finger slid inside her, scooped out hot liquid, and he began a slow, torturous circle around her clit. "We had an agreement, Cat. You knew from the beginning what kind of man I am and what I expect from my woman. I tell you don't fucking leave my side then you don't. I tell you to strip naked and dance on the damn table because I like seeing you up there you do it. Most of all, when I tell you trouble is close, trouble that can get you injured, raped or killed, you listen."

Fury edged his voice and he exploded, yanking her legs up over his shoulders, dipping his head low. His mouth clamped down on her and he began to devour her, eat her as if she was his last meal. His mouth was a weapon of total destruction and he knew exactly how to wield it. She couldn't move. She couldn't stop him. His tongue plunged, his teeth bit, tiny nips that stung, but sent blasts of radiant stars bursting through her body like white lightning.

The breath left her lungs in a rush. He pushed her up fast and high and she felt her body gathering—gathering. She reached for it. Needed it. A sob escaped. Then he was gone. Lifting his head. Leaving her desperate. Leaving her in need.

His eyes glittered with menace. More cat spilled into him. The driving demand to dominate. His face glistened with the evidence of her need. She tried to find anywhere at all to grind against something, but the way he held her legs over his shoulder prevented her from finding release, but left her open to him.

"You should have learned by now, Kitten, I'm not a man you cross. Not when it comes to your safety." His voice was low. Growling. Twice she felt the brush of fur when his hand stroked down her belly to her mound.

"Please, Eli." She tried not to sound as insane as she felt. As if on fire. He had a look on his face that scared her more than anything. He could torture her slowly and he'd enjoy every second of it. She could see the dark intent on his face.

He blew on her. It didn't cool the heat at all; if anything, his warm breath fanned the flames. Her entire body jerked. Before she could catch her breath, say anything, promise anything, he ducked his head a second time, clamping his mouth on her, only this time he added his fingers.

His thumb stroked her clit and then his tongue followed, flicking and pulsing against that sensitive bundle of nerve endings. She nearly came off the table. She fell back, unable to sustain her weight but needing to keep from going over the edge. Her hands started toward his hair.

He raised his head instantly, the glittering eyes moving over her face broodingly. He was still angry. It was there in the set of his mouth, his jaw. "Don't you fucking touch me," he snarled. "You're in enough trouble without making it worse. If you have to hold on to something, hold the edge of the table and keep your hands to yourself."

That hurt. He didn't want her touching him. She liked touching him. She needed it, that closeness and intimacy between them.

"Eli, please," she cajoled softly. "Don't be angry with me. I don't like it."

Eli watched her face intently. All the while she pleaded with him, her hips undulated, bucking softly, in need. Her body was coated with a fine sheen of perspiration. He'd driven her up fast, and left her there. He wanted her there, right on the edge, but unable to fall over. Not without his say-so. Not without his consent.

His leopard felt every bit as mean as he did, not willing to give an inch on this issue. They both could have lost the one they needed beyond all others. Rafe Cordeau could destroy them, not just their lives, but Eli and his leopard. Just thinking about the possibility had Eli snarling all over again. Heat banded, coloring his vision, streaking it with reds and yellows. He made a halfhearted attempt to push the leopard down as he bent his head to his feast once again.

As his tongue plunged, he brought his hands up to her breasts, soft, full mounds, tugging mercilessly on her nipples. Pinching and rolling, deliberately rough. She thrashed wildly. Begged. He felt her body tense. Immediately he lifted his head, looking at his prize sprawled out so prettily for him. He removed her legs from his shoulders gently, held her open to him, opened his jeans to release his throbbing cock and positioned the head right at her entrance.

He took a moment to enjoy the sight of her, the anticipation, knowing the burn would come and she'd be even higher, needing him more. He slammed home, burying himself to his very balls. Flames streaked up his body, and she screamed, clutching the edges of the table until her knuckles turned white.

"Look at me," he demanded, slowly pulling back. "Right now, give me your eyes. I want to see you." He waited until she complied. She was dazed and half out of her mind with need—need for him. "Did you really think I'd let you off this easily?"

He pulled out of her and she cried out. Moaned. Shook her head back and forth, her hips trying to follow, to catch him and force him back into her. He straddled her instead, grateful that when he'd bought the table, he'd made certain it was thick and sturdy. She was naked, bare to him, and he was still clothed, his jean-clad thighs pressing around her hips.

Her gaze clung to his and fear skittered there. Not of him. Of the pleasure he was forcing on her. Forcing her to take his way. Forcing her to accept anything he wanted to give her. To do to her. Both knew all she had to do was say stop, but she wouldn't. She was beyond that. She needed whatever he was giving her just as desperately as he needed to give it to her.

His hands caught those soft breasts, so full. So tempting. He bent his head and took possession, claiming her body for his own. He didn't need to, she was already his. She wanted to be his. He was rough, his teeth and tongue and mouth suckling at her skated right along that edge of pain, but the wildfire was already so far out of control, that every powerful pull of his mouth on her nipples and breasts sent shock waves through her body.

He reached out with one hand and caught up a bottle of scented oil he'd set out on the table behind her. His eyes blazing down at her, he tipped the bottle up and poured the contents between her breasts. She gasped as the cool oil pooled on her heated skin.

Eli used his hands to spread the oil up and over the curves of her breasts, kneading it into her soft skin, rubbing it into her nipples. With every stroke of his hands, the oil heated, so that her skin tingled and then it began to send even more flames over her. The sensation seemed to sink into her pores, made its way into her body, traveling through her as the feeling increased.

He gripped his cock with his oiled hands, watching her eyes go wide. Sensual. She couldn't take her eyes off his hands and the glistening thick shaft as he fisted himself and slowly gripped and released until every part of him was coated with the heated, slick oil. He shifted his position, still straddling her.

"Open your mouth. Don't move your hands. Stay right like that."

She couldn't keep still. She was too far gone, the flush and need stark on her face. Her hips moved continuously and her soft little moans and pleas didn't stop, not for a moment. She was desperate for release. He was only adding to that need, to that hunger, with his erotic display. She wanted his cock inside her.

He pushed her breasts together, forming a soft tunnel, nestling his cock there, surrounded by her softness. He pushed forward with his hips while she tilted her head up, her mouth closing over the crown, drawing him into that hot, moist haven. He threw back his head for a moment, savoring the feeling of paradise. She made the most of the pause, desperate to have him so hungry for her he'd cooperate. He let her tongue him, suckle and then when he felt the tightness in his balls, he drew back and began to slide through the hot oil. Over and over. Letting himself find that edge of control. Feeding himself to her hot, eager mouth and then depriving her until she let go of the table with one hand.

Instantly he stopped. Drew back. Let her know with his eyes that everything would stop if she didn't obey him.

"Eli, please," she said softly. "I need you."

"That's right, baby. Me. And when I fucking tell you to do something, I want it done." Even as he growled it at her, he let himself feel that soft cradle, her hot mouth one more time. Who the hell could resist?

"You can't use sex against me," she wailed.

"Is that what I'm doing?" Abruptly he released her breasts and slid off of her, dragging her body to the end of the table again, angry all over again.

He felt his leopard surge toward the surface, as angry as he was, the need for dominancy overcoming good sense. The slide of fur shimmered for a moment so close he actually had to fight it back. When he flipped her over, dragging her hips over the edge so her sweet little ass was pushed toward him, he smacked her harder than he intended, her buttocks flushing a deep red immediately.

She tried to stand, gasping in shock, turning her head, but he lifted her hips and drove into her. She screamed, nearly convulsing with the pleasure. He held her pinned there, thrusting hard and fast, pistoning over the small bundle of supersensitive nerve endings, a relentless, brutal pace, forcing her body to accept his. The oil added to the burning and stretching along her sheath, he could tell by the way she moved, as if her delicate muscles were trying to retreat, but she was hungry for it, desperate enough to push back into him with every forward thrust of his body.

He gave in to his temper, to the male's temper, and with every third deep stroke of his cock he left a handprint on her pretty bottom. Between he soothed her with his palm, although she didn't deserve it. He wanted her to remember this moment, remember that he wasn't going to tolerate his woman putting herself in danger for any reason.

In the end, Eli wasn't certain if his method would work. With each fall of his hand, hot liquid bathed his cock and her mewling cries crescendoed.

Catarina felt perspiration gathering over her body. There wasn't a cell in her that wasn't on fire, wasn't in need. She could barely breathe, even her lungs burning. Eli surrounded her, was in her. He'd opened up some secret part of her she'd kept hidden from the world, a primitive, wild uninhibited woman who reveled in everything he did to her. Who needed more. Wanted more. Wanted him. Like this. Wild and out of control to match the wild and out of control she was.

She didn't have a clue where he began and she left off. They seemed to be one person instead of two. She felt his pleasure as surely as she felt her own. It burned through her like a firestorm, rushing through her veins, dragging over her nerve endings until her mind burned with such need she thought she might die of pleasure. She felt him with her, moving in her, but more, moving in her mind, as if he'd somehow merged them together into one being.

"I love you so much, Eli," she whispered, knowing it was true. Knowing whatever had happened between them in the past, he was the man for her.

"Oh, God, baby," he groaned. "You defeat me every damn time."

His surrender. She heard it in his voice. She felt it in the way his hands stroked and caressed her body. The way his cock swelled inside of her, hot and hard, filling her with . . . him.

She closed her eyes and gave herself to him, surrendering everything. The tidal wave ripped through her with hurricane force, sweeping both of them over the edge of sanity for just a few moments, throwing them into subspace where she floated, unafraid, in pure bliss, anchored to him—to Eli.

He collapsed over top of her, pressing his lips to the nape of her neck. "You're going to lead me on such a dance, Kitten."

"I'm going to love you so much, honey, you won't care," she whispered back.

His arms circled her waist, holding her to him. "I already love you so much I don't care," he admitted.

She turned her head to look at him over her shoulder. "Strip naked and dance on the table? Really?" She laughed softly.

He grinned at her. "It was worth a try."

"Well. I might consider it for your birthday," she said. "Let me up. I still need my shower."

"Make me coffee first. Mine never tastes as good as yours." Eli didn't move.

She pushed back against him just to feel more delicious aftershocks. "I'm covered in oil. I think a shower is more important than your coffee." She was going to make his coffee because she enjoyed making it for him. He was usually grumpy in the mornings until she put that cup in his hands and he took his first sip. Then he looked at her as if she was the most wonderful, perfect woman who'd ever been born. She wasn't passing that up, not even to shower first.

"Then we'll just have to stay right here, locked together," he murmured against her spine. "Because I can't move without coffee."

Catarina burst out laughing at his grumpy tone. "You're such a baby, Eli."

He heard the capitulation in her voice. "You're going to make my coffee, aren't you, Kitten?"

"I shouldn't. Not after you smacked me on the butt."

He rubbed her left cheek with gentle strokes. "I didn't hurt you."

"If you'd hurt me, Eli, I would have let loose my leopard and you'd be ripped up a bit," Catarina assured.

"That's good, Cat, that's what I want from you. Stand up to me when I get too mean." He eased out of her and once again bent to kiss the base of her spine.

She wasn't going to tell him that when he was mean, his cat was involved, and that might not be the very best time to defy him. Male leopards definitely insisted on dominance with their females. She was figuring it out slowly, but she was getting it, just as Emma had assured her she would.

Pulling the edges of the shirt around her, she straightened. Eli's hands instantly went to her waist, steadying her. She loved that about him. The little things he did, even more than the big things, made her love him more. He always saw to her comfort—especially after they made love.

He tipped her head up and kissed her slowly, gently, his

golden eyes almost liquid as they looked into hers. "I do love you, Catarina," he said softly. "More than my own life. I do love you."

She leaned into him. His strength surrounded her. Protected her. She realized in that moment, that's what Eli did. He made certain she was protected, but he allowed her to stand on her own. He wanted her to be as confident in herself and in her ability to survive any situation without him. He'd been working toward that end almost from the moment she met him.

"I love you right back the same way, Eli," she said softly. "More than my own life." She'd give up everything to know he was safe. Alive. Healthy.

He dipped his head as if he might kiss her again, but his lips veered to her ear. "Make my coffee, woman."

She went straight to the coffee machine, laughing as she did so. "Go clean up and I'll have it ready when you come back."

She put extra love into his favorite caramel drink. She always teased him, saying the caramel sweetened him. He said it was the extra shots of espresso. Whichever it was didn't matter, only that smile he gave her when he took his first sip.

Eli returned looking casual in his drawstring pants and light shirt. She knew he wore them, like most shifters, to be able to get out of them fast. His arm swooped around her waist as he took the coffee from her. She watched as he took that first sip and then looked down at her.

"You're a fucking miracle, Catarina," he said, meaning it.

She brushed a kiss over his jaw. "When we have children, Eli, you're going to have to watch your mouth. But this one time, I'll admit, I rather like being your fucking miracle."

He blinked. His mouth twitched. He leaned down and brushed another kiss over her lips. "You don't get to swear. It doesn't sound the same. And for your information, I have been toning it down."

She burst out laughing again. "No way. You let go with two f-bombs in one sentence. That is not toning it down."

"Two exceptions, Kitten." He nuzzled the top of her head with his chin. "When you make me so angry I want to shake you until your teeth rattle, or put you over my knee and make it so you can't sit down for a week or two, I get to drop as many f-bombs as necessary to keep from doing either."

She mulled that over. "Okay. I'll agree."

"That was one exception."

"That was two. Rattling teeth. Not sitting for a week. Two."

"You make me want to do both at the same time, so one," he argued, drinking more of his coffee.

She rolled her eyes. "Fine, that's one. What's the second one?"

His smile made her stomach roll. Let loose a million butterflies. She reached up to brush the pads of her fingers down his jaw, her heart turning over.

"When you make me so crazy, burn so hot, lose my mind when I'm inside you so that I can't do anything else."

Her fingers curled in his hair. Stroked caresses. Anchored there. She loved that his hair was just a little too long and she could curl her fist there. "I like you crazy and burning hot."

"Out of my mind," he reminded, in his sinfully hot voice.

"That too," Catarina conceded. She looked up, into his eyes. Loving him. She knew he could see it and she didn't hide it from him.

He groaned softly. "Go take your shower, baby, before we start all over again. You're so damned tempting, at this rate, I'll never get anything done. We're supposed to be starting a ranch."

She laughed again, just because she was so happy. "We don't actually have any livestock yet, Eli, we can't exactly call this a working ranch. You're going to go sit in your favorite chair on the porch while I shower."

"Well. That's true," he conceded. "But I'm planning."

Catarina shook her head and left him in the kitchen. She didn't dare kiss him again because she knew if she did, she wouldn't stop and he'd need another shower. She had never considered, growing up, not one time, that anyone could be so happy.

She turned music on, her favorite playlist, while she showered. That was another thing Eli had done. Another gift. The moment he discovered she loved music, he'd given her an iPod and showed her how to fill it with the songs she enjoyed. There was a small speaker that she could attach it to, making it easy to listen to her music while she showered.

She liked the water hot, and she stood for a long while under the heavy spray, feeling the way the hot water soaked into her skin and made her feel languid and lazy. Eli never made her feel as if the things she wanted when they made love were wrong. She liked when he was edgy and rough. She liked when he pushed her out of her comfort zone. She liked bossy and arrogant and dominant. She didn't feel as if it made her weak at all.

She reveled in the way they came together. And she really wouldn't mind stripping naked and dancing on the table if he used that one sexy, commanding voice when he told her to do it. She was definitely getting a tattoo on her lower spine, just because he liked caressing her there. He often pressed his lips there.

She didn't want to linger too long there in the shower. She was already thinking about what she'd cook for his breakfast. She enjoyed cooking for him as well. He gave her so much and that was one way she knew she could give back. He enjoyed the meals she made for him. She and Emma had exchanged recipes and she was experimenting with some of them to make them even better.

She wrapped her hair in a towel and dried off, taking her time. Her body still felt sensual and sensitive, especially her breasts. She was a little sore between her legs, but that wasn't unusual. Eli was large and thick and they went a little crazy sometimes. She liked rough and he usually was very rough. Still, those little tinges only served to remind her of his possession. She loved being possessed by him.

She dressed carefully, choosing clothes that came off fast and easy. She had caches scattered around the ranch, just as Eli did. It was something most shifters did, just in case they were caught somewhere and needed clothes and supplies. The everyday clothes they wore were clothes they could shed as fast and efficiently as possible.

She loved her boots. Loved them. Shifters didn't wear boots that often because they were much harder to get off. Still, she loved them, and when Rafe was out of her life, she intended to wear every single pair lined up in her closet. That thought made her very happy.

She pulled on a skirt, tugging it to her hips. The band was wide and comfortable, the material falling in graceful ruffles to her ankles. The skirt was one of her favorites, so soft and swingy, very feminine. She knew Eli liked it. He'd chosen it for her when they'd ordered clothes off one of her favorite Internet sites. She'd looked at it all the time, but she never actually ordered anything until Eli had encouraged her.

When everything with Rafe was finally settled, she wanted to get a job in town and make her own money so she wasn't reliant on Eli for funds. She knew instinctively that it would be a fight. Eli was a macho alpha male and he believed he should provide for his woman.

She stared at herself in the mirror as she unwrapped her hair and it fell to her waist. He loved her hair long. He loved her to wear it down. She always did in the house, just to please him, but when she went running with him or climbing, she clipped it up. True, it was convenient to have it up, but mostly she put it up so he'd take it down. She loved the way he did that, all impatient, a frown on his face and then his hands would be in her hair, fingers threading through the strands so possessively.

She brushed all the tangles out, taking her time, looking at the woman she'd become. A few months ago she could never have looked at her body and been confident and proud of herself. She'd been ashamed of her lack of formal education. She'd found fault with every curve. She brought her hands up to her breasts. Now, she loved the sight of the body that pleased Eli so much. He worshiped her body.

Eli's marks were everywhere on her skin, on her curves, those dark smudges that told her the path his hands and mouth had followed. She loved seeing those signs of his possession. The sight always made her feel even sexier.

She chose a lacy white camisole to wear so she wouldn't have to wear a bra for support. The camisole fit snugly around her breasts and was tight around her rib cage. It was short, baring a strip of her midriff, the real reason she chose it. Eli could never resist touching her bare skin. The zipper on the side allowed her to get out of it fast, so she knew if he decided to practice shifting, she'd be much faster than he would think and she might actually best him.

She rarely wore panties at home, especially when she knew they'd be shifting. It was just one more item of clothing to get rid of, slowing her down. A thong or boy shorts could cost her precious seconds, just as a bra could. She made a mental note to consult with Emma about what she did when it came to clothing.

She left her hair down to dry, brushed her teeth thoroughly and made her way to the kitchen to begin cooking. Of course Eli was outside on the porch. Dawn was breaking. He loved to watch the light streaking through the dark. She made the dough for the beignets before she made her own coffee. Eli had grown fond of the warm treat with his coffee after breakfast and she always made them fresh.

She took her time making her coffee, looking around her kitchen. Eli had told her she could do anything she wanted with it and she had. He'd bought her the stove and

pots and pans, the rest was her design and the touches that
made life easier for her when she was working. The touches
that made her feel as if the kitchen truly belonged to her.

Eli had given her that as well. Love welled up. Overwhelmed her. She needed him. Needed to be close to him.
More and more she found herself drawn to him. Just like this.
Her breasts ached and she found it was a wonderful sensation
because the thought of Eli put that there. Her feminine core
pounded with heat, and again, she loved the soreness that
came from Eli's thick cock, stretching and burning her. She
was glad that with every step she took, she could feel him.

Pushing open the screen door, she stepped outside. It
was still dark, the light barely filtering through, but mostly
that was because of the black clouds churning in the sky
overhead.

The scent of blood hit her just as her gaze swept the
porch. On the far side of the porch, away from the door,
something heavy hung from chains. Swaying. Her heart
stopped for a moment and then began to pound. She wanted
to run to the swaying body—and it was a body—she could
see that now. Not just any body, but Eli.

20

CATARINA froze. She forced every muscle to lock in place. There was no way to take her horrified gaze from Eli's golden one. His face was swollen. Blood streaked not only his face and head, but his chest as well. Clearly, while she'd been showering, daydreaming, Eli had been tortured.

Eli's eyes had closed after that one brief acknowledgement of her presence, but she had the feeling he was alert. Ready. Coiled to strike. She didn't know how that could be possible, and maybe it was only because she was so terrified and needed to believe it, but she did. That gave her the added confidence to look around her.

She knew he would be there. She had thought he would come alone, but he hadn't. His three top lieutenants, all leopard, were with him. They stood on the ground, just past Eli's body. One held cables in his hands, another the hose. She felt her leopard rise. Fury shook her, replacing terror. But she didn't move a muscle. Only her eyes moved.

He was there somewhere, waiting in silence, wanting her terror to mount. She could feel his anger. The weight of it crushing her, just as it had crushed her when she'd been a helpless child seeking love and approval in his home. She couldn't afford to be crushed by him. Not now. Not when Eli hung from chains and the three leopard lieutenants had obviously been given carte blanche to torture him. She lifted her chin, inhaled, and knew immediately where he was. She turned away from Eli, hating to lose sight of him, but she had to face Rafe.

The moment her gaze found him, at the opposite end of the porch, standing upright in the shadows, he took a step toward her. He was a big man. Built strong and powerful. His features were cut from the same powerful cloth. His cold stare could stop a grown man in full battle mode from moving an inch toward him—even if they had a gun in their hand. She'd seen it happen more than once. Rafe Cordeau had that kind of power. He was handsome. She'd never really noticed that before. And he had charisma. She had noticed that.

"So you found me again," she greeted softly.

"I told you I would always find you, Catarina," he answered, his voice equally as soft.

The tone made her shiver. He never sounded angry. Not like Eli. Rafe didn't give away emotion. His expression was blank, his eyes cold and his tone low and carrying, but with no inflection one way or the other.

"Rafe, I hope you believe me when I tell you that if you hurt him any more—if you kill him—if you do anything at all to him, I will kill myself. You will never have me. Never have any part of me. I'm done with you ruling my life by hurting others."

"He touched you. He's been inside of you. No man lives if he's been inside of you," Rafe said.

"Then I won't live either." She didn't raise her voice, or lose control. This was too important. If Rafe had spent all this time and money hunting her down, it was to dispose of her himself, or to take her back. If he wanted her, she had to make him believe he couldn't keep her alive if he killed another person she cared about. "I can't live like that. I couldn't live with you knowing what you'd done to April."

"I didn't do that to April, you did. You've always known the consequences of running, and you did it anyway."

She shook her head. "I was a child, Rafe. You made me take that responsibility and guilt but it wasn't mine to take. That was you. You chose to hurt her. You took pleasure in hurting her. You knew she was my friend and you killed her in front of me. Did you think I would want to stay with you after that?"

He took another step toward her, glided fluidly, like the leopard he was. She saw his leopard now in his eyes. The need to dominate because she was arguing, defying him. His eyes glittered, focused on her like he would on prey.

"It doesn't matter what you want, Catarina. You belong to me. You always have. The moment I knew that bitch of a woman had something so precious, I knew I would take you from her and protect you." Again there was no inflection in his voice.

The sound of water and then Eli crying out had her spinning around. They were shocking him, running electricity through his wet body. She forced herself to remain still. Lifting one hand she shifted only her arm and hand, a difficult feat that had taken weeks of practice to accomplish. A paw formed where her fingers had been, long, curved razor-sharp claws springing out of them.

She didn't hesitate, bringing the claw to the artery in her neck. Blood trickled. Rafe leapt toward her, covering the distance between them in the blink of an eye, yanking her arm down and away from her jugular.

"You won't be able to stop me, Rafe. They hurt him, I'll do it. I'll kill myself. I'll find a way. That's the deal."

Rafe swore, the first sign of emotion he'd shown. He lifted his hand and instantly the water cut off and Eli stopped twisting and jerking.

"Please let go of me." His touch confused her. His grip on her was gentle, not hard. He held her arm firmly but without any force. She couldn't sustain the shift to just one body part and her leopard subsided, staying just below the surface in case Catarina needed her again.

"Promise me you won't try to harm yourself. We'll work out a deal."

She nodded. "As long as you don't kill or torture him, or harm anyone else I care about, I'll listen to what you have to say, Rafe."

Rafe waved his three lieutenants back, ensuring Eli's safety for the time being. "We'll go in the kitchen and talk," he said, making it an order.

"I don't trust them to stay away from Eli. Get him down from there, first."

"Not a chance, Catarina. I'm giving you this one concession. Go into the kitchen where we can talk alone."

She turned her body toward the screen door, allowing her gaze to sweep over Eli. His head was down as if in defeat, but his eyes had narrowed to slits. She saw the blaze of power there and it steadied her. He had a plan. So did she.

Catarina lifted her chin. "Give me your word that they won't touch him while we're in the house, Rafe."

"Will you believe me?"

She lowered her lashes. "I always believed you, Rafe. You're all I've ever had."

He might say he knew she was precious and he wanted to protect her, but he had known she was a shifter long before he ever removed her from that house of drugs and pain. His home, any home would have been better for a child to be raised in. But he'd left her there until she'd had her first period. Until he feared her leopard might emerge. He hadn't taken any chances, forcing her to live with him then.

She knew he could have taken her earlier, but he hadn't wanted the inconvenience of a small child. He would have had to hire a nanny, someone who might suspect what he did. More—and she suspected it was the real reason—he didn't want to risk her being attached to anyone else.

Catarina knew the soft statement *I always believed you, Rafe* had gotten to him. She saw his eyes change, the leopard backing off just a little.

"No one will harm him." Rafe lifted his head and pinned his lieutenants with his cold, steely eyes. "I don't want him comfortable, but do nothing more until you're given the order."

She hesitated. There was something in what he said that she'd missed. *How* he'd said it. She wasn't certain what to do. She needed to comply with Rafe's demands, make him believe she was listening to him, that there was a chance she'd go peacefully with him, but now she was afraid to leave Eli alone with Rafe's shifter lieutenants.

She glanced again at Eli out of the corner of her eye. His nod was nearly imperceptible, meant only for her. She squared her shoulders and moved immediately to stand at the screen. Waiting. Forcing Rafe to open it for her. To acknowledge she was a grown woman and had to be treated with respect. Eli opened doors for her, Rafe needed to do the same.

She stood there nearly a minute before Rafe's hand moved past her to yank the screen open. She swept through it like royalty.

"Would you like a coffee? I can make almost anything."

His gaze scanned the room, landed on the dough she had ready to make the beignets with. He inhaled deeply, dragging in the scent of sex. He couldn't fail to notice it. Fury burned across his expression, making her shiver, and then it was gone and his cool mask was back in place.

"Sit down, Catarina," he said. It was an order, but as usual, he couched it in low, soft tones.

He wanted to build her terror. She could see it was important to him that she feared him. Most of his employees were frightened of him for good reason. If they did something he didn't like, he took them into a room and scared the hell out of them without ever raising his voice. They did it again, they disappeared, never to be seen, and Rafe's leopard was a very satisfied hunter.

She complied, moving to the chair at the end of the table. She should have known it wouldn't work to try to keep a distance from him. He simply toed a chair close and straddled it, face-to-face with her, his demon eyes burning into her.

"You left again. I told you what would happen. Why did you leave me?"

"You killed April."

"That's it? That's the reason?"

She pressed her lips together and then tugged her lower lip between her teeth briefly to show him she was nervous. "You didn't like me very much, Rafe. I tried so hard and no matter what I did, you pushed me away from you. I hated what you did to April, but even after that I tried to take care of you the only way I knew how, but then you . . ." Deliberately she trailed off. Ducked her head. Looked at her hands, twisting her fingers together in the way she knew he didn't like.

Rafe preferred stillness and he'd been on her all the time about learning to be absolutely still. Now, she realized he'd been preparing her for her leopard in his own way.

He reached out and gently laid his hand over hers to stop the movement of her fingers. "Be still, Catarina," he said, in the same low tone, but his dominant male leopard retreated even a little more.

Without the leopard driving him to dominate or kill, Rafe would be easier to manipulate. She nodded her head and allowed her hands to relax under his. She remembered his hands forcing hers into the well of April's blood and she nearly jerked away from him, the memory was so vivid. She could actually smell the blood for a moment, but she held it together.

This was for Eli. She could do this because Eli made her

aware of her own strength. She had outsmarted Rafe once and she could do it again, because it didn't matter right then that she wasn't formally educated. It didn't mean she wasn't intelligent enough to turn the table on Rafe Cordeau. She knew she was.

"You left me because you think I didn't want you?"

She swallowed hard. It was difficult to tell him, because it was the truth. She had tried so hard and felt so alone and unloved. She'd gone to try to see her stepmother, hoping the memories of her childhood were skewed and maybe the woman did love her. Then she'd lost April, and she'd retreated from everyone, horrified, ashamed and guilty. She'd needed Rafe to reassure her. To come to her and hold her. To make things right, even when intellectually she knew there was no right to what he'd done. He hadn't. He'd left her alone with her nightmares, guilt and shame.

She knew Rafe could hear the ring of truth in her voice, she could see it in his eyes, in the way he looked at her. His thumb slid over the back of her hand.

"Don't stop, Catarina. I need to know everything. I need to understand. If I understand what happened, what drove you away from me, it will help determine how all this ends and if that man will live out his life safely or not."

Her stomach muscles clenched. Hard knots formed. It took a lot of control to breathe normally and not give in to the desire to jerk her hands away. The worst of it all was she felt sorry for him. He seemed so alone and she'd hurt him. She didn't want to see that, but she did.

"Do you remember the dinner you had with the Lospostos family? I was so careful. I wanted you to be proud of me. More, I wanted you to look good to them. I chose every dish so carefully and prepared it. It took me hours. Even the bread was made from scratch. Everything was perfect. They loved it. They loved the dessert. And then you forced me to read that poem. You knew I couldn't read. You wanted to make fun of me. Worse, you wanted them to make fun of me."

The memory brought heat to her face. She would never

be able to look back on that night without feeling the embarrassment of her lack of education. Rafe had done it on purpose, and no matter what he said now, he could never take the moment back.

"You said I was good in the kitchen, but not good for much else. I heard you. You laughed. They laughed. You implied I had a subpar IQ and couldn't learn anything in school."

She allowed her lashes to lift because she knew he'd see genuine pain there. She didn't want to show it to him. The only person she trusted enough to see her that vulnerable was Eli, but this was for Eli.

Rafe's fingers tightened around her hand. "I had no choice, Catarina. None. They had noticed you. They asked too many questions and they wanted to meet you. I couldn't have them speculating on whether or not you meant something to me. That would have put you in danger."

"You want me to believe you humiliated me in front of your friends because somehow that would keep me out of danger?" Catarina poured incredulity into her voice.

She kept her gaze from shifting toward the kitchen door through sheer willpower. She'd have to check on Eli soon. She couldn't stand not knowing if he was all right or not. There had been something in Rafe's look when he'd directed his men to leave Eli alone. She didn't believe that Eli was entirely safe.

"They aren't friends," he said, leaning toward her, his eyes steady on hers. "They are dangerous people I'm forced to do business with. I have one weakness. Only one. You make me vulnerable. If others know it, especially a crime family as dangerous as the Lospostos, you can be used as a weapon against me. What that means, Catarina, is they may take you and torture you. They may send you back to me in pieces. I wasn't willing to risk you for your pride."

She heard the truth in his voice and she didn't want to. Her heart already bled for him—this man lost to his past—to the parents who abused and corrupted him. There was no redemption, no going back from what he'd done.

She licked her lips, forcing her mind to stay on Rafe and away from Eli. She knew Eli had a plan and she had to trust him, although what he could do hanging from chains with three male leopards who obviously hunted humans with Rafe in the swamp was beyond her comprehension.

"Rafe, I grew up in your home."

"It's your home too, Catarina." His tone, still low, was very firm and decisive.

"I'm quite a lot smarter and more observant than you ever gave me credit for."

"I'm well aware of that, although I've always known you were intelligent. I just underestimated you. I thought if I kept you from school, it would slow you down a little. Instead, you accelerated. That was my mistake and one I won't make again with you."

She didn't know if that was praise or a warning. "The point is, I used your computer for my education, not my own. I hacked you. I know your business. I know what you do."

"I'm very aware of that." Now he did sound proud of her.

That pride made her heart ache all the more. "I know the arms deals. The drug deals. The prostitutes and even contract kills you arranged. I know where your money is. I'm a danger to you and to every business partner you have."

"I've been aware of that for some time, Catarina." He sat back, for the first time letting go of her. "You never once cooperated with law enforcement. You didn't go to them. You refused to give them anything this time, even when you knew I would find out where you were the moment they brought you to a police station. You knew I would come after you. And you knew I'd find you. Still you didn't take their deal. That's not fear, Catarina. That's loyalty. I've never once had anyone loyal to me. Anyone looking out for me. Not unless I paid them. You gave that to me."

It wasn't altogether a lie. There was more truth in his statement than she wanted to believe. He'd killed, and still there was a part of her that protected him and she didn't understand why. She kept thinking she could find a way to save him. He'd grown up in what could only have been a nightmare world, but so had Jake Bannaconni. Jake had found a morality, lines he would never cross; Rafe had turned to killing to ease his own pain.

"What about those people you allow your leopard to hunt in the swamp, Rafe?" she asked quietly.

His eyes flickered, darkened. She saw the threat of his leopard there. The focused, piercing stare of the hunter. "I don't kill those people, Catarina. My leopard does. It's the only way I can restrain him. Every one of them was an enemy."

"You brought women to our home to sleep with you. You hunted them. How could they be the enemy?"

"You go too far," he hissed. "Do you have any idea how dangerous this conversation is for you?"

"I want to understand the things I didn't as a child. The things about you that scared me. I'm giving you all the reasons I ran from you, Rafe. You were everything to me. My whole life. There was no one else. Only you. You didn't hold me. You didn't reassure me when I needed it. I tried to hold on. I tried to understand. But I knew what you were doing and it frightened me, especially when I felt her. My leopard. I was afraid she would hunt with yours. That she was a killer."

He studied her face. He reached out and touched her hair gently. So gently. His fingers slid through the silky length and then he tucked it behind her ear. She realized he really thought he could persuade her to leave Eli and go back with him. To do that, he had to know he'd have to kill Eli. Eli would never let her go, and if there was one thing Rafe was good at, it was reading other men. He'd know that. Somewhere in Rafe's mind, he believed he could make her see that it was the right thing to do. The thought that Rafe was that far gone saddened her.

"You don't understand about leopards, sweetheart. They need freedom to be who and what they are. They're at the top of the food chain. If I don't let mine run free and hunt the way he was meant to, his mood affects me and I become dangerous. Better a prostitute than some innocent woman."

"Did your leopard hunt my mother?"

"She wasn't your mother. She intended to use you for prostitution. She told me so herself when she came back demanding more money for you."

Her heart stuttered in her chest. She couldn't help herself. She wrapped her arms around her body and rocked herself gently back and forth. "I need a drink of water, Rafe."

"I'll get it for you. This is a lot to take in." He stood, his eyes on her just in case, and walked to the sink.

She waited for him to fill a glass with water before feeling quickly under the table for the weapon taped there. The moment her fingers found it, she dropped her hands to her lap, twisting her fingers together. She knew he would focus on that. He hated that she couldn't keep still when she was nervous or agitated.

Rafe set the water in front of her. "You were born for me. Every leopard has a mate, and you're mine. I've always known it. This man who came into your life, I can understand why you would think you needed him, but he isn't for you. He was never for you. Still, I do understand that you care for him."

"Rafe, you've killed too many people I care about. David Belmont and Bernard Casey didn't know a thing about me. They're dead. Some stranger was murdered as well. I didn't even know his name."

"Some things are necessary, Catarina. You're old enough and intelligent enough to understand that. You've got your explanations. It's time to come home now."

"And if I won't go?"

"You'll go. You'll go because you belong there. You'll

come with me, because if you don't, that man out there is going to die."

"We both know he'll come after me." She said it quietly, watching his face.

He hit her. He hit her hard, open-handed, across her face, knocking her right out of the chair. Stars burst across her eyes. Pain radiated from her cheek to the top of her skull and down across her jaw. She hit the floor so hard it knocked the wind from her so that she couldn't get air.

Rafe had often exploded into violence, one moment absolutely cold and controlled and the next, cold and vicious, capable of murder. He was on her so fast she didn't have time to even roll away from him. He slammed the toe of his shoe into her side, kicking her several times.

Pain blasted through her body. She couldn't think. Couldn't rise. Couldn't get away from the savage attack. It was so fast, so unexpected, all she could do was curl into a ball and try to protect her stomach and ribs. Instinctively, both hands covered her abdomen as her knees drew up for added protection.

He crouched down beside her, gripping her hair and yanking her head toward him. He slapped her three more times, the sound loud, the blows hard. When she managed to look at him, his eyes were all cat, his leopard close.

"You let him fuck you, right here. Right in this room where you cook him meals that should have been mine. Did you think I wouldn't smell the two of you? You let him touch you. You knew you belonged to me. You had no right allowing him to put his hands on you let alone his dick in you. You allowed his leopard to claim yours. Your leopard belonged to mine. Did you really think for one moment, I'd leave that man alive?" He snarled the questions at her, but his expression didn't change.

She didn't move. She didn't dare. He was too far gone into his world of violence and madness. She reached for air, prayed that Eli had somehow executed his plan and had gotten away from Rafe's lieutenants.

Rafe reached under the table to find the gun taped there. He pulled it out and showed it to her. "Were you looking for this? Were you planning to shoot me, Catarina?" He slapped her again. Hard. Once, twice. His expression never changed.

She'd seen him deliver this kind of punishment to those who worked for him, but he'd never laid a hand on her. She knew why everyone was so terrified of him. The viciousness when he appeared so remote and cold was worse than any anger he could display.

She felt her leopard rise close to the surface, fur pushing at her skin as the animal tried to save her. *Not yet. Not yet.* She tried to soothe the little female. She needed just a few more minutes. Rafe wasn't going to kill her. He planned on killing Eli, probably in front of her, that would be the only way he'd be satisfied. She would take whatever punishment Rafe gave her in order to give Eli the chance he needed to escape.

Rafe dragged her up by her hair. "You're coming home with me. That bastard is going to die, and it will be a very long time before I forgive what you've done. Don't you ever threaten your own life again, Catarina. I can hurt you in ways you can't even imagine, and I will if I have to. There are other people you don't want dead. Think about them before you ever do something like this again."

Pain crashed through her. She could barely think. She allowed him to shove her toward the screen door, keeping her hands wrapped around her middle, her fingers settling on the side zipper of her camisole. She'd practiced. She was fast. Very fast. Eli had been relentless, making her practice stripping and shifting on the run over and over for hours each day. She had thought he was a little overboard but now she was grateful.

Rafe kept his fingers around her upper arm. Hard. Digging into her flesh. A vise she knew she couldn't just yank away from. But her leopard could. She just had to figure out a way to rid herself of the camisole.

He opened the screen and thrust her outside, coming right behind her, never losing contact. Dawn had spread light through darkness. Her gaze went straight to Eli, his body still hanging, battered and streaked with blood. For a moment her heart pounded. She thought he was dead. She bit back a scream of denial.

Rafe shoved her toward the end of the porch. She stumbled, keeping her gaze on Eli. When she stumbled, Rafe let go of her. She tore the zipper down and ripped the camisole over her head, shoved the skirt from her hips and kicked it away as she leapt past one of Rafe's lieutenants who was sitting absolutely still in the chair on the porch. He hadn't even registered in her vision before.

Already she was shifting, catching the scent of blood, of death. She took one leap and landed on the wide wooden railing just in front of Eli. Only it wasn't Eli hanging there. It was another of Rafe's lieutenants. She saw that in an instant and knew the one sitting so still was also dead.

Elation swept through her as she leapt from the porch and streaked across the open yard for the trees. She knew every inch of the way between their property and Jake Bannaconni's. She also knew Eli had to be battling the third leopard, which meant her female would have to outrun Rafe's male.

She didn't look back. The little female valiantly ran for the fence that bordered the two properties. She knew where Jake's men, all three shifters, had been working to repair a broken fence line so their cattle would remain on their land. She headed for that spot, hoping the men would get an early morning start and they would help her.

She ran full out, but she hadn't counted on the damage Rafe had inflicted on her body. Every step hurt. She had to fight to breathe. He'd definitely hurt her ribs, and she felt each vicious kick he'd inflicted on her. She wasn't nearly

fast enough and she knew it. With a little sob, she pushed
the female harder.

Something large slammed into the female leopard's
side, sending her tumbling, rolling over and over. She
landed winded, shaking her head, trying to come to her
feet. The heavier male was on her fast, too fast. His teeth
bit down hard, lifting her, claws raking at her belly. She
curled to protect herself. He shook her much smaller body
and dropped her to the ground.

Catarina's leopard rolled, came to her feet and ducked
under the male's attack, slicing at his sides with one claw,
ripping him open as she leapt sideways out of the way. The
male snarled, his eyes going yellow green. Her leopard
eyed him warily. They stared at one another, the female
trying to recover her breath.

She couldn't outrun him. She couldn't outfight him. But
she might be able to outmaneuver him. She was much
smaller, and she had a few moves Eli's male had taught her.
The key was not to panic and not to waste energy.

The male charged, exploding into action. She held her
ground until the last possible second, springing into the air,
swiping at his eyes with one claw, turning direction in midair to land a few feet away and behind the howling male.
Blood streaked his side, not a killing wound, probably just
shallow, but she'd scored there. Now blood streaked his
face, and she saw one eye was damaged.

The male turned his head slowly and her heart nearly
stopped. Rafe was not in control of the beast and his leopard,
a true killing machine, targeted her for the kill. She could
see the rage and fury in his eyes. He wasn't going to simply
demand her submission, he was going to annihilate her.

ELI watched Catarina go into the house with Cordeau. She
looked so scared. So alone and vulnerable. He kept his
head down, but his eyes were on the three men who had

been having such a good time torturing him. They'd made several mistakes. They should have knocked him out. They should have tied his feet. The chains were wrapped around his wrists. And they thought with three against one the odds were in their favor.

One came at him from the front, his arms the legs of a leopard. He let the man get close, let him rake claws down his chest, a streaking, painful fire, but his legs whipped up and caught the man's neck between his powerful thighs in a vicious grip, preventing shifting, preventing anything but trying to survive. He wasn't going to. Eli killed him before the second leopard could leap the distance to try to come to the aid of his friend.

Eli lifted his body up, drove hard to rise above the hook and free his chains. He dropped to the ground and caught the second lieutenant around the neck with the chains, twisting with his enormous strength, relentless, brutal, taking the air from him, cutting it off, strangling him with the very manacles they'd used to bind him after they'd stunned him.

The other lieutenant recovered from his momentary shock and ripped his clothes from his body, shifting as he did so. Eli swung the dying man around to face the snarling leopard, giving the animal a target. The leopard leapt at him, his body hitting his friend with alarming force, smashing the chest, knocking Eli and the now dead man back. As he allowed the body to drop to the ground, Eli took the opportunity to shed the chains and his clothes in seconds. He shifted, his large male leopard already in combat mode, facing the leopard that had landed hard and was shaking himself.

Eli's big black panther charged the lighter spotted leopard. The male leapt to the side with blinding speed and whirled to try to leap on Eli's back. His panther met the leopard in midair, raking and clawing, using his teeth to try to secure a smothering hold, but the leopard was too experienced and twisted at the last second. He ran. Eli followed.

Eli knew he had no choice but to kill the leopard before

Cordeau returned to kill him. And he would. There was no question no matter what he told Catarina. Cordeau knew better than to leave him alive. Cat's leopard was Eli's leopard's mate. Cat was Eli's mate. Cordeau would have to destroy him in order to have any claim on Catarina or her leopard. He knew, if Eli was alive, Eli would never stop coming after him and Catarina would be driven to try to find him.

Cordeau's leopard had to be brutal. He'd driven the man mad. Some leopards, like their masters, were bad-tempered and edged a little toward insanity. Clearly, Rafe's leopard had needed a strong hold on it, but he had allowed the personality to take him over. He'd become a reflection of his leopard—a killer.

Eli knew every inch of his property. He followed the leopard closely until he realized the animal was deliberately drawing him away from the ranch house and Catarina. At once he spun around and raced back. Better to face two leopards than allow Cordeau to steal Cat away. He knew Cordeau's lieutenant would circle back to help his boss, but it didn't matter. He needed to make certain Cordeau didn't have the chance to take Catarina.

As he approached the ranch house, he heard the murmur of voices coming from inside. Cordeau sounded gentle and cajoling, as if he was trying to persuade Catarina to choose him over Eli. He didn't dare go confront Cordeau, not when he could use Catarina as a shield. He had to let them come back out. Cordeau would want Cat to see Eli's death. He would want her to blame herself. It gave Eli time to set a scene that would separate Catarina from Rafe, just enough to allow Eli to attack and still ensure Catarina's safety.

He knew he'd been damned lucky he'd killed the first two shifters fast, before either had made a sound. The third leopard had been so intent on killing him, he hadn't warned Cordeau with so much as a roar. Eli shifted and quickly put the body of the first man he'd killed into his chair on the porch, using a cord to lash him upright. A cursory glance might fool Cordeau for a moment. Using the chains, he hung the second shifter in the position he'd occupied recently.

The wind shifted just slightly and he had time to only partially shift and go vertical, leaping straight up to the roof as the leopard charged him from behind. He finished shifting as he landed and just that fast, launched himself in a silent attack on his pursuer.

He landed on the leopard's hind end, slamming him to the ground, raking with claws and driving his teeth into the leopard's neck. The leopard, using his flexible spine, turned with a show of strength, and raked at his face, rolling to try to get the heavier panther from his back. He smashed Eli hard into the ground, hard enough that Eli lost his hold on the neck and was forced to defend his own belly.

Both leopards rolled and came to their feet, reared up on hind legs, slashing and biting at their opponent. The leopard retreated first, falling back a few steps, sides heaving and bloody. Eli watched him warily. Circled slowly to the left. The leopard seemed to be favoring one side, down close to his hind legs, as if when Eli dropped from the roof, he'd managed to injure the heavily muscled leopard.

Cordeau's lieutenant suddenly made a run for the house, trying to burst past Eli's larger black panther. Eli realized immediately what he was doing. He wanted to warn Cordeau that Eli had killed the other two leopards and was much stronger and more combat experienced than any of them had counted on.

Eli cut him off, slamming him to the ground. The leopard rolled toward the tree line and Eli followed, raking at the injured hind end again, trying to hamstring him with vicious claws. He kept pushing him away from the ranch house, driving him back toward the trees. With each swipe of his claws, he dug deeper, did more damage until the leopard had no choice but to turn and defend himself.

Eli was on him in a second, using his superior strength and speed, rearing up with the leopard to rake the belly and get a strangling bite on his opponent's throat. He drove his teeth deep into the throat, and held him there. The leopard writhed, raked, fought, but Eli refused to relinquish his deadly hold. At no time had the leopard made a sound to warn his boss, and Eli realized that there was a scar deep in the leopard's throat, as if he'd suffered an injury there.

It took a long time for the fight to go out of the tawny leopard. He hung, panting, his eyes wild, the knowledge of his imminent death in his eyes. Eli held him and watched the life drain out of him, not able to take a chance that he could warn Cordeau that Eli was on the loose and hunting.

When he was certain the leopard was dead, Eli dropped him to the ground, shifted just enough to check for a pulse and then whirled to race back toward the house. He knew the moment he set his paw on the porch that Cordeau and Catarina were gone. The panther scented the female and also the male trying to take his mate. He let out a roar of challenge. The sound reverberated through the early morning air.

Eli pushed into the screen to smell blood. Catarina's blood. She was injured. The black panther whirled and rushed after his mate, running full speed, following the scent of stark fear and blood.

21

CATARINA stilled inside the small female as she watched the much larger, brutal male crouch low, his eyes fixed on her with deadly intent. The eye she'd injured wept blood, but rather than looking hurt, the large cat appeared evil. Invincible.

She refused to turn tail and run. If she was going to die, she would die fighting, keeping Rafe away from Eli for as long as she was able. More, if she injured him, she'd be helping Eli, because she knew, without a doubt in her mind, that Eli would be coming for her. He had wanted her to learn to fight so she could break away and flee, or if that failed, to stay alive long enough for Eli to come for her.

Catarina stared defiantly into the male's green-yellow eyes. Deep inside, she felt her little female coil. Become ready. She waited in absolute stillness, none of the fidgeting Rafe hated so much. Fidgeting would get her killed. She needed to see every nuance, every change in expression.

When he charged, he was going to try to end her fast—or at least end her rebellion.

His roped muscles bunched beneath the loose fur. He crawled, belly low to the ground, slinking forward an inch or two and then freezing again. His muzzle pulled back in a snarling grimace, showing his teeth. His ears had gone flat, pulled to the side of his head to protect them during a fight. The eyes never changed. Never left the little female.

Heart pounding, Catarina waited, forcing air through her lungs, holding her female in place, soothing her with the knowledge that their mate was alive and would be coming soon. Eli had prepared her for this. His male had prepared her female. She just had to do exactly what she'd been taught, and that meant conquering the terror that threatened to grip her, threatened to freeze her in place.

Rafe's male's tail switched. The wind ruffled his fur. She watched his eyes. The hatred and anger receded just a little, and Catarina knew Rafe was fighting for dominance. The cat wanted her female's submission. Rafe didn't mind beating her, or allowing his male to beat up the female leopard, but he still didn't want her dead, and that was an advantage—a small one—but still an advantage.

The male launched himself at her. His speed was breathtaking. The female tried to whip around, out of the way, but the leopard anticipated her movement and was on her in seconds, slamming her to the ground with his heavy body, his claws ripping into her sides, raking deep as his teeth sank into her shoulder, just behind her neck.

The pain was excruciating. Her leopard went still. Trembled. She was too new, too inexperienced, and the male was frightening. Terrifying. She simply disappeared, allowing her human to take her place.

The change happened so fast, so smoothly that for a moment, Catarina didn't realize what happened. Pain crashed through her body. She smelled blood. Felt it running down her back and the sides of her body. She felt the hot blast of the leopard's breath, the weight of his body as he pinned her to the ground, mauling her. Desperately she placed both hands over her stomach, trying to curl, to bring up her knees, as the claws shredded skin right down to the bone, but the leopard held her mercilessly in place.

She was going to die and there was nothing she could do about it. Rafe's leopard killed countless women. She heard screams, horrible wailing cries of pain and fear rising on the wind. It took a moment to realize it was her voice. Her agony. His terrible claws slashed and burned through her body. She couldn't even curl up into a little ball no matter how much she tried. There was no way to protect her head.

"You're okay, Catarina."

Rafe's voice was gruff. He sounded as afraid as she felt. The weight of the male leopard was gone, but she couldn't move. She drew her knees up under her, trying to find a way to breathe. Blood was everywhere, her body slick with it. She hurt everywhere, as if the heavy leopard had battered her, and maybe he had.

"Catarina, I need to look at you." Rafe injected more command into his voice.

She forced her head to turn toward him, flinching with the pain of just that small movement. Her shoulder and neck felt torn. Rafe's eyes were dark with worry.

"You can't ever allow your leopard to leave you facing another leopard," he lectured in a harsh tone.

She realized immediately he'd been terrified for her. Like Catarina, Rafe had feared his leopard would kill her before he could get the large cat under control. Rafe controlled his fears by going to someplace cold and barren where nothing touched him. Nothing but Catarina.

His hands moved over her body to inspect the savage wounds on her right side. "These are deep. You're going to need stitches. Infection is a problem with this kind of wound. We'll put you on IV antibiotics immediately. Can you move a little so I can look at your other side?"

Now that he was doing something to aid her, his tone had gone to brisk and matter-of-fact. His momentary lapse was gone and Rafe was once again in complete control.

She could barely breathe let alone answer him. Tears streamed down her face, although she wasn't certain if she was really crying or if it was an involuntary reaction to pain. She'd never felt agony like this in her life. She didn't know a person could live with such pain.

Rafe didn't wait to see if she could manage on her own. He gripped her arms to shift her to one side, but his hands slipped through the blood and fell away. He cursed and looked at the puncture wounds on her shoulder. She was losing a lot of blood there as well. His cat had been savage in establishing dominance over the little female. The moment the little leopard had disappeared and the male had a human under him his instinct was to kill. Rafe had used every ounce of his own strength and iron will to pull the leopard back and allow him to shift.

"Let's get you out of here. I have a vehicle just outside the tree line. You need medical attention, Catarina. It's going to hurt when I lift you. If you feel yourself passing out, just do it."

She was surprised at the gentleness in his voice. He had never been a gentle man, but he was afraid for her. She knew she was in trouble just by his voice.

His arms went around her and he lifted her. She screamed as sheer agony ripped through her. Her sides felt as if someone had ripped them apart, exposing bone and organs to air.

Rafe suddenly cursed and nearly tossed her away, but at the last minute he went down on one knee and shoved her away from him. She hit hard and rolled, leaving smears of blood in the grass. The action took what little air remained in her lungs so she couldn't even cry out.

But she saw him. The huge black panther charging toward them. His golden eyes were deadly and focused

wholly on Rafe. Already Rafe was shifting, rushing toward
the black leopard as he did so to give his leopard momen-
tum. He was fully cat by the time the two males came
together in a terrible crash of heavy bodies.

Roars of challenge filled the air. The sounds were terrible. Fur flew. Droplets of blood sprayed high in the air and
surrounded the two combatants. They reared up on their
hind legs like two primal beasts, raking with hooked claws
and biting with terrible teeth. They dropped apart and
charged again, leaping into the air, changing direction in
midair, using flexible spines to try to get a killing position
on the other over and over.

They were both experienced fighters and strong males.
Roped muscles moved fluidly beneath the loose skin that
protected them from the teeth and claws of their adversar-
ies. They hit each other so hard, driving first Rafe and then
Eli from their feet, the sound horrible each time their bodies came together, like two freight trains crashing. The
ground shook at times.

Catarina lay a distance from the two snarling, fighting
leopards, her eyes on them, but her vision was hazy. She
had thought she would be afraid for Eli when this moment
came. She'd always known it would come. Always. Eli and
Rafe would fight to the death right there in front of her.
Before she'd been absolutely certain of the outcome—
certain Rafe would kill Eli. Now, she wasn't afraid for Eli.

She blinked several times in an attempt to clear her
vision. It took a moment to realize she was sinking into
unconsciousness. She didn't want to do that. She had to
know Eli survived. She felt an overwhelming sadness for
Rafe, but even at the end, when he could have easily shouted
to Eli that she was in trouble and needed medical attention,
he had chosen to fight as a leopard because he'd rather she
die than allow her to be with someone else. That wasn't
love. Eli would have allowed Rafe to get her help if that was
the only way to keep her alive.

He didn't know the condition she was in, and she didn't want him to know. He'd sacrifice himself for her. She had to hold on because she wasn't losing a man like Eli. She knew he would defeat Rafe and find a way to get her to safety.

"Catarina." The voice startled her.

She turned her head away from the battling leopards and blinked several times to focus. Jake Bannaconni crouched beside her. His chest was bare, and she didn't look any further down his body. She kept her eyes on his face.

"God, honey. I've called for our helicopter. We'll get you to a hospital. You have to hang on for me."

She licked at her lips. Tasted blood. She couldn't talk and wondered if the leopard had ripped out her throat. Her gaze shifted back to the fighting males. Blood streaked their fur coats. Sides were heaving, desperate for air. Other leopards were there, ringing the two males and she realized her screams and the roars of the leopards had carried on the wind to Jake's ranch and they'd come.

"I'm going to try to stop this bleeding, Cat," Jake said. "It may hurt, but I have to get it stopped."

She nodded, or at least she thought she did. Her body shook with chills. She was cold and her brain wasn't functioning very well. She couldn't really think, and Jake's voice sounded as if it came from a great distance away. She felt his hands on her side, pressing something into the wounds, pressing it so hard her body seemed to rip apart beneath the pressure. She couldn't scream. She opened her mouth but no sound emerged. He did it a second time. Then a third. Black edged her vision.

"I'm sorry, honey," Jake whispered, his voice crooning.

She hadn't known he could sound so sweet, not unless he was talking to Emma or his children. He didn't use that voice on anyone else, at least she didn't think so. He kept his distance from most people. She thought he tolerated her for Emma, but his voice indicated affection.

"I'm going to turn you. It's going to hurt."

There was distaste in his tone, as if the thought of hurting her more was absolutely abhorrent to him. His hands
were gentle as he turned her away from the ring of leopards
watching the terrible battle. The movement made her sick.
She knew she was going to vomit.

Jake was suddenly there, holding her head to one side,
pulling her hair out of the way. The moment she emptied
her stomach, he shifted her away from the mess and once
again pressed something deep into the wound on her side.
She wanted to pass out. She even reached for that oblivion,
but it didn't happen. She felt the terrible pressure again, as
if he'd poured gasoline on the fire that burned into her side.

"He raked you on both sides," Jake explained. "He got
you with his claws. Three deep rakes on each side. I know
it hurts like hell and you're losing too much blood, but he
didn't hit anything vital."

His voice steadied her. She was really listening to the
sounds of the battle between two large males in their prime
fighting to the death. Eli. Rafe. Only one would walk away
alive, she knew that. No one would interfere in the battle
between the two leopards. That was the shifter way. That
was their justice. But Rafe was rogue, and these shifters
would kill him even if he won the battle with Eli. She
wished they'd just get it over with. She didn't understand
the strange code of shifters, nor did she care to, not when it
put Eli's life on the line.

"I've got to look at your shoulder and neck, honey."

He was already sitting her up, moving her body against
his. It was strange to be in such an intimate position with a
man other than Eli. Neither wore clothes, and yet she felt
nothing, not even embarrassment. She didn't think about it
once the thought moved through her head. With Jake holding
her up, she could at least look again at the two leopards.

Rafe was a short distance from Eli, his leopard's evil
eyes fixed on the black panther. The tawny head was down,
sides heaving in and out as the leopard tried desperately to

drag in air. He took a step and staggered. Eli's leopard hit him fast, hard, driving him from his feet. The sheer savagery of the attack left her breathless.

Even through the heat and haze of battle, the black rage rising like a tidal wave, Eli smelled Catarina's blood. The scent was overwhelming, sickening him. He couldn't rush to her side and see the extent of her injuries, not with Cordeau's killing machine of a leopard determined to rip him to pieces.

Eli's male was nearly as bad. The fight was savage. Brutal. Crushing. His male wanted not just to kill the tawny leopard, he wanted him to feel every crushing blow. Every deep slash and rake of claws. Every bite. Leopards went after the soft parts of the body in a fight, including the genitals, and Eli's male knew every trick in the book.

Cordeau's male relied on brute strength. He'd hunted humans. Humans without guns or weapons of any kind. Humans lost in the swamp. Mostly females who were terrified. Eli's male had honed his battle skills in the rain forests, fighting with teams to extract kidnap victims. Roughhousing. Mock battles. Learning technique and always, always conditioning.

There was immense satisfaction in every blow he dealt to the rogue leopard. Every brutal injury he bestowed on the beast. Until Jake and the others had arrived, all in leopard form, and yet Jake had hastily shifted to human form and rushed to Catarina's side. That meant something was wrong. Like most leopards traveling, Jake had kept a small pack around his neck with clothes, yet he hadn't taken the time to don them. That meant Catarina was in dire circumstances.

Then he heard Jake call in the helicopter. He'd faltered in that split second and he was damned lucky that Cordeau was struggling to stay on his feet. He should have dealt the killing blow right then, but Eli could barely breathe with fear. He couldn't lose Catarina. He hadn't considered that it might happen. He had every confidence that he would defeat Cordeau. There was no other option.

Cordeau couldn't have Catarina. She was a treasure and the man hadn't protected her, and even now, when he could have called out to Eli that she needed aid, he'd chosen to battle instead. That meant no more dealing out punishment. That meant killing Cordeau fast. The black panther understood, knew his mate was in trouble and instantly charged the leopard who had attempted to take her away from them.

He hit the side of the large cat and drove him over, feeling something give in the other animal. The leopard screamed in pain and rage. In fear. The heavier black panther didn't hesitate. He ripped at the unprotected underside of the tawny leopard, attacked the softer exposed male parts drawing rivers of blood. When the leopard had no choice but to turn in desperation, Eli was on him, driving his teeth deep in and holding him there in the killing stranglehold of their kind.

Desperate, Cordeau's cat fought to get free, fleeing uppermost in his mind now. Self-preservation had finally kicked in. The tawny male used his last remaining strength to stagger a few steps, trying to dislodge the black leopard, but Eli's male clamped down all the more viciously, determined to end the fight. Determined to destroy his rival. Determined to get to his mate to see how bad her injuries were.

Cordeau's male's fur was dark with blood. He fought one more savage moment, trying to turn, to use his flexible spine to hook claws into Eli's male, but the black leopard countered the movement, his bite relentless. He cut off the airway and simply held on, a ruthless, merciless kill. Eli felt no remorse and even less compassion.

He knew Catarina would hurt over this kill, but he also knew it was necessary. Cordeau had allowed his leopard to go rogue, and in doing so, the same madness infected him. No shifter could allow that. No shifter would allow it. Hunting human men or woman in the swamp was absolutely murder and they all knew it. It was forbidden, against every law they had.

Cordeau couldn't see the inside of a courtroom. He had to die and his body had to be burned and then buried deep where no one would ever find the evidence. His three lieutenants had to join him. Catarina might not like it, but she would understand. She had to understand, because he wasn't losing her over Cordeau's death and his part in it.

Cordeau's large male gave one more shudder and then went limp. Eli's panther knew better than to drop him. He kept a relentless, merciless pressure, a stranglehold that would suffocate the other cat, but he couldn't let go too soon, although the need to get to his mate was nearly overwhelming.

Eli had discipline and he used every ounce of it. Waiting. Feeling the life drain from the cat until he was completely a dead weight. Still he held on. Elijah's leopard ventured close. Eli fought down the urge to attack, realizing his leopard was still in battle mode. Elijah must have known it, because he was careful to approach with caution. He shifted just his arm and hand, checking Cordeau's animal for signs of life. His cat shook his head, and Eli knew Cordeau was gone.

His black panther dropped the other cat and he spun around, uncaring of his injuries. Uncaring that he was exhausted from the intense, brutal battle between the two male leopards. He shifted as he ran, reaching Jake, reaching Catarina.

His heart stuttered in his chest when he saw her. It nearly stopped. Terror lived and breathed in him. He hadn't known terror. Not even as a young boy when his parents had died. Grief. Overwhelming sorrow. But not terror. Not like this.

"Get dressed fast, the helicopter is coming. I'll go with you to the hospital," Jake instructed, preventing Eli from wrenching Catarina out of his arms. "Hurry. I'll need to dress as well. The boys will clean up here."

Elijah tossed him a pack, and Eli yanked the jeans free, dragging them up over his hips. Only then did he realize his body was streaked with blood as well. He hadn't felt the blows. Not any of them, but of course Cordeau's cat had scored on his male. He didn't bother with shoes or a shirt, he reached for Catarina, needing to hold her to him.

She cried out when her side came in contact with his, an involuntary cry that made it seem all the worse. Her face was twisted with pain and her skin felt cold and clammy. Leopards were always hot-blooded and to feel the chill in her skin added to his growing fear.

"She's lost a lot of blood," Jake said, his voice calm as he pulled on his jeans and dragged a shirt over his head. "I've put pressure bandages on the wounds on her sides, but she'd already lost so much."

Catarina's eyes were closed. Eli bent his head to her. "Look at me, Kitten. I want to see your eyes." He used his commanding voice, the one that always made her shiver. The one she obeyed without question.

Her lashes fluttered and lifted. His heart tripped. Tight knots formed in his gut. She was fading away from him. Instinctively his hands tightened on her, holding her to him. He bent his head, his eyes drilling into hers.

"You will not leave me. You understand, Catarina. You will not leave me. I need to know you understand." His tone was implacable. He wouldn't lose her. He didn't allow fear into his voice, but it was there, deep inside, eating him up. He could barely breathe with terror edging his mind. "Say it. Say it to me right now."

Her lashes fluttered, but she didn't look away from him. Her gaze clung to his as if he was her anchor, and he intended to be. He knew leopards who had shared a past could eventually be so close they were psychically connected. He pressed into her mind. Used his male shamelessly to press into her female's mind. He had to find a way to keep her with him, keep an unbreakable thread between them.

He heard the helicopter now, the *whop-whop* of the blades as it cruised through the air to get to them. Jake was on the radio giving orders. None of it mattered. She hadn't answered him.

"Catarina, you fucking promise me right now. You won't leave me."

She gave him the faintest of smiles and it broke his heart. Her tongue touched her lips. Clearly just moving hurt, but for him, she reached for her voice. "Can I promise that?"

"You can." He was adamant. Demanding. Arrogant even. "If you give me your word, I know you'll keep it."

The helicopter was down, and Eli cradled her as close as possible to keep from jarring her as he ran with her through the clearing to the open field. Her teeth came together and he could see the pain in her eyes, but she didn't cry out again. She was limp, a rag doll, not holding herself at all, her arms and legs clearly lead, all strength gone.

He pushed down fear as Jake climbed into the helicopter and held out his arms for her. Eli shook his head and made the leap, landing in a crouch, Catarina against his chest. Eli couldn't take the chance of losing contact with her.

Almost before he was seated, the helicopter was in the air, turning in a wide circle back toward town and the hospital. Jake was on the radio, calling ahead for an operating room and doctors he trusted.

"I know it hurts like fucking hell, Kitten," Eli whispered, his head bent to hers, his mouth against her ear. "I know you're suffering and it feels easier to let go. I'm asking you not to. I'm telling you I need you. For me. You have to live, do you hear me, baby? I need you. I don't want to do this without you."

He didn't give a damn if he was baring his soul to her. Hell, it was the raw truth. He *couldn't* live without her. He hadn't been alive until she came into his world. Her laughter had brought him to life. Damn her, she wasn't going to leave him alone now that she was wrapped so tightly around his heart.

She moistened her lips again. *I hear you, Eli,* she whispered. Or did she whisper it? Did he hear her soft whisper in his mind? Had he managed to find a way to connect them? If so, he wanted to grab hold with both fists and hold her so close there was no way for her to slip away.

The helicopter landed on the pad on the roof of the hospital. The gurney was waiting, just as Jake had instructed. Eli was reluctant to place her body on it, knowing they would take her from him, but he had no choice. He ran with the gurney, his hand hard around hers, his eyes on hers, demanding. Forcing her compliance.

She kept her eyes open, but there was so much pain he felt sick. She was so cold he felt her slipping away. Her pulse beneath his seeking fingers was thready and weak. *Don't leave me, baby. Stay for me. I need you. Need you so much.*

She was gone. They took her through double doors, forcing him to stay back. He felt her slip away from him. Felt the breath leave her body. Felt the moment her heart stopped beating and the pulse went quiet in her body. He *felt* her leave him. He knew he wasn't making it up when he heard the voices shouting instructions, all a calm, but frantic fight for her life. He almost lost it, shoving at the two men who stepped in front of him, but Jake was there, one restraining hand on his arm.

"Let them do their job, Eli," Jake advised. "Both surgeons and their team are well aware of what she is."

"She's pregnant. I know she is. I didn't tell them." Eli shoved both hands through his hair in agitation. "Maybe a month."

Jake immediately approached one of the two men who had stopped Eli from entering the surgery rooms. The man turned and rushed through the double doors.

"They'll take care of it," Jake assured again.

He'd been there with Emma. The same waiting room. He remembered standing in front of the window, his world bleak and gray. Waiting to know. Waiting to hear if she was alive. He'd prayed for the first time in his life. He knew what Eli was feeling, a gut-wrenching sorrow. An agonizing fear. Terror that the one person who made up his world could be taken from him.

Eli was grateful Jake was there, but he couldn't talk. He needed quiet. He needed to find the invisible thread that he'd made psychically with Catarina. No one had come to tell him she was dead, so they had to have got her breathing again. He would know if she tried to fade away again, and he would do everything in his power to stop her. She had to love him that much. Enough to endure whatever was necessary in order to stay with him.

He wouldn't survive her loss. Not intact. It was impossible. She'd made her way into his heart. Snuck in when he wasn't looking. It was impossible to be with her and not fall deeply, madly in love with her. But that hadn't been enough. She'd taken his soul.

His throat felt shredded. Raw. Aching. He didn't even know why. His eyes burned and his body ached, especially his chest. He glanced at his reflection. A man stood there. A stranger. His thick chest was streaked with blood. He wore no shoes, only a pair of soft blue jeans that set low on his hips. His hair was wild. His face was swollen from multiple cuts and bruises and his chest had rake marks down the heavy muscles. His eyes . . . his eyes had gone a dark gold, all sorrow. All fear.

He'd all but forgotten Cordeau and his lieutenants had tortured him before he'd gotten free. It didn't matter now. The nurses and the one doctor who approached him fell back when he swept his cold gaze over them. He knew he scared others there in the small waiting room, but he didn't care. He didn't care about anything but keeping Catarina alive.

He was in a cold sweat at the thought of losing her, his guts twisted with fear. He knew Jake hovered close, probably out of fear that if anything went wrong, the male leopard would take over in an effort to protect Eli. He couldn't imagine what damage a grieving male leopard would do in the small hospital waiting room.

He felt his leopard close and it should have been a comfort, but all it did was make him feel more desolate, more alone. When had it happened? How? From the first moment he'd walked into the dojo and saw her working out, something inside of him, something that had always been closed off, shut down, *broken*, had suddenly come to life. She was that life. Her warmth. Her laughter. Her intelligence. The way she took care of him. The way she delighted in caring for him.

His hand gripped the window ledge until his knuckles turned white. *Don't fucking take her from me.* He didn't even know who he was without her. He'd walked through his life, feeling no joy. No happiness. How could he ever go back?

There was a small commotion at the entrance to the waiting room and he turned his head. Emma entered. Jake's face immediately became a mask of fury. Surrounding her in a solid shield were Joshua, Trey and Elijah. They had the look of bodyguards and the two people who had remained in the room fled.

Emma ignored Jake and went straight to Eli. He couldn't swallow the sudden lump that rose in his throat. The sight of her pregnant body choked him. Maybe it was the compassion on her face. He gave her the death stare, the one that always kept everyone away from him, but she kept coming, ignoring his silent warning, just as she ignored Jake's anger that she wasn't at home where he expected her to be. Eli's eyes burned and he turned his head back to stare into the window. He could still see her reflection in the glass, that beautiful face, reminding him exactly what he could lose.

"Eli, she'll fight. That's who she is."

He shook his head, pressing his fingers to his burning eyes. "You didn't see her, Emma. She was torn up. He'd beat her before the leopard got ahold of her. She's so small. Vulnerable. I should have gotten to her faster."

"Don't." She pressed her head against his side, heedless of the blood. Her fingers gently circled his forearm. "You don't understand women. I do. She loves you with every breath in her body. She'll fight for you. She isn't weak and fragile. She's strong. I listened to her when she told me about living in that house with him. No child should have survived such a nightmare, but she not only survived, she educated herself and she found a way to escape. That took courage, especially after the things Jake told me were done, killing a friend in front of her and convincing a young girl the blood was on her hands. Catarina is courageous. She's a fighter. She doesn't stop. You have to believe in her and trust her right now."

He knew she was trying to help. And maybe it did help. He was grateful they had friends that would take the time to come and see how Catarina was doing. He forced himself to look down into Emma's face, knowing she would see his anguish. His pain. The looming gut-wrenching sorrow. He was totally vulnerable in that moment—absolutely naked and he didn't give a damn.

"I'm certain she's pregnant. Not very far along, but . . ." He shoved his hand through his hair in agitation. "I don't care so much for myself. Right now what matters is that she lives, but she'll tear herself up thinking she should have done something more to protect our child."

"Eli." Emma's voice was soft. "You know better than to do this. You can't control what's happening in that operating room, and you're making yourself crazy. You and Jake think you can control every aspect of your environment, and you just can't. Don't think about things you don't know will or won't happen. Just send her strength. Send her your love."

He didn't answer her. She was right of course. He did want control of everything in his environment, especially Catarina. His parents had kissed him good-bye and left the house laughing. He'd stood at the window waving. They never came home and his life changed completely. It wasn't that he'd been in bad homes. He just had been moved from home to home, and no one cared about him after that. He hadn't cared after that. He wouldn't allow himself to care. Until Catarina. She found her way into his heart, into his soul, and now he stood in a fucking waiting room because he hadn't kept her safe enough.

The waiting seemed endless. Jake stalked across the room and tugged Emma away from him, putting her in a chair, and sliding a second one close so she could put her feet up. Joshua handed him a wet towel without saying a word. Eli used it, wincing as he wiped at the rake marks on his chest. The slashes were deep and yet he hadn't noticed he was injured.

It was useless to put on the T-shirt they'd brought, not with blood seeping from the various wounds on his body. It didn't matter to him. Nothing did. He kept his gaze on the double doors where they'd taken her. Waiting. His heart in his throat.

He heard the measured footfalls coming toward them from the hallway leading to the surgery rooms. His pulse thundered in his ears. He felt bile churning in his gut. Still, he didn't move, every muscle locked in place. His leopard pushed close, too close to the surface. Beneath his skin the wave of fur sent an itch rushing through him. His eyes went cat, heat waves banding.

Every scent came to him, pouring off the doctor as he stepped through the doors. Her blood. Her scent. He didn't go to the doctor. He couldn't take a step, not without his cat forcing a shift to protect him.

"Mr. Perez?"

Eli nodded. That was all he could manage. The rest of his body was locked in place. Frozen with fear. Coiled and ready to strike.

"I'm Dr. Mulligan. Jake called me in to help with Catarina. She's alive and she's doing very well. The woman is a fighter." There was satisfaction in his voice.

Eli's entire body seemed to shut down. He was afraid he might actually collapse. The thunder in his ears roared louder and little jackhammers tripped against his skull. He forced his body under control because the doctor continued to speak and he needed to listen.

"There was a severe loss of blood. Broken ribs. She was battered, but she protected the baby. There wasn't so much as a bruise on her stomach or abdomen. Her ribs, hips and back took the brunt of the attacks. We had no shortage of blood. Jake called it in fast, and Dr. Mason and I were set up for her. She'll be sore and weak for a while, but she's going to be fine."

Eli glanced around the room. There were only shifters. "Her leopard?"

"I'm certain the leopard is okay as well. There were no signs that there was any damage, but of course we had no way of examining her cat."

"Thank you." He could barely get the words out. He glanced at Jake, who was holding Emma close to him. "Thank you both." Dr. Mason had done the surgery on Drake, and Eli remembered him from that operation. He was grateful Jake had called both shifter doctors in to try to save Catarina.

Jake gave him a small salute, one that said "what are friends for." Emma was crying with relief, and that's what really mattered to him. Jake turned her into the shelter of his body and held her gently. He might be angry that she came, but there was only gentleness in his touch.

"I need to see her." Eli made it a demand.

"She's in recovery right now. In a couple of hours . . ."

"I need to see her," Eli said again. This time his voice was a low growl. His leopard needed to see her as well.

Mulligan was a leopard. He knew the signs of a male at his limit. He nodded his head. "I'll show you the way."

"Elijah will stay," Jake said. "He'll have anything you need, Eli. Let Liam take care of your wounds while you're with Catarina in recovery. You're scaring the hospital personnel looking like that."

He couldn't answer. He couldn't breathe without her. He needed to see her. That was all that mattered. Until he did, his leopard prowled too close. Until he did, air wouldn't move through his lungs. He nodded a little curtly to Jake to indicate he understood and stalked through the double doors and down the wide hallway.

Dr. Mulligan hurried after him. "She's strong, Mr. Perez."

"Eli. Any man who saves Catarina's life can use my first name."

Mulligan smiled for the first time. "I'm not altogether certain I was the one who saved her life. She was a pretty determined woman."

He opened a door, and Eli actually caught hold of the doorjamb to keep his legs from going out from under him. Only Catarina could make him this weak. She lay on a hospital bed, so pale she was nearly as white as the bleached sheets she was on. Her eyes were closed, her long lashes two thick feathery crescents standing out starkly against her white skin.

She had bruises everywhere. Her face was swollen and shadowed with blue and black. She was swathed in bandages. But she breathed. In and out. He sagged there, gripping the doorjamb to keep from sliding to the floor. She breathed. She was restless, fighting the sleep, or maybe reliving the attack, her body moving constantly as if trying to flee. Shadows flitted across her face. The nurse fussed over her, clicking soothingly, but that didn't stop the agitated movements.

"Let's get you cleaned up," Mulligan said briskly. "The nurses in here like things sanitary. If you're going to stay, you can't be bleeding all over the floor."

He nodded. He was going to stay whether they liked it or not, but he could cooperate now, his Catarina was breathing.

Ignoring the doctor and the nurse sitting so close to his woman, Eli crossed the distance to her. He laid his hand very gently over her small one, the one fisting over and over in the sheet. They were still giving her blood and intravenous antibiotics. Shifters carried venom and bacteria in their claws. He'd need a round of antibiotics as well.

He leaned down, uncaring in that moment that the doctor and nurse could see the stark, raw love he had for Catarina so naked on his face. "Kitten, I'm here now. Just relax and let me take care of things. I've got you now."

Her lashes actually fluttered. He held his breath. Cobalt blue stared at him for a moment and then all the wild color was gone. But her body relaxed. Went still. Beneath his hand hers relaxed and stopped gripping the sheet.

"That's right, baby," he said softly. "Just rest for me."

The nurse smiled at him for the first time. Mulligan stepped up to him with the look of a leopard, threatening to throw him out if he didn't cooperate. Eli cooperated.

22

CATARINA woke to the feeling of hands moving over her body. Almost from the moment she'd come home from the hospital, Eli had awakened her with his need to feel every inch of her body. He was always gentle, but as time went by, his touch brought her far more than reassurance of his love. She needed him inside her. Dominating her body. Giving her the scorching fire that always brought her pleasure beyond belief.

He had been so careful with her, forcing her to stay in bed the first few days after her hospital stay and then carrying her to the porch or the sitting room, placing piles of books beside her. He waited on her hand and foot. Each night he held her tight, so tight she could barely breathe. Always, at some point, in the middle of the night, she awakened to his hands moving over her body to feel her heart beat. To assure himself she was alive.

She relaxed into his touch as the pads of his fingers

moved over her face, tracing her bone structure. His lips feathered over each eye and trailed along her cheekbone down to the corner of her mouth. That was new. She looked at him, seeing him there in the darkness. His masculine face, lines carved deep. So beautifully male. His eyes had already gone from a dark whiskey to pure gold.

Instantly her body stirred. Came alive. Every nerve ending awoke. She felt an electric burn sizzle through her veins. His lips moved over hers with the same tender touch, back and forth, rubbing along her lips as if he had all the time in the world.

She shivered beneath his touch. She couldn't help it. No matter how gentle he was, there was an unmistakable possessive feel to his hands. He knew her body, and he knew it intimately. Even the lightest of touches could bring fire to her body, let alone the sweet assault on her senses he'd been conducting nightly.

His mouth moved against hers again, this time coaxing. A little firmer. More demand. His tongue ran along the seam of her lips, while his fingers smoothed up and over her breasts, one palm directly over her heart so he could feel it beating into his hand.

She opened her mouth to his and the world shifted around her. His kisses had always been able to bring her to her knees, but now, after waiting what seemed to be forever, his tongue ignited a firestorm inside of her. She felt the burn pour down her throat, straight to her swollen, aching breasts, radiate outward to spin through her body down to her groin. Instantly her womb clenched. Her sheath spasmed. She went wet and a little desperate, the fire no sweet ache, but a roaring monster of hunger and need.

Eli kissed her over and over, each kiss more aggressive, more passionate and more primitive than the last one. All the while his hand stayed over her heart. His other hand wasn't so still. His fingers stroked the curve of her breast. The pads of his fingers circled her nipple, round and round until she wanted to scream in frustration. She tried to move just enough that his wandering hand would swipe over her taut, needy nipple, but he kept her trapped with one heavy leg draped over her thighs and his chest partially pinning her to the mattress.

His kisses sent more flames licking along her nerve endings until she was kissing him back fiercely, just as demandingly. Nearly as primal as he was. Then his kisses changed and more liquid spilled from her body. He went dominant, demanding, taking rather than asking. She loved that trait in him the most. The way his mouth was starved for her, the way he devoured her, eating at her as if she was his last meal.

His mouth was wicked. Sinful. Beautiful. A miracle. His fingers found her nipple and tugged. Instantly the shocking current of electricity rushed to her clit. Her hips bucked hard against him.

Eli lifted his head and looked down at her, his eyes golden, glowing in the darkness at her. Predatory. Possessive. Nearly all cat. She should have been afraid, but she wasn't. Only hungry for him. Desperate for his touch. She wanted rough and fast, but already he dipped his head and kissed his way down her chin to her throat.

His mouth covered her pulse there. His tongue stroked over the beat. He kissed it again, his lips rubbing back and forth to the rhythm of her heartbeat. She couldn't help the small sound that escaped her throat.

"Easy, baby," he murmured against her pulse. "I want a long journey. I want to feel every fucking pulse in your body, with my hand. I want to feel your heart beating in my palm and in my mouth. You just lay there and take it, because you scared the holy hell out of me and I need this."

There was no hurrying Eli when he didn't want to be hurried. His tone was back to the Eli she knew and loved. Rough. Dominant. Absolutely arrogant and confident. She was going up in flames, and he simply took his time. She knew what he was doing—reclaiming her body for his own. She felt possession in every stroke of his fingers, every touch of his hand.

Eli ignored her shifting, restless body and proceeded, trailing kisses from her throat to the cleft of her sternum. He paused to dip his tongue there. He traced the curve of both breasts and then ran his tongue in the deep valley. Her body shuddered with pleasure. She wanted his hands on her. Her breasts were hot and aching. She craved the feel of his mouth and teeth, the pull and massage of his large, rough hands.

Her head tossed on the pillow. She couldn't stop writhing. Her body dripped for his. Wet and wild and on the very edge of control. He could do that without even trying. She felt the hard, thick length of his cock, just out of her reach, pressed tight against her hip. She felt the small pearly drops leaking into her skin and her mouth watered.

"Eli. Let me."

"Shhh, baby. Not yet. You don't get to take this from me. I need this." He lifted his head to look at her.

She saw the warning in his leopard eyes. It only made her need stronger, her craving increase. She loved that look. She loved to know that he was every bit as hungry and in need as she was. She loved to push him right over the edge of his control. His warnings only served to give her more incentive.

She had her hands and she brought them to his hair, curling her fingers into the shaggy mass as his mouth finally—*finally*—moved to her breasts. She cried out as hot pleasure speared through her. His mouth settled over her left breast, drawing it into a vortex of scorching heat. His tongue lashed her nipple, flicking back and forth. He used the edge of his teeth and she wanted to weep with need. Her body did it for her, spilling more nectar along her thighs.

Without warning, his thumb and finger caught at her right nipple in a hard pinch that sent fiery sensations sizzling through her body. The pleasure bordered on pain and made a straight line for her sheath so that she nearly convulsed with its onslaught. His mouth moved over her breasts, teeth nipping and tongue laving. She wanted more, always more, and she arched her body, offering him her breasts, willing him to feast there. He suckled, first her nipple, then along her delicate skin, leaving his mark everywhere, leaving his prints and even the small burn of his teeth. She reveled in his claiming, cradling his head close to her, giving herself up to him.

He demanded a full surrender and she gave it to him, nearly sobbing for relief as she did so. Her body was so tight and hot, the tension building without respite. He licked over her heart. Pressed his ear there, while his fingers and thumb slid back and forth over her nipple in the same rhythm.

She felt the jerk of his cock against her hip, a throbbing of heartbeats between them. Her feminine channel clenched desperately to be filled. "Eli, I'm burning up."

"I know," he whispered back, his lips against the underside of her right breast. "We'll get there. I just need to feel you're alive."

"I am alive, but if you don't hurry that could change."

He laughed softly, his breath warm against her left breast. She felt the stinging nip of his teeth and the slow slide of his tongue. "So impatient, my little Cat. We'll do this my way."

Secretly, she was glad her Eli was back with all his arrogant dominance. He'd been too sweet to her, too controlling of her every move. In bed was one thing—outside of it, she knew if he kept it up eventually she'd kick him in the shins, hit him over the head and totally defy him and run free when he wanted her to sit on the porch and read.

Eli kissed his way straight down from her breasts to her belly button. He made a side trip exploring each rake mark on her sides over her ribs. Six altogether. His touch was magic. Healing. His tongue soothing. He could make her forget the raw scars and the terrible moment when she'd been certain she was going to die under the rogue leopard's teeth and claws.

Still, the leisurely way he licked and kissed her body, sipping at her as if she were a fine wine, stroking her skin with the velvet rasp of his tongue like a leopard might do, drove her insane with desire. She was drenched. Hot. Needy.

Eli framed her womb with his hands and kissed her belly over and over. "You saved our child, Kitten. You couldn't have known, but you instinctively kept our baby safe. It's going to be beautiful, just like you."

She closed her eyes. She hadn't known. Her leopard had still been too inexperienced to tell her, and she hadn't felt the pregnancy, but Eli had known the moment he'd gotten her pregnant. She brought her hand to her face and looked at the ring there. Jake and Emma had come with a justice of the peace and Eli had married her a week after she'd gotten home.

Catarina blinked back tears and reached once again for the silky mass of Eli's hair. "I love you so much sometimes I don't know what to do with it," she admitted, the sound so low it was barely there. No one in her life had given her compliments until Eli. No one had ever said they loved her until Eli.

Love and the admission of love were still strange and terrible yet wonderful things, just as the feeling was. It was overwhelming to her at times. Like now. In this moment. When Eli had to claim every inch of her. When he had to love every inch of her, showing her what she meant to him. It almost felt as if he was worshiping her body right along with claiming her. She never quite knew what to do with his sweetness and always, *always*, she wanted to curl up and hold herself still in fear that she might lose him. She couldn't imagine how he felt waiting to hear if she was alive or dead. She would let him have whatever he wanted just for that alone.

Eli lifted his head from where he'd been communicating

with their child. He had no idea if the baby was a boy or girl. He'd know soon enough because her leopard would tell his leopard. But right now, his heart was full, shattering with her soft admission, knowing how hard it was on her to tell him.

His eyes met hers. Catarina. All cobalt eyes and long, silky hair. He had no idea a man could love a woman so much. He knew he was driving her crazy with his too close, hands-on control, but until that feeling of being unable to breathe left him, she was going to have to give him time.

"You're everything to me, Cat," he told her. It was true. He'd found that out when he thought he'd lost her. "I can't breathe without you. I'm still trying to catch my breath."

She stilled under his hands. Her eyes took on a deep violet vibrant hue. She got it. She knew what he needed and why. He felt her body settle, although her breathing remained ragged. He bent to kiss her belly where his child snuggled.

"You're such a miracle. A real fucking miracle, Cat."

She laughed. "Honey, seriously, you have to clean up your language just a little bit. You can't say *miracle* and drop the f-bomb at the same time."

He loved the sound of her laughter. It filled the room with warmth and joy. She gave him things that were so intangible he couldn't tell anyone else exactly what they were, but he couldn't live without them. Without her.

"I dropped a few of those f-bombs when I was pleading for your life in that waiting room," he growled, unrepentant. He dropped his head back to the important matter of hearing and feeling her heart beating in every part of her body.

"You didn't?" Her breath hitched as he shifted his body to slide lower.

"I did." He pushed her thighs apart and looked down at her body. "You're so damned beautiful, Catarina, sometimes I can't believe you're really mine."

"I hate to be the one to tell you, but I'm covered in scars."

Eli had scars too. Cordeau's lieutenants had taken him down with a stun gun, chained him, and Cordeau had used his claws to rake him open from his chest to his belly and then he ordered his men to get started on the real torture.

"You're beautiful, Cat, with or without them. Jake has found a plastic surgeon, a shifter, one of us, so we'll see him."

"I'm pregnant." Instantly her hands covered her belly, still flat, her body still not giving away their secret. "I don't want cosmetic surgery enough to endanger our child."

He loved her for that alone. "We'll do whatever you want, baby." He dipped his head to trace her hip bone, to find the soft indentation where he could feel her heart pounding through her body. He closed his eyes, savoring the sound and feel of life.

Her breath hissed out of her lungs as he wedged his shoulders firmly between her thighs, stretching her legs with his width, leaving her open and vulnerable to him. He scented her, the call of his mate. Already the taste of her was in his mouth. Still, he needed to feel every pulse point. For the moment he was content to just feel her heart right there. Waiting for him.

He kissed her other hip, lapped at the little indentation and then kissed his way down her thighs. First one, then the other.

"No. Eli." Catarina wailed her protest. She lifted her hips as if trying to follow him. "You're making me crazy."

"Always in such a hurry," he murmured, lifting her leg, bending it, pressing kisses to the back of her knee. He felt it there. Life. He took another breath and his lungs expanded. Sometimes when he woke up beside her, he was choking, his lungs burning. But there it was, the air that he needed. Her. Catarina.

He kissed his way to her foot. Lifted it, pressed a kiss to the sole and back up her other leg. She trembled. Writhed. So alive, his woman. So responsive to his every touch. So impatient.

He took his time on the inside of her thighs. He inhaled, taking her scent deep into his lungs. Maybe if he could keep her scent in his lungs long enough he'd believe she was safe and no one would try to take her from him—not even death. He licked along the inside of her thigh and discovered the sweet, spicy taste, unique to her—his addiction. He craved her taste. He dreamt of it. Woke with it on his tongue.

He lapped it up, taking his time, feeling the beat of his own heart in his cock, telling him he was alive because she was. He lifted his head to look at her as he once more wedged her thighs open with the broad width of his shoulders. Her blue eyes gleamed violet at him. He laughed softly at her glare and dipped his head to blow warm air into the seething, scorching-hot sheath waiting to surround him like a tightest fist.

His body reacted, shuddering at the thought of so much pleasure. He plunged his tongue deep and she came apart just as he knew she would. He loved the abandon, the way she gave herself to him without reservation. So responsive. So sensitive. So willing to let him take her to paradise. He loved giving her that. He loved seeing her pleasure. He loved it more than when she gave it to him, and that was saying something. He lapped at the honey spilling from her body, his private reserve of nectar.

He took his time, changing his rhythm, licking and sucking slowly, languidly, leisurely, and then when her hips were helplessly bucking, he used his tongue to invade, to push deep. He used his mouth on her clit, suckling, flicking with his broad, flat tongue, adding the edge of his teeth until she was screaming for release.

Eli didn't give it to her this time. He wanted to be inside her. Surrounded by her. He knew when he entered her she'd come apart instantly, shatter around him, and the way her delicate muscles would work his cock would be exquisite. He needed that. Needed to feel that small death and rebirth.

He moved fast, startling her, cupping her rear, dragging her to him as he knelt between her legs. He entered her in one fast, hard surge, driving through the soft folds, feeling her stretch to accommodate the thick, hard invasion. Her breath hissed out of her lungs, out of his. She screamed as her body clamped down like a vise around his, surrounding him with a tight, hot, velvet grip. Her muscles milked at him, grasped hungrily, greedily.

He threw his head back and forced his body under control when it wanted to let go and fly free with hers. He withdrew, inhaling as the friction of her tight sheath sent fire racing through his body. Surging forward again, he forced his way through the rippling, shuddering muscles, pressing down along her sensitive clit.

She screamed again and clutched at him, her nails driving into his arms. He let go of his control and took her the way he'd needed to these past couple of weeks. Hard. Hungry. Primitive. He claimed her body for his own. He was rougher than he intended, but she liked rough, and the harder and deeper he drove into her, the more of herself she gave him. Hot liquid surrounded him, her sheath so tight and exquisite he knew he was going to burn in hell or heaven. It didn't matter which to him, only that he burned.

He felt the flames licking along his legs, scorching his thighs, rising like a wall of fire to burn through his balls. Her body grew hotter, fed those flames, clamped down so hard, so unexpectedly, strangling his cock with the burn, with the pleasure-pain. He couldn't even separate the two sensations they were so tied together. Ecstasy. Paradise. Hell. It was all there in the miracle of her body as it milked his, demanding his seed.

He felt the roar of it, heard it thundering in his ears, the fiery flames consuming him as he emptied himself into her. He swept her with him into the fire, so that her body shuddered with her violent release. He took everything she was into his keeping, and he gave her everything he was.

He knew he'd never be the same. He didn't want to be. This woman had changed his life in ways he hadn't known she could, but he wouldn't ever go back to life without out her. He kissed her over and over. He left his mark on his neck. Her breasts. Little strawberries that stood out on her pale skin, little marks of his possession.

Eli buried his face in her neck, holding her tight, his body over hers, arms, hips, chest and legs aligned as best he could. He lay there for a long moment, feeling her heart pounding against his, knowing he had to move, but something wouldn't allow him to.

She wrapped her arms around him instead of pushing his heavy body off of her. The tight ball of fear deep inside him, the one always one moment away from threatening to consume him, thawed around the edges. That was his Catarina. She was so accepting of him, of his controlling, dominant ways. He knew he had to ease up a little. He could see the little signs of impending rebellion, but still, she hung in there with him, trying to give him time to come to terms with his fear of losing her.

Her hands glided up his back. Went to his hair. Her fingers threaded the silky strands, then caressed and tugged. There was such a feeling of contentment lying with her, her body melting into his. Her scent wrapping him up and her hands moving over him so gently.

"Honey." Catarina turned her head so she could press kisses along his temple. "Nothing's going to happen to me. I'm safe now."

"You aren't, you know." He lifted his head, reluctantly sliding off of her. Immediately he turned on his side and swept her close, pressed her tightly against him, his arm an iron band around her waist. "Cordeau had partners. They only know he disappeared. They could decide you're a threat to them. Most likely they will."

"We've already decided that we're going to let Jake and his people deal with them," she replied softly. "Eli, I'm alive. I'm with you, exactly where I want to be. We have our home, a baby on the way and things are good."

Eli pushed her long hair from the nape of her neck and kissed her there. He kissed his way over her shoulder to the much smaller puncture scars Cordeau had left behind.

"My leopard needs to run. She needs her mate. And I need to cook you breakfast. That's important to me, honey. I want to wear your flannel shirts and nothing else. I need to be me again. And you need to be you again. Once our baby is here, there won't be much kitchen table, on the bar or sink or out on the porch fun. We need to make every minute count."

He smiled against her shoulder. She had the little sexy voice that managed to set nerve endings on fire without much of an effort.

"I'm buying more flannels."

"You wouldn't have to if you'd stop ripping all the buttons off. I definitely have to learn to sew."

The amusement in her voice warmed him. Still. He sighed. "Kitten, I don't know how much freedom I can give you right now. I bought a Jeep for you, a four-wheel drive. They're going to deliver it any day now. I wanted you to feel like you could go anywhere you wanted to go, but honestly, I can't let you out of my sight."

He waited. Holding his breath. He hated that he was the needy one. That he knew he should give her everything she wanted, including freedom. She deserved it. She'd more than earned the right to make her every decision. But he couldn't breathe without her.

Eli knew when it happened, the exact moment when the air had left his lungs and wouldn't fully return. They'd taken her from him. They'd rushed her through the double doors and he'd felt her heart stop. Felt the breath leave her lungs. Felt her pulse still. It had been there inside of him. He knew she was being taken from him, and his world had changed. Everything had changed.

He buried his face against her shoulder, inhaling the

subtle female scent that was unique only to her. God, he loved her. He loved her with everything he was. Every cell in his body. He knew if he kept holding her so close she would eventually fight him. How could she not? Where was his control and discipline now?

"Eli, I'm yours." She said it so simply it was eloquent. She turned in his arms to face him. Her fingertips traced the lines in his face. "I belong to you, just the way you belong to me. When I need anything, you provide it for me. When you need something, I provide it. That doesn't mean it's always going to be easy, but when you love someone, that's what you do."

He searched her blue gaze, the bottom dropping out of his stomach. Her features were so delicate. She looked fragile. Vulnerable. But she had steel inside of her. His woman had steel.

"If you need me to stay close to you, then that's what I'm going to do. There's nowhere I want to go right now. I love being home with you. Spending time with you. Looking at you." She brushed a kiss over his jaw. "But I love taking care of you too. I want to cook for you again. I *need* to do that. Make your coffee. I want to wake you up with my mouth around your cock. I love your body just as much as you love mine. I don't need to stay in a chair or in bed anymore. But I don't need to be away from you either."

Just her voice could harden his body, but when she started talking about waking him up with her mouth and the images in his head turned erotic, his cock came back to life. He found himself smiling. Breathing. Happy. She understood him and she loved him enough to give him the things he needed, even if she felt a little smothered for a while.

"I'm looking forward to a cup of your coffee. And breakfast. I haven't had a decent meal since you've been laid up," he admitted. His voice was a little rough with emotion, but he was already looking forward to morning. He knew she would do exactly what she said. She'd wake him up in that sexy, hot way of hers. His cock jerked in anticipation.

"I love the idea of the Jeep, Eli," she said. "But I don't know how to drive a stick shift."

He hugged her to him. "We have a big ranch, baby, and I like teaching you new things." He made certain it didn't sound like he was talking about driving, because he wasn't.

Her smile lit up her eyes. "I love learning new things. You can teach me anytime, Eli."

More than anything, he loved that she meant it.

Keep reading for an excerpt from
the next Sea Haven novel
by Christine Feehan

EARTH BOUND

Available July 2015 from Jove Books

PAIN was a strange entity. It could live and breathe, existing in every cell in one's body. It could cripple, rob one of breath, of dignity, of quality of life. Pain could be the first thing one felt when waking and the last thing one felt when falling asleep. It was an insidious enemy. Silent. Unseen. Deadly. Gavriil Prakenskii had decided some time ago to make pain his friend.

If he was going to survive, if it was even possible with pain as his companion, he would come to terms with it—and he had. Until this moment. Until pain wasn't about the physical or the mental, but all about the emotional. That was an entirely different kind of pain and one he was completely unprepared for.

His life was one of absolute discipline and control. He planned his every move and his contingency plans had backup contingency plans. There was never a moment that he wasn't ready for. There was never a time when anything shocked or surprised him. He stayed alive that way. He had no friends and he thought of everyone he encountered as an enemy. The few people he had ever allowed himself to feel even a drop of friendship with had eventually betrayed him, and he simply counted those painful moments as important lessons to be learned.

He was used to deceit and betrayal. To blood, torture, pain and death. He was used to being alone. He was most comfortable in that world because he understood it. He was thirty-seven years old and he'd been in that world since he was a child. He knew more ways to kill or torture a human being than he could count. It was instinctive, automatic and a natural part of him. He carried death with him the way others might carry their identities, because he *was* death. If he came out of the shadows, even for a moment, it was to deliver that killing blow.

Few ever saw him. He lived in a shadowy world, and moved through it like a phantom, a ghost in the night, leaving dead bodies in his wake. He wasn't real, was nothing more than a shadow someone might catch a glimpse of. Insubstantial. Without substance. He hadn't been human in years. Yet here he stood in the early morning, dawn streaking long rays of light through the velvet black of night, with his well-ordered world crumbling around him so that he felt the earth actually move under him.

His palm itched. Not a small nagging itch, but a full-blown do-something-this-minute-to-alleviate-it itch. Gavriil pressed his hand tightly into his thigh and held it there, his heart suddenly beating hard in his chest. Life sometimes threw curves at the most unexpected times—yet he should have known this might happen.

He had walked into a place of power. Energy rippled in the air and came up through the ground. It was in the wind and in the very water he felt flowing beneath the ground. This place, this farm he had come to, was dangerous, and yet he hadn't heeded the warnings—hadn't expected the danger would be to him or what form it would take. He had come, and now someone would pay the price.

A young woman came toward him through a field of corn, the stalks taller than she was. She moved with grace, a fluid easy manner, occasionally stopping to pull one of the ears down and inspect it.

He couldn't take his eyes from her or the way the plants leaned toward her, as if *she* were the sun, not that bright ball beginning its climb into the sky. She was dressed in frayed vintage light blue jeans and a dark blue plaid shirt buttoned carelessly. The top and bottom buttons were undone, and he had a ridiculous urge to slip them into the closures for her—or maybe open all the rest.

Her auburn hair was very long, probably past her waist, and very thick, but she had it pulled back away from her face in a careless ponytail. Her face was oval and rather pale, but her eyes, as they surveyed the cornstalks, were a striking cool, forest green. Even in the dim early morning light he could see her intriguing eyes, surrounded by long dark lashes. Her mouth was full and luscious, her teeth white and small.

Even dressed in her working clothes, there was no hiding her figure. Full breasts and a small tucked-in waist emphasized the flaring of her hips. She was a pixie, ethereal, just as unreal as he was, and she was so beautiful it hurt.

He knew her. He had always known her. He'd known she was somewhere in the world waiting, and the itch in his palm and the pain paralyzing his mind told him this woman belonged to him and only him. How completely unexpected and unacceptable was that?

He'd come to the small town of Sea Haven off the northern California coast to warn his youngest brother, Ilya, that he was on the same hit list as the rest of the family, and to see his other three brothers who had settled there. Seven brothers, stepping stones, their parents had called them, torn apart when they were children. They'd been forced to watch the murder of their parents, and then they'd been taken from one another and kept separated in the hopes that they would forget all about one another. Now, all seven were on a hit list. Gavriil had known it was coming, he just wished they'd had more time to prepare.

He watched the woman as she continued toward him. He was deep in the shadows and utterly still so that there was no chance of drawing her gaze. She had just changed his entire plan. His entire existence. As she stepped out of the cornfield and the light bathed her face, he could see her flawless skin, the curve of her cheek and high cheekbones.

She looked far too young for a man like him. It had nothing to do with age and everything to do with who and what he was. Still. His palm itched, and that sealed her fate. He wasn't about to throw away the only thing in the world he could truly call his own. He didn't have much to offer her. He was hard and callous and damned cynical when it came to the world around him. He could be ruthless and merciless as well—and he would be, he knew, if anyone tried to stand between this young woman and him.

He didn't even care in that moment, with the dawn breaking, spilling a fire of red into all that glorious hair, that he didn't deserve her. Or that he didn't even know her or she him . . . He didn't care that he was far older and as lethal as hell and had no business with a woman like her, or that his body was in pieces and he looked like a rag doll sewn together. None of it mattered to him.

She belonged to him, this woman. She was created for him. She was the one woman he could bind to him. Gavriil pressed his thumb into the center of his palm. He was broken and there was no fixing him. He was a killer and there was no taking that back either. He didn't get a do-over— and that emotional insight, that pain, was a burden far worse than the physical one he bore.

She was the youngest woman on the farm where his brothers lived. Lexi, they called her. She turned her head abruptly toward the back of the property and just as suddenly switched directions.

The moment he'd stepped onto the property, the large farm with his brothers and the six women living on it, he'd felt the ripples of power and knew the farm was protected, not only by his brothers, who were dangerous, but by elements. Earth. Air. Water. Fire. He even felt Spirit.

Had he been less powerful in his own right, without his own gifts, he would have been far more cautious about following her through the thick foliage along a broken path. Nothing could deter him from his chosen course. He was stalking his prey, moving like the ghost he was through the heavy foliage as she made her way toward some secret destination.

Gavriil knew she was going somewhere important to her, and that she didn't want anyone to know. She moved stealthily and occasionally darted little glances around her, as if she suspected someone watched her. He knew he wouldn't set off her radar. He didn't give off enough energy to do that, not even when he was slipping up on his prey and about to deliver the killing blow.

He glided rather than stepped. He had learned to walk softly in his school as a young boy, but pain was an even better teacher. Taking heavier steps jarred his body. She was moving faster now, heading straight for a vehicle, a small open wagon, and she'd gone quite pale.

Something was wrong. He glanced around him, looking for wildlife, a bird, a squirrel, anything at all. The skies were suspiciously empty. He didn't trust it when a forest, in the early morning hours, was silent. Even the insects had ceased their continuous racket. Something was terribly wrong. He felt it with every step he took. He could tell she felt it as well, but she didn't believe.

LEXI Thompson hurried along the faint path leading to the back of the property where she'd left the little trail wagon parked. She wanted to take another look at the adjoining property that was up for sale—now in escrow. Thomas and Levi had put a bid on it and the owners had sold quickly without negotiating too long. She was very excited about the possibilities the acreage represented.

The farm was doing so well. The new greenhouse was already producing far more than she expected the first year out. The orchards with their fruit trees were yielding large crops and the fruit was fantastic. Her lettuce field had been ruined by a helicopter landing right in the middle of it when some men had come to kidnap her sister Airiana, but she still had managed to save some of the crop and Max had managed to save Airiana.

The bottom line was, Lexi needed more space—and someone to help. All the other women had jobs away from the farm. In the beginning those other businesses had been necessary to support the farm, but this year they'd gone from running in the red to being comfortably in the black, and she intended to keep it that way. She worked hard every single day, from sunrise to sunset and sometimes more. She poured herself into the farm, and at times it was frustrating, backbreaking work. There was only one of her and she needed help if the farm was to continue to sustain them.

She sighed softly. The problem was, her sisters loved living on the farm and eating the food, but each of them had their own businesses—ones they loved—outside the farm. She wasn't certain how to approach the others to tell them she needed more full-time help.

Lexi stuck her thumbnail in her mouth and bit down on it repeatedly, a habit she continually vowed she'd quit. When she realized what she was doing, she snatched her thumbnail from between her teeth and rubbed her palm down the side of her jeans.

She was suddenly uneasy, and she stopped and took a careful look around. She spent most nights sitting on her porch swing, apprehension growing in her. She knew she was paranoid, especially ever since her sister of the heart, Airiana, and her fiancé, Max, brought home four very traumatized children.

The children's parents and a sister had been murdered and the children abducted by a human trafficking ring. Had not Airiana and Max rescued them, they would have been killed.

Knowing children were on the farm, that they were vulnerable and at any moment something terrible could happen to them, had made her more paranoid than ever. She realized her thumbnail was between her teeth again and she blew out her breath in total exasperation.

She detested being the weak link on the farm, with her panic attacks and paranoia. She tried to make up for her failings by working long hours and making a success of their family business. She couldn't sleep in her house, or her bed. She'd tried and she just couldn't do it.

To her everlasting shame, when she was so exhausted she knew she had to sleep, she would sleep in the porch swing, or in the sleeping bag she had stashed in the corner of the porch, out of sight. Sometimes she even slept on the roof. She knew it was silly, but the house didn't feel safe to her. Nothing felt safe.

Fortunately, she lived alone, so nobody knew how truly paranoid she was. There were weapons stashed all over her house, taped under tables and behind the cushions of the furniture, so many she was afraid to have the children visit her home. But she wasn't actually certain she could harm another human being. Well, she had, but it had made her sick.

She lived on the farm with warriors, yet she, the most paranoid of all, felt powerless to harm others. She could barely kill a snail eating her precious crops. She felt weak beside the others, the weak link they all had to rally around and protect. Things were tense on the farm and it seemed as if they needed warriors more than breadwinners.

The trail wagon was right where she'd left it when she

took her early morning walk through the gardens and various crops, the keys still in the ignition. She slipped inside the open vehicle and paused with her hand on the keys to take another long look around her. She was even more uneasy than usual.

Dread filled her. She could feel the emotion as if it were an actual being, pouring inside her like an insidious monster, robbing her of her ability to breathe, to think, to do anything but sit still, her mouth dry and her heart pounding too fast. She jammed her fist into her mouth for a moment—the absolute wrong thing to do.

When she was in a full-blown panic attack she couldn't even move. She was frozen to the spot, useless to her family. A liability. She worked out every single day. She went religiously to self-defense training. She could shoot a gun and throw a knife accurately at any target—even moving targets. What was wrong with her that she couldn't be like her other sisters?

She swallowed a sob and forced her mind to work properly. *Nothing* was wrong. Nothing. No one could get on the farm with their warning system. Each of her sisters of the heart was bound to an element, and the three men residing with them were just as gifted. Should anyone wishing them harm come to the farm, Air would call to Max and Airiana. Earth would tell her. Water would summon Rikki. Judith, bound to Spirit, would feel any disruption at all. Fire called to Lissa. And Blythe just knew.

No one could possibly slip through the power rippling throughout the farm, not with the men, Judith and Blythe amplifying it, she reminded herself.

She forced air through her lungs, always grateful her family rarely witnessed these moments of weakness. She'd been certain the addition of the men to their family farm as well as all the self-defense and weapons training would help her through the panic attacks, maybe even make them stop altogether. It hadn't happened.

"What's wrong with you?" she murmured aloud and started the ignition. "You're such a freakin' baby."

Straightening her shoulders, she drove determinedly toward the back entrance, the gate that led to the road that came into their property through a forest. She felt as if the towering trees were guardians watching over those living on the farm. She loved that they were surrounded on three sides by forest. Some of their acreage remained part of a mixed forest, but behind them the trees were thick and untouched. She drove down the road to the entrance to the next property. She coveted that acreage—she had from the moment it had come up for sale.

Lexi turned off the engine and sat for a moment just drinking in the sight of all that beautiful soil, untouched. No one had ever lived or worked the property, and she'd often pushed her hands deep into the dirt and felt the rich loam just waiting to grow something beautiful.

Usually when she came to this spot, any residual feelings of fear vanished, but it didn't seem to be working now. She still felt as if she couldn't quite breathe, as if air was just out of reach. Her lungs burned and her stomach churned. She slipped from the trail wagon and walked to the gate of the property bordering hers, crouching down to push her hands into the rich soil—another trick that helped when her mind refused to calm.

The moment the soil closed around her hands, the peace she so desperately needed slipped into her. She knelt there beside the gate, pushing her hands deep, feeling a connection to the earth that set her heart soaring free. She felt the ebb and flow of the water running beneath the ground, the heartbeat of the earth, the very sap flowing in the trees. The connection was strong—deep—and she knew it would always be her saving grace.

The ground around her hands shivered and her eyes flew open in sudden alarm. She moistened her lips and looked down at the soil where she'd buried her hands. Her heart skipped a beat and her mouth went dry. She could see the boot prints stamped into the soft ground. Worse, on the gate was a symbol. She'd seen the symbol hundreds of times. It was burned into the wood, a brand, a sheaf of wheat tied with a cord. The same symbol was burned into her upper left thigh.

Bile rose and she fought it down. She would not lose it, not now, when everything she had fought for was at stake. Levi, Rikki's husband, had told her not to leave the farm—that it wasn't safe yet. Her sister Airiana had a madman after her, so the farm was on lockdown. Their combined gifts protected the farm itself, but not if they went off the property.

"Did you think I wouldn't find you, Alexia?"

Her body froze. The air rushed out of her lungs. She closed her eyes briefly. She knew that voice—she would never get it out of her head. Sometimes when she rocked on her front porch swing in the middle of the night, wide awake, she would hear his voice—that hated, horrible voice, commanding her to her knees. Commanding her to pray for forgiveness. Commanding her to perform unspeakable acts to atone for her sins and then flogging the skin off her while demanding she thank him for saving her from her corrupt, disgusting body.

She lifted her head slowly, keeping her hands buried in the soil, trying to find her breath, her resolve. She'd trained for this moment, and yet now that it was here, just his voice alone had her body solidly frozen. Her mind refused to compute beyond terror.

"While you're there on your knees, you might consider begging forgiveness."

She closed her eyes briefly, terrified to look up, but knowing she had to. A thousand plans were formulated and then discarded. Duncan Caine. He always made her feel so powerless. His punishments were the worst. He was enforcer to one of the branches of the cult the Reverend RJ had started. The Reverend and Caine were cousins and cut from the same depraved, sick cloth.

She swallowed hard, desperate not to give him the satisfaction of being sick all over his polished boots. She was not going back with him. She'd told the police all along to look for Caine, that he was still alive, but they assured her he was killed in a shoot-out with the police when they'd raided the farm and arrested several key members of the cult.

This man had crawled through her bedroom window in the middle of the night with her parents right down the hall. He'd held a knife to her little sister's throat and told her he'd kill her sister if she didn't come with him. She'd gone, and she was grateful she didn't struggle. Caine's men surrounded her home, ready to murder her parents, her older brothers and her little sister. She'd gone quietly with him to protect her family.

She'd been eight years old and her life had changed forever. She'd been beaten, starved and raped, forced to "marry" Caine and become his "wife." The one saving grace had been the farm. He'd forced her to work from sunup to sunset, and she'd loved every second of her hands in the soil, coaxing the plants to grow. She could forget her life and pretend she was a girl on a farm with no endless nights of hell to worry about.

Caine and the other cult members had learned that with her working the farm, they prospered. That didn't stop the beatings or the cruelty; if anything, Caine wanted her cowed and completely under his thumb. He'd dug a hole in the ground and forced her into it several times after beating her senseless. The problem he found with the punishment was that she healed fast and didn't seem to mind being in the ground with the soil all around her. So he'd found a metal box, and when he was especially drunk and feeling mean, he would force her into it.

"Did you really think anyone could keep you from me? Your betrayal has brought God's wrath down on you and you will be punished. I've searched for you, a cheating, betraying wife. Jezebel. God sent me to save you in spite of yourself."

He reached down and grabbed her ponytail, yanking her head up so that her eyes were forced to meet his. He wore his beard bushy to cover his weak chin, and his eyes blazed fire like a madman's. He'd been the demon in every one of her nightmares. He was the devil, evil incarnate.

He leaned close to her, pressing his foul-smelling mouth next to her ear. "I killed them all, one by one. I told them you wanted them dead in order to be with me. I knew that's where I made my mistake. You didn't cleave to your husband as you should have because the sins of your former life were too great for you to overcome as long as those sinners lived. You had to be shown the way. You had to be punished."

He slapped her face hard, knocking her backward, bringing tears to her eyes. When she would have been driven back by the blow, his hand holding her ponytail kept her from falling. He rained blows on her, using his fist as well as his open hand.

Lexi barely felt the attack after the initial slap, managing to kick out with her legs, as she'd practiced over and over in the gym with her brothers-in-law. She hit him hard in one knee and a thigh with the heels of her boots. He cursed at her as he fell into the gate. She rolled, astonished that the move actually worked.

Slamming her fists as deep as possible into the soil, she directed the seismic energy straight at the man who had turned her life into a living hell. She put every ounce of fear and anger, helplessness, and despair he'd made her feel into the blow. All the pain. The grief at the loss of her family. All of it went into the terrible strike directed at him.

The earth shook beneath her fists, the ripples spreading out, rushing beneath the ground straight at its target. Caine struggled to his feet, dragging himself up using the fence post.

"You bitch. You're going to pay for that." He winced when he tried to take a step and his knee crumpled out from under him.

A vein appeared in the ground, zigzagging like a snake, widening as it approached Caine. Her eyes widened in horror and she pulled her fists out of the earth fast, but it was too late. The crack became an abyss, opening directly under Caine and the gate, dropping them both into the fissure. The crevice wasn't extraordinarily deep, and it slammed closed on Caine's legs, crushing them, trapping them in the ground. He screamed and screamed.

Horrified, she stumbled backward. Two men raced toward her from the other side of the fence, leaping over it, one breaking off to try to aid their leader while the other rushed her. He held a very large knife in his fist. She recognized both men. They had been training under Caine, doing enforcing and punishing members who committed any infraction against the cult when she'd been there.

Peter Rogers was the man desperately trying to dig Caine free, while Darrin Jorgenson came at her with a knife.

"Kill her. Kill the bitch," Caine screamed over and over, tears running down his face. His upper torso flopped over the ground, his face suddenly buried in the dirt.

She tried to make her brain work, tried to remember what Levi had told her to do, but she couldn't think, couldn't move. She stood waiting for the death blow, thankful that at least she'd managed to stop Caine from taking her away with him.

There was no sound. None. Later, when she thought about it, she felt as if the very earth had taken a breath. Time slowed down. She saw each step Darrin took as if he were in slow motion. She literally could see every breath he drew and the lines of fanatical hatred on his face.

She didn't take her eyes from him, watching him come closer and closer, waiting for him, relieved now that it was over.

A hole blossomed in the middle of Darrin's forehead, a bright red crater that knocked him backward, the blow hard enough to jerk his head back and send his body flying through the air to land in a heap on the ground.

Lexi stared at the body, uncomprehending. A hard arm circled her waist and dragged her backward, thrusting her behind a man she'd never seen before. He was tall, with axe-handle shoulders, a thick chest and shaggy hair. At first she thought it was Levi, Rikki's husband, but he moved differently and he was . . . bigger. More muscular.

He strode toward Caine and Rogers, covering the ground as if he moved above it rather than on it. He was smooth and fluid and something out of a movie with his long coat swirling around him. He raised his hand as he approached the two men and squeezed the trigger of his pistol just once. Peter Rogers dropped to the ground like a stone. Lexi jammed her fist into her mouth to keep from making a sound.

GAVRIIL crouched down beside Caine, lifting his head by his hair, staring into his eyes. Evil stared back at him malevolently. Caine's legs were crushed, but Lexi had managed to keep the crevice from killing him. Caine looked past Gavriil to Lexi and spat on the ground.

"You whore. You're dead. I'll kill you slow. Your devil won't save you. No one can save you. Your name is written in the book of the reaper in blood."

"Save it for your parishioners in hell." Gavriil kept his voice soft, so there was no way Lexi could hear. Deliberately he dropped Caine's head harder than necessary so that Caine's face landed in the dirt. He leaned down, putting his mouth close to Caine's ear. "I'll be coming back without her and I know more ways to make you welcome death than you can possibly imagine. Stay alive for me, will you?"

Gavriil rose, turning back to Lexi. Her face was stark

white, her eyes enormous. "Are you all right? Any broken bones?"

She still couldn't move, not even when he reached her, holstering his gun in the shoulder harness and reaching out to run both hands over her, searching for damage. Terrible tremors wracked her body and she couldn't catch her breath. She didn't dare look at him or she'd cry. If she looked at Caine or the two dead men, she'd throw up.

"Lexi, talk to me. Look at me. Look at my eyes." His fingers smoothed over a bruise already marring her cheek. The pad of his thumb removed a small trickle of blood at the corner of her mouth.

There was something commanding, compelling in his voice—not at all like Caine, but more in a velvet-soft, mesmerizing, *worried* tone. As if her health were the most important thing in this man's world. Lexi forced her gaze upward, over his broad chest where the thin black shirt he wore was stretched tight over well-defined muscles beneath his open coat. Her gaze continued upward, past his strong, shadowed jaw and straight nose until she found herself staring into eyes as dark as midnight. Beautiful eyes. Eyes she was certain she'd seen before. Her breath caught in her throat.

She let herself fall into his dark blue gaze, her only refuge. The world around her receded until there was only this man and his amazing eyes holding her safe.

"Do you know who I am?" His voice was infinitely gentle. A wisp of sound with no impatience, no threat, only concern.

She shook her head mutely. She couldn't find her voice. Her hands trembled and she twisted her fingers together to try to get the shaking under control. She was definitely in shock. Violence was abhorrent to her, although she *had* defended herself. She just couldn't look at the dead bodies, or at Caine, still alive, still a threat.

Her gaze, in spite of it all, began to shift toward him.

"Have you heard the name Gavriil before? Or Prakenskii?"

Gavriil deliberately spoke softly in a Russian accent as he framed her face with his hands. "Look only at me, *angel moy*, nowhere else. Only at me."

He watched her eyes widen. She nodded, some of the shock receding.

"I'm here and I'm going to take care of this. Don't look at them. Don't look at him. I need to know if you're hurt."

She swallowed hard, her breath still shallow and labored, her eyes still bouncing a little, but she didn't pull away from him and her gaze was steadier on his.

"No. No broken bones. He's very good at beating up a woman but making certain she can work the next day."

"You know this man?"

"I'm the whore's husband," Caine shrieked. "She's a Jezebel. Look what she's done to me. She made a deal with the devil. She's a witch, worshipping Satan, holding him hostage between her legs."

Her face went completely white. She looked as if she might faint. Gavriil held her head firmly to prevent her from looking at the man claiming to be her husband. "Don't look at him. He's nothing. He can't hurt you, not ever again," Gavriil said, keeping his voice as gentle as ever. "I need you to go sit in your wagon there for a moment. I'll be right with you. Can you walk?"

She nodded and Gavriil turned her around, away from Caine and the obscenities he continued to shout in between screaming and crying and desperately digging at the dirt holding his legs captive. Gavriil waited until she had crossed the road to slip into the trail wagon before once more crouching down beside Caine. He held Caine's hair in a vicious grip, dragging his head up.

"We'll have a conversation very soon, you and me, but not right now. Never call yourself her husband again. Not out loud and not in your mind." As he held up Caine's head by his hair with one hand, the other took a fistful of dirt, shoving it in, packing it tight and then holding his hand over his mouth and nose. "I don't have soap with me, so this will have to do."

Gavriil was strong and he made certain Caine could see the casual way he cut off all air one-handed before he dropped the man's head on the ground again and left him to try to pry and spit the dirt from his mouth. He kept his body between Lexi and Caine so she couldn't see the man or what he'd done to him. He leaned into the trail wagon.

"He's not my husband. They told me the marriage wasn't legal. I was eight years old and he kidnapped me. He's not my husband," she denied, tears shimmering in her eyes. A few trickled down her face.

"I'm well aware of that," Gavriil said, and used the pads of his fingers to brush the tears away. "I don't want you to think about him ever again. He's totally insignificant. A worm. Less than that."

"He'll never stop coming after me. He won't. I have to call the sheriff right away and tell him what I've done," Lexi said. "They'll send me away from here and I don't know what I'll do. I can't start all over again. I just don't . . ." She trailed off, tears swimming in her eyes.

"There's no need to call the sheriff," he said gently. "I want you to let me take care of this. You go back to your home and call Levi, Thomas and Max. Tell them what happened, but don't let anyone overhear. I know Max has children. We don't want to frighten them after all they've been through."

"They'll make me leave," she whispered again, her hand going protectively to her throat.

"Who? No one can make you leave," Gavriil assured her, struggling to understand.

"I'm in witness protection. I'm supposed to call a number and they'll come and get me. They'll take me away from everyone and I'll never get to see my sisters or the farm again." Tears tracked down her face. "He's got followers, others who will come for me. They kill entire families. They killed mine."

Gavriil felt everything in him go still. It took control not to look back at the man who had kidnapped a child and then murdered her family, forcing her to become his "wife." "Look at me, Lexi. Right now. Don't think about anything else. Just look at me."

Lexi's tear-drenched eyes met his. He smiled at her, more a showing of his teeth than an actual smile, because he wanted to kill the son of a bitch right then. He watched her take a deep, shuddering breath.

"We'll handle this. You'll never see these men again. We'll figure out how they found you and we'll make certain it doesn't happen again. The farm is safe. They couldn't get on the farm without any of you knowing."

She frowned and looked around her, back toward the farm. "But you did, didn't you?" she asked suddenly, comprehending. "You were following me."

"I belong on the farm," Gavriil said, keeping his voice as gentle as he could. Caine was back to shouting obscenities at Lexi, clearly not learning his lesson. "The warning system already in place recognized me—recognized that I belonged here." He reiterated it, wanting her to begin to accept it as fact.

She nodded slowly. "Thank you for saving my life. They would have killed me."

"I'm sorry I was slow getting here. I don't move quite as fast as I used to." His body was screaming at him, protesting every step he took, every move he made now.

Lexi's frown deepened and she leaned toward him, her hand smoothing over his jaw. "You're hurt."

He stilled inside. No one ever saw his physical pain. He didn't allow it to show on his face, in his eyes or body. Only someone who saw into him, saw beyond the surface, could have seen pain in him. There was no doubt this woman was his. He took her hand and pressed his palm to hers. "Wait for me at your house. I'll come to you. Send my brothers to me and don't think about this anymore. Don't call or talk to anyone else until I've come to you."

"But my sisters . . . We made a pact to tell each other everything."

"We'll tell your sisters," Gavriil said. "But I'll be with you. Remember, I'm the one who did all the damage here, not you."

"Caine has to go to the hospital," Lexi pointed out. "The cops will know for certain then." She looked down at her hand, still enveloped in his.

"Let me worry about that. You go get my brothers and wait for me."

"Gavriil, they'll all come to my house. They'll know. We always know when one of us is in trouble."

He nodded. "That's okay. Just don't allow any of them to call the sheriff." His gaze was steady on hers. "Will you do that for me?"

Lexi's gaze clung to his. "That's the least I can do after you saved my life." She started to look past him to Caine, but Gavriil blocked her view.

"Don't. Don't give him that satisfaction. He's nothing to you. Just look at me and then go." He tightened his fingers around hers. "Don't see him. Only me."

Lexi pressed her lips together and nodded. Reluctantly he let go of her and watched as she drove away. He turned back toward Caine and there was nothing at all left of the warm, gentle man. The one striding toward Caine was utterly stone cold, inside and out.

From #1 *New York Times* Bestselling Author
CHRISTINE FEEHAN

THE LEOPARD SERIES

"The Awakening"

Wild Rain

Burning Wild

Wild Fire

Savage Nature

Leopard's Prey

PRAISE FOR THE LEOPARD NOVELS

"Dark, gritty and sexy." —*Joyfully Reviewed*

"Loaded with plenty of surprises, heat,
thrills and suspense!" —*Fresh Fiction*

"Sultry…vivid…tantalizing [and]
unforgettable." —*Fallen Angel Reviews*

christinefeehan.com
facebook.com/christinefeehanauthor
facebook.com/ProjectParanormalBooks
penguin.com

M1237AS0113

THE CARPATHIAN NOVELS FROM
#1 *NEW YORK TIMES* BESTSELLING AUTHOR

Christine Feehan

DARK BLOOD

DARK WOLF

DARK LYCAN

DARK STORM

DARK PREDATOR

DARK PERIL

DARK SLAYER

DARK CURSE

DARK HUNGER

DARK POSSESSION

DARK CELEBRATION

DARK DEMON

DARK SECRET

DARK DESTINY

DARK MELODY

DARK SYMPHONY

"Feehan...finds more readers
with every title."
—*Time*

penguin.com

M475AS0314